Loud Sparrows

Weatherhead Books on Asia

contemporary chinese short-shorts

selected and translated by

aili mu

julie chiu

howard goldblatt

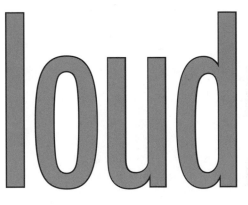

sparrows

columbia university press   new york

This publication has been supported by the Richard W. Weatherhead
Publication Fund of the East Asian Institute, Columbia University.

COLUMBIA UNIVERSITY PRESS
Publishers Since 1893
New York   Chichester, West Sussex
Copyright © 2006 Columbia University Press
All rights reserved

Library of Congress Cataloging-in-Publication Data

Loud sparrows : contemporary Chinese short-shorts /
selected and translated by Aili Mu, Julie Chiu, and Howard Goldblatt.
    p.   cm.   —   (Weatherhead books on Asia)
ISBN 0–231–13848–2
1. Short stories, Chinese—20th century. I. Title: Contemporary Chinese
short-shorts, in the series Weatherhead books on Asia. II. Mu, Alili.
III. Chiu, Julie. IV. Goldblatt, Howard. V. Series.
PL2653.L65   2006
895.1'3010805—dc22
2005046671

Weatherhead Books on Asia

COLUMBIA UNIVERSITY

LITERATURE

David Der-wei Wang, Editor

YE ZHAOYAN, *Nanjing 1937: A Love Story*, translated by Michael Berry

MAKOTO ODA, *The Breaking Jewel*, translated by Donald Keene

HAN SHAOGONG, *A Dictionary of Maqiao*, translated by Julia Lovell

TAKAHASHI TAKAKO, *Lonely Woman*, translated by Maryellen Toman Mori

CHEN RAN, *A Private Life*, translated by John Howard-Gibbon

EILEEN CHANG, *Written on Water*, translated by Andrew F. Jones

AMY D. DOOLING, editor, *Writing Women in Modern China: The Revolutionary Years, 1936–1976*

HAN BANGQING, *The Sing-song Girls of Shanghai*, first translated by Eileen Chang, revised and edited by Eva Hung

HISTORY, SOCIETY, AND CULTURE

Carol Gluck, Editor

TAKEUCHI YOSHIMI, *What Is Modernity? Writings of Takeuchi Yoshimi*, translated by Richard Calichman

RICHARD CALICHMAN, editor, *Contemporary Japanese Thought*

Contents

XI. Nourishment

XII. Weirdness

XIII. ?

XIV. Elegy

XV. Looking Backward and Looking Ahead

Foreword

90 + 1: Sparrows and Me

In the spring of 1958 Beijing residents plunged into a campaign against sparrows, led by Mao Zedong. Schools suspended classes. For three days and nights the entire city of Beijing sank into madness, waving flags and raising an earsplitting hue and cry around the clock. I beat on broken enamelware and empty cracker tins on my balcony from dawn to dusk, shouting until I was hoarse. My eyes were bloodshot, my arms sore from pounding. But for a boy not yet nine years old, it was the supreme revelry imaginable! With nowhere to land and rest, the sparrows eventually dropped dead from exhaustion, hunger, and thirst. It was said that more than four hundred thousand sparrows were killed in the Beijing area alone.

The title of this book, *Loud Sparrows,* calls to mind this childhood experience: although loud sparrows were not particularly harmful, the loud human disturbance brought about their death. Sparrows were replaced by bedbugs as one of the four national pests the following year, but the birds' rehabilitation came too late. The extinction of sparrows led to a plague of insects that was at least partially responsible for the famine that caused more than 20 million people to die of starvation.

And so sparrows entered the history books. Contemporary China, itself a huge book filled with sound and fury, abounds in extraordinary happenings and is stained with blood and tears. This constitutes a boon for Chinese writers: calling upon little imagination, they can tear any page from this book and turn it into a work of art. The line between fact and fiction, after all, is blurred—history has been read as fiction and fiction regarded as an extension of history.

Wang Zengqi is one of my favorite Chinese authors (some of his short-short stories appear in this collection). In the essay "What Is a Short-short?" he wrote: "Short-shorts are an extended branch of the short story genre. But this branch also tests the limits of the genre. While hewing close to the genre and possessing the general characteristics of short stories, a short-short differs from them. Generally a short story has more prose elements, whereas a short-short story contains more features of poetry. Short-shorts are a cross-bred new genre combining short stories and poetry." The originality of Wang Zengqi's view, especially his evocation of the relationship between short-shorts and poetry, opens up a new horizon for this sparrow of short-shorts to take flight. His own short-shorts prove the point. They are, in fact, reminiscent of haiku—hinting by allusion but with restraint.

Short-shorts, as official jargon has it, work well in China's actual conditions. Their source and course are distinct in Tang and Song *chuanqi* and Ming and Qing *biji*, and from *A New Account of Tales of the World*, to *Strange Tales from a Chinese Studio*. In today's China, where commercialization carries the day, the proliferation of short-shorts is, more than ever, out of control. Debates over mobile-phone short-shorts have grown especially loud lately, and I am a little confused. This will not be a reenactment of the sparrow annihilation campaign of 1958, will it?

Fortunately there are insightful scholars like Aili Mu, Julie Chiu, and Howard Goldblatt, who have chosen the finest examples of short-shorts and translated them for this collection. These unique and discerning representations allow English readers to catch glimpses of daily life, to conjure up pictures of Chinese history, and to savor the exquisite ingenuity of Chinese literature.

If sparrows are but a metaphor, every writer faces the challenge of reality, namely, how one catches this sparrow.

One day in the early 1970s, when the Red Guard generation had lost its way, as the Cultural Revolution was ebbing, I borrowed an air gun and went hunting with two friends in the outskirts of Beijing. Large flocks of sparrows, obviously the offspring of those that had survived in 1958, were flying noisily in the air. Who would have thought they had such indomitable reproductive powers? Finally, some of them landed, dotting the lines of an overhead wire like notes on a sheet of music. Holding my breath, I raised my gun, with my left eye closed and the right one aimed at a loud sparrow through the sight. I pulled the trigger. I missed. The sparrows flew off. We went home empty-handed.

Bei Dao

Introduction

As much as the consumption of short-short stories (also known as short-shorts) has become a global phenomenon, nowhere in the world has the genre been as enthusiastically received as with contemporary Chinese readers. In Taiwan, efforts to promote short-shorts began in the 1960s, but it was the section of "very-short pieces" in *United Daily*'s literary page that set off the wave of creative writing in the genre in the early 1980s. Columns dedicated to short-shorts in newspapers soon became the venue where amateurs brushed shoulders with well-known writers. Under the slogan "everyone writes,"[1] amateur writers from all walks of life have participated in the development of the genre, although established writers remain its driving force. Both kinds of writers have been anthologized by literary presses since the late 1970s, and publishers of popular literature also pitched in, putting out collections of short-shorts with sensational titles.[2] Appearing in newspaper features sections as early as the 1950s, short-shorts in Hong Kong have provided the public with amusement and food for thought on a daily basis for more than 40 years. If short-shorts of 1,600 characters or less were created in the days of manual typesetting to meet the need for fixed-length features, they were later produced in great numbers as literary commodities. In the last decade they have finally made it into Hong Kong magazines and journals dedicated to serious literature, as a fictional genre separate and distinct from short stories, novellas, and novels. But the height of the genre's development has been reached on the Chinese mainland, where, among more than 400 literary journals and magazines, the *Journal of Selected Short-shorts* (first published in 1985) makes up half the total number of subscriptions. For nearly 10 years the journal has boasted a subscription figure of over 500,000, reaching its peak of 640,000 in 2001.[3] The success of the journal gave rise to quite a few similar publications, which pushed the circulation to more than one million and the number of readers well beyond that.[4] At a time when literature has become increasingly marginalized with a shrinking market, this is nothing short of a miracle.

What has led to this phenomenon? Indicative of the changes in contemporary life, the genre underscores the complexity of experiences and sensibilities as Hong Kong, Taiwan, and mainland China join the global drift into the postmodern era. While closely associated with a passion for speed—easy consumption and instant gratification—and a desire for greater diversity, the popularity of short-shorts is probably, as the Taiwanese writer Yin Di points out, a consequence of excesses:

> This is an era of "explosions," with an excess of people, cars, plastic products, and political gestures. . . . The city, in particular, suffers from too much talking and too much eating. Painters paint too much, writers write too much. A sense of restraint is needed in everything we do, and minimizing is the first step toward self-restraint. That which can be said in 1,000 words had better not be said in 10,000 words.[5]

As an antidote to super-sizing and overdose, short-shorts are not at all hostile to becoming a commodity. The genre, in fact, embraces the market and has become a favorite in it, enjoying the ride of growth and increasing popularity. In the third decade of "modernization" and development toward a market economy, Chinese cities, like their counterparts elsewhere, are undergoing a rapid process of commodification in various aspects of life and culture. Being perceived as less profitable, established literary genres are losing ground to TV programs, movies, and other popular multimedia productions. While many literary elites are still steeped in resentment of the market and its ways, short-shorts readily participate in the change toward commercialization of social, cultural, and political discourse. From Hong Kong to Taiwan to mainland China, most short-shorts have been published in newspapers and magazines that target the general reader and are marketed as commercial products. The *Journal of Selected Short-shorts* represents the success of this effort. Running the journal as a business operation, the editors at *Garden of Flowers* facilitate the genre's adaptation to commercial interests through such mechanisms as content arrangement, image manipulation, novelty in binding and printing, and marketing strategies.[6] They also make sure to anthologize best works regularly, hold annual award competitions, national writers' forums, and international conferences, to theorize and popularize the genre. Through the promotion of mass education and participation, they establish a firm reader base among both urban and rural residents of different ages, genders, and occupations, especially among educators in tertiary and secondary institutions and their students.[7] While bringing up new loyal cohorts of the genre (both as readers and writers), these entrepreneurial editors create the need for the consumption of their own literary products.

The relative freedom of the market impacts the development of the genre positively in many ways. For example, the effort to capitalize on the "celebrity appeal" of better-known writers helps to promote the "literariness" of the genre; the easy access to short-shorts from other parts of the world, especially those from Japan, Russia (or the former Soviet Union), the United States, Germany, and France, facilitates creative thinking and experiments with writing techniques.[8] The bite-size short-shorts also take on an interactive character with their frequent and periodical appearance in popular media. Often written as responses to issues of the day and read alongside reports of the latest happenings, short-shorts can be entertaining and responsive to what is happening in people's daily lives. While benefiting from the market, short-shorts also contribute to it by providing valuable products of consumption to satisfy readers' varied needs. The mainland writer Wang Meng therefore attributes the popularity and success of the short-short to its constructive responses to the challenges the market economy has brought upon literature.[9]

The present anthology brings together ninety-one short-shorts written over the last three decades by some sixty writers from Hong Kong, Taiwan, and mainland China. In preparing this anthology we have scanned newspapers, popular magazines, literary journals, personal collections, and literary anthologies.[10] We are aware that any effort to anthologize is to remove the short-shorts from their original interactive context, both social and historical. Nevertheless, by making these representative works available in English, we provide direct access to the contemporary Chinese experience and a chance for an enhanced understanding of Taiwan, Hong Kong, and mainland China today. It is also our wish that the anthology will become a means by which Chinese writers contribute to the genre's development in world literature.

The organization of the anthology brings in a touch of "interaction" between stories, and between the anthology and you, our reader. The ninety-one selected stories are divided into fifteen categories to confirm rather than confine their many possibilities: Grooming, Change, Choices, Governance, Games, Controversy, Anticipations, Creatures, Sharing, (In)fidelities, Nourishment, Weirdness, ?, Elegy, and Looking Backward and Looking Ahead. To validate the many facets of the leading motif for each group of stories, the categories are accompanied by "cautionary tales" against extremism. The "tales" were written by How-ard Goldblatt in the form of flash fiction, that is, extremely short fiction. These flash pieces, instead of directing reading, are intended to create mood, whet readers' appetites, evoke their emotions, appeal to their intellect, and set the stage for their reading. This cross-cultural creative intertextuality, we hope, will constitute shared imagination, experience, and humanity beyond artificial national or cultural boundaries.

Interspersed among the ninety-one stories are notes on the genre by writers. We include them not just to enrich the reading experience but also to ease the anxiety that may have been caused by the absence of rigid definition. Obviously the selected writers and critics of the short-shorts have found their own ways to define the genre. By presenting how they imagine the art form and how they realize their imagination in practice, we hope to bring anchorage to the basics of the genre: free-dom of form, expression, and function.[11]

As much as this anthology differs from other works of fiction in such established genres as short stories, novellas, and full-length novels, the facts remain: short-shorts are stories, and they belong to the extended family of narrative. Possessing all the features of fiction, a short-short is, as the famous Chinese saying goes, small as a sparrow but has all the vital organs. Wang Zengqi, a veteran writer from the mainland, catego-rizes short-shorts as a "branch of the short story genre" that "tests the limits of the genre." Cross-bred with poetry, a short-short differs from a short story in that it contains more features of poetry, yet "has a style freer than that of narrative poetry and a plot-orientation stronger than that of lyric poetry."[12]

Short-shorts are hybrids that resist definition. In the last three decades many names emerged to highlight one of their essential features. There has never been a literary genre, observed Xiu Shi, with as many varied and colorful names as the short-short. It has been named with refer-ence to its duration (one-minute fiction), length (a story of a thousand words), image (palm fiction), related media (snapshot fiction), and sub-ject matter (urban legends). While such names as "sudden fiction" and "palm fiction" indicate an obvious foreign influence, names like "hav-ing-a-puff fiction," "the transitory mustard seed," and "urban legends" bespeak local imagination and the genre's Chinese heritage. Our collec-tion of terms has exceeded forty, and we are still counting.

The love for the genre and the challenges the art form presents result in the plurality of this volume—with voices from both sides of the Taiwan Strait and writers of varied backgrounds. Many selected writers are famous for their works in established genres. They include, from mainland China, Wang Meng, one of the region's most reputable novelists and the former minister of culture; Wang Zengqi, a writer of many talents and among the best practitioners of the short-short genre; Ah Cheng, a prominent writer of stories, essays, and film scripts, and best known for his series of "king" novellas; and such eminent short-story writers and novelists as Lin Jinlan, Feng Jicai,[13] Liu Xinwu, Mo Yan, Cao Naiqian, Zhang Kangkang and Chi Zijian. From Taiwan we bring to you, among others, Chen Kehua, a medical doctor by profession and a poet and short-short writer by passion; and Yuan Qiongqiong and Ku Ling, Taiwan's most celebrated writers of short-shorts. Closely associated with the popular media, Ku Ling, as TV talk-show host, and Yuan, a writer of pop-song lyrics and scripts for films and TV drama, are known for their insights on relationships and abilities to draw material from real life. The selected writers from Hong Kong include the "Godfather of Hong Kong Literature." Liu Yichang, writer of Hong Kong's first stream-of-consciousness novel and chairman of the Hong Kong Writers' Federation; Zhong Ling, poet, essayist, literary critic, and educator of Buddhist visions; the veteran fabulist Xi Xi, whose touch of childlike innocence always inlays her incisive criticisms of life; and Ye Si, whose reflections on Hong Kong's "postmodern" specifics—its food, clothes, and traveling—bring Hong Kong to the world and vice versa. Extremely conscious of form and well versed in the art of fiction, they are willing to experiment and discover. Because they often produce representative works of artistic excellence and insights, this volume contains multiple selections from many of these writers.

A significant number of the selected stories are, however, from not-so-famous writers. These writers are nevertheless dedicated to the art both professionally and personally. Well trained and working in local literary and art circles such as municipal or country literary federations (Zhang Jishu, Zhan Jing, Liu Guofang, and Ling Dingnian) or as editors of national or local literary journals (Qin Yong and Bai Xiaoyi), they have been working in the form for years. Their persistent effort has produced many top-notch works that have been anthologized within and outside China. While asserting a critical spirit, humanist ideals, and traditional virtues, and while giving vent to popular dissatisfaction in their writing, these writers also nod to the opportunities commercialized society affords. They have been instrumental in making short-shorts a literature both of commitment and of entertainment. Through their professional affiliations and functions, they have helped to bring professional writers off the pedestal and lay writers up into the "ivory tower."

Yet a number of the selected stories are from practitioners of the art who make their living in professions other than literature. They publish their work in popular media for the love of the art. The writer of "Lover" and "Mothballs" is an eye specialist; the author of "Parting" is a local educator; "Home" was written by a first-class cook in a Qingdao rest home; the story of the crow and the fox comes from a county official in Shanxi Province; and the writer of "General" works in the security department of a local bank. Coming from outside the literary establishment and living among common people, these writers have easy access to popular sentiments and tastes, and are therefore in an advantageous position to articulate them. Their stories, unlike avant-garde works, which are impenetrable for most readers, have direct relevance to readers' lives as living social and cultural beings. The immediate aesthetic appeal of their down-to-earth playfulness can be easily consumed by the majority of the population. The inclusion of these writers brings readers to the substrata of unofficial histories, undocumented memories, unspoken human predicaments, and intimate life-worlds. In so doing, the volume achieves a fuller presentation of contemporary Chinese life in general and of the art form of short-shorts in particular.

Many of you, our readers, may find the art form of Chinese short-shorts reminiscent of the economy of Hemingway, the profundity of Shinichi Hoshi, the irony of O Henry, the poignancy of Chekhov, and the alienation in Kafka. Those with some training in Chinese cultural traditions may enjoy the familiar "art of leaving blank," that is, the art of articulating the most important by what is left out, like the expressive blank areas often found in traditional Chinese brush painting. Because of Chinese writers' conscious effort to learn from other cultures, to incorporate different traditions, and to creatively reconfigure formal properties, the short-shorts in this anthology pleasantly frustrate expectations and challenge the boundaries of literary conventions. Like a video recording played in reverse mode, Cai Nan's "Looking Back at the Moment of Death" allows the reader to fast search and to play slow motion or normal speed in reading. Chen Kehua's "Lover" and "Mothballs" explore the intensity of one single moment at the expense of the plot. As Chen Hengchu's "Promotion Report" blurs the line between literary and nonliterary discourses, Wu Yiming's "Number

Eight" obscures the distinction between verbal and visual arts. While Wang Meng's highly condensed prose on ordinary phenomena bursts with metonymical revelations, Wang Yanyan's lyrical reliance on imagery replaces "story" with feeling. Zhong Ling's "Contemplating Water," with its Zen touch, is as enigmatic as Mo Yan's "Horse Talk" is fantastic and elusive. The wild humor of Chen Shixu's "What's Up, Lao Cao?" is matched by the fuzzy logic in Xu Haiwei's "The Principle of Rebound." In "Division," our capacity to reason is thwarted and our faith in absolute egalitarianism shattered as we ponder the mathematical problem of mosquito bites. Through its own aesthetic strategies, every story in this volume discloses some crystallized human moment, yet lingers and haunts with no attempt to exhaust the subject matter it broaches. With their characteristic open end, the selected short-shorts manifest distrust of the ultimate or absolute and signal a redistribution of power from author to reader.

In our effort to embrace diverse aesthetic representations and strategies, we include in this volume stories of various lengths (from about 125 characters to about 1,600) and of mixed genres (fables, parodies, romances, fairy tales, dramatic monologues, classical tales, anecdotes, prose poems, and popular or historical accounts). The narrative texts, often in the first or third person, may take the form of a letter, a report, a monologue, a sole narrative or one interspersed with dialogues or flashbacks. Their dominant motifs are beyond the scope of our categorization; the techniques of displacement, allusion, condensation and substitution are commonplace.

Such tolerance of formal flexibility, however, serves not only to rejuvenate calcified forms. The aesthetic freedom that short-shorts enjoy also affords endless artistic possibilities and makes it possible for the genre to encompass more diverse voices and perspectives. Such autonomy in art, to use Janet Wilson's expression, brings to light the necessary "constitutive features of the society," that is, the society's capacity to "accommodate plural voices and promote alternative ways of thinking."[14]

The first serious rendering into English of the multifarious genre, this volume, with stories ranging from portraits of psychological depths to allegorical treatments of social and cultural formulations, presents a gamut of human emotions and situations. Penned by a variety of authors who are no longer concerned with authorial expositions, the selected works focus on fragments, contingencies, and individuals trying to cope with basic issues of life. Despite the differences in political systems and developmental stages among mainland China, Hong Kong, and Taiwan, short-shorts from all three regions share increasingly similar frustrations and hopes in the intimate private lives of individuals.

In the section entitled "Choices," for example, the revelation in Taiwan writer Ku Ling's "Jailbreak" not only resolves the structural puzzle of the story but also unveils, most intensely, modern man's existential dilemma. In the same section, mainland writer Chang Gang shows, with his "'Left' with No Chance," the absurdity of contemporary conditions where the "right" choice is wrong. Hong Kong writer Xi Xi's "Sunday Morning," conversely, uncovers a postmodern loner's expected and limited choices through a set of multiple-choice questions with the obscurity of a poem. In the category of "(In)Fidelities," Ku Ling embeds, with his "Confession of a Photographer," a paradox of modern life in the illogicality of a successful career; in "Grooming," two other Taiwanese writers, Yuan Qiongqiong and Chen Kehua, evoke universal sentiments by investing with new meaning the trivial acts of ear picking, nail clipping, and preserving winter clothes with mothballs.

Many of the short-shorts in this volume can also be read as testimonies to past ideological crazes and to the present economic and sociopolitical transformation in Greater China. For example, mainland writer Ah Cheng's "Observe" and "Chimney Smoke" both remind and warn us of how politics is literally the decision concerning the apolitical body. In its surrealistic style and with self-deprecating humor, Lin Jinlan's introspective "A Knock on the Door" mocks Chinese intellectuals' sense of righteousness and infallibility. Unmistakably the change of sovereignty in Hong Kong looms large in Che Zhengxuan's "Last Stop, Mongkok." Turning to the seven stories in the section titled "Sharing," we may note that each story involves the term in a most unconventional way. Six point to the negative impacts of tradition or modernization, with Ah Cheng's story about "sharing" garbage particularly suggestive of a contemporary malaise—a fast-developing society trapped in an underdeveloped mentality and caught up in a vicious recycling of the unwanted. Both Zhong Ling's "Killer Well" and Liu Yichang's "Wrong Number" were inspired by actual events reported in the news. Coincidentally both representations of the news stories lend philosophical depth to the random play of probability in the life and death of human beings.

What is the current status of contemporary Chinese short-shorts? In Hong Kong, short-shorts are retiring from popular media to the ivory tower of serious literature. In Taiwan, short-shorts are still going strong in both newspaper features and literary anthologies, the former a major source of the latter. Both commercial and literary presses have published series of better-known writers' personal collections of short-shorts. In both areas educators are making use of the genre to promote creative writing among students from primary to tertiary educational institutions. In mainland China, short-shorts have yet to be fully recognized in elite literary circles or accepted as a distinct literary form, which raises the question of what the future holds for short-shorts in China. One might argue that the elevated position of short-shorts in Hong Kong affirms, from a different perspective, its legitimacy and value as a new art form for a new age. But can the evolving popular genre bridge the gap between highbrow and lowbrow literatures? Will it suffer the fate of diminishing readership as other print literature has, especially when the even shorter mobile-phone literature has embarked on its commercial venture? Can the art form be expected to assume a dominant position in the literature of the twenty-first century? These questions make the dynamic phenomenon of short-shorts all the more fascinating.

In hindsight we may take some hints from history. Early Chinese fictional narratives were short. Huan Tan of the Eastern Han (A.D. 25–220) refers to them as "short works." Such narratives fashioned into Liu Yiqing's (403–444) *New Account of Tales of the World* in the Six Dynasties (220–589), in the Tang (618–907) *chuanqi* (transmissions of the marvelous), in the Song (960–1279) *huaben* (oral fiction) and *biji* (skeleton texts), and in *Strange Tales from a Chinese Studio* of the Qing (1644–1911). Lu Xun admired the capacity of mini-short stories to capture the universal through the particular and practiced the art in his own writing. It is not an exaggeration to say that the short-short as an art form has been practiced by most modern and contemporary Chinese writers, among them such familiar names as Yu Dafu, Xiao Hong, Shen Congwen, Xu Zhimo, Xu Dishan, Bingxin, Wang Renshu, Sun Li, Ye Wenling, Cong Weixi, Jiang Zilong, Jia Pinwa, Liu Shaotang, Su Shuyang, Chen Jiangong, Su Tong, and Bi Shumin. Even in short stories by such avant-garde writers as Can Xue, we can see the continuation of the "short works" literary tradition.

Another contributing factor to the genre's future dissemination is that short-shorts are both device-independent and compatible with today's technology. Offered in booklet format, they can be toted around in a bag and consumed at ease. The declining readership of written media may also be a blessing in disguise for short-shorts, as the latter offer relative freedom from censorship not enjoyed in other media. Further, a short-short fits either on one page or a few pages or on one computer screen, which facilitates consumption. As a genre that encompasses yet escapes all genres, short-shorts have found a home in high school and college classrooms, attracting millions of fans among young readers.[15] The deliberate cultivation of the young in this art form has been occurring not only in China. As teachers of language and literature at the university level, we have found in short-shorts excellent teaching material for graduate as well as undergraduate courses, in such disciplines as language, literature, translation, Chinese studies, and cultural studies.

When people of different backgrounds contribute to the popularization of an art form as a creative process in which both professionals and the majority of the population can participate, it seems clear that a conceptual change is imminent: the Writers' Association in China recently accepted a few dozen professional writers of short-shorts as formal members. While it may be overly optimistic to interpret this act as an official acceptance of short-shorts as the fourth member of the narrative family, alongside full-length and mid-length novels and short stories, such recognition clearly marks a change of attitude: first, that serious literature can exist in formula entertainment commercialism, and, second, it does not have to be an enemy of art. We hope that upon reading this volume you will reach the same conclusion.

We end this introduction with a few words on the title of the volume, *Loud Sparrows*, inviting readers to contemplate the agency of art and to anticipate short-shorts' continuous aesthetic enactment of alternative imaginations. For us, the volume's translators and editors, and for many who have experienced recent Chinese history, the emblematic bird is more than simply "small but complete." A species of songbirds, sparrows in China were condemned, together with rats, flies, and mosquitoes, to the category of "four pests" and suffered a tragic fate in the 1950s. Although the bird has been fully rehabilitated in the following decades, achieving the status, in 2002, of state-protected species, its journey toward extinction seems to have accelerated in recent years with a new set of arch enemies, namely, the excessive use of pesticides in farming and the incessant appetite for barbecued wild game on the dinner table.[16]

The tragic fate of Chinese sparrows is indicative of the suffering inflicted by the blind pursuit of development and modernization, especially on the marginalized, throughout the past half-century. Keenly aware of the extreme swings of the authoritarian pendulum, we were drawn to an art form whose formal properties necessitate the aesthetic disruption of understanding and whose narrative strategies trigger new ideas and perceptions. We found, in the art of short-shorts, a way to experiment with and think through the tragedy of the past and the misgivings of the present. With this volume we hope to bring to our readers the bustling sounds of life, voices of difference, and proud assertions of individuality from all corners of a Greater China undergoing historical transformation.

We thank the National Endowment for the Humanities for its generous Collaborative Research Grant that made possible the three-way collaboration between Aili Mu (Iowa State University), Howard Goldblatt (University of Notre Dame), and Julie Chiu (Lingnan University, Hong Kong). All three actively participated in the selection and translation of the stories. Howard doubled as the team's editor, who read and edited the preface, the introduction, and all translations included in the anthology. The friendly help and support of the *Garden of Flowers* journal in Zhengzhou, China, were indispensable to the completion of the project. We owe our special thanks to Chief Editor Yang Xiaomin and his colleagues, particularly Qin Yong. We are indebted to Chung Ling (Zhong Ling), Dean of Humanities of Baptist University, and to Leung Ping-kwan (Ye Si), Head of the Chinese Department of Lingnan University, for sharing with us their enthusiasm for and insights into the writing and reading of short-shorts in Taiwan and Hong Kong. We also thank Yin Di, founder and editor-in-chief of Erya Press in Taiwan, for his help in obtaining copyright permissions. Our deep gratitude goes to Sylvia Lin for her voluntary help in the story selection process and for her suggestions at various crucial stages of this project. This volume benefited tremendously from comments by the two anonymous reviewers, ranging from organizational suggestions to detailed editorial recommendations. We sincerely thank them for their contribution.

Aili Mu, Ames, Iowa
Julie Chiu, Hong Kong

Loud Sparrows

I. Grooming | *Howard Goldblatt*

It was the most spectacular comb-over any of them had ever seen.

"World-record caliber," a man standing close to him whispered to his friend. "Got any scissors on you?"

With the man's head slumped to one side, the eight-inch-long slurve of ratty brown hair stood up like half of a Soviet symbol, the tips twitching like the tendrils of a sea anemone.

A young woman, noticing the smirks on the two friends' faces, took a bobby pin from her hair and held it out to them, motioning with her lips where she thought it might be delicately placed.

The next offering, from an older woman sitting in the next seat back, was a long-handled comb, then a baseball cap, followed by a red hair-tie a teenage girl slipped off her wrist.

The bus stopped, roughly, and the man woke up. He glanced at his reflection in the window, smiled, and stood up. "Excuse me," he said, as he stepped over to the exit and off the bus.

A Lover's Ear | *Yuan Qiongqiong*

Translated by Howard Goldblatt

He noticed that she carried an ear pick in her purse. She told him that her ears itched from time to time, and she carried it with her so she could clean them whenever she felt like it.

He asked if she would mind cleaning his ears for him. They also itched from time to time.

They had strong feelings for each other by then, and had already done lots of things. Cleaning each other's ears had not been one of them.

In fact, she had used her ear pick only on herself, never to clean anyone else's ears. She had felt that cleaning someone else's ears was the height of intimacy—except, of course, when it was done professionally. Her mother had been the only other person ever to clean her ears. It seemed to her that if a relationship was lacking in passion or in trust, there was little chance that one person would clean the other's ears.

She giggled nervously. "Now?" she asked.

They had agreed to meet somewhere else this time, an open, well-lighted place with lots of people, someplace public. She had insisted on it. She had told him she didn't want to go to his place or to her place this time. There was so much passion in their relationship at this point that whenever they were alone they fell immediately into each other's arms. That left them no time to do anything else.

He smiled back and took her hand. Holding it tightly, he looked her in the eyes and said softly, a little conspiratorially: "Yes, now." The same tone of voice he used when he wanted to do *it*. He would say: "I'm putting it in."

For some strange reason she blushed. Two women at the next table were talking about a man. No more than three paces separated the tables, so every word they said came through clearly.

He was sitting across from her, but it was a small table. She told him to lay his head down on the table, right side facing up. His head was so large it took up nearly half the tabletop. That made it easy for her. She could see all the way down into his ear canal. He had fleshy ears and a wide opening to his ear canal. Strange how you could know everything about someone you were in love with, how you could see their most private parts, yet surprisingly never really notice their ears. Since the light was fairly weak, everything looked a little fuzzy. She asked if she was hurting him. "No," he said.

When she had finished with the right ear, he turned his head to the other side. Neither spoke while she was cleaning his ears, so they could hear every word spoken at the next table. One of the women was saying to the other: "What in the world could have happened? With all that love, I just don't understand it." They were discussing a relationship that had gone sour for no apparent reason. She was concentrating so hard on cleaning his left ear that her eyes began to blur; just then her hand slipped. "Ouch!" he complained tenderly, as though the pain itself were an expression of love. "Oops," she blurted out. "I'm sorry." Drops of blood oozed from the inside wall of his ear. She didn't have the nerve to tell him. "I'm not going to do it anymore," was all she said.

He sat up and felt around in his ear with his pinky, his eyes narrowing as he savored the feeling. Then he gave her a wicked little look and said: "That was sort of like putting it in, wasn't it?"

They broke up not long after that.

Their breakup was accompanied by a very unpleasant scene. It took her a long, long time to get over her feelings of loathing for him and pity for herself. Her only reaction to the news that he had gotten married was indifference—not a trace of emotion. He had become totally irrelevant to her life.

From now on, she reflected, his wife can clean his ears for him. Inexplicably, this thought saddened her—she suddenly felt very, very sad.

1988

Mothballs | *Chen Kehua*

Translated by Julie Chiu

And so they don't say another word. He takes her hand and carries it into his overcoat pocket. They walk off together.

Such cold, dry weather is rare in Taipei. His tan overcoat, with its turned down collar, gives off the faint smell of mothballs, carried in the air by the wind. Only just taken out of the closet, it seems. As she leans close to his shoulder, she thinks: A man's body cannot smell any better than this.

Clean, neutral, with few associations.

Some say a man who smells of tobacco is sexy. She finds that too direct. Like a worker who has baked himself under the fiery sun all day. His body smells of unadulterated flesh. It is bright and glaring, imposing even, but falls short of a subtle, elusive stimulant. And any man who wears cologne or eau de toilette, even for the right occasion, is still somewhat effeminate, although he may be using a brand specifically created for men—unless he is the obvious couldn't-care-less type from a wealthy family, or a fair-faced young revolutionary with his high ideals, cynical and extremely narcissistic. She can't really explain it, but for her, men's perfumes can only be justified when matched with utter cynicism.

But he is none of these types.

Mothballs boast of a homey smell: in a few days, when it gets warm again, he will fold up his overcoat and put it back, throw in a few mothballs, and wait until the next winter to wear it again. If it isn't cold next year, then he'll wear it the year after next. It will always smell the same.

She thinks: The way a man treats his overcoat, and the way he treats his love—to what extent are they similar?

He must be the practical type. This particular overcoat isn't at all trendy, and a man who can wear it must have a certain steadiness of personality.

She thinks.

Right now her hand is held in his, tucked inside his big, wide pocket. She distinctly feels a large, supple, moist hand trying to warm up her chill. In the tightening and loosening of his grip, in the squeezing and letting go, he sends to her powerful electric currents. Aimlessly, the two of them walk on, holding hands, not exchanging a word, shoulder to shoulder, walking on, she taking in the smell of mothballs from his overcoat—suddenly she sees that she will remember it all, all that this moment is about. Walks like this are rare in anyone's lifetime.

Indeed, the smell of mothballs is a mind-settling smell of home, yet, she knows, it is his home.

1989

Short-shorts belong, after all, to the family of fiction—small as a sparrow, they have all the vital organs. With all the features that fiction has, short-shorts differ qualitatively from essays, stories, prose, and satire and should not be blended in with them.

Wei Jinshu

A Shaved Head | *Wang Meng*

Translated by Aili Mu

In the heat of midsummer, Lao Wang wanted to get a haircut. "How about having my head shaved?" he asked his wife.

"No, no," she said anxiously. "Your head has to be smooth and round, round and smooth to have it shaved," she reasoned. "That's the main condition. Your head, shaped like a winter melon, an eggplant, a bullet, wouldn't look right shaved. It would offend public sensibilities. Besides, this isn't the Cultural Revolution. During those years you shaved your head so Red Guards wouldn't be able to grab you by the hair. Now the government is well regulated and society is stable. The people have set their sights on getting rich and living a comfortable life. What's the point of having your head shaved?"

Lao Wang was not convinced: "Why can't I just shave my head to be cool and comfortable? A man in his seventies wouldn't affect the public's sensibilities one way or the other if he wore a pigtail. In describing his mood in retirement, an old colleague once told me, 'Now I can't move forward by being modest or lag behind for being conceited.'[1] Why should a person who couldn't care less about modesty or conceit be afraid of having his head shaved?"

For the sake of family harmony, Lao Wang postponed his head-shaving project. On Sunday he discussed the issue with his children, who were divided into two camps. Supporters argued that shaving one's head is the same as wearing long hair, a matter of fashion. The best diver in the U.S. shaves his head, so do the State Department spokesman, the head of a certain country, and some renowned scholars. It is a man's privilege, his sex appeal, an expression of aging without decline, a symbol of freedom and liberty, the victory of Papa Wang's strong will, an instance of society's progress and cultural diversity. . . .

The opposition retaliated: To be beautiful is not only women's but also men's first need. It is the privilege of the young as well as the old, and a special obligation! Hair is the most beautiful part of a person's body, like a peacock's feathers or other fine hairs on the human body. Great men are not afraid of a bald pate. As a polio victim Roosevelt had to sit in a wheelchair. But because he was Roosevelt, he looked good even in a wheelchair. It added to his bearing. But Papa Wang has spent his whole life without accomplishing much. If he shaves his irregular head, he is bound to invite ridicule. Why can't you be practical and realistic about things?

Lao Wang was bored. Bravely he walked to a nearby barbershop. With resolve and indignation, he told the barber, "Shave it off!"

The barber, radiating youthfulness, didn't seem to hear him. She complimented him, "You have fine hair. Some hair oil will make it even nicer, what do you say?"

Thus, not only did Lao Wang save his hair, he even had it dyed black, had a treatment, and returned home dandified and one hundred yuan poorer. He told his wife there was a barber in the shop who looked like a Hong Kong starlet.

2005

While looking up to the ivory tower of serious literature, the short-short faces up to the needs of the consumer reader.

Xiu Shi

Lover | *Chen Kehua*

Translated by Julie Chiu

In the dark, a certain something was gnawing on his fingers, he felt.

But he was extremely sleepy, so many dreams so heavy on his eyelids.

But then the gnawing got aggressive. Virtually his whole arm was dragged over, that certain something fiercely munching.

It didn't hurt, but the feeling of its teeth's sharp edges was distinct.

Yet from start to finish he did not even open his eyes—as he came to think about it now, he wondered how he could have taken it with such insouciance, allowing the wantonness of an invisible finger-gnawing beast that lurked in the dark?

Gradually he sank into the depths of a dream, a patchwork of feelings and echoes. It was a chaotic dream. His sleep was troubled.

He woke up the next day sensing a peculiar calm and brightness in the air. He came to an awareness that he was all by himself.

He began to examine himself. A residual expression on the face from the happy days; shallow greenish bags under the eyes; lean, sunken cheeks; a stiff neck; flabby arms. And all ten fingers.

Then he realized that someone had clipped his nails last night while he slept.

Each perfect curve, neat and glossy, meticulously manicured. With fresh eyes, he gazed at his fingers for a long while, confused and curious, but for no reason. He wanted to cry.

That was it between him and his lover. Before that, they had both been scratched in the heart.

Yet soon his nails grew long again. To be exact, they simply shot out.

1989

Losing the Feet | *Zhong Jufang*

Translated by Julie Chiu

Her feet always carried a certain smell. Some might say a bad smell.

Spring, summer, fall, or winter, it vanished and then emerged again, now obvious, now faint. Like a shadow to a body, it twirled and lingered, never to be dispelled.

Some people say the feet of a person who sweats a lot smell. The problem may lie in the material or design of the shoes, or in the person's physical condition. And so on and so forth.

The smell was never too strong, not the kind that would turn people away. Every time she took off her shoes, or even slippers or sandals, the smell would be in the air. Other times, the smell was undetectable. People generally paid attention to her beauty, talent, temperament, and attire, but not to the inconspicuous smell. She seldom took her shoes off in public. And so only a few people had been exposed to that unique smell.

I was one of the few.

I was not a family member, boyfriend, or husband. I was a clerk in a shoe store.

She probably cared a lot about the smell of her feet. She never asked anyone but me to fetch shoes for her fittings, not wanting even one more person to find out about the smell.

She loved shoes that looked simple but were unique, and placed comfort over fanciful designs. Did not love high heels. Never very fussy, but particular about her demands. Before every purchase, she studied not only the surface but also the soles and stitches. If she found the material or craftsmanship not to her satisfaction, she would give up the shoes even if they were of excellent design and at a fantastic bargain. She was a customer who knew what she was buying.

Days went by, and I knew she patronized only our store. Maybe she minded having someone else smell her feet. Sometimes, when she couldn't find any patterns in the store that she liked, she asked to have a pair custom-made. I wasn't particularly familiar with custom-making, but she insisted on having me take her measurements. She said it with such urgency, fear spreading across her face, as if she were terrified that her new boyfriend was about to discover the odor. I could only comply.

It was an autumn evening, cool, crisp and bright. I traced the shape of her feet with a pencil.

Her feet were neither too big nor too small. Long, slim, and a bit bony. Full, round heels. Very neat feet, with toes of just the right size, nails nicely manicured. Her feet were a little fairer than her legs and face, with markings of the sandal straps, probably just tanned by the sun.

A pair of very attractive feet, with a unique smell.

Every day I encountered many women and many pairs of feet. Some had a very pretty face and legs, but misshapen, dirty toes pointing sideways. But her feet radiated life, clean, luminous, and soulful. One look at them settled your mind, bringing it calmness and clarity. It was as if in a split second, all turmoil was lightly flattened and quieted by her feet.

I remember clearly my first encounter with her. She was probably still a student, with a ponytail and a big cloth bag over her shoulder, rather casually dressed. I said to myself: Just another teenage girl. One of the fifty-plus who came in and out of our store every day.

She took a long look, not at the shoes, but at us—every clerk who worked there. She studied us very carefully, but, not wanting us to be conscious of her scrutiny, she let her glances fall on a few shoes before drawing near to one of the clerks to steal a good look. I was serving a woman, squatting to put a shoe on her foot. She walked up to me and sniffed me out. Ah yes, I had the feeling that I was not watched but sniffed. It was a weird feeling and sent a shiver down my spine. I turned to look at her.

We exchanged a look. Her eyes shone with steady intelligence, lucid and bright. Then she made up her mind: she would try on some shoes, and I would serve her.

Altogether there were seven clerks, male and female. I was neither the oldest nor the youngest. Nor was I the best-looking one. I had been working there for about six months, bored with the dullness and trivialities of the job. I was twenty-five, not sure what else I could do. But she singled me out, and I stayed. It has now been seven years.

The day she took off her shoes I was aware of her smell, not strong but not mild either. Never had there been another pair of feet with the same smell. I offered to tie her shoelaces. No need, she said, and did the laces herself. Once her feet were in the shoes, the smell was gone. Burning with anxiety, I wondered if the smell was real or imagined. Then came a moment when all my thoughts and worries were cleared, about me only a solitary void, a quietude I'd never known before.

She nodded and said she would take that pair. Feet out of the shoes, the smell returned; feet into her old shoes, the smell disappeared. In the obscurity of coming and going, I felt as if I had passed through several lifetimes.

After that I was the only one who served her. I could tell she was a competent woman with high expectations. She came once or twice every month. She didn't always buy something, but when she did she made quality choices. One time, she rushed into the store in flip-flops and a plain, formal dress, her hair done up in a gaudy bun. She looked a little flustered. She said she'd scoured her apartment but couldn't find a single pair of shoes to match her dress. Which was why she'd come in such haste.

That was the only time I saw her rattled. But even then, the smell and shape of her feet remained unchanged, graceful as always, wiping away the chaos of noise and colors, as always. When she kicked off her flip-flops and stretched out her feet, all the sounds and figures and actions came to a halt—all was mellow and joyous, all was bright.

In the days that followed, her attire changed and there was increased sophistication and style in her grooming. Even her male companions changed—from the nice big boy to the unkempt fellow, from the giddy and garish to the quiet and refined. Her eyes began to show fine lines in the corners. Her hair was cut shorter and shorter. With each visit, her face radiated greater beauty, and her speech became more apt and elegant. What remained unchanged were her feet and the smell they carried.

After changing girlfriends several times, I had gotten married two years earlier and had taken a part-time night job.

My wife said there was no future in a shoe store; I wouldn't starve but wouldn't thrive either. In seven years I'd been promoted twice. Now I was manager, and that was as high as I could go. I was only in my early thirties, and I needed a better career. So I worked at night as a broker of foreign-exchange futures. I attended a six-month course and moonlighted five nights a week, managing only three or four hours of sleep.

My part-time job brought in twice the income I received from the shoe store. My wife told me to quit and concentrate on my broker work.

I didn't. I still saw her once or twice a month, sometimes to take her orders for custom-made shoes, sometimes simply to chat, as we were now pretty well acquainted. She seemed to still mind the smell of her feet being detected by others. Once, when she was trying on some new shoes, a fat woman sat down beside her and showered praise on the shoes she was wearing. She moved away immediately and did not remove her shoes until the woman had walked off.

Then early one summer, after a morning visit, she disappeared.

The store had just opened when she came in and bought a pair of white sandals. Everything was as usual. But after that, time passed— one month, three months, six months—and she didn't show up. I knew she'd never show up again.

I quit my job in the shoe store. That night I went home and washed my face, took off my shoes, and bared my feet. All of a sudden I noticed the same smell that her feet used to carry, and the smell was coming from my own feet.

The world became calm and steady, an endless expanse of bright, lucid purity. . . .

1998

Fad | *Zhang Zheng*

Translated by Julie Chiu

Tang Ying was obsessed with the thought that her clothes weren't hip enough. She spent five or six renminbi a month subscribing to magazines like *L'Officiel*, *Fashion*, and *Haut Couture* but still felt dissatisfied with her personal style. Hep, maybe, but not hip. When she got off work, she stood in front of the big dressing mirror and felt just, well, bummed out.

When it actually happened she couldn't recall, but one day she discovered a whole new continent! Some two hundred meters from where she lived, a British girl, in the prime of her youth, had moved in. Blonde, green-eyed, this girl wore clothes that, let's face it, had never been seen in China before. Not by Tang Ying, not even by those stupid editors of *Fashion* who, compared to this girl, were real dingbats. What was she wearing that day? The top was some sort of bat cut. Its folds were tucked neatly at the waist but spread in rays all the way down to the heels. A non-jumpsuit jumpsuit. Ultra cool! The outfit was made with a decent silk fabric which, as the girl walked, rustled, and showed off her slim figure and her lovely buns and thighs. Tang Ying was mesmerized! This girl's my height and build! How can I claim to be a modern woman? Tang felt as if someone had rubbed red chili peppers on her cheeks!

So every day she waited at the street corner by the park so she would walk up to British Girl from the opposite direction. She made sure she'd come face to face with the girl, and would openly look her up and down. That was far from being polite, for sure, but she didn't care!

Somehow Tang Ying felt that British Girl also looked her up and down, with a faint, mysterious smile on her face. Tang Ying spoke no English and had no intention of striking up a conversation. All she wanted was to figure out those super-moda outfits!

Tang Ying was a smart girl. She shut herself in one Saturday night and the whole next day. Big mirror in front of her, she worked for twenty-five solid hours, cutting, checking, madly treadling the sewing machine. And so the real thing was born, a trendy outfit that would turn British Girl's green eyes red. Tang even sewed a vivid, velvety panda on the chest. Sell it at a hawker's stall, and you could ask at least two hundred renminbi.

The next morning Tang Ying was up at five o'clock. She put on the outfit, which had been placed under the mattress and pressed for the night. She carefully did her hair, letting it hang gracefully on her shoulders. She drew on eyebrows and put on light makeup. Here's a face that could fell a city! Even Tang herself was charmed. Yes, beauty is right *here*! Tang could feel her heart pounding. Ah, that's bliss, that's joy! Thus have psychologists explained abnormally fast heartbeats at moments like this.

At 7:40 British Girl walked out of her apartment complex and headed for the subway to go to work. All full of herself, Tang walked toward British Girl. Crisp, familiar footsteps echoing in her ears, Tang straightened up and tried to keep her steps slow and steady.

God!

When their eyes met at the street corner by the park, Tang and British Girl both put their hands to their mouths. They stood there stiffly, five or six meters apart, staring at each other, insuppressible cries of shock bursting from their lips. British Girl was wearing a lotus-colored *qipao* exactly like the one Tang had just changed out of. Even the peach-blossom pattern was the same!

1987

II. Change | *Howard Goldblatt*

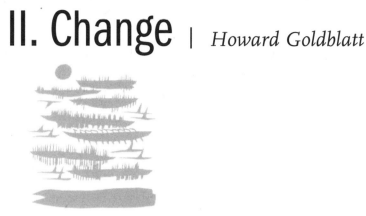

In every election since 1968 I've written in the name Robert Kennedy for president. That first time didn't seem at all quixotic. You simply don't change horses in midstream.

Over the next eight elections I looked at the choices and saw no reason to abandon my pursuit of "statement." My friends all thought I was nuts.

Then last year they appealed to my fears of where we were headed, reminding me of the critical juncture at which the country stood and the micro-slim margins in some states in the previous election. Their arguments convinced me it was time to change. So this time I wrote in Martin Luther King.

Wrong Number | *Liu Yichang*

Translated by D. E. Pollard

I

Chen Xi was lying on his bed looking at the ceiling when the telephone rang. It was Wu Lichang. She suggested going to see the five-thirty film at the Lee Theater. He perked up at once, and briskly set about shaving, combing his hair, and changing his clothes. As he changed he whistled the tune of an old patriotic song, "We Are the Bold Chinese." Having finished changing he stood in front of the wardrobe and looked himself up and down in the mirror; he decided he would have to buy himself a designer tracksuit. He loved Lichang, and Lichang loved him. As soon as he found a job they could go to the marriage registry office and name a day. He had just come back from America, and though he had got a degree, finding work was still a matter of luck. If his luck was good it shouldn't take long, but if his luck was out he might have to wait a while. He had already applied for seven or eight jobs, and the replies ought to be coming back any time now. That was in fact the reason why he had been hanging about at home all day: he was waiting for the firms where he had applied to give him a ring. Normally he wouldn't go out unless absolutely necessary, but in Lichang's case it was different: going to the cinema with her was not to be missed. It was already four-fifty; he had to get a move on to get to the Lee Theater in time. Lichang would be annoyed if he was late. So he took the distance to his flat door in big strides, opened the door, then the steel security grille, went outside, closed both the door and the grille behind him, took the lift downstairs, went out of the building, and made his way with a song in his heart to the bus stop. He had just got to the bus stop when a bus approached at high speed. The bus was out of control; it crashed into the bus stop, knocked down Chen Xi and an old lady and a young girl, and squashed them flat.

II

Chen Xi was lying on his bed looking at the ceiling when the telephone rang. It was Wu Lichang. She suggested going to see the five-thirty film at the Lee Theater. He perked up at once, and briskly set about shaving, combing his hair, and changing his clothes. As he changed he whistled the tune of an old patriotic song, "We Are the Bold Chinese." Having finished changing he stood in front of the wardrobe and looked himself up and down in the mirror; he decided he would have to buy himself a designer tracksuit. He loved Lichang, and Lichang loved him. As soon as he found a job they could go to the marriage registry office and name a day. He had just come back from America, and though he had got a degree, finding work was still a matter of luck. If his luck was good it shouldn't take long, but if his luck was out he might have to wait a while. He had already applied for seven or eight jobs, and the replies ought to be coming back any time now. That was in fact the reason why he had been hanging about at home all day: he was waiting for the firms where he had applied to give him a ring. Normally he wouldn't go out unless absolutely necessary, but in Lichang's case it was different: going to the cinema with her was not to be missed. It was already four-fifty; he had to get a move on to get to the Lee Theater in time. Lichang would be annoyed if he was late. So he took the distance to his flat door in big strides, opened it . . .

The telephone rang again.

Thinking it was someone from one of those firms he had applied to, he rushed back to answer it.

A woman's voice came over the line:

"Is Uncle there, please?"

"Who?"

"Uncle."

"There's no such person here."

"Is Auntie there, then?"

"What number do you want?"

"3-975 . . ."

"You want a Kowloon number?"

"Yes."

"Wrong number! This is Hong Kong side!"

Slamming the telephone down angrily, he covered the distance to the door in big strides, opened the security grille, went outside, closed the flat door and grille behind him, took the lift downstairs, went out of the building, and with a song in his heart headed for the bus stop. When he was about fifty paces from the bus stop, he was startled to see a bus approach the stop at high speed and, out of control, crash into the bus stop, knocking over an old lady and a young girl, and squashing them flat.[*]

1983

Learning to Talk | *Wang Meng*

Translated by Aili Mu

When Lao Wang's grandson started to talk, he created many original expressions. For example, he called his mom "Momsy," his dad "Heady," a horse "ah-ohs," a train "hoot-toot," milk "white-white," and an apple "chubby." For a while the whole family, young and old, changed their accustomed way of speaking accordingly. Unanimously they addressed the mother as "Momsy," the father as "Heady," a horse they called "ah-ohs," a train "hoot-toot," and so on. The grandson's language became their language. Feeling its originality and creativity, they were all ecstatic and eager to use it.

Before long the boy started kindergarten and learned to talk from his teacher. All his "mistakes" were addressed: he now called his mother "Mommy," his father "Daddy," a horse "a horse," milk "milk," and an apple "an apple."

While his grandson was experiencing healthy growth, Lao Wang felt lost and was bored stiff.

2002

A Seat | *Liu Guofang*

Translated by Aili Mu

Li Yan's workplace was in a new development, far from her home. She had to take the bus to work.

Li Yan was fearful of riding the bus.

[*]Author's note: Today's newspaper reported a fatal accident at a bus stop in Taikoo Shing.

Li Yan boarded the bus midway. The bus departed from the terminal, and did not make it to where she waited until after five or six stops.

By this time the bus was crowded. Even standing space was tight, let alone any chance of finding a seat. The bus continued on its way. There were seven or eight more stops, with people getting on at just about every one. The bus became more and more crowded. At times Li Yan had people clinging to her from behind, pushing her from the front, and leaning against her on both sides. Li Yan was short, and every so often, it was so jammed she could hardly breathe. Most people on the bus worked in the new development. They were from various institutions and enterprises, and had more or less the same work hours. Riding the bus together every day, they pretty much knew one another. Occasionally, Li Yan would display envy of those who boarded at the early stops. "You folks have got it made," she said. "Get on early and take a seat."

Those in the seats smiled and said: "Then why don't you come to our stop and board there?"

"What a pity," she replied, "that I don't live there."

At times, it was not only crowded, but the passengers were knocked about when the bus braked suddenly. One time, Li Yan was leaning against a seat when the driver jammed on the brakes. At the mercy of momentum, people bore down on her from behind, and since her chest was right up against the back of the seat, she felt as if her breastbone was nearly crushed. After being freed, Li Yan grumbled to an acquaintance beside her: "You can't even get a seat on this damned bus!"

Another acquaintance commented: "If you want a seat, go get an official post. As soon as you're an office holder, you'll get your seat."

While the acquaintance was talking, beyond the window, one car after another passed the bus. "That car belongs to the Department of Finance," the acquaintance announced to Li Yan. "That one belongs to the Department of Public Health, and that's Mayor Wu's car. Those officials don't need to ride in a crowded bus. They have their seats in cars."

"According to you," Li Yan replied, "none of the people riding in crowded buses hold official posts."

Someone else chimed in: "There's absolutely no one on this bus who holds an official post. Ask around if you don't believe me. Not even someone at the deputy department head level."

Li Yan didn't ask around, but she later understood that there were, indeed, no officials among those who took this crowded bus to work.

After a year or two of taking the crowded bus, Li Yan was finally able to have her seat. Naturally, it wasn't that she became an official and was able to ride in a car, but because she got married. Her husband lived near the bus terminal, so when Li Yan set out to work, the bus was parked at the terminal. She boarded with plenty of empty seats and very few people, chose a good seat, and sat all the way to work.

During that period, there were no complaints from Li Yan. When people seemed envious of her having a seat, she would say: "You ought to move to our neighborhood. If you did, you'd have a seat every day."

Unexpectedly, however, a few days after Li Yan uttered these words, the situation changed again.

One day, she was sitting in the bus on her way to work. All the seats had been taken after three or four stops. Then a fat man boarded. Someone saw him and cried out: "Mayor Li, what are you doing on a crowded bus?"

The fat man replied: "Haven't you heard? The municipal government has issued a regulation stipulating that senior officials are not allowed to take cars to work. They must use public transportation."

This news prompted the man to say: "Come over here, Mayor Li. You can have my seat."

The fat man went over and sat in the man's vacated seat.

At every stop after that someone cried out. One said: "Chief Hu, so you're on this crowded bus, too! Here, you can have my seat."

Another said: "Secretary Jia, please, take my seat."

And yet another said: "Minister Sun, you can have my seat."

As there were senior officials boarding the bus the whole way, so also were there people giving up their seats. In the end, Li Yan noticed that most of the seats were taken by heads and other bosses of various institutions and enterprises.

Yet another stop. Li Yan saw her own boss, Chief Tang, board. He stood right next to her. Chief Tang was older than Li Yan and was a senior official. Much as she hated it, she had to do it—she got to her feet and said: "Chief Tang, here, take my seat."

Chief Tang's hindquarters immediately hit the seat.

The situation soon became routine, and once again, Li Yan had no seat.

2004

A short-short is a keen sensibility—to capture a story from one aspect, one frame, one contrast, one exclamation, one fleeting moment—a wisdom, a beauty, an intriguing occasion, and a fresh idea.

Wang Meng

Self-Murder | *Cai Nan*

Translated by Aili Mu

I discovered Myself one morning. It was a morning like all others. I awoke at six-thirty, and was startled to see a man sitting at the foot of the bed. I sat up abruptly, rubbed my eyes, and asked guardedly yet sternly: Who are you?

I am you, the man answered with a smile but without moving.

Who am I? I then asked.

You are me, he replied.

I sized up the man in front of me: black Pierre Cardin suit and light yellow silk tie with a white floral pattern, and wearing a pair of cheap, off-brand leather shoes—my outfit exactly. Then my eyes scanned his face: broad cheeks, thick lips, narrow eyes—my look exactly. Recognizing him as Myself, I reached out to shake hands with Myself.

Seated at the head of the bed, I began talking excitedly with Myself. I said that since I'd been in this city too long, I planned to go on a long trip this summer. It's bad for a person to stay put for too long, and I wanted to get out. I told him that the manager of my company did not like me because I did my job well without giving a damn what he said. He couldn't fire me because his daughter, Miaoling, was madly in love with me, and so I still occupied the position of office head. I'd told him I wanted to get away, but he wouldn't let me, nor would Miaoling. The former worried about work, while the latter hated parting company with me. I'd long nurtured the thought of how wonderful it would be if I could have a double, one who goes to work, the other out to have fun! Today my thoughts had turned into reality. Things could not have been better!

While I was delivering my long monologue, Myself's hands ached from my iron grip and the shaking. Seeing my childlike countenance, Myself smiled magnanimously: I'm here, so you go ahead, don't worry.

I packed up and began my planned trip. First from north to south, then from east to west, the distances I traveled were long and the places I visited far away. Like a bard, I chanted my passion onto mountains and waters. At each stop, I called home at night to hear Myself's report on progress at work and in romance. Myself told me that he sat in my chair every day and worked as hard as I once had. He served the manager with modesty: helping him in negotiations, assisting him in business, chatting and playing chess with him. He even escorted him to dance halls and sauna baths, and entertained young women with him. The manager praised him, saying it was as if he'd become a new man. Myself also reported that the relationship with Miaoling was developing as I'd expected, steady and passionate. They had embraced, kissed, and were about to get to such essential issues as marriage and how to obtain housing.

I was pleased by the progress. With Myself as a substitute, I could travel without a care in the world and receive my handsome salary at the same time. I might even be in line for a promotion. Myself's talents earned my full admiration.

My suspicions of Myself did not occur until after I'd called home five times in succession and no one had picked up the phone. I'd changed from calling home once a day to once at each new location. That is to say, I lost contact with Myself for a long time during my visits to five cities. Each time I called I was greeted with a short recorded message: I'm accompanying the manager to a new development. Please leave a message. Or: I'm at the movies with Miaoling. Please leave a message. Or: The manager has taken me on an inspection tour. Please leave a message. Or: I've gone with Miaoling to check out the new house. Please leave a message. Later on it was: We've gotten married. Please leave a message. We're on our way to the hospital. Please leave a message. . . .

My mind, a weedy expanse, was soon crowded with doubts: Had it been a mistake to give Myself such a free hand? Are we, I and Myself, one person, or two? Will the manager's appreciation of Myself undermine my own position? Am I wearing a green hat—a cuckold—because Myself has married Miaoling? Plagued by these doubts, my interest in the pleasures of travel diminished and I grew weary of beautiful landscapes and sentimental affairs.

Just before embarking on the trip to my final destination—Tibet—I turned and headed for home, relinquishing the chance to explore this mythical, enchanting land, and boarded a plane for the trip back to the city of my departure.

Myself was not in when I got home. I could tell from the accumulated dust on the desk and bed that Myself had not been there for some time. I called my office; Myself wasn't there either. I asked, and was told, that he was in the manager's office.

I decided to show up at work. I headed straight for the manager's office. I knocked, went in, and saw Myself seated in the manager's chair, talking to a member of the office staff who had once been my subordinate. Both were surprised to see me, especially my subordinate. He shot a glance at me, then at Myself; perplexity was written all over his face. I had to lie—I came from the countryside to see my brother.

After my subordinate left, Myself told me, while pouring tea, that the former manager had been killed in a car accident and that Myself had been promoted to manager. The one-time subordinate who'd just left was the new office head. Myself also informed me that Miaoling was two months pregnant. . . .

I threw my tea cup to the floor; hot water splashed on my feet. I grimaced in pain. There was no doubt in my mind that I and Myself had separated, that I was me and he was him. It was no longer possible for us—psychologically, biologically, or practically—to be recombined into one again. I was overcome by sadness.

Back home, I shut myself up and thought for a long time. A plan emerged. I prepared a meal, called Myself on his cell phone, and left a message: Please come home for dinner tonight.

Myself showed up as expected, bringing with him a bag of fruit. After exchanging greetings, I took out a bottle of Qingke wine from Qinghai. I and Myself drank to our hearts' content. I talked about the ancient paths of the Shaanxi plains, the solitary mist of the Great Desert, and the pleasantly soft Suzhou dialect; Myself spoke of the vicissitudes of life, the ups and downs of the business world, and institutional reform. Two bottles were soon empty. By then drunk, I asked Myself: Who are you? Myself answered, I am me. Then I asked: Who am I? You are you. With these words, Myself fell to the floor, drunk.

The end had arrived—now, in great agony, I felt that I was indeed me and he was indeed him. It looked as if there was only one way to deal with the problem of recombining. And I knew I had to take that action.

After dragging the drunken Myself all the way to the bathroom and throwing him into the tub, I fetched the chain saw I'd bought for this purpose, and went to work on Myself. . . .

I dismembered Myself. I murdered Myself. I saw Myself's blood fill the tub.

Light on my feet, I went to work the next day. Sitting in the manager's office, I phoned Miaoling to tell her that today was my birthday.

1998

Last Stop, Mongkok | *Che Zhengxuan*

Translated by Julie Chiu

"It's right over there, on the top floor of the tenement building." Sai Keung raises his arm and points to a penthouse apartment on 997 Shanghai Street. His hands are covered with fine, interwoven wrinkles, obviously not those of a teenage boy. The delicate gentleness has long since evaporated. Aged hands are not necessarily annoying, but this pair is particularly tedious. "Look for a sign that says 'Stud Keys' next to a doorbell, and that'll be it. Tell 'em Sai Keung sent you. Got it?"

Two red, two green, and one blue neon tubes were pointing to the flat.

"Hmm" emerges from the vibrating vocal chords of the teenage girl with him.

"Look me up later at the newspaper stall outside Fat Cow's Hot Pot!"

Without a word, the teenage girl heads toward 997 Shanghai Street.

Sai Keung crosses the street and makes for the newspaper stall without even looking to see if a car is coming.

Sai Keung throws down twelve dollars and picks up a copy of *Flashing Flame and Warrior*. He thumbs the pages with deft fingers, the deftness mocking the wrinkles on his hands.

"Stud Keys" is a great name. From a literary point of view, it's a subtle symbol that tacitly embodies a wealth of meanings. The imagery isn't bad either. The name was conceived before the handover of Hong Kong's sovereignty. During that period, the police made major efforts to take down neon signs of the sex trade, and touched up the scene quite a bit. But the unchanging law is, when the strength of angels is enhanced one point, devils always catch up tenfold. What comes down will go back up—later if not sooner. The comeback devil shows even greater power, and will not be harmed again, not even a single hair.

The many signs that emerged in the period were of high literary quality. "Empress Electricity," "Apollo Lightings," and "People's Nuts and Bolts" were among the best of those days. Those palace-style signs must have been the work of the old-timers who patronized Tak Yu Teahouse, the ones who brought their bird cages with them to *yam cha*—sample tea. Though they had little education, they all knew lines like "In the morning, a maid by the Yue river / At night a concubine in the Wu palace." Or "Dawn sees the twelve mansions ready with makeup / At Immortal Lookout her gaze is turned toward the Emperor." But they have all gotten old now. Their days of taking birdcages to the teahouse are gone. Tak Yu Teahouse has been torn down.

Then came some imitation palace-style signs, but they were way too inferior. Signs like "Dundas Restaurant" and "Art Nouveau Photography" were all appropriated from the shops downstairs and turned into their own revered brands. These names were far from original.

Gone is the general. With the strength to bare the branches of a champion tree, a cold wind is flipping the "Stud Keys" sign, which looks as if it will fall down at any moment.

The teenage girl's client is a man in his seventies. He screws her once, done in less than three minutes.

The deep wrinkles on his hands swim over the girl's breasts, abdomen, buttocks, thighs, calves, and toes. In the yellow light of the neon sign, the wrinkles seem incised in her fair, young skin, too. Her moans die down as his aged panting comes to a dead standstill. It is exactly two minutes and fifty-nine seconds.

When she showers, the teenage girl rubs her body for a long time, but in the gloomy yellow light the traces seem impossible to wash away.

She turns off the tap and walks out of the bathroom. One piece after another, she puts her clothes back on, which have been scattered all over the floor. First, a tiny, low-cut golden blouse, then a black mini-skirt ten inches above her knees, and finally a pair of boots with four-inch heels. After getting paid for her work, the girl leaves with her little handbag stuffed with cosmetics, a cell phone, and a pack of cigarettes.

She walks over to the newspaper stall by Fat Cow's Hot Pot. Sai Keung is still clutching his copy of *Flashing Flame and Warrior* in his aged, tedious hands.

"Big Brother Keung, I'm done," the teenage girl says.

2002

Parting | *Wang Kuishan*

Translated by Aili Mu

On the day Mangzi had to return to active duty, Xiao'e accompanied him to town to see him off.

They reached the train station before the ticket window had opened, so they squatted in the square in front of the station and talked. After a while, Mangzi stopped talking and just stared at Xiao'e, utterly infatuated. "Would you please stop gawking at me like that?" Xiao'e said. "That's a greedy look!" Mangzi smiled and replied, "How did you know I was gawking at you if you weren't gawking at me?" Xiao'e made a spitting noise and said, "Shame on you!" Mangzi whispered, "I really want to kiss you again." "Are you crazy?" Xiao'e cried. She stood up. Mangzi followed her lead and stood up, too. He paced up and down. Then, apparently having made up his mind, he said, "I'm not going to take the next train." "Why not?" "I'll take the night train. There's one a little after ten o'clock." "We talked it all over," Xiao'e said, "and now you won't leave as planned. You change your mind from one moment to the next." Mangzi showed a naughty smile and repeated, "I'll wait and leave at night." He then lowered his voice, "I have to kiss you again when it's dark, then I'll go. I won't have any peace of mind if I leave without doing it." Before Xiao'e could give her consent, Mangzi made straight for the street. Knowing how stubborn he was, she followed him.

They strolled around the shopping arcade. When Mangzi saw lovers walking hand in hand, he wanted to follow suit. He made a few attempts but didn't dare reach out. They then strolled through a park. On the park benches, lovers were in each others' arms; some were even hugging and kissing in broad daylight. Shocked at the sight, Xiao'e turned and walked away. Mangzi, distressed to see her backtrack her way out, shouted, "Xiao'e, Xiao'e, don't leave. Please don't leave!" With his rural, mountain-area dialect, and loud voice, Mangzi drew a peal of laughter from nearby park visitors.

Time dragged on until mid-afternoon, when they returned to the square in front of the railway station.

"There's a train a little after five," said Xiao'e. "You might as well take it."

"No!" Mangzi said resolutely. "I refuse to do that. I'll be damned if I don't wait for the ten o'clock train!"

Xiao'e thought for a moment, then asked him: "What will I do after you leave in the middle of the night?"

"Why not spend the night in an inn?"

"That's easy for you to say. You can't find one for less than eight to ten yuan. Do you have that kind of money"

"If that's how much it costs," Mangzi said, "we'll just have to spend it."

Xiao'e glared at him, "Braggart!"

Mangzi chuckled.

Suddenly, someone cried out, "Mangzi! Mangzi!"

They turned and saw Mangzi's father. Anxious to know if something had happened, Mangzi asked, "Dad, what are you doing here?"

"Weren't you going to take the nine o'clock train? Why are you still here?"

Mangzi blushed and said, "I couldn't get a ticket."

Mangzi's father said, "Your mother was worried that something might have happened when Xiao'e didn't return. She sent me to fetch her."

Mangzi flew into a rage. "What could happen in broad daylight!"

In the face of Mangzi's anger, his father hemmed and hawed, "Your mother forced me to come. I said not to worry, but she wouldn't listen."

Ill-humored, Mangzi told his father, "Go on home."

"Why so soon? Since I'm already here, I'd like to see you off and then go back home with Xiao'e."

Mangzi knew his plan had fallen through. He stood up sullenly and headed for the ticket window.

Xiao'e followed on his heels.

While he stood in line for the ticket, Xiao'e took advantage of the bustle of the crowd to press her handkerchief into his hand and then secretly leave her hand tucked into his.

To her surprise, Mangzi, unappreciative of her effort, pushed her hand away. She smiled, nudged him, and offered her hand again. This time, he took it and squeezed, squeezed hard. Although she gasped in pain, she didn't pull back, preferring to let him have his way.

Mangzi left on the five o'clock train.

Before he walked off to the platform, he tossed off a casual comment: "It's hard for us country folk to get anything done!"

His father gave him a stern look and said, "What's so hard? There are buses to get you to town, and there are trains to get you back to your unit. What's hard about that? Why, in the old days . . ."

Xiao'e laughed up her sleeve.

1997

I have always felt that in my own (and other people's) existence, there are spots of glittering light that are capable of suddenly illuminating or scorching the soul. When this happens, it draws forth in me a singular rush of inspiration, filling me with the desire to try my hand at a "one-sentence story." We call it life at a glimpse. . . . To me, the most important trick is to "leave blank" . . . to draw on the wondrous charm of "leaving unsaid."

Liu Xinwu

The Beat | *Liu Xinwu*

Translated by Julie Chiu

Metronome in hand, he walked into the residential area.

As he crossed a grassy area, he noted that the stone bench under a silk tree was unoccupied. So he sat down to rest.

He took the metronome out of the package and began to play with it. He let it strike a fast beat. The sound it produced made him laugh. He then switched to a slow, leisurely beat and stood the gadget on the bench.

An old man walked by. One glance and he knew: this was someone who was prone to starting up conversations with strangers. He quickly looked away, but the old-timer chose to stop right in front of him. In fact, he even bent over and asked, in a gentle voice, "Learning to play the piano. . . . How old?"

He picked up the metronome and set it in his lap. The old-timer sat down beside him. "Not in school yet? . . ."

He muttered a vague answer. Obviously pleased to have finally found someone to talk to, the old-timer began to run at the mouth, "It's been three years since our Jingjing studied the piano. She's already passed the grade 5 exam. . . . Oh, Jingjing's my granddaughter, my daughter's daughter. . . . In the past, people only took the son's daughters as granddaughters, and daughter's daughters were called "outside" granddaughters. . . . Men and women are equal now. . . . They all have your own blood, so why bother distinguishing between "inside" and "outside"? Don't you agree? . . . Is yours a daughter or a son? . . . Doing Thompson or Czerny? . . . Jingjing and her class gave a performance recently at the East Gate Youth Palace—I learned about it from an ad in the newspaper. . . . Aye, a pity I don't own a piano, or they'd have come by more often. . . . But I'm thrilled all the same! . . . Do your parents have a piano? . . . So many people are learning the instrument these days, there's no way pianos will get cheaper. They'll just stay at these high prices. . . ." Getting no response, the old-timer heaved a sigh.

The summer sun filtered through the branches and fell on the metronome, which was still knocking out a dance beat. He suddenly sensed a pleading tone in the beat, and his heart softened. The old-timer sitting beside him was no longer a nuisance. He cocked his head to look at the old-timer, and found him looking back at him, his head having obviously been cocked that way for quite a while. He smiled at the old-timer, whose ready smile became even broader.

But he still didn't know what to say to him. The old-timer opened his mouth to speak again. "A steady guy, you are, staying all this while listening to me babble. . . . Jingjing's family—her dad in particular— never sits with me this long. When he's at my place, he's so busy he won't even sit down on the sofa. . . . Not that he's chosen not to sit; he simply can't. Either his pager is beeping nonstop or his cell phone is buzzing like a wasp. . . . He comes like a gust of wind, and goes like a waft of smoke. . . . Well, I won't say he means any disrespect; he's a filial son in both families. Still, he leaves new pajamas for his mom at my place or a T-shirt for me at his mom's. . . . My daughter and grand-daughter are willing to sit with me awhile, but they both have so many exams to take. They're forever short one certificate, and there's always the next higher level to reach. . . . Busy folks who wish they could grow a pair of wings! . . . But you—you're a steady guy! . . . ."

He knew he wasn't really such a steady guy. He switched off the metronome and put it back in the package. He smiled at the old-timer again, saying, "It's a beautiful day. . . . Not so hot. . . . I've got to go. . . . See you again!"

And so he left, surprised to note that he hadn't been like a gust of wind or a waft of smoke. And he'd never leave the metronome in the wrong place. . . . The thought made him smile.

. . . He climbed the apartment building steps. . . . He pressed the bell and could hear the happy voice inside. . . . The door opened, revealing the joyful face of an old lady. . . . She took the metronome. . . .

. . . Inside the apartment, a brand new piano stood by the wall. The metronome was immediately taken out of the package and put on the piano, beside a tri-colored horse figurine, an imitation of glazed ceramics from the Tang Dynasty. . . . A closed copy of *A Beginner's Piano Course for Children* was sitting on the music stand. . . .

He looked around him, his face showing amazement. The curtains, cushions, sofa cover, and table cloth—everything that used to be brown or a batik blue and white—were now a soft pink or yellow tone. . . . Still made of batik-dyed fabric, but basically a cheerful red and white pattern sprinkled with spots of green. . . .

He could not help marveling: "Mom, everything's gotten younger here!"

His mother took the *Piano Course* down and passed it to him. "It only came in the mail today. . . ." He took the book and turned to the title page, where he saw his younger sister's scribble: "For dear Mom, as she moves into her second childhood. . . . "

. . . Mom sat on the piano bench and set the metronome in motion. As her eyes followed the "tadpoles" on the *Piano Course*, she picked out a simple practice tune. . . .

He realized that he'd been standing all along. . . . He was feeling shy. . . . He anchored himself deep into the sofa. . . . From the side, he watched his mother's coarse hands crawl up and down the keyboard, and noted the peculiar lights emanating from her eyes. . . .

Retired, his mother had spent all her savings to realize a secret dream that had never faded in her heart. . . . The old days, in their small, fine details, all came back to life. They swelled his heart, surging, drifting, flying. . . .

The metronome directed the simplest, most innocent notes. Following the beat of the tune, he could feel particles of dust shaken off from the heart in his chest. . . .

2000

III. Choices | *Howard Goldblatt*

"I simply can't make up my mind. They're all so cute. Just look at all that fur! And those eyes . . . oh, my, what are they doing? Stop it!"

"They're only playing. You know, babies . . ."

"That doesn't look like playing to me. I said stop it!"

"Please don't stick your hand in there."

"Ouch! Let go!"

"Oh, my God, what's happening? What have you done?"

"What have *I* done? What are *they* doing?"

"They've never . . . "

"Help! They won't let go of me!"

Whack! Smack! "There, that did it."

"Would you look at that! Those little bastards!"

"Yes, I see. So, tell me, which one do you want?"

"Left" with No Chance | *Chang Gang*

Translated by Aili Mu

A certain marketing company had placed an ad for a couple of assistants. Brimming with confidence, dossier in hand, I went to apply.

A good many people were there ahead of me when I reached the company's office, all in high spirits, as if the high-paying job was theirs for the taking. As I looked them over, I couldn't help feeling that I was certainly no less qualified than any of them and had absolutely no reason to feel inferior. With that thought, I took my place at the end of the line, filled with confidence.

The line began to move, and each applicant handed an admission slip to the guard at the door, who tore it in half and let the person in, sort of like having your ticket punched at the train station.

"By every indication, this company employs strict hiring practices, and that's good news," I said under my breath as I waited patiently. Finally, half an hour or so later, it was my turn, so, bracing myself, I went inside.

I walked down a corridor that abruptly forked off, one corridor to the left, another to the right. I was wondering which way to go when I spotted a small sign: "Those with a bachelor's degree or higher from a top university, please go to the left. Everyone else go to the right."

I cheerfully went to the left, turned a corner, and saw another sign: "Those who are 5'8" or taller, please go to the left. Those shorter than that, go to the right." I was elated. What a fascinating company, I was thinking, and what a brilliant scheme for weeding out most of the people. I continued on to the left.

I'd taken only a few steps before I reached yet another sign: "Those who speak a foreign language well, please go to the left. Everyone else go to the right." Again it was off to the left for me.

There were more signs, one after the other: "Those who are computer experts, please go to the left. Everyone else, go to the right." "Those who are articulate, please go to the left. Everyone else, go to the right." "Those who are socially adept, please go to the left. Everyone else, go to the right." "Those with a pleasant appearance and refined demeanor, please go to the left. Everyone else, go to the right." "Legal residents of the city, please go to the left. Everyone else, go to the right."

For me it was: left, left, left, and I congratulated myself for meeting all the qualifications. Deep down I swelled with pride as I surmised that after this winnowing process, I and my like were probably the only ones left, the crème de la crème.

"Those who know how to cook the books, please go to the right. Everyone else, go to the left." This, I could see, was the essential quality, and I was gladdened by the knowledge that this was a company that valued integrity and honesty, one solidly opposed to cooking the books. I strode proudly to the left,. and before I knew what had happened, I found myself standing in the middle of a busy street.

2003

We can say that short-shorts are an extended branch of the short-story genre. But this branch also tests the limits of the genre. While hewing close to the genre and possessing the general characteristics of short stories, a short-short differs from them. Generally, a short story has more prose elements, whereas a short-short story contains more features of poetry. A cross-bred new genre from short stories and poetry, a short-short cannot be as extensive as narrative poetry nor can it be as rhythmic as lyric poetry. Written in prose, it has a style freer than that of narrative poetry and a plot orientation stronger than that of lyric poetry. Yet a short-short is, after all, a story. A short-short defies definition. It is all the more enjoyable, fascinating, and lovely because of its indeterminacy.

Wang Zengqi

Sunday Morning | Xi Xi

Translated by Howard Goldblatt

It's summer.
Sunday Morning.
At wake-up
( ) the clock strikes seven
( ) it's nine o'clock
( ) no telling what time it is
( ) it's noon
( ) it's right back to sleep for a while
Sit up in bed.
The window narrates what is happening outside.

The weather today is
( ) clear and mild
( ) bright sunshine
( ) overcast
( ) drizzles, sometimes heavy
( ) a storm is on the way
Turn the feet over to their slippers.
Wash up and brush the teeth.
Look in the mirror and see
( ) a pall of loneliness
( ) a toothpaste ad
( ) boundless wheat fields
( ) a lotus in full bloom
( ) a pair of eyes crossing
Sit down in a chair.
Go to the kitchen and pour a glass of ice water.
Thoughts turn to what to eat and drink
( ) some bread with sugar and peanut butter
( ) the teahouse is sure to be packed
( ) God, no more instant noodles
( ) an apple
( ) there's nothing to eat in the fridge
When putting on jeans, coins fall out of the pocket and roll all over
the floor.
In the end, two can't be found.
The explanation for that is
( ) bad things happen to Leos
( ) troubles have ended
( ) try harder to save some money?
( ) there'll be a fountain here
( ) the earth is still young
Come to a decision. For this afternoon
( ) the hamper full of dirty clothes can wait till Monday
( ) go swimming at Sai Wan beach, with its big waves
( ) sing in the rain
( ) write an application letter for an interesting job
( ) start writing a great novel
There's the doorbell.
The door opens and it's

( ) a broom salesman
( ) someone here to collect the building management fee ·
( ) someone here to repossess a record player over lapsed payments
( ) a telegram
( ) nobody in the hallway
( ) a roomful of hydrogen balloons that float in

1975

Jailbreak | *Ku Ling*

Translated by Howard Goldblatt

I lay still in the tall grass, waiting until night fell.

It was impossible to come anywhere near this place in the daytime, so all anyone could do was gaze from a distance at the mottled but sturdy two-story-tall surrounding wall, which was topped with barbed wire. Looking up at it from ground level gave one the feeling that it could even hold back the clouds in the sky. I dragged out a couple of ladders I'd hidden in a nearby patch of tall grass, then tied them together tightly, the friction from the thick, coarse rope chafing my hands. But just thinking I was on the verge of scaling that wall was invigorating; quickly leaning my ladder up against the wall, I climbed shakily, the rickety bamboo rungs creaking with each step, the noise shattering the night calm.

Just as I reached the barbed wire, a searchlight beam began to sweep the area, throwing a scare into me as I curled up to avoid being spotted. This action nearly caused me to lose my balance and fall backward, forcing me to dig my fingers into the top of the wall, and flail my legs wildly to right myself. But the ladder fell sideways to the ground anyway, the sound fortunately muffled by the grass. I tried to ignore the pain in my hands as I made my bid to scurry over the barbed wire before the searchlight made its return sweep.

Blood had begun to drip from my forehead, running into my eyes and clouding my vision, and as I reached down with my hand to wipe my eyes, I discovered that my arm was bleeding too. By the time I'd crossed over the barbed wire and was crouching on the top of the wall, I was aware of at least ten places on my body that were cut and bleeding. I could actually hear the sound of blood dripping at my feet, running down the wall to the ground. I suddenly began to feel faint and couldn't hold out much longer. There was no ladder for me on this side, and the wall was two stories high. . . . The searchlight was heading back this way. I clenched my teeth and leaped off the wall, sensing immediately that I had torn a hunk of flesh off my back that had caught on the barbed wire as I jumped; then, as my feet hit the ground, I knew at once that I had broken my ankle, for I heard the sound of it snapping.

My good luck had deserted me: guard dogs started barking all around, lights in some of the surrounding buildings were flicked on, and I could hear people running this way and that. I struggled to get to my feet, in spite of the broken ankle; in the dim starlight a huge square opened in front of me—it wasn't nearly as small as I'd imagined it to be. Two more searchlights began sweeping the grounds, turning the area from night to day; now I knew where I had to go. Limping badly, I began running as fast as my feet would carry me, as though my life hung in the balance.

The wind whistled past my ears; mixed in with it were the shouts of the guards, the barking of guard dogs, and the ear-splitting wails of the sirens. Ahead, my destination came more and more clearly into view. I kept running, frantically, completely ignoring my injuries, including the broken ankle. Just then they opened fire! Bullets whizzed all around me and kicked up dust at my feet. Telling myself they weren't shooting to kill, I headed straight for the nearest light. Effortlessly I opened the steel door and entered a dimly lit corridor, where I was suddenly greeted by the reverberations of thunderous shouts coming at me from both sides—the guards were obviously hot on my trail, for I could already hear their labored breathing. Finally, I came to a door, which I flung open before collapsing into the room, totally spent. . . .

The guards stood in the doorway, glancing back and forth at one another, having no idea what they ought to be doing as they stared at me lying on the floor of the cell like a man whose fondest wish had been granted. After spending thirty years locked up in this place, I was ill-equipped to fit into the alien world beyond these walls when I was given back my freedom. So, finally, enduring any and all hardships that came my way, I broke back into jail.

1994

A Cup of Tea | *Yu Yingmao*

Translated by Aili Mu

The meeting was well under way.

It was very hot. Outside, cicadas were singing nonstop in the Chinese parasol trees. Eight conference desks were clustered in the middle of the conference room, a row of vacuum bottles lined up on top of them. The electric fan in one corner buzzed as it oscillated from side to side. People were sitting at the desks, a steaming hot cup of tea in front of each of them.

Bureau Chief Hu, who had just assumed office, strode into the room. Today he was to meet everyone at a formal meeting. We all rose and turned our eyes toward our new boss. With a nod and a smile, Hu sat down in the chair next to me. Everyone else then took their seats.

Director Li of the General Office resumed his reading of a document: "We must improve relations between the leaders and all the comrades, between the officials and the masses . . ." His voice was a bit hoarse, so he paused, picked up his tea, and drank. His voice mellowed at once: "We must establish a new relation between office holders and the masses, like fish in water . . ."

Water? This damned weather! Instinctively I reached for my tea. My hand no sooner touched the handle of my cup than I withdrew it—I suddenly realized that Bureau Chief Hu didn't have a cup of tea. It would be outrageous if I ignored him and drank my tea. I looked around and saw an encirclement of porcelain cups from Jingde Township standing at equal distance to each other on the desks, with one gap—the one in front of Hu.

Looking at the empty cups in the tray on top of the file cabinet across the room, I thought to myself, "I ought to make a cup of tea for Bureau Chief Hu." Then I noticed that Xiao Li, on Hu's left, was taking his tea as usual, one sip after another, as if a drought victim named Hu were not sitting beside him. A puzzling thought ran through my head: Why aren't these people, who are much more experienced than I, thinking of making Hu a cup of tea? They must . . . Should I do it? Hu is new to the job and the first in command. Will the others think I'm trying to soft-soap him? I just began my career and mustn't give anybody a handle against me with things like this. . . .

I decided to sit still and listen wholeheartedly to director Li: "We must prevent the submissive, the bootlickers, and the toadies from sneaking into the third echelon of cadres . . ." Hearing this, I brought out my handkerchief unawares and wiped off the sweat that dotted my forehead, feeling fortunate I hadn't acted rashly just now.

The cicadas were singing even more loudly outside; the wind from the electric fan was hot and suffocating. The delicate fragrance of the green tea made its way directly into my nostrils. I sniffed, looked at Bureau Chief Hu, beside me, but ended up not daring to touch my tea again.

"So hot! This damned weather!" Hu took off his shirt, wearing only a singlet now.

"Hot!" the others echoed. Someone stretched, causing his rattan chair to creak.

I felt ill at ease, like being on pins and needles, so uncomfortable. Should I just sit here? What will the bureau chief think of me? In the future . . . Do it! I can disregard the fact that he's my boss and just treat him as an elder. No one can criticize me for pouring a cup of tea for an elder, can they?

But there are so many eyes watching.

Do it? Not do it? Not do it? Do it?

Lao Zhang, opposite me, took another sip of his tea, smacking his lips to relish the taste. The noise appeared to catch Bureau Chief Hu's attention. He looked up at Lao Zhang, and as he was turning his head, cast a seemingly casual glance at my cup. That made me even more uneasy. What did that glance mean? Was it a look of reproach? Dissatisfaction? This is bad. He must have . . . There's no time to lose; I'd better make him a cup of tea right away. I'm sitting next to him, after all. Ai!

I finally decided to pour Bureau Chief Hu a cup of tea. But as I stood up, I knocked over my chair, which clattered to the floor. All eyes turned on me like spotlights, including those of director Li, who stopped abruptly in the middle of a sentence.

Lao Zhang and Xiao Li were whispering . . . I felt as if the rays from their eyes were gradually turning into expressions of loathing; I thought I heard Xiao Li say to Lao Zhang: "I could tell he was the slavish type right from the beginning!". . . .

I lost my nerve in that instant. Instead of going for a tea cup, I turned and headed for the toilet instead, saved by some quick thinking. . . .

When I returned from the toilet, Director Li had reached the end of the document: "In a word, we must construct a relaxed, harmonious atmosphere of mutual care and respect between the leaders and the comrades . . ."

I sat down again but couldn't hear a word.

Do it. It's only a cup of tea.

Don't do it! Better to offend one than to enrage all. Office holders nowadays are reshuffled as frequently as if they were on a merry-go-round. Who knows when Bureau Chief Hu will wash his hands of it all and get transferred to a new post? But I'm stuck here and have to make the best of it, just like everybody else.

Do it? Don't do it! Don't do it? Just do it!

Director Li had finished the document by now. He picked up a vacuum bottle and went to add water to everybody's tea.

He cried out in surprise when he walked up to Bureau Chief Hu, "How come there's no tea for our bureau chief?" He turned to me and said, "You . . . how could you . . . sitting right beside Bureau Chief Hu."

I blushed with shame while Hu responded politely: "I don't drink tea. Seriously, I don't." He cleared his throat and began his summary of the meeting. In a raspy voice, he sounded even more hoarse than Director Li had at the beginning of the meeting. So Li went to the end of the desks, brought over a cup, and rinsed it many times with hot water before taking a pinch of green tea leaves from the tea box and putting it into the cup. He then poured hot water over the tea and carried the cup to Bureau Chief Hu with both hands.

No one but me paid any attention to all this. Bureau Chief Hu was methodically summarizing the meeting, while the others were listening attentively. The only other sound in the room came from the electric fan, which sounded like an old cow panting loudly. The steam from the tea and cigarette smoke filled the room with a hard-to-describe smell.

I felt caught in a very awkward position. I was angry with myself for having been swayed by selfish considerations and having lost an opportunity. Why hadn't I just gone ahead and poured Bureau Chief Hu a hot cup of tea when he walked in? No one said anything when Director Li did it; no one so much as batted an eye. I was a little angry with Director Li. Why do you have to bring everything out into the open in front of Chief Hu? What did I ever do to you? What will Chief Hu make of all this? I have to explain everything to him. Yes, that's the only way out.

When Bureau Chief Hu's summary ended, the cup in front of him was still full—he hadn't touched it. Was he angry with me? I lagged behind deliberately after the meeting and caught up with him after the others had left: "Bureau Chief Hu, I wonder if I could report something to you?"

"What's it about?" He stopped and looked at me solemnly.

"I . . . I wanted to pour you a cup of tea, but . . ."

"A cup of tea?"

Puzzled, he looked at me, unable to make heads or tails of what I was talking about: "A cup of tea? What tea? What happened?"

"This afternoon, when I was sitting next to you . . ."

"What's there to report about that?" Then, as if truth had just dawned upon him, he burst out laughing: "My doctor forbade me from drinking tea because I'm on traditional Chinese medicine. If I wanted tea, the cup was close at hand, I could have poured it myself, couldn't I? Ha ha ha!"

He left, but I stood there in a daze for a long, long time. Finally, I pounded my head with my fist in endless remorse: Stupid me! Why did I have to speak to Bureau Chief Hu about it? Won't he think that instead of the job, my mind is always on trifles, petty stuff that doesn't amount to anything? Ai . . .

1987

In the Haystack | Cao Naiqian

Translated by Howard Goldblatt

Silence all around; the moon goddess casts her light on the ground. On the moonlit side of the haystack, he and she tamp out a nesting spot.

"You first."

"No, you first."

"We'll go in together, then."

He and she climb into the nest, bringing the hay sliding down so that it buries them both. He reaches out with his muscular arms to prop it up again.

"Don't worry, this is fine." She cuddles up in his arms. "You must hate me, Elder Brother Zhou."

"I don't hate you. The coal miners have more money than me."

"I won't spend any. I'll save it up so you can find a wife."

"No, thanks."

"But I want to."

"I said, 'No, thanks.' "

"And I said, 'I want to.' "

He can tell she is on the verge of tears, so he holds his tongue.

"Elder Brother Zhou," she says after a long silent moment.

"Hmm?"

"Give me a kiss, Elder Brother Zhou."

"Don't be like that."

"But I want to."

"I'm not in the mood today."

"But I want to."

Once again, he can tell she is on the verge of tears, so he leans over and pecks her on the cheek, gently, softly.

"Not there, here." She puckers up.

He gives her a peck on the lips, cool and wet.

"How did that taste?"

"Like oats."

"Wrong, you're wrong. Try again." She pulls his head down.

"It still tastes like oats," he says after a thoughtful pause.

"Don't be silly. I ate some hard candy a while ago. Come on, try again." Again she pulls his head down.

"Hard candy, it tastes like hard candy," he hurries to say. Neither of them says anything for a long while.

"Elder Brother Zhou."

"Hmm?"

"Why don't I do this for you tonight?"

"No, no, the goddess of the moon is right outside, so you can't do that. It's not something girls of the Wen clan cave dwellers do."

"Then make it next time, when I come back."

"Um."

Once again, there is a long silence, except for the footsteps and sighs of the moon goddess.

"Elder Brother Zhou."

"Hmm?"

"It's fate."

"Yes, it is."

"Our rotten fate."

"Mine, maybe. Yours is all right."

"No, it isn't."

"Yes, it is."

"No, it isn't."

"Yes, it is."

"I said, 'No, it isn't.'"

He can tell she is crying now. He also feels hot tears rolling down his cheeks and splashing onto her face.

1988

Returning Home on a Stormy Night | He Weiping

Translated by Aili Mu

The mind-sets of those who return home early and those who return home late are different. She belonged to the latter category. The street had long been deserted, with only wind, snow, and footprints in abundance.

After this turn, the gate would be there. Her heart was racing—I hope it's still open. I hope . . . Her hands and feet were icy cold. Under the dim streetlight in the whirling snow, the gate at the corner of the street was tightly shut.

She tightened her muffler, looked all around as far as she could see, hoping someone else from the compound was coming back late. There was no one.

She'd have to shout to be let in. She walked up next to the wall. Now the question was, who? Jindi was her best friend, but she'd gotten married and moved out the month before. Why didn't I go to see this movie last month? She immediately realized how ridiculous she was being. Forget that. I'll call for Aunty Liu, the compound resident who greeted her more warmly than most. But she resented the fat old lady for being a bit of a snob and seldom speaking to her. Many years earlier, when she'd been sent to the countryside after high school, her mother had been inconsolable. While she was crying, Aunty Liu had said, "You'll be one of the poor and lower-middle peasants once you're in the countryside, so your children will be poor and lower-middle peasants, too." Aunty Liu had been quite nice to her since she'd come back to work in the city, but she couldn't forget that remark. I can't ask for her help. Besides, since we're nearly strangers, it wouldn't seem right to call her.

So it would have to be Ma Pingping, a fourteen-year-old boy. His parents worked in another province, and he lived with his grandma. He'd pestered her to tell him stories ever since he was little, and she'd never let him down. She took aim at Pingping's house, but then discovered, as if for the first time, how high the wall was! Her call for help couldn't reach that far, could it? And what if it could? A fourteen year old wouldn't wake up even if you banged on a drum right next to him.

I'll call for Pingping's grandma then. Nobody's kinder than her. Of all the people in the compound, she was most concerned about her not being married, and often tried to fix her up with dates. But she was fed up with dating. The probing eyes of those impeccably dressed young men made her feel small. She was keenly aware of her deplorable plight: the vast countryside had claimed the best years of her life; she was now over thirty. As the saying goes, every girl is pretty at seventeen or eighteen. She'd have made some effort if she were five years younger, even three, for she was quite smart. But it was too late now—just like returning late from this movie, all doors had been shut on her unexpectedly. She didn't want to resign herself to fate and just marry anyone; that started the gossip about her being a nit-picker. Only Pingping's grandma hadn't joined the gossip. But ask an old lady of over sixty to open the door for her in a snowstorm at night? That would never do!

The cold was really getting to her. She then realized that the wind was blowing harder and the snow was falling even faster. Everywhere she looked she saw a world of white. When her gaze moved to the end of the street, she spotted a black dot moving toward her. Her eyes popped wide with delight—how wonderful it would be if he lived in the compound! She would thank him a million times whether he gave a damn or not.

It was a middle-aged man carrying a basket. But he had no intention of going into the compound and passed quickly by.

She felt like stamping her feet and cursing, but didn't know who to curse—the man, herself, the weather, or her bad luck? Fixing her eyes on the man's receding figure, she was overwhelmed for a moment by a feeling of envy. He was bringing things home; someone would open the door for him—his mother, his wife? His must be a very warm home. She, too, had a home, with a bed, a comforter, and a stove. Although it was a little lonely, it was at least warm. But she couldn't get in. It was close by yet beyond reach. That damned movie!

She didn't think she could survive the night out there. Go ahead! Just call for help. It doesn't matter who answers. She swore that from now on she'd be very nice to whoever came to open the gate.

Finally she let loose—"Open the gate!"—and pounded it with her fists.

The gate creaked open.

It wasn't bolted after all.

1986

It is said that the intensity of pressure a phonograph needle places on a record is greater than that of a train on the rail. This is because a phonograph needle is pointed, which concentrates its pressure. A short-short story, because of its size, does not have the advantage of massive weight, but when it concentrates its energy it can create great intensity and attract a large readership.

Shao Baojian

Tied Together by Fate | *Chen Huiying*

Translated by Howard Goldblatt

It is a chair.

A chair with a back and four legs, made of wood, with a velvet seat cushion.

The chair enjoys a steady existence on the rooftop not far from the adjoining building.

When the fog lifts and the sky is clear, there is an unbroken vista of trees: greens and emeralds and browns and reds, and some naked branches. The chair faces the woods.

As the housepainter paints the wall, he turns his head to look out the framed window, where he sees a chair on the rooftop.

Who was it who moved the chair up there? A woman, ideally. For some reason, the way the chair is so wispy and delicately crafted, a woman comes to mind. Why has a woman moved a chair up onto the rooftop?

So she can sit out there under a clear sky? A woman exhausted from her household chores. Back in the village, Ah Xiu is like that, isn't she? After she's done the dinner dishes, she moves a rattan chair into the doorway to sit and cool herself with a palm-leaf fan. In the fall and winter, of course, she's forced to stay inside.

Does she come alone? Or does she play with a baby in her lap as she leans back in the chair? Could the woman be young and pretty? Ideally she's in her late twenties or, if she's taken good care of herself, her early thirties, no more than thirty-two.

Ah Xiu is twenty-two, I'm thirty. She's my second wife. The first one? She died. I attribute her death to vanity. Obsessed with getting to Hong Kong, she passed herself off as an entertainer, a singer. Damn! I ate too much. Why do they want this place painted pastel orange? It'll put you to sleep. One room using three different tones of orange. Lucky for them they hired me, since I have such a good eye for color.

The chair is up on the rooftop. At lunchtime I went up and sat there awhile. A new house is going up nearby. Happily, I can still see the green mountains. It's springtime. There are new blossoms on the kapok trees, even buds on the wampee trees. It's springtime.

The door to the rooftop opens. Apparently the builders are back on the job. Should I go and move the chair downstairs? I feel like going for a walk today, and that's not like me. I throw open the windows.

It's not such a big deal to climb up to the rooftop from the street, is it? A mere three storeys. Of course it's even easier walking the three flights down. The builders might just come up that way to harass me— a worrying thought. The woman—that's what we'll call her for the time being—puts a piece in the puzzle, and smiles. A corner of the sky is still missing.

If they put a tall ladder against the building, they could climb up and easily reach in through the window to take the Walkman, the alarm clock, and the wristwatch lying on the headboard. This piece doesn't fit, so I'll keep looking. What about this one? Would I buy another Walkman? I should get one that plays CDs rather than cassettes. The alarm clock? This one isn't all that good. If I'm going to buy another one it ought to be a radio-alarm, so I won't have to wake up to monotonous buzzing. I won't buy another wristwatch, since I already have several in my jewelry box.

I vaguely recall having seen the woman. Not tall, actually on the short, pudgy side, with long hair, if I'm not mistaken. Men always fall for women with long hair. Ah Xiu has long hair; as they say, there are no ugly girls at twenty-two, except she has a strange body odor, not one you could call ill-smelling, but I take ten or twenty bars of good soap along with me every time I return. Scented soaps: orchid, jasmine, sandalwood. She turns around and gives them to her sisters as gifts. Face-saving means more to her than the man who shares her pillow. A vague recollection: short and pudgy, sort of languid.

How does she like to sit when she's up there? Letting the sun warm her? She probably doesn't go up there often; if she did, she'd likely have brought a canvas deck chair or one made of rattan, something on that order. That kind of wooden chair obviously comes from the dining table.

Some paint has dripped onto my paper hat, there's even a drop of it on my eyebrow. Slightly cool. This pastel orange makes me sleepy. Soft and gently.

Ah Xiu has fallen asleep in the crook of my arm.

The woman: The builders are still at it. Not yet 3:15, the time for afternoon tea.

I think I'll go up and move the chair. Climbing up to the rooftop from the street and then walking down the stairs is a piece of cake. What if it really happened? I'd say to him, Hi, how are you? But . . . but, how could that be? Me, I'd scream . . . what's the big attraction? Ha, I'm bored silly, let's sing a song, what do you say?

The key's inside the room. It's not easy to get at it just like that. If I close the door, they won't be able to open it. I'll walk barefoot in the mud out there screaming for help. Could I hurt myself that way?

My window was broken the last time, and my cassette recorder went missing.

But it isn't time for afternoon tea yet. I'll wait till tea time to go up and move the chair.

Sometimes I can't help wondering how Ah Xiu passes the time when I'm not around. Does she move a rattan chair out into the doorway when she has nothing to do, hoping there'll be someone she can talk to?

Mother has always been hard of hearing, so she probably can't hear what Ah Xiu is saying.

That chair, if the woman I vaguely recall, sort of short and pudgy, sits in it and stretches out her legs, her belly forming a little hillock, her arms probably hang straight down, plump and meaty, languid and oh so comfortable, sort of like a cat.

Meow, meow.

A cat is supposed to stretch lazily.

When she stretches lazily, her breasts and shoulders swell.

Three-fifteen. Tea time.

Not me, there's still a corner I haven't painted. You guys go ahead.

The woman fits in another piece. She stands up, looking quite relaxed, stretches lazily, her breasts and shoulders swell and give her a woman's figure.

It's tea time. I think I'll go move the chair.

Yes, I've seen that woman, and she's nothing at all like Ah Xiu. Too short, too fat, too old, too worn-looking. The painter sizes her up ruthlessly.

As the woman moves the chair, she looks over at the new house and sees the painter staring at her through the window. At that moment she realizes that 3:15 isn't tea time for all workmen.

1991

IV. Governance | *Howard Goldblatt*

"Sergeant, get in here!"

"Sir?"

"Who are those people?"

"Which people do you mean, Sir?"

"The ones massing on the parade ground, the ones holding little bottles with candles in them."

"I'll check, Sir."

. . .

"Well?"

"They're new recruits, Sir."

"What the hell are they doing?"

"They say they're demonstrating."

"Demonstrating? About what?"

"About how things are being run around here. That's what they said, Sir."

"This is the military, for cryin' out loud, not some cushy democratic institution!"

"What do you want to do, Sir?"

"Tell you what, send the chaplain down there to get them to go back to their barracks. I'll give him fifteen minutes before . . ."

"But there are too many of them, they won't be able to hear him."

"Then give him one of those battery-powered bullhorns."

The Busy Secretary | *Zhan Jing*

Translated by Howard Goldblatt

Secretary Wang was hounded nearly to death seeing to the needs of seven or eight bosses, from bureau chief to deputy bureau chief, and from department head to deputy department head. On this particular morning he had to place a dozen phone calls—some long, some short—rush a dossier through the mill, draft a document, and run from one office to another—altogether a dozen or more—handing out directives, asking for instructions and delivering reports, and so forth and so on.

Ah, so much to do. Fortunately Secretary Wang was quick of hand, fleet of foot, and nimble of mind. He could write up dossiers while talking on the phone; carry on simultaneous conversations with one person on the phone and someone else in his office; keep one eye on the person he was talking to and the other on someone he was greeting; take notes and write drafts while keeping both eyes trained on his superiors; use half his brain to think about one thing and half to think about another. He'd no sooner inhale a mouthful of cigarette smoke than it would emerge with an outpouring of words.

His hindquarters were forever brushed by closing elevator doors, his shoulders always bumping into doorways. When he was on the move, it was somewhere between a walk and a run, sort of like speed walking. He'd frequently be strolling along and then abruptly turn on his heel and head in the opposite direction; he'd often be comfortably seated and then suddenly jump to his feet.

At eleven o'clock that morning, he realized he hadn't relieved himself all day, and couldn't hold it in any longer. Secretary Wang rushed off to the toilet.

Xiao Huang, a clerk, was squatting in the toilet doing his business when he saw Secretary Wang rush in, unbutton his pants along the way, and squat next to him.

Xiao Huang was about to strike up a conversation, but Secretary Wang was done, hitching up his pants and on his way out the door.

"That was fast," Xiao Huang commented.

"Can't afford not to be," Secretary Wang replied.

Secretary Wang rushed out the door, and almost immediately rushed back in.

"Overlook something?" Xiao Huang asked.

"No." Secretary Wang squatted down. "Forgot to shit."

2000

Compared with longer short stories, short-short stories (as an art form) stir emotions more readily and inspire a keener observation of life. A fine short-short story is created when a smile, a cry, or a leaf touches you, excites you, and obliges you to give it expression in language.

Yuan Yaqin

Cloth Shoes | *Ah Cheng*

Translated by Aili Mu

Wang Shulin bought two pairs of cloth shoes each year: one unlined, the other lined with cotton. The former he wore from April to November, the later from November to March.

Since the unlined pair had to last longer, he needed to be extra careful, so he went barefoot when it rained, carrying his shoes in his hand. Rain was really hard on shoes. Letting the shoes soak in rainwater and washing them with water were different, even though in both cases they came in contact with water. The logic behind this was over Wang Shulin's head, but he knew he'd better not let his shoes soak in rainwater.

Here's how cloth shoes are made: you paste worn-out pieces or odd bits of cloth in layers on a wood board, dry the cloth under the sun into the so-called cloth crust, peel the crust off the board, cut it into smaller pieces according to a sample sole, stack four or five of the cut pieces together, and stitch them with hemp thread in thick lines, to form the sturdy sole of a shoe. There is, of course, still the work of hemming and putting on the heel, etc. The front uppers of shoes require strong cloth. They need hemming, too: black inside, white outside.

Wang Shulin's grandmother had to make six pairs of shoes each year, three unlined and three lined, for Shulin and his two sisters. The unlined shoes for girls even had straps. In fact, shoes come off boys' feet more often because they run and jump a lot. But for some reason they don't have straps. The girls looked pretty in their cloth shoes with black uppers and white edges.

Before Grandma made the shoes, she had to first make the hemp thread by twisting two thin fibers into one. She would roll her trouser leg up and rub the hemp fibers on her thigh with her palm. That made her thigh as smooth as jade. After a while, her thigh would turn pink. If she needed to attend to something, she always let down her trouser leg before she stood up and walked off. Later on, Shulin's eldest sister helped Grandma with making the thread on her own thigh. When she needed to attend to something, she didn't let down her trouser leg first. She simply stood up and left. Grandma would shout, "Let down your trouser leg. Don't you know how that looks!" Shulin was puzzled: Why was it okay to show your thigh sitting but not standing?

To make a sole, Grandma first bored a hole with an awl for the needle and thread, then wrapped the thread around the handle of the awl a couple of times and pulled hard. She always said her wrist and shoulder hurt after making a few pair of shoes. Twelve pairs!

A hole in the front upper of a shoe was usually mended with a piece of leather; a nearly worn-out sole would be resoled. Retiring a pair of shoes was a major affair. When the elder sister outgrew a pair of shoes, they went to the younger sister. Shoes too small for both sisters would have their straps cut off and go to Shulin. Shulin's schoolmates always made fun of him.

On the afternoon of August 17, 1966, Shulin's school notified all students and teachers to gather at Tiananmen Square that evening. When Wang Shulin got home, he clamored for a new pair of shoes, saying there was an important event that night. After thinking it over, Shulin's mother let him try on the new unlined shoes Grandma had just made for him for the next year. Grandma said, "Stamp on the floor to see if they fit." Shulin stamped his feet a couple of times, said they fit well, and left for school.

On the night of August 17, hundreds of thousands of people were gathered in Tiananmen Square. They sat on the ground at assigned locations, frequently singing revolutionary songs. There was a constant stream of people going to the makeshift toilets. Later on, the revolutionary masses grew tired and sleepy. They lay down and went to sleep. In the morning on the 18th, when people began waking up, trips to the toilets resumed. The Square came alive gradually, with occasional revolutionary songs.

At daybreak, people with sharp eyes spotted figures on Tiananmen's gate tower. The rosy clouds of dawn were glowing in the east. Word from the area around Golden Water Bridge came to Wang Shulin: "Chairman Mao is on the gate tower!" He turned around and relayed "Chairman Mao is on the gate tower" to the people behind him. He turned back and gazed for a long time without being able to tell which one was Chairman Mao, until he heard "Chairman is in an army uniform." "The East Is Red" started up, a million or so people seethed with excitement, shouts of "Long live Chairman Mao!" resounded through the skies, and the news reached the whole world.

Later on, the million or so people surged to Tiananmen's gate tower. Then they left the Square to march along Changan and Qianmen boulevards. Roughly fifty thousand pairs of shoes were trod off people's feet and abandoned in the Square, among them the pair of next year's unlined cloth shoes belonging to the first-year middle-school student Wang Shulin.

1998

A short-short story is a "wave," not a "river." . . . It starts with a ripple, develops into a wave, and ends with echoes and effects that send shock waves through readers' hearts.

Shao Baojian

Promotion Report | *Chen Hengchu*

Translated by Howard Goldblatt

I

Li Li; Male, twenty-five, graduate of Beijing University, Department of Chinese Literature. Began writing at the age of twenty. More than twenty stories published to date. This comrade has demonstrable leadership qualities. Recommend promotion to head of literature section.

Personnel Office, July 1958

Obviously someone with potential, should be actively cultivated. Send down to the grass roots for a period of training and see how he performs.

Bureau of Culture Party Committee, August 1958

2

Li Li, male, thirty-one, assigned to Bureau of Culture upon gradua-
tion from college. Sent down as factory worker in 1959. In addition
to assigned jobs, wrote many literary works that reflect daily life and
worked with a group of amateur writers. Endowed with a strong sense
of professionalism and organizational skills. Recommend promotion
to head of factory culture section.

Personnel Office, September 1964

Although this comrade has strong professional abilities, he remains
deficient in his political studies. Too much the intellectual. Continue
to evaluate.

Factory Party Committee, October 1964

3

Li Li, male, forty-six, graduated in Beijing in the 1950s. After gradu-
ation served as cultural worker in a government office and a factory.
Labeled a "counterrevolutionary" during the Cultural Revolution. Verdict overturned in 1978. Assigned at own request to teach language and
literature at factory school. Based upon impressive publication record
and years of specialization, recommend assignment as chief editor of
Workers' Literature.

Personnel Office, February 1979

This comrade's professional level is commendable. Unfortunately
he is not a Party member, and it is inappropriate to assign someone outside the Party as chief editor of a Party-supported literary magazine.

Factory Party Committee, March 1979

4

Li Li, male, fifty-one, college educated, joined the Party in 1982. Has
maintained faith in the Party for more than thirty years under a range
of circumstances and has written many influential literary works. Has
rich practical work experience, advanced cultural and literary cultivation, and keen organizational skills. Recommend assignment to Cultural Bureau as Vice Commissioner.

Cultural Bureau Party Committee, April 1984

This comrade is indeed a rare talent. However, given the current demand for more youthful cadres, he must be considered too old and therefore inappropriate for this position of leadership.

Ministry of Organization, June 1984

1987

Purchase Request for a Kettle | *Xu Shijie*

Translated by Aili Mu

"Is this Xiao Wei from Tianjin? Please come to the General Affairs Office. Your request has been processed."

Puzzled, Xiao Wei asked, "What request is that?"

"The, um . . ." The sound of shuffling papers came through the phone before Chief Wu read to him, "purchase request for a kettle."

"What? Are you serious? That was last winter, and it's only now been processed? The air in our office was uncomfortably dry because of the stove, and we desperately needed a kettle. But now—" Xiao Wei cast a glance at the wobbly electric fan and could not suppress a wry smile. "So, it took half a year to process a kettle purchase request. Tell me, Boss Wu, did this go all the way up to the ministry level?"

Xiao Wei never dreamed that getting a kettle could be such a chore. He'd first brought the matter up with the GAO in mid-November, the year before. A section chief named Zheng had given his immediate approval. But when there was no sign of a kettle, Wei went back to the GAO two weeks later. This time Section Chief Zheng was away, and another man, Chief Wang, was reading *Leisure Time*. He put down his magazine, took a drag on his cigarette, and said, in a bureaucratic tone:

"A kettle may not cost much, Xiao Wei, and requesting one doesn't seem like a big deal. But if other sections found out and put in their requests, that would be a real hassle."

Xiao Wei was annoyed. "But they don't need one. They work in an office building with central heating. We're the only ones who work in a bungalow and rely on a stove for heat."

"Don't always put things in terms of 'they' and 'we.' You need to be more mindful of solidarity."

Xiao Wei's nose was bent out of shape from rage. So he went to see the number one man, Section Chief Wu. But the answer he got there surprised him. "Well, um, since those two don't agree, you'd better submit your request to the higher-ups for consideration."

This "consideration" took more than five months, but the paperwork finally came down. Too late for last winter but still in time for this year. To avoid any further delays, he rushed over to the GAO to fill out the purchase order in triplicate.

Teacup in hand, Chief Wu was studying the request, thickly covered with remarks, when Xiao Wei entered. He ran his fingers through his thinning gray hair, the strain showing in his lusterless eyes as he looked over his reading glasses at Xiao Wei. "This is a tough one," he said, obviously embarrassed. "Bureau Chief Zhao has not given the final word."

"Are you kidding me? A simple thing like a kettle needs the approval of a bureau chief?" Xiao Wei could hardly believe his own ears. He went up closer and glanced down at the request. There it was, Bureau Chief Zhao's signature. "Wait a minute! Hasn't Bureau Chief Zhao signed off here with 'I agree'?"

"It's precisely this 'I agree' that complicates things."

"How so?"

After another sip of tea, Chief Wu replied slowly, "On the, um, request, Chief Zheng jotted down 'Agree to purchase,' while Chief Wang wrote 'Do not agree to purchase.' Director Li and Director Zhou merely circled the two comments. Deputy Bureau Chief Sun wrote, 'Make the purchase to show concern for our subordinates,' and Deputy Bureau Chief Qian noted, 'How ridiculous that a kettle request must journey through all levels of the bureaucracy! Our administrative structure is in need of a good shake-up. We'll start with this request, as an object lesson for the cadres.' So, um, I wonder whose opinion Bureau Chief Zhao actually agreed with."

"Oh . . ."

1982

A Capable Man Can't Handle a Small Case | *Liu Jing*

Translated by Aili Mu

Who would have thought that the man known as Capable Wu, the chief of south town's police precinct, could also be stuck with a hard nut to crack?

Come to speak of it, it wasn't such a big case at all. A quarrel between a hairdresser and her proprietress ended with the former being slapped by the latter—a tiny law-and-order case that shouldn't have presented a problem to Capable Wu.

Narrowing his eyes into slits, Chief Wu asked, "This shitty little affair, that's it?"

Just then the phone rang.

It was Li, his childhood playmate. You'd be wrong to dismiss Li just because he couldn't even get into a vocational school. Now having money to burn, he occasionally shared his wealth with old pals like Chief Wu. He was saying, Chief, in all these years I've never bothered you with anything, have I? Chief Wu replied, jokingly, You son of a gun, with your pockets stuffed with money, when did you ever give a thought to a petty government official like me? Li said, Don't talk like that. At the moment there's something I'm afraid only you can help with. Chief Wu said, You make it sound like the sky is falling. Li asked, Is there a hairdresser who's come to you to lodge a complaint? Lodge a complaint? Chief Wu replied. It was just a cat fight between a hairdresser and her proprietress over ill-gotten gains. I was just about to fine them each fifty and let them go. Li said, That's not the way to do it. China is a country of laws, and if people go around hitting each other, what do the laws amount to? Hairdressers are people, too, aren't they? If someone has slapped her, she should be punished, shouldn't she?

Chief Wu began to see to where this was leading. He asked, Why are you so concerned over such trifles all of a sudden, instead of trying to increase your wealth?

The truth is, that hairdresser is one of my wife's distant cousins. Right after she suffered the abuse, she called my wife, who immediately issued a command: See that my cousin gets justice, or don't think about coming home! Chief, take pity and help me out. I'll be happy to pay for a few extra appreciation banquets.

So, that's how it is. As he gave his promise, Chief Wu shot a glance at the hairdresser, who happened to be looking his way. Even though the look in her eyes appeared to be shy and timid, her ears were pricked up, as if trying to listen in on the conversation.

Chief Wu brought over a chair for the hairdresser and, after a second thought, brought over another one for the proprietress.

"This case . . ."

Before he could go on, the phone rang again. This time it was Wang, one of Wu's middle school classmates. Wu's family had been very poor back then, whereas Wang's father had been the Deputy Secretary of the Municipal Party Committee. So Wang had often helped Chief Wu out, taking him home from time to time for a meal and an overnight stay. Ever since then, Chief Wu had cherished a deep sense of gratitude toward the Wang family. After getting his job, he often went to see Wang's father. As for Wang himself, Chief Wu treated him like his own brother. Wu answered the phone by saying, So, tell me, what's on your mind? Wang, feeling no need to beat around the bush, went straight to the point: The hairdresser who's just lodged a complaint in your precinct is the daughter of one of my cousins. Just last night I received a call from my cousin in the Northeast, entrusting her daughter to my care. Who'd have thought that she would be abused today? As an uncle I'd be humiliated if my cousin got wind of this. So please give me a little face when you handle the case.

Of course. While giving his promise, Chief Wu shot another glance at the hairdresser: the shyness and timidity on her face had been replaced by a faint smile.

Before Chief Wu could proceed, the third phone call came in. To his surprise, it was from Wang's father. Over the past two years he had been transferred from the Municipal Party Committee to the Municipal People's Congress. Even though his words might not count as much as before, the People's Congress had a function that no government departments, institutions, or enterprises dared to overlook: regular evaluations of professional ethics that directly affect each organization's reputation, its rewards or punishments. If Chief Wu offended the old man and negatively impacted an evaluation, Chief Wu might forgive himself, but the bureau head certainly wouldn't. These considerations aside, Wu's personal gratitude toward Wang's father dictated that he must treat this call seriously. The conversation started casually, with questions like why Wu hadn't come to dinner for some time. But what he said next startled Chief Wu. The old man said,

I hear your precinct detained a non-local hairdresser today. Well, she is, in fact, the only descendent of a cousin of mine. Both her parents unfortunately passed away, but on their deathbed they asked me to look after their darling daughter. Today I failed to protect her from an unwarranted slap in the face, and how could I have a clear conscience toward my cousin in her grave! So, my nephew, you must settle this case on my behalf.

Stunned by news of the complex relations, Chief Wu was enlightened when he viewed them from different angles. He promised: Uncle Wang, don't you worry, I know just what to do.

At this juncture, the hairdresser sat cross-legged, looking sidelong at Chief Wu one moment and glaring at her proprietress the next. Disdain was written all over her face.

Chief Wu poured a cup of water and offered it to the hairdresser. "Have some." Then he turned and said to the proprietress, "Give me a straight answer. Why did you slap her?"

The proprietress jumped to her feet and said, "You bastard! Do you know why I'm still in business after you've investigated my salon so many times? Tell your bureau head to come here. I have something to say to him! And if that doesn't work, call Mayor Liu . . ."

An explosion erupted in Chief Wu's head, and he froze. . . .

2002

Ears | *Sun Xuemin*

Translated by Aili Mu

Deputy County Magistrate Fang did not understand why Xiao Ren, his secretary, walked into his office without knocking. Sitting in his revolving easy chair, Fang was holding a thick red-and-blue pencil, its red tip pointing diagonally toward the ceiling, looking very imposing.

Xiao Ren took a look at Fang, said something, and then made straight for the phone.

The phone was on Fang's desk, just a few inches from his red-and-blue pencil.

When Xiao Ren picked up the phone from across the desk, feelings of displeasure suddenly arose in Fang: What's he up to? There are telephones in the outer office. Besides, Xiao Ren has always been polite, disciplined, and good at pleasing his superiors. . . .

Fang, however, came to see that something was wrong with his ears. Just as he realized this, he experienced a sudden spasm of pain on his eardrums. After a loud burst of cacophonous ringing in his ears, he turned stone deaf.

Fang was thunderstruck.

The first thing that came to mind was that no one should know about his condition. Historically Fang had been a man with a reputation for keeping his cool.

Fang took a look at the two words "Be Cautious!" in tablet style calligraphy under his glass desktop, and then stood up, betraying no feelings. He made himself a cup of oolong tea, set it on his tea table, and then sat down on his sofa.

Ears! Ears!! Ears!!! Those damned ears! What could have happened? At fifty-nine, he was still a young man!

No wonder Xiao Ren came running to answer the phone. Xiao Ren must have thought he didn't want to take the call or he was deep in thought and didn't hear it. Yes, that must be it. But who made that call and what was it about? . . .

Fang looked at Xiao Ren as if listening attentively, wearing an ambiguous smile.

The receiver in hand, Xiao Ren turned toward him and said something. He nodded and waved his hand: "Um . . . that . . . that'll do." He was trying to be evasive, but Xiao Ren began to speak into the receiver excitedly.

What on earth is that about? Ah—!

Finally, Xiao Ren left.

Go to the hospital and see a doctor, then? No, no, that will never do. That would send rumors flying all over town. Have you heard? Deputy County Magistrate Fang's ears, his cranial nerve, his insight, his quality of thought, his ability to make decisions are all . . .

Besides, even if he went, was there any guarantee of a miracle cure?

But how could he lead without his hearing? The deputy county magistrate in charge of industry has a tremendous amount of work. . . .

Fang worriedly paced in his office and didn't even see Xiao Ren come in again—imagine his surprise when he saw Xiao Ren on the phone when he turned back from the door.

He repeated the same tactics: nodding, waving his hand, babbling that . . . that'll . . . that'll do, and looking very skilled and impressive.

All together in one afternoon, Xiao Ren answered four calls for him; that is, Ren was his mouthpiece four times. Fortunately, that afternoon no one came to visit or report on work or ask for instructions.

Hmm, Xiao Ren couldn't have figured out that I have an ear problem, could he?

Fang went to bed early that night, but sleep simply would not come. A large part of his world disappeared when he couldn't hear his wife's nagging. He got up after midnight and sat quietly under his desk lamp.

The resident correspondent of the municipal newspaper came for an interview the next day. Xiao Ren brought the correspondent into Fang's office after having knocked; Fang had not heard him.

The correspondent handed him a document for him to check and approve.

It was a news report with an eye-catching headline: "Steady Progress in X County's Industrial Reform—Four Accomplishments in One Day."

That gave Fang a start. Four accomplishments? How come I wasn't aware of any of them?

As he quickly read on, he came to see why.

No, he became confused. These issues, concerned with the economic structure of the entire county's industrial base, had been under discussion for a long time; piles upon piles of papers about them were there on his desk. Why on earth couldn't he resolve any of them when he had good ears and eyes?

Looking back, Fang was somewhat apprehensive. He darted a glance at the correspondent, pondering over how to start and continue the interview.

1992

I believe that short-shorts are more a state of imagination. There would be no short-shorts without the involvement of imagination. Life is a most important source of creativity in writing short-shorts, but it is not the only source. Sensitivity and imagination are just as important. Life and imagination are inseparable, like fish and water. It is because of this that most of my short-shorts are a state of imagination in flight.

Cai Nan

V. Games | *Howard Goldblatt*

I'm sitting here watching the end of the Super Bowl (Pats win, again) and thinking about games. Boy, talk about possibilities.

There are games you play by yourself. There's solitaire ("borrring"), there's pinball, and there's Tetris. That's just a sampling. You probably have your personal favorite.

Lots of games for two: ping-pong, tennis (singles, obviously), boxing (a wild "game," not to be confused with "wild game," which, in my opinion, is a sick game, if it's a game at all), ice dancing (no, that's a sport [kind of], not a "game"), and more. There aren't so many with one against everybody else: golf is the most obvious.

How about the team games? Too many to count, I'm afraid. From two players to eleven, maybe more. There are dry games (beach volleyball), wet games (water polo), smart games (chess), silly games (cricket—sorry), timed games (football, both ours and theirs), games that seem to go on forever (roller ball—think James Caan), graceful games, brutal games, and clunky games, not to mention some I don't even like to think about (jai alai—whoosh!)

But you probably think it's time to stop, especially since this is supposed to be a story, right? Okay, I'm game.

What's Up, Lao Cao? | *Chen Shixu*

Translated by Aili Mu

Note: This is not a morality tale.

Zhang Yi found himself a new girlfriend, her name was Ding Ding. She was pretty, and Zhang loved her very much. "I'll do anything you ask," he vowed. "Nothing will stop me, not a mountain of swords or a sea of fire, if it makes you happy." "Really?" she said with a tilt of her head. "Do I have your word on that?" With his hand over his heart, Zhang Yi promised, "I swear. I'm lower than a dog if I go back on my word. Test me anytime you want." "Great!" Ding Ding said. "But don't worry, I won't ask you to climb a mountain of swords or swim in a sea of fire." Talking and laughing, they went into the movie theater.

Once the movie started, the darkness of the theater was relieved only by a beam of light from the projector. There in the seat ahead of Zhang Yi and Ding Ding was a shiny bald head. Struck by an inspiration, she leaned over and said, "What you promised, that you'll do anything I ask, you haven't changed your mind, have you?" "How could you doubt me?" Zhang replied. "Okay, slap that bald head." Shocked, Zhang was slow to react. "Isn't that a bit too much?" "I knew you'd go back on your word," Ding Ding said grudgingly. "Says who?" Zhang said anxiously. With that, he reached over and smacked the head. Startled, bald head spun around. Darkness blurred his angry face, but his heavy breathing was unmistakable. "What's up, Lao Cao? Here for the movie, I see." Keeping his anger in check, bald head said gloomily, "You've got the wrong person." "Oh, sorry about that," Zhang quickly apologized. Bald head turned back to the movie, and a nasty scene was averted. Zhang nudged Ding Ding with his foot, quite proud of himself. Ding Ding nodded to show she was pleased.

Assuming he had passed the test, Zhang Yi sat back to watch the movie. To his surprise, before it ended, Ding Ding repeated her request: "Would you slap the bald head again?" "Are you kidding? Didn't I just . . . ?" Ding Ding cut him short. "It's okay if you can't do it, I won't force you. I know what you're like." Gnashing his teeth, Zhang defended himself: "Don't belittle me like that." With that he reached out and smacked the head again. This time bald head's rage was inevitable. He jumped up, turned, and was about to pounce on Zhang Yi, who kept his composure and fended off the attack. "How can you say you're not Lao Cao?" he asked in a studied tone to show he was puzzled. "You're Lao Cao from the office across the street. Why deny it?" "Deny what?" bald head growled, keeping his voice low. He took out his ID card. "Take a good look. Am I your Lao Cao or aren't I?" Zhang Yi pretended to study the ID card by the light of the projector for a long while before returning it to bald head. "Amazing!" he muttered. "You look exactly like him." Bald head snorted derisively, but let Zhang off a second time.

Zhang was relieved when the movie ended. Smugly, he said to Ding Ding, "Believe me now?" He did not get the answer he expected. "Not so fast," she said. "I'm not finished. How about slapping him one more time?" They were now outside the theater, and bald head was standing on the steps in front of them, his scalp almost glowing under the bright lights. "You're gambling with my life this time," Zhang Yi complained, pulling a long, sad face. Seeing the pathetic look on his face, Ding Ding snorted her scorn and started to walk off. Zhang Yi reached out and took her arm. "Don't go, I'll do it." And so the unfortunate bald head was slapped for the third time. Left with no choice, bald head put up his fists to settle matters once and for all. Zhang Yi, on the other hand, was overjoyed. "Lao Cao," he shouted, "Lao Cao! So this is where you've been. Inside the theater, I slapped another man on the head twice, thinking it was you."

This story was told to me by a friend. It may not sound like much, but there's a lesson here: There's no nut you can't crack, so long as you've got the wisdom.

2003

General* | *Liu Jianchao*

Translated by Aili Mu

"In fifteen years, I will be a general," my elder brother said to me after reading a yellowing copy of Sunzi's *Art of War*, with the help of a dictionary. Standing by the window, he looked solemnly into the bound-

---

*In Chinese chess, the term *jiangjun* (general) also means checkmate. The title carries both meanings.

less expanse of sky, his right hand tapping his left palm with the book. He was twelve that year.

My brother signed up to join the military upon graduating from high school. Three pilots were to be chosen from among the eight hundred graduating students countywide. My brother was one of the six finalists. He opened his trunk, took out a few dozen books that he treasured and had forbidden me from touching: "I leave these to you. Study hard. I'll come back for you when I'm a general." My brother, however, did not pass the political background check. He cried for an entire day. Then he threw the quilt our mother had made for him over his shoulder and went to the county chemical plant, some eighty li distant, to be an apprentice. His monthly salary was twenty-three yuan.

My elder brother's master was mean. In addition to his regular work, he had to do the man's laundry and fetch his food, and, on Sundays, he had to go to his master's home in the countryside to help with farm work. The master, who was addicted to cigarettes and was fond of playing chess, frequently pressed my brother to play a game of chess, with the loser buying the winner a pack of Gold Leaf cigarettes. After buying food, nearly all the rest of my brother's salary went to "treat" his master to cigarettes. One summer vacation, I went to see my elder brother with a small sack of steamed white buns. There was nothing in his room but the quilt Mother had made for him. A reed mat spread across the floor; books on chess were piled up on it. Stripped to the waist and sitting on the floor, my brother could stay up all night, practicing chess with the manuals. "The current situation is like this: the certainty of beating my master is in my hands," he proclaimed. That noon, he lost three straight games to his master. My heart ached and I was in tears when his master's dirty hands removed three steamed buns from the sack. My brother consoled me, "You're too young to understand that deceit is necessary in war." On the day when his probationary period ended, my brother challenged his master in the factory canteen: "Let's play for a carton of Gold Leaf cigarettes a game." Excitement swelled among the onlookers as he placed three cartons of cigarettes on a table. His master produced a wad of food rations from his pocket: "This is enough for salted vegetables for a whole month!" My brother, squatting on the bench, cupped his chin with one hand and deployed his forces with the other. His moves were so devastating that sweat dripped from his master's face on that cold day. Some of the onlookers provided counsel for his master. It didn't help. My brother won three straight games without breaking a sweat. He collected the food rations, tucked the cigarettes under his shirt, and walked out of the canteen with composure and grace. Bug-eyed and slack-jawed, his master did not recover from the shock for a long time. My brother became famous in the factory.

Fifteen years later, my brother became a father rather than a general. He gave his daughter the resounding name of General. My sister-in-law's displeasure showed in her pout. By the time General entered elementary school, the factory where my sister-in-law worked ran into trouble, and many of the employees sought to transfer to my brother's factory, seeking the help of influential persons or relations. My sister-in-law urged my brother to speak to his boss. As he paced the room, hands behind his back, he said: "Under current circumstances, my factory's returns aren't bad, that's a fact. But it's an industry with a severe pollution problem, and it's only a matter of time before we're made a bad example of. Your factory, on the other hand, makes products for national construction and will definitely be supported." Just as he had expected, his factory was shut down within a year, whereas my sister-in-law's factory was well on the rebound. Her admiration for him knew no bounds, and she looked after him even better than before. When General was entering middle school, a home-buying craze hit the cities. Double-income families borrowed money to build homes in new developments for workers in the county seat. My brother remained unmoved by the temptation. When construction on their houses was complete, old neighbors on the same street invited him to a house-warming party. As he was enjoying the food and drink, he took a walk through the new house and uttered three words: "What a pity." The host asked him to explain, so he dipped a finger in the wine and drew a map. With one hand on his hip, the other holding a chopstick, he elaborated: "The current situation is like this: The Yunmeng River, one of the major rivers feeding the Huai River, stretches across half our province and passes through four cities. It is the major cause of floods in spring and summer. The world these days is in a continuous fight over resources, especially oil. A decade or two from now, the focus of the strife will be the water supply. The water in the Yunmeng River is of high quality and wasting it will only invite floods. It is only a matter of time before water conservancy projects get under way. Considering the geographical location of our county, harnessing the power of the Yun-meng River will occur at the Hulu opening. Building a dam there will mean that the new developments for workers will be among the first to be flooded. Won't it be a pity to have invested so much man-power, material, and money, only to have to tear down your houses and resettle in three or four years? Not liking what he was hearing, the host asked my brother to leave. Sure enough, three years later, resettlement projects began at the new developments for workers. My elder brother became a household name.

Although heaven did not bestow upon my brother any important post, it put him through some very hard times. His daughter, General, died in a traffic accident during a spring outing. His wife, frantic over the loss of her daughter, fell from the second floor while she was hang-ing out laundry. Even after three months of treatment she wound up paralyzed from the waist down. As the bills piled up, my brother spent all his savings, sold off all his belongings, and still accumulated a debt of twenty thousand yuan. Yet the only effect on him, it appeared, was that his hair began turning gray. Whenever he had some free time, he took his wife out in a wheelchair for a "walk." My sister-in-law would be holding two things in her arms—a small folding stool and a set of Chinese chess. My brother would park the wheelchair, unfold the stool, lay out the chess board, and welcome all challengers. My brother never muddled through a game, regardless of his opponent's skill level. Once he had his opponent cornered, he'd shout "Checkmate!" After that, he'd take out a pack of cigarettes and put one in his mouth; my sister-in-law would strike a match to light it and smile broadly. My elder brother would take a deep drag and then slowly let the smoke out through his nostrils and mouth—his complacent bearing was truly that of a digni-fied general.

1997

The whole life of a person is a full-length novel.
A day in the person's life is a short-short story.
But if this day in the person's life, being trivial and disorganized, is mechani-
    cally recorded, who would enjoy reading it?
Of the 365 days in a year, few can be turned into short-short stories, and they
    will be the only few.

Yin Di

Number Eight | *Wu Yimin*

Translated by Howard Goldblatt

It had rained steadily for days on end, submerging the roadway. Each passing motorbike sent spray both ways, a magnificent sight.

A kid was on the curb, just standing there, doing nothing I could fathom; but I quickly got my answer. When my motorbike hit a pothole hidden under the water, a crafty smirk spread across the kid's face; he turned and shouted to a kid in the house: "Number seven!"

I cut a sorry figure as I pushed my motorbike up next to the kid, wanting to give him a piece of my mind, but not quite sure how. He was gleefully watching something, and I looked in time to see another motorbike coming our way, impressively sending spray in both directions.

The sight of an adult and a child, both soaked to the skin, standing on the curb, apparently caught the rider by surprise. Before I could figure out what I was feeling, the surprise on his face quickly turned to panic . . .

"Number eight!" the kid and I shouted in unison.

1979

A good short-short is short but not small, light but not slight.

Ku Ling

Observe | *Ah Cheng*

Translated by Aili Mu

Lao Zhang was full of vitality, had a full head of black hair, not the look of someone who had reached retirement age. But retire he did. His age was an undeniable factor, plus the repeated directives from on high.

Lao Zhang's colleagues hated to part with him. This cast a chill over the festivity of the farewell party. Lao Zhang ended up consoling his friends.

Lao Zhang said, There's no party that doesn't end, right? I'm not comparing working for the Party to having a party. What I mean to say is, as much as we enjoy working together, someone has to leave first. That I'm the first to leave doesn't mean I'll be the first to die. I may well survive those of you who keep working for the Party. I'm not saying I'll stop working for the Party. I can still do that. Not long ago, a research institute sought me out for an article on psychology. I told them, I don't understand your Fu-le-da (Freud) formula. What was it called? Fu-le-yi-de?—Must be Fall-and-yield! I told them, the human heart is made of flesh. It's the same everywhere. To subdue is to understand the makeup of the body. On my departure, I want to offer you some practical advice: Come see me whenever you run into sticky cases. I'm not saying I'm better than you. I don't mean to be cocky, but I've been in the business for nearly fifty years, after all.

In his retirement Lao Zhang didn't know how to keep caged birds, nor did he know how to play cards or chess. He could only look on, not understanding what he was seeing.

Lao Zhang refused to go to *qigong* classes. He said, One of my kidneys has twice the amount of their *yang* energy.

So Lao Zhang stayed home most of the time, looking first at the east wall, then at the west wall, then the west wall, then the east.

Of course, he also looked at his son. To use a term at work, he "observed" him.

Lao Zhang had often worked the night shift, so he seldom saw his family. It hadn't been easy over all those decades. He'd had a son rather late in life and hadn't been able to care for him. Now that he was retired, he had the time to do it.

Soon, Lao Zhang observed that his son masturbated.

Lao Zhang found an occasion to say to his son: You've been playing with your 'shotgun,' haven't you? Don't blush. What man hasn't? It's obvious that a 'shotgun' needs to work, and it's better to do it yourself than to force someone to do it for you out on the street. Your father wouldn't be able to show his face if you committed a crime out there. You're no longer a child. Although the Party advocates late marriage, you've reached the age to marry legally. See if you can find the right person. As the saying goes: Playing with your 'shotgun' weakens your kidneys; when your kidneys are weak and tired, you either have the will but not the strength or the strength but not the will, to carry out your revolutionary work. There's truth in that, isn't there? You know what I mean, don't you? I'm telling you this for your own good. I'm afraid you'll not only weaken your kidneys but also take on a load of guilt. You're my only son. It's all right to play with your 'shotgun' once in a while, but don't make it a long-term solution.

Lao Zhang knew that however thorny an issue might be, 80 percent of it got resolved once people talked it over. He hated the way some people bottled things up all their lives. That complicates the simple, and hurts both others and yourself.

Someone came from work. He asked how things were going with Lao Zhang. While making him a cup of tea, Lao Zhang said, Everything's fine. I thank the institution and my colleagues for thinking of me.

The visitor said, Lao Zhang, we'd like to hear your opinion on something.

Lao Zhang replied, If it's work related, ask away. I've got plenty of experience.

The visitor said, The station house brought in a criminal a few days ago, a political case. The leadership at the higher level, anxious over the case, is getting impatient. So are we.

Lao Zhang smiled: An intellectual who refuses to cooperate, right?

What should we do about it?

Lao Zhang said, Observe. Determine through observation how he plays with his shotgun.

What does that mean?

Lao Zhang said, You intellectuals! Playing with your shotgun means self-pleasuring. Three fingers in the spring, four in autumn, a full hand in winter, but only two fingers in the heat of summer. The human heart is made of flesh; everyone plays with his shotgun when imprisoned. Once the playing begins, the means of subjugation are at hand. Playing can lead to the loss of morale and the resignation of hope. Bring the offender in for interrogation right after he's finished playing, and you'll see very different results. Or simply confront him with his masturbation. Educated people are thin-skinned. Once his dignity is in the dust and his prestige swept away, things will be easy. It's unwise to beat an intellectual, for that only boosts his morale. There are, of course, some who can't take a beating. You must observe.

1998

The short-short is a self-sufficient universe. Never embarrassed, never impoverished, it is blessed with all the necessary elements. Humble by nature, it calls itself mini, it calls itself short-short.

Wang Meng

Confinement | *Yuan Bingfa*

Translated by Howard Goldblatt

Wei was sent on assignment to the provincial capital. On the train he was absolutely amazed by the man sitting on the other side of the pull-down table.

What amazed him was that the man was strikingly similar to Wei: The nose, the eyes, the mouth, the shape of his face, even the hairstyle were identical. In other words, the man could have been Wei's clone.

Incredible! As the train jolted and swayed, Wei studied the man carefully.

As luck would have it, the man across the way chose that moment to look up. Upon seeing Wei, he, too, was absolutely amazed. Obviously he also had noted the incredible likeness.

Once they'd gotten past the amazement, Wei was the first to speak:

˙ "What's your name, my friend? And where do you work?"

The man said his name was Qiang and that he held a position at one of the provincial universities.

When Wei heard that, his first thought was: Crap! He's trying to make himself look important. Holds a position at a university, indeed! At best, he looks like a salesman.

The man named Qiang asked Wei the same questions: his name and his work unit.

He said his name was Wei and that he held a position at a university in another province.

When he heard that, Qiang thought to himself: This fellow Wei and I have never met before, but he looks exactly like me and also works in education. I mean, incredible!

Wei asked Qiang: "What degree do you hold, my friend?"

Qiang replied: "Doctorate."

Qiang asked Wei: "How about you?""

Wei replied: I have a postdoctoral fellowship."

Qiang said: "Impressive. Really impressive!"

Wei handed Qiang a cigarette. They both lit up.

Qiang studied Wei through the cigarette smoke. The conversation and manner gave him no indication of Wei's refinement, no matter how hard he looked.

Qiang said to Wei: "I am a Ph.D., but my wife holds a post-doc fellowship."

Wei said: "My wife doesn't hold a post-doc fellowship, but she frequently goes abroad to lecture."

Qiang said: "My wife doesn't go abroad to lecture, but her doctoral dissertation won an international prize."

When he heard that, Wei took a drag on his cigarette, then said: "My daughter attends a university."

Qiang said: "My daughter is studying for a master's degree at a foreign university."

Wei said: "Just by looking at you, my friend, I wouldn't think you had so much going for you."

Qiang said: "You're not doing so badly yourself."

At that point in the conversation, both men laughed out loud.

After the laughter died down, Wei said: "We were fated to meet, given how much alike we look. Owing to that act of fate, if, in the future, I become a great man, I'll ask you to play me on the stage or in a movie."

Qiang replied: "I hope so. But if, somehow, I become a great man before you, isn't it only right that you play me on the stage or in a movie?"

"Wei replied: "Yes, of course."

Again they laughed loudly.

The train arrived at its final stop while they were laughing.

As they walked off the platform, Wei was thinking: That fellow, could he be me?

Precisely what Qiang was thinking at that very moment.

1998

Here's How the Flu Spreads | *Qin Yong*

Translated by Aili Mu

In a not very big nor particularly small office, Secretary Li Si was just an ordinary guy, and, like every ordinary guy, he had hidden desires. At this moment, for instance, Li Si keenly wished he could catch the flu.

It was the morning of April 5, sunny and bright. Li Si was standing in front of the desk of his boss, Director Liu Aiguo, listening to Director Liu say to him: "Xiao Song just called in sick. Says he has the flu. During the flu season, I want everyone to take it easy."

Li Si knew that Xiao Song was not sick. He must have gone to the provincial capital to see his girlfriend over the weekend and didn't make it back in time. But Li Si had long since passed the age when he'd say whatever was on his mind. He returned to his office without a word, took out the attendance record, and conscientiously entered: "April 5, Song Peng has the flu, taking a day's sick leave." Then he casually turned back the pages, where he read the following:

February 14, Liang Sisi has a bad case of the flu, took a day's sick leave.

March 8, Director Liu Aiguo has the flu, took a day's leave.

March 19, Director Gao Gang took a day's sick leave (flu).

A desire, therefore, crept into Li Si's head: We're in the middle of the flu season. If Xiao Song, a college graduate recently assigned to the office, can catch the flu, why can't I get it for once? At heart, Li Si was the type who lived life with the utmost care and caution, and this thought brought him a bit of excitement. At work that day, Li Si kept turning these questions over in his mind: Which day should I choose to get the flu? What do I do on that day?

The date eventually was set: April 8. April 8 was special to Li Si. On that day the year before last, he'd met a pretty girl named Zhang Ying; on that day last year, the girl named Zhang Ying had become his wife; this year, on that date, he wanted to treat Zhang Ying to a romantic surprise. Creating romance requires time. So Li Si decided: Catch the flu on April 8.

On April 7, a timely spring rain put a chill in the air, which gave Li Si the excuse he needed to display some sluggishness. From time to time, he had that suffering look of someone who wanted to cough but couldn't. Sure enough, someone came up and asked: "Li Si, are you catching a cold? You're not wearing enough . . ." Li Si conspicuously felt his forehead with his hand, then shrugged it off: "It's nothing. I'll be okay tomorrow." Before he could say anything more, he covered his mouth with his hand and released a muffled yet audible sneeze. . . .

It was, after all, a season when it was easy to catch cold. With the flu on his mind, Li Si actually caught it. At midnight on April 7, his nose started running and wouldn't stop. He was sneezing badly and loudly spouting nonsense. This worried Zhang Ying, who felt his forehead—it nearly burned her hand! She rushed him to a nearby hospital, where test results indicated that he had a case of pneumonia caused by the flu. He was hospitalized immediately.

On April 8 Li Si was lying in a hospital bed. All alone and bored, he started counting the drips in the IV: "One, two, three, four . . ." When he reached a thousand and twenty-four, his boss and colleagues from the office rushed into his hospital room to see how he was doing. After Director Liu Aiguo made a short speech of sympathy on behalf of his office mates, they left some bags of fruit on the bedside cabinet and rushed out. Following two days of treatment and another day of observation, Li Si showed up early at the office Monday morning. When he opened the office attendance record, out of habit, he saw this line:

April 8, Li Si's flu led to pneumonia, hospitalized. The whole office went to see him. A one-day holiday for everyone.

Li Si felt weird, as if he'd found a fly in some food he'd carefully prepared.

At that moment Song Peng came in. Staring at Li Si from a distance, Song Peng said, "Out of the hospital so soon? Are you fully recovered? Now everyone in the office except me has had the flu . . ." With this, Song Peng opened his mouth and released a loud sneeze in Li Si's direction.

2003

The Upholder of Unity | *Wang Meng*

Translated by Howard Goldblatt

Unity Ai noiselessly entered Old Wang's house, where he said to Old Wang in a hushed voice, "Don't pay any attention to him, Old Wang. A man of greatness has to be magnanimous. A sensible fellow like you shouldn't let it get to him."

Old Wang had no idea what this was all about. He blinked once or twice, but since he was just then making some furniture, he went back to work without responding to whatever it was Unity Ai was saying.

"Actually, you've known all along. You're not one to get all caught up in petty things. You're at a different level altogether."

Old Wang lowered his head as he cleaned up his plane.

Unity Ai bent over and moved up closer: "You know that Old Zhou said you're wearing a phony nose."

Old Wang's only response was a sort of grunt.

Unity Ai put his face up even closer, until Old Wang could feel his hot breath on his ear. "Old Zhou said that you found the nose you're wearing in the garbage bin by his house and that you used pigskin paste to stick it on your face."

Old Wang looked up.

"Old Zhou also said that you sold your real nose to smugglers so you wouldn't have to pay any taxes."

Old Wang frowned.

Unity Ai said, "Don't be angry, now, don't be angry. Everyone knows that you've got a first-rate nose, a real treasure, an original, and all that his comments prove is that he's a know-nothing. You're not one to get all caught up in petty things, not you . . ."

Old Wang lowered his head again as he tried to figure out what was going on. "I wonder what's on Old Zhou's mind that would make him go around saying bad things about me."

As he was leaving, Unity Ai made sure he got his point across: "Unity is all-important. Yes, sir, unity is all-important."

Unity Ai took his leave of Old Wang and went looking for Old Zhou in his role as the "upholder of unity."

1982

VI. Controversy | *Howard Goldblatt*

"Tonight's question for our five panelists is: What if they gave a war and nobody came? An intriguing thought. Senator?"

"Well, I say they'd have to have it anyway. You can't throw a big war and then just walk away, can you?"

"Professor?"

"Of course you can. That's the whole idea of not coming. They'll have to cancel the damned thing if none of the invitees show up."

"General?"

"Hell, I say go round up as many no-shows as you can and mix 'em up. Just because war is hell doesn't mean—"

"Thank you, General. Madame Secretary?"

"We have to attempt a negotiated settlement, no matter how long it takes."

"And finally, you, young lady."

"Who are 'they'?"

A Tail | *Wang Zengqi*

Translated by Howard Goldblatt

Old Huang, our personnel consultant, was an interesting fellow. The position of personnel consultant did not exist at the factory until he assumed it. He'd worked in personnel so long he knew pretty much everything there was to know about the employees. But over the past couple of years, as age began to overtake him, his health started to fail, and he was always complaining about aches and pains and rising blood pressure. So he asked to become a consultant, and since most of his consultations came in the area of personnel matters, everyone called him the personnel consultant. Although it started out as a nickname, it had a decidedly formal ring to it. He never missed a meeting concerning personnel matters if he could help it. Sometimes at these meetings he spoke up, sometimes he didn't. Some of the people liked what he had to say, some didn't. He was an eclectic reader and an inveterate storyteller. Sometimes he'd tell one of his stories right in the middle of a serious meeting. This is one of them.

An engineer named Lin was slated to become chief engineer at a factory, but the leaders were anything but unanimous in their decision. Some approved the promotion, some opposed it, and even after a series of meetings the issue remained unresolved. The opinions of those who approved should be obvious, while those of the opposition can be summarized as follows:

1. Bad background: he came from a capitalist family;

2. Unclear social connections: he had a relative living outside the country—a cousin in Taiwan;

3. He was suspected by some of having had rightist tendencies during the Anti-Rightist campaign;

4. He didn't get along particularly well with the masses: his ideas were sometimes too penetrating.

The strongest opposition came from a personnel section chief by the name of Dong. This particular fellow was very excitable, and every time the issue arose, he made the same unreasonable comment over and over again as his face turned bright red: "An intellectual! Ptui! An intellectual!"

The personnel consultant listened to him each time without taking a stand one way or the other. One day the Party secretary asked, "What's your opinion, Huang?" Huang answered in measured tones, "Let me tell you a story . . .

"Once upon a time there was a man named Aizi. One day Aizi was on a boat that docked alongside a riverbank. In the middle of the night he heard the sound of weeping down in the water. He listened carefully. A group of water denizens were weeping. 'Why are you weeping?' Aizi asked them. 'The Dragon King has given an order,' they said, 'that all animals with tails will be killed. We're weeping because we all have tails.' Aizi was greatly moved by their plight. He looked down at each of them and noticed that there was a frog among them. It, too, was weeping. Aizi was puzzled. 'Why are you weeping?' he asked the frog. 'You don't have a tail.' The frog looked up and said, 'I'm afraid he'll dig up my past as a tadpole!'"

1983

The ancients said, "The best existence is shapeless; the best sound voiceless."
Li Lijun

Black Hen, White Hen | *Ji Dongliang*

Translated by Julie Chiu

I was covering a story in Ma Village that day. There in front of a restaurant I walked into Buffalo Ma, who was coming through the door wiping his mouth, his face flushed. When he spotted me, he came over and tried to drag me in for a drink. I've still got this errand to run, I said, but he wouldn't let me go. Come on, just one drink, he said. We need to talk. And so I sat down with him.

I'd come to the same village just two months before. My newspaper had received several letters complaining that Ma Village was becoming more and more like the old society, that Buffalo Ma was more a landlord than any landlord in the old days. They also listed a series of crimes he committed. The one remark burned in my memory was that Ma was a modern-day Liu Wencai.[1]

According to these letters, Ma had recently become a grandfather, but then his daughter-in-law didn't have enough milk. So he started looking for a wet nurse, promising to award the chosen one with two cement cave-dwellings that were built for the poor. So all the nursing women in the village competed for the job. They flocked to the village entrance, bared their breasts, and stood waiting to be screened as the fragrance of milk drifted in the air, filling every corner of the village.

I was sent by my editor-in-chief to look into the matter. The moment I stepped into the village Ma learned of it. He insisted on taking me to lunch, and I insisted I wasn't hungry. When I carried out my investigation, none of the villagers dared say anything. So I had to talk to Ma face to face. He didn't dodge the subject at all. Yes, he admitted, it did happen, it did, but not the way you've described it. You got the sequence of events wrong, and it is in the sequence of events on which my principle rests. You see, I relieved most of these people from their poverty before they came to help me in return. Isn't it human nature to want to return favors? Doesn't the radio remind us every so often that even a Communist is flesh and bones? What did I do but help the poor by giving out some welfare money and dwellings? And give them a couple of worn-out garments you city folks donated. Why make a mountain out of a molehill? What is this compared to what you do in the city, where every official embezzles welfare money in the tens of thousands?

But you're using public resources for the poor to serve your own good, I said. He stared at me and said, You can't put it that way. You don't understand. Every year, when the relief goods come down to the region, people take turns getting their share. What's wrong with that? Mind you, I rarely take any of the stuff home. His explanations stunned me. They went beyond my wildest imagination.

So I wrote a story on the case, and, when it appeared, Buffalo Ma spread the word that he'd have every drop of my blood drained out. Later he said to people, Who is that fuckhead to call me corrupt? Me? Corrupt? Isn't he God-damned speaking too highly of me? Compared to the corrupt lot, I'm a fucking nobody. Well, if he's got the balls, why not kick up more shit for my lot, so people will really scorn him? When these words reached my ears, I took them seriously, but what could I do?

Now he was proposing a toast, saying, no fight, no friendship! Empty this glass of wine and we'll be friends.

I don't drink, I said with a smile.

One sip will do, he said. Just touch it to your lips, how's that?

I looked at him, picked up my glass, and emptied it. He clapped his hands and said: Thanks!

Then he filled his own glass. He drank the wine and said, I'm so very happy today. You and I have sorted it all out, and I—I'm still the village head. I just got reelected.

What? You're still the village head—really? He nodded and said, When election day drew near, I organized a primary election. I worked out a riddle and said, All right, you all want to run for village head, right? Fine, solve my riddle, and you're qualified. Well, guess what riddle I came up with for them.

I shook my head. He downed two more glasses before he spoke again. I asked them, Which do you think is worth more, a black hen, or a white hen? They were all stupefied, rolling their eyes, and thought long and hard. Nobody got it. So I said: What, do you really think you can be village head? Who can you lead? In the end, they all backed out of the election. Well, even if they hadn't, it wouldn't have mattered. Seventy percent of the villagers have the surname Ma, so how could this village be run by anyone but me?

He glared at me and said, Look, you're an educated man, so you must know which is worth more, a black hen or a white hen.

I shook my head and said I didn't know.

Are you joking? he asked. From the look in his eyes I knew he was very happy with himself.

I said I really had no idea.

Thrusting out his neck, he said, You really don't know?

I said I really didn't know.

He threw his head back and said, The black hen, of course.

I asked why. Well, he said, the black hen is capable of laying white eggs, but the white hen is not capable of laying black eggs—that's why! He leaned back in his chair and laughed out proud and loud.

I raised my glass and emptied it: No, the white hen is worth more.

He sat up straight and asked: Why?

I said, The white hen lays white eggs, but the black hen lays no black eggs. So, isn't it obvious? If even the black hen can't lay black eggs, why should the white hen?

He gazed up at the ceiling, holding his head in his hands, deep in thought: Right, you're right. Then he grabbed my arm and said, You're really something. An educated man. It's a good thing you're not a native of our village, or where would someone like me be?

At this he clinked glasses with me.

2001

My One Comment Too Many | *Yi Ming*

Translated by Aili Mu

I rode the bus to take care of some business the other day. It wasn't too crowded, but there were no empty seats. A few people were standing, holding on to the handrail and swaying back and forth.

A young man with a number of large bags was studying a map in his hands, his eyes occasionally revealing a vacant, helpless look. He hesitated for quite a while before he asked the conductor shyly, "Where should I get off to go to the Summer Palace?" The conductor, a girl in short hair, was cleaning her fingernails. She looked up at the young man from out of town and said, "You're heading in the wrong direction. You need to take the bus across the street, going the other way."

There was nothing wrong with what she said. The young man had made a mistake. Get off at the next stop and take the opposite bus across the street—end of story. But the conductor wasn't quite finished. She added, "What's the point of looking at a map if you can't read it!"

The young out-of-towner had plenty of self-restraint; he simply smiled. An old man nearby, however, wasn't happy with what he heard. He told the young man, "You don't have to take the opposite bus. Four more stops and change to bus 904, and it'll take you where you want to go." That would have been quite enough—helping the young man and redeeming the image of Beijing residents at the same time—had the old man stopped there. But he couldn't keep from adding one last comment: "There isn't a single well-bred youth in today's society!"

The old man's added words were certainly inappropriate. There were many young people on the bus, and his attack had been too broad. Sure enough, the young woman next to him couldn't hold back: "Uncle, how can you say all young people are ill-bred? In fact, ill-bred youth are in the minority. What does your generalization make of people like me?" The young woman was fashionably dressed: a tank top with spaghetti straps, face heavily made up with bright colors, and hair dyed red as fire. She sounded like someone of good breeding, addressing the old man politely. So why had she felt it necessary to utter one last comment? "People getting on in years, like you, may look benign, but they've got a bellyful of spite!"

It would have been odd if no one had spoken out against the young woman. A middle-aged woman said: "How can a girl like you talk to your elder like that? Mind your manners. Do you talk to your parents that way?" How proper the woman's criticism was. Once the girl's parents were brought into the conversation, the girl shut up. That would have brought the matter to a close and everyone would have gone on their separate ways. But bear in mind that the woman's final words were yet to be spoken: "Look at you, dressed up like a whore. I'll bet your parents have no control over you!"

It's easy to imagine what happened next. Simply put, people's lives were on the line. Amid all the bickering and shouting, the bus reached a stop. After opening the door, the conductor cried out, "If this is your stop, hurry up and get off the bus. Don't let this stop you from what you should be doing." Naturally, she did not forget to add one last comment: "If you keep this up, you can all get off my bus! We're not going anywhere until you do! I'm pissed!"

Pissed indeed! And she wasn't the only one. Everyone was the target of curses: the conductor, the young man from out of town, the fashionable young woman, the middle-aged woman, the weather, their own children, a chaotic chorus.

The young man from out of town had remained silent until then. Apparently unable to hold back any longer, he shouted, "Stop it! It's all my fault. I read the map wrong and made everyone suffer. Please do me a favor and stop fighting, will you?" Hearing his plea, the other passengers would have been embarrassed to keep it up, and things quickly quieted down. But the young man threw in one final comment: "I'd have stayed home if I'd known that Beijing residents were such unreasonable bastards!"

I ended up not being able to attend to my business that day. I went first to the local police station to record my testimony, then to the surgical department of a hospital to dress the wound on my head, caused by the ticket box the conductor threw at me. Please don't think that I joined their fight; I was there to stop them. I urged them to calm down, to talk things out, saying that this was a trivial matter not worth shedding blood over.

My one comment too many went like this: "So the conductor spoke inappropriately. Can't you simply consider her a stupid bitch and not stoop to her level?"

2004

Gen Xiaocao's Bamboo Pole | *Deng Hongwei*

Translated by Aili Mu

I was riding down the People's Bridge one afternoon a few years ago, when Gan Xiaocao came walking up the other way, dragging some bamboo poles behind her.

I asked, Where are you going? She answered, To work. Work where? The bank. I was puzzled. "You need bamboo poles to work at the bank?" Gan Xiaocao giggled, beaming like sunshine.

Gan Xiaocao said, "It's too early for work. I'm going to my dorm first to set up a mosquito net."

With this, she passed me and went up the People's Bridge, tugging the bamboo poles that scraped along the ground.

I cocked my head and looked back. My gaze traveled up the long bamboo poles and caught Gan Xiaocao's plump hips, swinging rhythmically in the sun.

For a moment, I wanted to run back and touch them.

But, of course, I didn't dare, not even with borrowed nerves. I could only open my mouth and murmur toward her hips that I'd joined the army and would be leaving town tomorrow.

I wondered if she heard me. She didn't look back, and her hips still swung vigorously as she sank to the other side of the bridge like the crimson setting sun.

I remembered my mother's words: Xiaocao has a large rear end and is very smart. She'll reap great happiness in life.

My mother was right. In the neighborhood, Gan Xiaocao had long been known for being smart. She was helping her parents in their grocer's stall when she was eight. Very quick-witted, she would know how much to charge or what the change should be immediately, without ever making a mistake, not even by a penny. She'd been a model student from elementary school through senior high. Owing to a momentary lapse, she failed the college entrance exam by one point. Luckily, two months after that, the bank was recruiting new employees, and she was hired as the top candidate.

Gan Xiaocao's parents, relatives, even her teachers, all said that she was lucky to have failed the college entrance exam. Going to college cost money. The goal was to land a job. It was better this way—it was easy and allowed her to start earning a salary a few years earlier.

After bumping into Gan Xiaocao at the People's Bridge, all I could think about that day was her plump hips. When I got home, I told my mother that Gao Xiaocao had got a job in the bank.

Mother said, "I told you so. Gao Xiaocao has a big rear end and will enjoy a wonderful future. She gave up a sesame seed and got a watermelon in return."

Throwing me a glance of disdain, mother continued, "When will you bring me a watermelon home?"

I thought her words were cruel. I was now a soldier. How could a mother insult a soldier's self-respect like that?

Three years later I left the army and returned home. I was given a job in the bank's security department and became Gan Xiaocao's colleague. I still bore a grudge against my mother's words.

Proudly wearing my new bank uniform, I came home and said to my mother: "Mom, here comes your watermelon."

Again with disdain, Mother said: "Gan Xiaocao's brought home a watermelon indeed—without even trying she became the daughter-in-law of Zhu, the county magistrate, and a director at the bank. Zhu's son has a big business. He bends his finger, and money rolls in. Now the whole Gan family is cashing in. They've sold their house in our neighborhood and moved into a villa."

Crestfallen, I went to work. Walking around the bank lobby with a gun over my shoulder and a baton in my hand, I stole glances at the eminent lady, Gan Xiaocao, in her office. I found her hips rounder and fuller than ever.

I knew I could never touch them. Only that damned son of the county magistrate Zhu could.

Gan Xiaocao wanted to be my matchmaker. She asked, "What do you think of Zhang Guihua?"

Zhang Guihua worked for the bank, too. Senior to Gan Xiaocao by one year, Zhang became Gan's good friend when she joined the bank. At the time, Zhang was dating the son of county magistrate Zhu. But for some reason, Zhang's parents simply wouldn't agree to the match. So Zhang Guihua asked Gan Xiaocao to help talk Zhu's son out of the relationship. Xiaocao obliged. But to everybody's surprise, she talked herself into the arms of Zhu's son.

Many believed that Gan Xiaochao had taken advantage of the situation, but she felt wronged. "I was just doing Guihua a favor," she protested. Nevertheless, she felt she'd been unfair to Guihua, who had dated a number of times without success.

Gan Xiaocao decided to set me up with Guihua. I shook my head and said, "How could Zhang Guihua be interested in me when she isn't willing to become a member of the county magistrate's family?" Patting me on the shoulder, Gan Xiaocao said, "Love is a mysterious thing."

She was right. Love *is* a mysterious thing: Zhang Guihua gladly accepted me.

Gently Zhang Guihua said, "You're the one I've been waiting for all these years."

Immensely flattered, I asked, "Why?"

"Because you're honest and kind. A person of integrity must be honest and kind."

I was so moved I burst into tears. I took Guihua home to meet my mother. "Mom," I said, "I brought you home a watermelon."

Zhang Guihua was puzzled. "What watermelon?" Scratching my head and smiling, I said, "It's too hot. Time for a watermelon." I ran to the end of the street and came back with a big watermelon.

Our love developed rapidly, along with the summer heat, increasing with each day. On the hottest day of that summer, it reached its logical conclusion. Unable to shake off the heat, we got naked and had a gratifying "sauna" in each other's sweat.

Zhang Guihua said panting, "You are neither honest nor kind. You are simply 'an introverted lecher.'"

Once, twice, we lost count of how many times we'd done it by the time we were married. Each time, I'd say to her, "Let me give you a 'sauna.' "

While she and I were busy giving each other "saunas," a major smuggling case that shocked even the central government came to light in our county. The county magistrate and his son were the guilty parties, and father and son were sentenced to long prison terms. All their property was confiscated. Gao Xiaocao came back, with her twin daughters, to our neighborhood to be with her parents.

That evening I was having another gratifying "sauna" with Zhang Guihua, but for some reason I couldn't help seeing Gan Xiaocao's plump hips. I paused and wondered, "How could a shrewd person like Gan Xiaocao end up like that?"

With her eyes closed, Guihua said, "She's the stupidest woman in the world. After dating the magistrate's son for a while I could tell he was no good, that he'd get into serious trouble one day. So I used my parents as an excuse to ditch him. He agreed to end the relationship but on one condition—that I introduce Gan Xiaocao to him. I came up with the idea of having her talk to Zhu on my behalf. To my surprise, she fell for it.

I shuddered abruptly, so did Zhang Guihua.

One of the bamboo poles from years back reached over and smacked me on the back.

I rolled over, dripping with sweat.

2005

The problem with a piece of chocolate is, once it melts in your mouth, it's gone. A short-short may be eaten in one bite, but even after it melts it does not go away.

Ji Wei-eng

Right to the Heart of the Matter | *Wang Meng*

Translated by Howard Goldblatt

A meeting to discuss cold drinks for summertime was held in a place called "M."

MA put forward his proposal to raise the quality level of osmanthus-flavored sour-plum nectar, and voiced his opinions on the issue of beverage production facilities in general.

MB made a recommendation regarding the opening up of additional sources of cold milk and liquid yogurt.

MC advocated an energetic expansion of the production and supply of bottled beer, ale, and light beer.

MD made known his ideas regarding the production of top-grade soft drinks.

ME demanded the return of the traditional thirst-slaking dried fruit from North China.

MX stood up, pounded the table, raised his index finger, and sounded a warning: "Gentlemen, friends, since we are discussing the issue of beverages, we mustn't forget for a single moment man's most basic, his principal, his most essential, his most important beverage, the one that can never be overlooked: not beer, not fruit juice, not yogurt, and not soft drinks, but H2O—that's water! Talking about beverages and ignoring water is a perfect example of reversing the relationship between principal and subordinate, which can only lead to chaos. At this rate, before long the people will be drinking urine, lime wash, maybe even lubricating oil. Why? Because they will have forgotten that water is *the* source, that water is at the heart of all things, that they must hold on to water at all costs! If we can tolerate this sort of trend, then what's left for us *not* to tolerate?"

All the others, from MA to ME, gazed at one another in blank dismay, not knowing what to do now.

MF was the first to rise to the challenge. "I'm in total agreement with MX's point of view," he shouted, "and I want to go even further by stating that it's not enough just to drink water, that in order to ensure its survival, mankind must also eat! Whether it's flour or rice, vegetables or seafood, makes no difference at all, so long as we eat. Just ponder for a moment the serious consequences of drinking water and not eating! Therefore, of primary . . ."

MA was clearly getting worked up. He unbuttoned his shirt to expose his chest, shouting as he did so: "I want to solemnly declare that I have never opposed the eating of food or the drinking of water, not in the past, not now, and certainly not tomorrow, or the day after, or the day after that . . ." His declaration thus completed, he took a biscuit out of his pocket, poured himself a glass of cool water, and began eating and drinking right there in front of the others.

MB entered the fray at that moment, calling the others to account: "I want you all to take note that it's not nearly enough just to eat food and drink water. We must also wear clothing! Clothing is necessary to keep us warm *and* to keep our bodies concealed from view. Without clothing we would be no better than beasts!"

And the debate goes on.

1982

As far as the creative process is concerned, short-shorts have more to do with improvisation, contingency, and opportunity.

Feng Hui

Sexual Harassment | *Lin Li-chun*

Translated by Lin Li-chun

He was engrossed in the newspaper, reading about the baseball betting scandal when a woman's loud, clear voice suddenly disrupted the quiet morning bus.

"If you don't stop touching me, I'll ask the driver to throw you off the bus."

Touching a woman on the bus? That's disgusting, he thought. At seven in the morning, the passengers were mainly professionals. Like him, they were casually but well dressed. How could any of the neatly dressed and clean-shaven men be touching a woman on a bus?

He wanted to see what he looked like. So he looked up from the Sports page, only to see eyes trained on him with disgust. He was confused, then he realized he was the harasser. The voice came from the young woman next to him in the window seat. He had no idea what was going on. He opened his mouth, but words didn't come before the driver, who had already stopped the bus, came over. A burly man with a ruddy face and fierce eyes.

"You'll have to sit in the back." The driver said to him with a voice loud enough for everyone to hear.

"I—"

"Get over there before I throw you off my bus." The driver pointed to the back of the bus and gave him a look that said he might get physical if he refused to move.

Hastily getting up while gathering his backpack and the newspaper, he ran toward the row of empty seats in the back. The driver had already restarted the engine, and he was thrown into the seat with the sudden lurch. His head bumped against the window and pain increased his confusion.

What was going on? He was reading the newspaper. He didn't touch the woman. Why did she say he did? What possessed her to make up a story like that, and what did she gain from it?

He wanted to look at her, to find out what she looked like. What kind of woman lied about a man touching her on the bus? Was she craving attention?

He looked up but could only see the back of her head. Dark wavy hair. That was all he could see. He stared, trying to find some meaning in strands of hair that glowed slightly under the morning sun. She was wearing sunglasses, wasn't she? He remembered glancing at her when he sat down next to her the first time a month ago. He'd been sitting beside her ever since, and she'd always worn dark sunglasses. She neither smiled nor acknowledged him each time he sat down. She didn't even move her briefcase, which was wedged between them, to give him more space. They never exchanged a word. After the bus arrived at the downtown station, he would get off first to grab a cup of coffee before heading to his office. He had no idea where she went. He wasn't curious about her. And he believed she wasn't curious about him either. But now she'd made up a lie about him, about herself, too. Why?

The bus entered the station. The passengers got up to leave, most of them shooting him a glance before getting off. They wanted to get another look at the pervert, him.

You pervert! That's you, you pervert. He felt his knees buckling. He had never been so humiliated in his life. It was like running out of the house naked or accidentally walking out of a store with unpaid items. No, it was worse, much worse than that, because he would've actually been naked or appeared to be shoplifting. He hadn't done anything. He hadn't touched that woman.

He got off the bus last. Shielding his eyes against the bright morning sun, he looked for the wavy hair despite himself. He wanted to see what she looked like, as if knowing her face would lesson the confusion and humiliation, as if she'd recant her accusation.

But she was nowhere in sight. He walked absentmindedly toward his office.

Life goes on, he told himself. Maybe she was indeed craving attention. A young woman in her late twenties, with nice legs, and she apparently had no confidence in herself. That was why she made up something like that. It wasn't directed at you. She could've said anything like that about anyone. He suddenly felt a strong surge of sympathy toward her. She obviously had a tough life.

Energized by the thought of pity, he was no longer upset; he was even whistling, for he felt magnanimous, as he was able to forgive that woman. But he couldn't concentrate on his work. Staring at his computer screen, where he could vaguely see his own reflection, he felt a strong urge to go into the men's room, to look at himself in the mirror, to see what it was that would cause a woman to falsely accuse him of sexually harassing her.

It was a drawn face with sad eyes that stared back at him. Only forty-three, he was losing the hair that had turned gray two years earlier. He wasn't bald; his hair was just thinner, which had been fine with him. Deep lines seemed to have been carved into the flesh between brows that were strangely bushy. There were also lines around his mouth. Did he have a face that said "I'm a pushover; go ahead, do whatever you want to me"? Or did he have a molester's face that made the woman pick him out because people would believe her?

Anger surged through him the longer he stared at himself. I'm just an ordinary guy, riding the bus to work, like everyone else. Why did she do that? How could she say those things about me? I touched her? I touched her? Why would I want to touch her? Her, with that pale face and scarecrow body?

After lunch he knew what he had to do. He went home, shaved, took a long bath, and changed into a new blue shirt and a pair of navy pants. He then went over to the bus stop, where he found a bench and sat down, pretending to read the newspaper.

It was six ten when the wavy-haired woman finally got off. With a quickening heartbeat, he watched her cross the street. He stood up.

"Excuse me," he said, conscious of his hoarse voice, which sounded as if he'd been shouting for a long time.

"Yes?"

"Miss, You . . . I need to talk to you."

"Do I know you?"

She looked at him with a curious expression, but didn't seem to recognize him.

"Yes—no, I don't think you know me." It suddenly dawned on him that she didn't know him, and that was the reason she had lied. She wouldn't have said he touched her if she'd known him. He couldn't believe she hadn't known who he was. He was incensed. She had told a busload of people that he'd touched her, and she didn't even recognize him when he stood before her. His anger was quickly replaced by his previous sympathy. She clearly wanted attention, and she didn't care who was sitting next to her. That was why she didn't recognize him.

Bolstered by the new knowledge, he said indignantly:

"I'm the guy from the bus. I want to tell you it was terrible to lie about me touching you."

She was silent momentarily, and then she said slowly: "So, you think I lied?"

"Of course you did. I'm not that kind of guy." He added, "I'm not a pervert."

"Oh, sure. Are you saying you never spread your legs wide enough to rub against my thigh with the movement of the bus? Are you telling me you didn't intentionally open your newspaper in such a way that your arm would touch mine? And why have you been sitting next to me for the past month, even though there are plenty of empty seats when you get on every morning?" She kept getting louder.

"I . . ." he stammered before a thought occurred to him: "All men are like that. We need more space when we sit, and we like to sit by pretty women. What's wrong with that?"

2005

Short-shorts are the art form of common people. By that I mean, they can be consumed by most people, most people can participate in the creative process, and most people can benefit from an art form of simple words and profound meaning.

Yang Xiaomin

VII. Anticipations | *Howard Goldblatt*

"Good evening, welcome to la Bœuf. My name—"

"Thanks, we're happy to be here. My name is Jack and this is Jill. We'll be your guests tonight. We'll now decide what, besides water, we want to drink. We've brought a list of our preferred wines, which you will ask that nice gentleman with the medallion around his neck to get for us, one red half bottle and one white. Thank you."

"But—"

"Now, about appetizers. You have them, don't you?"

"Yes, but—"

"Ah, yes. We'll have this and some of this."

"But—"

"Thank you."

. . .

"Would you come here please, we want to tell you how everything is, now that we've had two or three bites of our entrée. The risotto is too salty, and medium rare is not rare, wouldn't you agree? But, never mind, we'll make do."

. . .

"Now, do you have any double chocolate cake? How about crème brûlée? Fine. And you'll want to know about coffee, won't you? None tonight, I'm afraid. You may bring us the check now."

"Thank you and come—"

"Yes, of course. I'm sorry, I didn't catch your name."

Bed-Wetting | *Zhang Jishu*

Translated by Julie Chiu

I started off as a good boy but turned bad as time went by. That was because I didn't used to wet my bed, but later on I did.

I changed because of my younger brother. He had wet his bed right from the beginning, and if he made it through one night without wetting the bed, Mom would reward him with a hot chestnut or buy him some candy balls. I could only watch with my mouth watering. I wondered what I could do to get a bite of all this good stuff. Finally I figured it out: I would wet the bed, too. Yet from not wetting the bed to wetting the bed, there was a process. The first time I did it, I got a spanking from Mom. She grabbed a feather duster and beat me with the knobby handle. With every hit on my backside, she said, "You never wet your bed before. Now the older you get, the more childish you become, eh?" I held my tongue, gazing at my mattress with a spot even bigger and more badly soaked than my brother could have created. The next day I did the same, and got spanked again. As I received my spanking, I thought: "I guess if I don't suffer some physical pain, I won't get the treat." The third day I didn't wet the bed, and got the same reward that my younger brother always got. As Mom handed me a hot chestnut, she scolded me with a laugh, "Shame on you. But still, we call that progress." As I munched on the hot chestnut, I couldn't help touching my recently spanked behind.

From then on I wet the bed every three or four days and continued to get Mom's little treats.

After I grew up, I started off as a good worker but eventually changed. In the beginning I took every task seriously and never cut corners. I was the most outstanding worker among my colleagues, but when it came to a pay raise or promotion, it was always somebody else who got recommended. Eventually I wised up. Inspired by my "wet-the-bed" experience as a child, I started "wetting the bed" at work. The outcome was surprisingly similar to what I had experienced in my childhood. I not only got promoted but also had my salary increased. One year I even attended the municipal confederation of model workers. A big red flower on my breast, I took a seat on the rostrum and "shared my experience"—imagine how my heart flew!

Now I'm approaching the age of retirement. Whenever I stop and look back, my heart is flooded with emotions and laments. Sometimes I tell the story to my son, and it always ends up with his teasing me. At that I always say, "Don't you laugh at me now. The day you understand your old man's story, you can call yourself fully grown."

My son's response: "I hope your story will be outdated soon! Or there'll never be progress."

"Yeah, well, I hope before my story gets outdated, you'll smarten up!"

My son casts a scornful look at me and turns back to his business. He goes *tap tap tap* on his computer keyboard, sending foreign words I don't recognize up onto the screen.

2003

The flame of complete combustion has a blue tinge. It is a beautiful color; it is a ferocious color. A piece of writing is powerful if its words are "completely combusted." Its impact may not have to do with whether it is long or short.

Chen Yizhi

The Principle of Rebound | *Xu Haiwei*

Translated by Aili Mu

An eminent monk went down the mountain to spread the Buddha's teachings. He saw a statue of Sakyamuni in a shop. It was cast in bronze with lifelike features and a peaceful countenance. The eminent monk was immensely pleased. It would be a blessing if he could take it back to the monastery, launch its Buddha radiance, and enshrine and worship it forever. The shop owner, however, asked 5,000 yuan for it, not a penny less. Besides, seeing that the monk loved it so much, the owner was especially firm about the price.

The eminent monk returned to the monastery and discussed this with the other monks, who became anxious and asked the eminent monk how much he was willing to pay. The eminent monk said: "No more than 500 yuan." The other monks whimpered uncontrollably, "Impossible!" The eminent monk chanted: "Heavenly principles still exist, so there must be a way. In this vast world of mortals and among all living beings, the abyss of greed can never be filled. Trying to fill it leads to more losses than gains. The Buddha has great compassion. He delivers all from suffering. He will save the man by letting him earn this 500 yuan and no more!"

"How is this deliverance to happen?" the other monks asked in bewilderment.

"Make him repent," the eminent monk answered with a smile. The other monks were even more puzzled. The eminent monk instructed them: "Just do as I say."

The eminent monk told his disciples to deck themselves out as ordinary folks.

The first disciple went down the mountain to bargain with the shop owner. He insisted on a price of 4,500 yuan, and returned with no result.

The next day the second disciple went down the mountain to bargain with the shop owner. He insisted on a price of 4,000 yuan, and also returned with no result.

And so it went, up to the ninth day, when the final disciple went down the mountain and offered a mere 200 yuan. Watching helplessly as buyers came and went day after day, each offering a price lower than the day before, the shop owner grew very concerned. Each day he regretted not selling the statue to the previous buyer at yesterday's price. He castigated himself severely for having been too greedy. By the tenth day, he said to himself: "If another buyer comes today, I will make a deal on the spot at whatever price is offered."

On the tenth day, the eminent monk himself went down the mountain. When he said he would pay 500 yuan for the statue, the shop owner was thrilled—who would have thought that the price could rebound to 500 yuan! The sale was completed, and when the shop owner calmed down a bit, he offered, as a gift, an altar for the statue. The eminent monk took the bronze statue but declined the altar, with thanks. While bowing with one hand in front of his chest, the eminent monk said with a smile: "Desire is boundless. Propriety exists in everything. Whatever one does, refrain from excess! Wonderful! Truly wonderful. . . ."

2002

A piece of good fiction must never leave the reader thinking, "So what?" The very short fiction, in particular, should end with the reader saying, in a moment of sudden illumination: "Ah, yes."

Shen Mingjin

Accidental Confidante | *Bai Xiaoyi*

Translated by Aili Mu

I noticed right off that a woman was looking at me. I chose to ignore her by looking at the rows of trees, which didn't seem happy. With a few dried-up leaves hanging on them, the trees were swaying in the wind and bringing a sense of melancholy to the compound. As if I could forget, I reminded myself again—I'm in a mental institution.

I was sitting on a bench under one of those trees. Some dead leaves swirled at my feet and then dispersed, but the woman was still looking straight at me. The combination of curiosity and cold detachment in her eyes made me shudder. You couldn't be confident or certain of what might happen next under a gaze like that. My only solace was that it was a woman sitting across from me. I felt that the right thing to do was admire her elegant hair and her lovely long legs while waiting to see what her intention toward me was.

So I wasn't surprised when she came over to talk.

"May I sit?" Her voice was very soft, but the animated expression on her face made me suspect some sort of trap.

"Please." I betrayed no emotion.

She sat at the far end of the bench, leaving enough room between us for two more slim persons like us. Maybe because we were sitting on the same bench, she could no longer stare at me, so she fixed her gaze on the trees in front. Availing myself of the opportunity, I turned my trees over to her and took a good long look at her, until, for no apparent reason, she began to tremble.

"Look at me, shaking like a leaf," she said, smiling at me and then turning her attention back to the trees. "Truth is," she added, "I'm not really afraid of you."

"Me neither," I replied. "You see, I'm not shaking." I thought about my response and wasn't sure if she got it. "There's nothing to be afraid of."

With a winsome smile, she leaned against the back of the bench, a sign that she was a little more relaxed.

Glancing around at the old buildings where danger lurked, I grew somewhat apprehensive: "What if the doctors see you? You know they don't allow . . ."

"You just said there was nothing to be afraid of. Well, I'm about to leave anyway."

"Sorry, I didn't mean that," I rushed to explain because I saw the space between her back and the back of the bench reduced drastically. "Please, sit where you are. There shouldn't be any problem."

"Are you always this tense? It's nerve-racking to have to worry about one's own image in others' eyes, isn't it?"—Who'd have thought she'd be lecturing me? "Try to relax. This is a mental institution, not a prison."

I bit my lip, at a loss for what to do, but trying hard to tough it out.

"When did you get here?" she asked.

"Not long ago."

"Are they treating you okay?"

"Who?" I asked, somewhat unnerved by her questions.

"The doctors and nurses, of course."

"They're okay."

"Well then, are you willing to stay?" It appeared that she'd accumulated a stack of questions and finally found a chance to ask them.

This was a question I had to treat very seriously because of the impact my response might have on her.

"I can stay pretty much anywhere." I thought my answer was quite clever.

"I like it here," she said resolutely. The look on her face made me speculate about her dissatisfaction with my attitude.

"Yes, the place isn't bad," I said.

"Everybody I meet here embodies a kind of sincerity I don't see elsewhere. You give me the same feeling."

"Maybe I'm somewhat different," I said.

"Please don't get me wrong, don't think I take you as simple-minded. I know why you look numbed. It's because you enjoy a rich inner world. When one is preoccupied with a single concrete matter, one's face usually gives people an impression of intelligence when, in fact, one might be dulled by a conundrum. Your innocent, almost bewildered look is in truth the place where wisdom resides, real wisdom. . . ."

Deep down I heaved a sigh of wonder. It was such a pleasure to hear what she was saying! For a moment I thought it would be wonderful to become a mental patient one day, so I could be with delightful people like her all the time. But now—I looked at my watch—it was time to leave, otherwise I'd miss the last bus to downtown.

"Sorry I can't keep you company any longer. It's been a pleasure chatting with you. But I must leave now, for home."

"What? You're going to run away?" She was surprised.

"You're mistaken. I came to see a patient today. But the doctor told me he died last month. He was a classmate of mine. I was sitting here thinking about him."

"Oh, my God, all this time I thought you were a patient." She couldn't help laughing. "My first time here and I made a fool of myself. . . ."

"What, you're not a patient either?" My eyes bulged. "All this time I thought . . ."

"Hai!" Her face was red with embarrassment. "We both . . . this is really funny."

"But I was unable to tell the difference between you and a mental patient."

"Me too," she said.

Since we were not mental patients, there was no point or reason for us to sit there together any longer. We didn't even ask each other's name. The only thing that left me with a sense of warmth was that she turned around and said "Bye."

1990

Matching Sets | *Wei Jinshu*

Translated by Dongming Zhang

"Please sit down." I pulled over a chair, welcoming my colleague, Xiao Wang, with a smile.

"*Crack.*" "*Bang.*" Xiao Wang sat down hard on the floor.

The grin froze on his face. He looked embarrassed as he faced the once four-legged chair now with only two legs remaining.

I smiled apologetically. "I'm very sorry. You're not hurt, are you?"

He clambered to his feet, whisked the dust off his clothes, and made a magnanimous gesture. "I'm all right, but your chair ought to be replaced with a new one."

I saw that his words were both true and reasonable. The chair was tattered and had uneven legs. Decrepit and dirty, it looked like an unearthed relic. Whenever someone sat on it, it creaked unceasingly, pointing to an impending crisis just as the wind heralds a rising storm.

Over the next two weeks I began to make a chair.

"I must make a chair that is sturdy and attractive," I quietly resolved.

The chair was finished. The mahogany pieces fit together perfectly. It was exquisitely carved, the bronze-colored paint gave off a delicate fragrance, and the surface was shiny as a mirror.

Visitors all said the chair was beautiful but that it no longer matched its companion, reminding me that originally there had been a pair of chairs, one on each side of the tea table. Now the newly made chair was beautiful. Its beauty outshone its companion, making the other chair appear shabbier and uglier than before.

So I returned to my tools to refurbish the other chair.

Two weeks later another chair was finished, and the two were exactly alike.

"These chairs are gorgeous!" my wife's younger brother exclaimed as he walked into the room.

No wonder the chairs appealed to the eye. Put side by side with the other worn-out furnishings in the room, they stood out as pearls among swine.

"The thing is, the tea table is so unremarkable. Maybe you ought to replace it," he said offhandedly before leaving.

That made perfect sense. Standing on both sides of the tea table, the chairs gleamed, but the tea table was too dark. They stood like two devastatingly beautiful serving girls accompanying an ugly lady, making anyone who saw them uncomfortable.

I spent a month tidying up the appearance of that "ugly lady."

"That should do it." I took a step back, quite satisfied with my masterpieces.

"No good." My neighbor, Mama Li, eyed the "serving girls" and the "lady," stopping at an old wooden chest: "I think it would be perfect if you replaced this chest with a wine cabinet. Chests like this haven't been in style for years." After several weeks the chest was transformed into a wine cabinet. After that, many people visited the room. Gradually the two-drawer table was replaced with a study desk; a nightstand was replaced with high and low sideboards; and an old bookshelf was replaced with a dressing table. A color TV, a refrigerator, a VCR, and other items were also added to the room, which had a bright, new look; everything matched perfectly, even under fastidious scrutiny.

Furnishings were replaced, and the family's deficit grew. Because of this my wife grumbled constantly, "You foolish old man, what evil has possessed you! You do exactly as others tell you to do, but what about our daily needs? Your wife is old; why not replace her, too?"

While my wife's remarks were spoken offhandedly, I took them to heart. Her angry words buoyed me. Exactly! The room was filled with exquisite things, but they were all used by such a clumsy, dirty woman. That really depressed me.

Success comes to the determined. After two years of hard work, my room finally had a young and beautiful wife.

Satisfied, I smiled complacently and boasted joyfully to my friends, who all expressed their admiration. One friend joked with me, "Your room leaves nothing to be desired. Everything except you has been replaced with a new one. Aren't you going to be replaced as well?"

Everybody laughed, including me.

Quite unexpectedly, my friend's prophecy soon came true. One afternoon I moved out as well, as another young and handsome man had moved in.

1992

Home | *Xiu Xiangming*

Translated by Aili Mu

Whenever I had a fight with my wife, our son would beg us to make peace.

But can a ten-year-old child eradicate the shadow of war between two grown-ups?

Changes, however, did occur eventually. It wasn't that my wife and I stopped fighting, but when our fights broke out our son would no longer mediate. Instead, he would pick up a pen and draw pictures with concentrated attention on a piece of paper.

My son would always draw a two-bedroom apartment with a red carpet, glittering sconces, a Simmons mattress, and a leather sofa. There were plants like kaffir lily and asparagus fern on the balcony. Goldfish flapped their fins as if they were flying. In the bathroom, the water heater spurted stream in floral patterns.

These were precisely the reasons for our fights. We three lived in a small room of twelve square meters in a single-storey building. Facing the street was our kitchen, formed by a wooden plank. With standing room for two, it looked like a ramshackle toilet.

Three-fifths of our twelve square meters were taken up by a book-shelf, a cupboard, a wardrobe, a sofa, a coffee table, a desk, and a bed. It isn't hard to imagine what space was left.

There were, consequently, many inconveniences in life. My wife and I were like thieves when we made love, for fear of waking up our son. It wasn't such a problem in the winter, when we could all huddle together. But in the summer the small room was like a furnace after having been scorched by the burning sun all day. Crowded together in bed, we felt like we were being cooked in boiling water, sweat oozing from our pores. For lack of a better solution, I slept on the carton for the TV spread on the floor. I suffered through the summer nights on this carton.

At first my wife only voiced complaints about me but then she began to quarrel and turned abusive, "I married a worthless wretch who can't even secure decent housing!"

"I'm forty-five now, I'll retire in five years. Am I supposed to live in this cowshed for the rest of my life?"

"How can this makeshift shanty be called home?"

As a matter of fact I was frustrated, too. Who wouldn't want to have more spacious accommodations? If by saving a little on onions and scallions I could afford to buy an apartment, I'd definitely tighten my belt. The reality was that even if I sealed up my mouth and stopped eating altogether, even a lifetime's savings would hardly be enough for a decent apartment.

Driven beyond endurance by my wife's endless quarreling and abuse, I had no choice but to retaliate. Our fights shrouded the family in constant disharmony; our son was in perpetual fear.

The strange thing was that he drew the same picture every day. The wall next to the bed was covered with his drawings of two-bedroom apartments.

Every time when, conscience-stricken after a fight with my wife, I came to put things into perspective for my son, I said:

"Son, drawing is like writing. You must work on what you're familiar with. You should draw our small room in order to draw well."

Our son would say, "I'm familiar with two-bedroom apartments, too. Niuniu and Yuanyuan from my class all live in two bedroom apartments. I've been to their homes. Niuniu's dad is a factory director; Yuanyuan's mom is a company manager. Their homes are really nice."

After this comment, his cheeks would move while he swallowed saliva, as if trying not to drool at the sight of delicious food.

I couldn't stop the tears running down my cheeks. I was so grateful to our son I wanted to hold him in my arms and kiss him. He'd seen so many beautiful apartments, yet he didn't blame me, as my wife did.

Whenever I fought with my wife, my son would draw that two-bedroom apartment with the airs of a painter wrapped up in his obsession.

It was probably my son's sincerity that moved God. I was eventually assigned a two-bedroom apartment. My institution paid 110,000 yuan for it.

My wife and I, however, were divorced a month before I got the apartment.

My understanding son chose to live with me.

In gratitude to him, I decorated our rooms, balcony, and bathroom exactly as he had drawn them in his pictures.

I slept in the large bedroom, he in the small one.

On the night we moved in, I said to him, "Son, now that you live in your own room, you will surely draw your pictures even better now."

The next morning when I came to wake him, I saw him sound asleep bent over his desk. He hadn't slept in his bed all night. There were more than a dozen pictures on his desk. The image, however, had changed. They were all of that tiny room we'd lived in before.

I woke him and asked, "Why don't you keep drawing the other picture? You've got what you wished for, haven't you?"

With his sleepy and vacant eyes, he looked first at the pretty new apartment, then at the pictures he'd created during the night, threw himself into my arms, and began to cry.

1999

Short-shorts are easy to write because they are short—with limited space and few characters. Many devotees of literature began their career with writing short-shorts. Short-shorts are difficult to write because they are short—without being simple or insubstantial. The short length results from fine craftsmanship and exquisite beauty.

Xiu Xiangming

Rendez-vous | *Si Li*

Translated by Julie Chiu

In June, often after a few days of sunshine, dark clouds gather and rain begins to pour, a sluggish rain that only slows its pace after midnight.

Supper had been eaten and the table cleared. Auntie Ah Man passed through the living room on her way to her own room. Her only son, a newlywed, was absorbed in a TV show, one arm around his wife, a cup of tea in the other hand. Embarrassed, the daughter-in-law twisted her body but didn't manage to free herself from his grip.

Auntie Ah Man heaved a soft sigh, thinking, That TV is the daughter-in-law's dowry, so go ahead and watch it if you want. But do you have to display such intimacy, as if you were in your bedroom? Anyone would be embarrassed to sit down and watch it with you.

Auntie Ah Man pulled the door shut. A curtain of rain hung on the window beside the bed. She sat down at her dressing table. Embedded inside the fine dark frame was an oval mirror. As she did several times a day, she leaned forward to admire her hair, which was tied in a bun. The mirror showed a fine looking face, still delicate and sleek. Eyebrows meticulously shaped and nicely drawn; eyes beautiful like those of the phoenix, the fine wrinkles in the corner ingeniously covered with powder. A straight nose, just about right. Lips nice and thin.

Reflected in the mirror, too, was a portrait of Uncle Fu, which hung on the opposite wall. He had long since passed away, leaving behind a handsome inheritance, with which she had raised their child single-handedly. So many years had gone by!

Auntie Ah Man put on lipstick, and her face lit up. She stood up, tugged on her beige top, which had been nicely washed and starched, and patted her light-colored pants. She slipped into a pair of low-heeled shoes that had been shined that afternoon. She opened the drawer and took out an envelope, her ID card, and her seal, and put them all in a slim handbag she'd taken from the wardrobe.

Auntie Ah Man tiptoed across the living room, where her son and daughter-in-law were sharing a passionate kiss. She found a big black umbrella by the kitchen door, opened it, and stepped out into the pouring rain. She walked slowly, carefully counting the stone steps down the hill. Cutting through a few alleys, she crossed a main street and arrived at the harbor.

In the distance, a clock hung high on a tall office building, its hands clear and distinct in the spotlight. It was five minutes to nine. Beyond the office building were numbered warehouses, linked by a walkway illuminated by streetlamps scattered along the way. The lights were reflected in the water in the harbor, giving the rainy night a touch of desolate beauty.

As Auntie Ah Man walked by the office building, she looked up at the big clock and checked the time against her wristwatch. She then walked on toward the warehouses. Warehouse Number One. Number Two. Number Three. Number Four. She stopped in front of Warehouse Number Five and looked around. Except for the sea and a couple of ships in the distance, there was nothing but rain.

She looked at her wristwatch. Two minutes to nine. She shifted her handbag to the hand holding the umbrella, freeing the other one to straighten her top and smooth her hair. She checked her watch again. One minute to nine.

There by Warehouse Number Ten, someone in yellow rain gear— hooded slicker, pants, and rain boots—was approaching. He held a flashlight, which he shone left and right as he walked.

Deftly, Auntie Ah Man took off her shoes and put her handbag on top of them. The handbag had already been zipped up so its contents would not get wet in the rain. She shut the umbrella and laid it horizontally atop her handbag. With nothing standing in its way now, the rain poured down on her. But somehow she felt heat rising slowly in her chest, her body getting warm and languid.

She looked toward the far end of the warehouses. The yellow mass was approaching Number Nine. She walked up to the harbor side, hesitated for a moment, and jumped fearlessly into the water, maybe with a voice in her ears—

Hey, hold it! Don't jump!

She held her breath and sank. After some struggling, she floated to the surface, and the yellow mass had already made it to the waterfront. She sank again, the water about her roiled by the yellow mass. A powerful arm was thrown around her, and docilely she let the man push her ashore.

Slumping down onto her umbrella, she immediately started wailing— I don't want to live! I don't want to live! Her beige top and light-colored pants were so soaked with rain and seawater they were wrapped tightly around her body, showing every curve. Beating her bosom with her fists, she yelled and screamed.

The man squatted down, took a close look at Auntie Ah Man, and swallowed the water in his mouth. He shook his head and said:

"Ah, woman, why must you always choose my shift to jump into the harbor?"

1990

If a poem is a flower, an essay a meadow, and a novel a tree . . . a short-short can be seen as a single leaf, drifting down from among the interwoven branches of a luxuriant tree. . . . One fallen leaf is enough to announce the arrival of autumn. A good short-short presents the big with the very small. A good short-short goes in search of a mood, like that of a fallen leaf in the wind.

Xiu Shi

VIII. Creatures | *Howard Goldblatt*

My Ten Favorite Places to View Animals

10. Sculpted hedges in my neighbor's yard
9. At a toddlers' playground
8. In trees
7. In a B movie
6. In a George Orwell novel
5. At the New Orleans Aquarium (especially the jawfish)
4. In my head
3. Clouds in the sky
2. In a Petri dish
1. At my house

Cat | *Yuan Qiongqiong*

Translated by Howard Goldblatt

"My cat, if I'm around, so is he. I have only him, and he has only me."

That's the way she always talked, her voice low, with a lethargic drawl and an affected languor. Even with his back to her he could easily picture her expression: head raised, face framed in black shoulder-length hair, eyelids drooping slightly. She was saying, "All by myself . . . live in such . . . a big house. Except for . . . my cat, that is." Soft and purry. She breathed a long sigh. "Ah, my Blue."

Her cat was always named "Blue." Who knows which generation of Blue this was. He had once been so captivated by the throaty, clipped way she spoke that his heart nearly melted. The man talking to her now was more or less the same: guarded, respectful, in a husky voice he felt made him dignified. "Me, I've never liked cats. They're . . . too much like women."

"Oh?" She responded, teasing, surprised, the sound trailing off into the air. "Me, too?"

He didn't have the patience to listen anymore, so he walked over to a corner of the room, keeping his back to her until he got there. When he turned around, she looked just as he had pictured her. Still beautiful, the petite, slim figure of a classic fragile beauty. She was having a one-woman art show, and everyone knew that her physical beauty was half the reason her paintings were causing such a sensation.

The man was young, no more than twenty-five. Young and innocent. He probably knew nothing about cats and nothing about women.

They had lived together for a while. Never much of a pet fancier, he had somehow gotten along with Blue just fine. It was a plump, furry little thing, so in the winter he'd put it on his lap to stay warm. Eventually Blue came to like him so much she got jealous. She had said the cat acted as though it were his.

She turned around while she was talking and spotted him. Fixing her eyes on him from way across the room, she smiled fetchingly. Up to her old tricks. He was unhappy with himself for still finding her irresistible. She walked up and said, "You never come . . . my house." That same old seductive purr. "All alone. Still." A string of high-pitched titters followed.

Instead of responding, he just smiled politely. A moment later he asked, "How's Blue?"

"Ah." Her eyes brightened. "This time, it's . . . Siamese. Really blue. Its eyes."

She truly seemed to have forgotten. How strange.

He could never forget. When he came home that day, Blue was lying dead on his desk, a wire coiled three times around its neck. No one would ever believe that those hands gesturing in front of him, so tiny, so delicate, held such strength.

"I see." He was at a loss for words.

She was calmly talking about her current cat. He observed the artless, contented look on her face.

He guessed he didn't understand women either.

1988

Closely knit short-shorts with a surprise ending are good. One way to go. Short-shorts that harmonize the ambience of poetry and the plot of short stories are good. Another way to go. Short-shorts, nurtured in the tradition of short sketches, loose but with very high attainments are good. Yet another way to go. There are many other ways that are good, but it is best that none is the best—it is stupid to spin a cocoon around oneself.

Lin Jinlan

Pets | *Ah Cheng*

Translated by Julie Chiu

A man in his sixties, Jin was a great lover of animals. The year China was liberated, he was keeping a German shepherd as a pet, which to his neighbors was intimidating and hateful. When the government gave the order to eradicate dogs, they were quick to report this "Japanese shepherd" of Jin's.

Terrified, Jin explained that his was a *Mongolian* shepherd, not even remotely related to the Japanese breed. But a Mongolian dog is a dog, too, and was among the creatures to be eradicated. With a rope looped around its neck, still wearing the soft, glossy collar Jin had waxed so many times, the dog was taken away.

A few years went by, and Jin kept his sorrow to himself. Every time he stood in his doorway, he'd have a vision that the dog had returned, rubbing up against his leg. He'd reach out to touch it, only to find that nothing was there.

Then Jin adopted a cat. It was a common breed, with white and yellow stripes, like a tiger. But a tiger has black and yellow stripes. Seeing that one of his neighbors had a cat like that, too, Jin felt heartened.

The cat was a neat thing. It went out to do its business. It even knew enough to cover it with dirt. What grave lesson had their ancestor learned, Jin wondered, that cats took such care generation after generation? Dogs are neat, too, but rather crude. They are always trying to get into a fight, like a silly boy who refuses to grow up. They'd never be like a cat, which, at the slightest suggestion of danger, shoots up a tree or takes refuge in a room.

When the cat washed its face, it put one paw up and moved its cheek around, its tongue licking back and forth. Imagine a man doing the same—his face would soon be dripping with saliva. Its face now cleaned, the cat grew very still, its gaze fixed on something in the distance. It was like a woman caught in the middle of a bath, anguished or stupefied, heat written all over her face.

Often Jin would bring home a fish head or intestines or something. He'd set it in a plate and stand by to watch the cat move its head up and down until it finished the food. When the eating was done, it would leap into his lap and lick his hand. He'd sniff his hand, and, strange, it didn't carry any fishy smell.

When the Three-year Natural Disaster occurred, Jin racked his brain but couldn't get any food for the cat. Desperate, he gathered a few leaves and fed them to the cat. It was so sickened by the food it went to the doorway and wiped its mouth on the doorframe. Jin laughed a bitter laugh: Ah, the cat could climb a tree if it fancied a meal of leaves. Why have I bothered to gather leaves for it?

Then the cat left for good. Jin worried himself sick for a few days before settling on this thought: if it's left, it's left. Just don't let it find itself on someone's plate. The cat has no faith or loyalty, unlike the dog. A dog is never ashamed of a poor master, like a son isn't ashamed of an ugly mother. But you can't eat integrity. These days only the faithless and disloyal can survive, so what can a beast do?

Shortly after the cat was gone, the mice came. Lying in bed listening to the squeaks and scurrying at night, Jin thought: Why all the bustle? Humans struggled to bring food into this house, and there's still not enough for us. So what are you looking for? It's a fool's errand.

One day in the first month of winter, Jin opened a drawer to find something and a big mouse shot out, turned a somersault, and got away. From inside the drawer, there came a strong mousey smell and a symphony of squeaks. The mouse had just given birth to a litter of baby mice.

Their tiny claws trembling, the baby mice hadn't even opened their eyes. Jin moved a lamp over and shone the light on their nearly transparent, wax-like bodies. My house has been turned into a maternity ward, Jin said to himself. Now what?

Worried that the baby mice might be cold, Jin carefully moved them over to a spot on his bed close to the stove. When he turned around, he saw the big mouse staring at him from under the bed. What are you going to do, little mother? Jin asked.

Jin himself didn't know what to do. The mouse refused to go. Jin took it that the mother was worried, so he went out through the front door and watched the scene from outside the window.

The mouse hopped onto the bed and, one after another, carried the baby mice off in her mouth, their tiny limbs kicking as she bore them away. Heaving a sigh, Jin said, Not even the mice trust us now. What's the point of being a human being?

Back inside his house, Jin started looking for the mouse hole. He found it. This family is freezing in that hole, he said. He moved his chests and cupboards to clear the space in front of the hole, and set his stove near it.

From then on, Jin walked around on tiptoes, as if he were a tenant afraid to rouse his landlord from his sleep.

Often, lying in bed with his arms folded behind his head, Jin gazed at the mouse hole, contemplating the pets he could not see, and thought: There's nothing much to eat here. Just you keep warm.

When the winter sun sent its rays into the room, Jin had fallen asleep. One by one, the pets came crawling out.

1998

No short-short is complete by itself. Complete short-shorts are created by the joint effort of the writer and the reader.

Shao Baojian

Sea Turtle | *Zhang Kangkang*

Translated by Aili Mu

D had a darling three-year-old daughter whose requests he never turned down. Since his workplace was nearly two hours away, he came home only on weekends to reduce the commute. Every time he was home, his daughter would ask him to tell a story before she went to sleep. Within a year he had told all the stories of big wolves and little bunnies he knew and his story tank had dried up.

But his daughter wouldn't let him go without a story. Clinging to his knees, she refused to go to bed; even her mother couldn't talk her out of it.

He was filled with anxiety. Although it was a weekend, he had to dash off an article in the evening. The head of the research institute had called upon him to speak at an academic conference—an opportunity to give full play to his potential and talent in front of his peers.

Daddy, tell me a story please, his daughter pestered him.

What story? He really didn't have the time. The speech had a great deal to do with the recognition of his competence and personal worth. He had gotten wind that an academic appointment was on the way.

Suddenly he recalled an anecdote in the newspaper that day. He had only glanced at it earlier, but now he could pass it off as a real story for his daughter.

Once upon a time, there was an island . . . D started off, trying hard to sound patient, soft-spoken, and interesting to his daughter. Every family on the island had a special breed of giant sea turtle as big as a small table and with a very hard shell and very sturdy feet. There were no buses, bicycles, or donkeys on the island. They rode on sea turtles when they visited one another. Sea turtles love bananas, so the owner of a turtle would sit on its back, dangling a banana over its head from a string attached to a slim pole. The banana would only be a few paces ahead of the turtle, which, craving the fruit, would crawl forward. When the turtle did that, the banana in the hands of the person on its back would move forward, too. But the turtle could not reach the banana, so it tried harder and harder, and as it advanced, so did the banana. The man on its back got to where he was going without a hitch. . . .

His daughter fell asleep without his being aware of it, wearing a faint smile.

D worked like a demon at his desk day and night, nonstop. The speech was a success. Well received by all, it was selected for publication in the annual conference collection. People were talking in private, saying that although he was an assistant researcher he had the competence of an associate researcher.

It was Saturday again before D realized it. He was so busy his head was reeling the whole week. He didn't realize that he'd forgotten to prepare a story for his daughter until he was on his way to pick her up from the kindergarten.

To his surprise, she blurted out before she went to bed, Daddy, please tell the story of the big sea turtle again.

Heaving a sigh of relief, D wondered why his daughter was so interested in the big sea turtle.

. . . The man sitting on the turtle's back got to where he was going without a hitch.

D muddled through the story, realizing he was not in the mood to relate to his daughter. He couldn't, in fact, take his mind off the issue of his own academic title. If he was promoted to associate researcher this time, his family of three could hope for the assignment of a two-bedroom apartment and a salary increase by dozens of yuan, a substantial amount. Yesterday his superior had assigned him new tasks: he must complete a two-hundred-page monograph elaborating W theory in a month, compile a new dictionary in three months, and write a book of commentary on W theory through collaboration in six . . . D had no idea how he could accomplish all this.

What did the man do after he got to where he was going? To D's surprise, his daughter, uncharacteristically, was still awake, her eyes twinkling like dark grapes as she asked the question, gazing up at him.

When he got to where he was going, D said, he turned the sea turtle over so it couldn't run away. The turtle had to wait obediently for its owner to finish his business, turn it back on its feet, and ride it home.

His daughter seemed to have more to ask, but D patted her on the head impatiently and handed her over to his wife.

In order to complete all the above tasks in the given time undisturbed, and to really establish himself in academia, D moved to the research institute altogether. He spent his days and nights in the library and the reference room, believing that this was the only way to be fair to himself and to be worthy of his superiors' trust. In a research institute with several hundred employees, many were too old or too inexperienced, and it was up to the middle-aged but still youthful, like him, to get real work done. However hard life was, he felt there was always hope ahead . . .

He went home for the first time half a year later, exhausted but relieved of heavy burdens. Upon seeing him, his daughter turned her eyes to her mom, the question on the tip of her tongue: Who is this man? For the first time she didn't pester him for a story before she went to bed. She rolled her big eyes a few times before she finally asked: I remember the big sea turtle you told me about the last time. In the end did the man give the turtle the bananas or not?

Stunned for a moment, D gave an equivocal reply—I assume so. Not satisfied, his daughter asked how many bananas the man gave the turtle. He answered, A big bunch. Then his daughter asked if the man fed the turtle every time. D was at a loss . . .

At work on Monday he was informed that the promotion quota had been filled and that he was not among the hopeful because he lacked seniority. His salary and housing situation would, of course, remain unchanged for the time being . . . He felt as if his body had come completely unglued. . . .

For some reason the sea turtle came to mind. It would be too cruel of him to tell his daughter that the man didn't give the turtle bananas. He didn't have the heart to do that.

2003

Flies | *Yuan Qiongqiong*

Translated by Howard Goldblatt

He phoned home and heard a loud swat while his wife was talking to him.

"What was that?"

"A fly, it landed on my face," she said. "Darn! I missed it."

"Still a lot of them?"

"Yes, more than yesterday."

He was on a three-day business trip. He called home the first day, and she said there were flies in the house. "Lots of them," was all she said. "They're everywhere."

It was something he couldn't imagine, since cleanliness was so important to her. The house was always spic and span. Hardly ever any flies, and never more than a couple.

"Maybe one of the garbage bags wasn't tied tightly enough?"

"Of course not!" She sounded injured, like he was blaming her. "I took the garbage out today, like I do every day!"

"Then try some bug spray."

"I did!" This time she sounded troubled. "But there are so many of them."

He was staying in a hotel. The surroundings weren't ideal, but at least there were no flies in the old but refurbished room. The wallpaper went all the way down to the floor, where some of the concrete was crumbling. The bathroom fixtures were bright and shiny, and of excellent quality, but for some reason they seemed befouled, maybe because of all the bodies that had used and bathed in and rubbed up against them. On business trips staying in hotels was unavoidable, but he always felt peculiarly travel weary in them just because of that feeling.

The house they lived in was old, too, ten years at least, and, because it hadn't been kept up, it had a run-down appearance. A magnolia tree in the yard grew tall and sturdy, but never flowered. Its limbs brazenly weighed down the eaves of the house and reached across the wall to the outside. They'd taken the place because of the low rent. Dense, green-to-the-point-of-black magnolia leaves blocked the window, keeping out nearly all the light.

The call came in the middle of the night and took several rings to wake him. Telephone calls in a hotel room can spark an abnormal reaction, as if someone has tracked you down in another world. It was his wife. He looked at the clock. Three a.m.

"There are swarms of flies," she said.

His room was dark, with just a trace of dusky light, and he detected a soft slur to her voice, as if she'd been drinking or was still half-asleep.

"How can that be?" he said.

"There are swarms of them," she insisted. This time he could tell she was crying. She sobbed and said in a barely intelligible voice, "Come home soon, okay?"

"Use the bug spray!"

"I did!" Now she was really crying. "They're everywhere . . . it's scary . . . I can't help feeling . . . feeling like the house is dying!"

"Don't be silly!"

There really was something putrid about the house. Neither the landlord nor the previous tenant had taken care of the place. So after they moved in, she wore herself out cleaning it from one end to the other. And yet some of the odors simply wouldn't go away: a dank rotting smell in the wood and the nauseating stench of little creatures in corners. She sprayed air freshener, but that didn't help. It was as if the house had developed its own odor, which was especially noticeable on rainy or muggy days.

He let her cry awhile before saying, "Put up with it the best you can. I'll be home tomorrow."

He couldn't get back to sleep after hanging up, so he turned on the bedside lamp and lit a cigarette. The faint three a.m. light lent the room a blurry resplendence; after spending two nights there, the room had taken on some of his own characteristics and had achieved a sort of passive familiarity, whereas, in his imagination, his home had grown fuzzy: they slept on a dark-brown, Japanese-barracks-style bed that was uneven and gave off the sour smell of years of accumulated sweat; cockroach droppings were embedded in cracks in the bedroom walls. Before they went to bed, she laid out a multicolored comforter as a sort of mattress, then they covered themselves with a silk quilt they'd had since their wedding; it was decorated with big, bright purple flowers.

Why, he couldn't say, but he imagined her sleeping on the dark bed, covered by the quilt, with its big, beautiful purple flowers, only her pale face exposed, which he found strangely enticing. He shivered as he envisioned the impossibly mysterious allure floating on the surface of an impenetrable, marsh-like darkness, bright purple flowers atop the black marsh, and her damp, pale face pulled into it by her black hair.

He returned home the next day. An ambulance was parked at the head of the lane and a crowd had gathered in the doorway of one of the houses. It was, he saw, their next-door neighbor's house.

It was afternoon, somewhere around two or three o'clock; lengthy, blinding rays of sunlight lit up the walls, the rooftops, and the people who'd come to see what all the excitement was about. The door was open, so he looked inside, shielding his eyes with his hand, like everyone else. His neighbor lived alone. He'd only seen her a time or two, but he recognized her lying on the stretcher two men were carrying out of the house.

She'd been dead several days, he was told, and yet her body, corrupted by the heat, didn't smell. Her mouth and eyes were open slightly; a few flies were perched on the taut skin of her face.

When he walked in the door, she was on her hands and knees scrubbing the floor. "I found a dead mouse," she said, crinkling her nose. "No wonder there were so many flies."

She told him there were fewer flies than the day before, but they weren't gone altogether. You could still see them in small clusters, little black dots on the walls. One was buzzing in the air. It landed on her neck; she turned her head, and it flew off.

His stomach lurched. He alone knew where the flies had come from, that after attending the corpse next door, they were coming across the wall and, like bees spreading pollen, landing on his wife, bringing death with them.

Meanwhile, she was on the floor, her arm twitching as she scrubbed, sweat streaming down her face, seeming to heat the air around her. Suddenly the tangible image of life she presented made him feel hopelessly humbled.

He walked past the flies. The little black dots didn't budge; they just gazed intently at the two people in the room.

1988

The Crow and the Fox | *Liang Dazhi*

Translated by Dongming Zhang

Lying in bed, the son clamored for his mother to tell him a story. So she repeated the story she had told again and again.

Passionately fond of literature, she had not yet published any of her writings, but occasionally a few were aired on the county's closed-circuit broadcasts. On this day she saw a notice in a magazine soliciting contributions to a grand literary competition with the goal of fostering new literary talent over the turn of the century.

Fascinated by the notice, she sent the magazine a short essay that had been rejected earlier by the county's closed-circuit broadcast. As a matter of course, according to the request, she sent a three-yuan application fee along with the manuscript.

She began the story:

A crow stands high on the branch of a tree, holding a piece of meat in its mouth. A fox living in a hole in the tree stares longingly at the meat. Standing under the tree, the fox compliments the crow on its beauty: "You beautiful crow, your feathers are so beautiful, your body is so strong, and I bet that your singing is very pleasant to the ear. Sing to me, if you will." The crow is very pleased with the fox's words. As soon as it opens its mouth to sing, the meat falls to the ground. The fox snatches the meat and dives into the hole in the tree.

"Understand?" She said to her son, "This story tells people that becoming drunk with praise can cause one to play the fool."

The son did not respond. She looked at him, not knowing when he had fallen asleep.

A few days after she sent out the essay, she received a notice from the organizing committee of the competition: Your contribution has been deemed acceptable. It has earned an award of excellence based on serious deliberations by the panel of judges. You have also qualified to participate in the second round of competition, which decides the first, second, third, and fourth prizes. Every writer who participates in the second round must pay 48 yuan to cover revisions, evaluation, certificates, recommendations, printing, and other expenses. Those not paying the additional entry fee will be disqualified, their submission removed from competition for publication, and their original award forfeited. In today's market-oriented economy, one must invest to get ahead. This is true in the creation of fine literature as well. We heartily welcome your participation in the final round of competition.

She thought it was totally unnecessary for the organizing committee of the competition to use such high-sounding, preachy words. Saying too much can make people think back to the fox's compliment to the crow. It's only 48 yuan. She and her son can simply go without milk for a month and a half. It's true that a talented literary figure doesn't breeze in at the turn of the century. She mailed in the 48 yuan.

Again her son clamored for a story. She said: "A crow holds a piece of meat in its mouth . . ."

"Mama, every night you tell me the story of the crow and the fox. Why is the crow taken in by the fox every time?"

The mother said, "Don't ask so many questions. Now, go to sleep."

She received an honorary certificate, which was only slightly larger than a business card. Her contribution, which had once been rejected by the county's closed-circuit broadcast station, won a prize. The certificate would facilitate admission to schools of higher education, a better occupation, and an increase in salary. Looking at the card, which fit in the palm of her hand, she wondered whether it would be accepted by the Ministry of Organization and Personnel.

Sent along with the certificate was a "notice to publish an anthology of excellent literary works from the turn of the century": Your contribution has been deemed worthy of publication. The author must pay a total of 188 yuan for layout, revision, proofreading, handling, and postage. Anyone not paying the fee will be disqualified, and their submission removed from publication.

She figured that 188 yuan was roughly the cost of milk for half a year for herself and her son. So be it, she thought to herself, we can forget about milk for the sake of literature. She went back to the post office.

The son said, "What happens to the crow in the end? How long can the fox fool it?"

"All right," she said, "I'll tell you a new crow and fox story."

She began:

A crow stands high on the branch of a tree, holding a piece of meat in its mouth. A fox living in a hole in the tree stares longingly at the meat. Standing under the tree, the fox compliments the crow upon its beauty: "You beautiful crow, your feathers are so . . ." The fox no sooner begins than the piece of meat falls into its mouth. The crow begins to speak: Mr. Fox, every time you compliment me, you desire only to eat the meat. Today, I've simply given it to you. There is no need for more talk. Your swindling act is shameful, for which you will be punished sooner or later. The fox thinks: Today I, an old fox, am lucky indeed. I receive the meat without wasting a word. It's my turn to enjoy this gourmet delicacy. Thinking this, the fox closes its mouth. But instead of a gourmet treat, a hidden nail pierces its mouth."

"Good, good." The son clapped his hands and said, "Now the fox will not dare trick the crow again."

Neither nodding agreement nor shaking her head, the mother patted her son to sleep.

She received an anthology of excellent literary works from the century from the organizing committee of the competition. To her surprise, it was comprised of several thousand essays like hers. She noted that her essay remained unchanged; even the two spelling errors she habitually made remained "with respect to the original."

"A crow holds a piece of meat in its mouth . . . ," she was once again telling her son the story of a crow and fox. She thought: how numerous the crows and foxes are in the world. So long as crows and foxes exist, the story of a crow and a fox will never end.

The next day she saw in another magazine a notice that invited contributions to a prize-awarding competition. She sent out "A New Story of a Crow and a Fox" with the application fee of 3 yuan.

2001

Waiting for a Windfall | *Wang Yanyan*

Translated by Aili Mu

A farmer of Song[1] had a tree stump in his field. A hare ran into the stump, broke its neck, and died. The farmer stopped farming to wait by the tree for more hares to show up. None came, and the farmer became a laughing stock of Song.

This story about me was beautifully written, simple yet solemn, like patterns on a Shang[2] vessel. Later, as the story disappeared into history, the patterns fading with time and dispersing into streets and byways, it became a fable painted in heavy colors.

My coming out from behind the scene was obligatory, after the wild beating of gongs, drums, and clappers; it could not be glossed over nor could it be explained. The official narrative was like the bright central room of a house—the acme of clarity, its depiction beyond my control. But the real story was locked up in the wing-rooms.

That year I felt the secret arrival of spring a couple of days earlier than usual. Year after year I anxiously awaited its coming, like a passionate young man waiting for his girl. I was able to capture its most delicate sound and smell. Since my waiting had no limits, time or space, the onset of spring, always miraculous and wonderful, had never let me down. My innate inexplicable anxiety dissolved in its colors, sounds, and scents.

That morning, in my small perilla-covered courtyard, I turned over a fallen mulberry leaf from the year before. Just as in my dream, the peony under the leaf was bursting forth, its ruby sprouts tender but sturdy, already displaying grace and beauty. Branches and twigs from last year's perilla reached out in the wind, stupefied over the harbinger of spring. I was filled with joy.

I stepped out of the courtyard and started my spring outing. I roamed around the village day and night. I'd shaken hands with thirty-two springs; each was forever fresher—and briefer.

When tender leaves emerged from parasol trees, straight as bamboo flutes, beautiful clouds floated in. Big birds with ash-blue wings abruptly stopped preying on sparrows—that was for cold days. Everywhere in the village flowers bloomed in a brocade of colors. When the fields seethed with more and more people working, I chose to lie down in the grass to avoid them. Visited by dreams or not, I lay there, wishfully thinking that spring would never end.

I could not escape a life in which work began at sunrise and ended with sunset, but I had my happiness in the blossom brocade of spring.

When the little gray hare hit the stump, it woke me from my dream. I knew he could not be saved because even the purple paulownia flowers turned pale. I brought him home. My family cooked him for dinner. This hare, being my only contribution to the family that spring, gave me a good excuse to roam the fields: to wait for more hares to dash themselves against a tree stump.

People in the village talked about my foolishness that whole spring. The scent of locust flowers hovering over the village carried more chitchat that year. Many passersby took a break at the well in the west end of the village, then took my story away with them after the sweet water had rejuvenated them. Gradually my story lost its details.

Later on, it became known to all that I no longer waited for hares.

Many springs later I was still a quiet guest in the warm embrace of this land.

Many more years later a man named Jimi understood what I was waiting for:

On the fourth day of waiting, gazing into the distance, I learned to appreciate the uncertainty of changing clouds;

On the tenth day of waiting I learned to distinguish the chirpings of small birds and the fragrances of different plants and flowers;

On the seventeenth day of waiting I could feel a butterfly's mood in the breeze;

On the twentieth day of waiting a bunch of hares smiled and presented me with a purple flower. We chatted for a long time before bidding one another good night.

2003

Little Stray Cat | *Zhong Ling*

Translated by Julie Chiu

Cold air stole in under the blanket and sent a chill down Marianne's silk-smooth back. She woke up, and as she wrapped the blanket tightly around her neck, she pressed her cheek against Martin's chest, gently rubbing his brown hair. Suddenly she opened her blue eyes wide and stared at their red blanket in surprise. Oh no! This was not what she and Martin called home; this was what she and Lawrence called home! The clock at the head of the bed said it was ten past eight. Immediately she shook Martin and said, "Wake up, my love, the sun's up!"

Martin shot out of bed, hurriedly got dressed, and ran toward the kitchen with his shoes in his hands. Her body wrapped in the red blanket, Marianne followed him. He had already opened the back door, but he stood there, petrified. Why, over the last night three feet of snow had fallen! There was no way he could cut through the back yard! They rushed back into the living room and, through the tall window, could see that the snow on the road had already been cleared. He could only risk going out through the front door.

His lips were busy kissing her good-bye while his feet were finding their way into the shoes. He opened the door, peeped out, and, seeing not a single soul on the road, dashed outside. She scurried to the window and watched her ex-husband's large figure make it to the corner and disappear. She breathed a sigh of relief. But suddenly she was staring again. Oh, my God! The path leading to the front door was clearly imprinted with his footprints. If her neighbors saw it, she might as well confess all to them.

Now it was Marianne's turn to dash around. She put on her clothes, grabbed the shovel, and got out on the front path to clear the snow. After a few sweeps of her shovel, she dug up something heavy and hard. It had a strange, irregular shape, looking like a big, black toy gun. Curious, she picked the object up and took a close look. It was a black cat, frozen into a hard mass and very dead.

Holding the dead cat in her hands, Marianne stood dumbfounded for a while. If she threw it into the bin by the door, by the time the garbage collector came six days later, it would smell very bad. It made her sick just to think of it. Oh, all right, she was going to shop for groceries later, so she might as well chuck it into the big rubbish bin outside the supermarket.

When Marianne was done with her rounds in the supermarket, she walked into Howard Johnson's, where she took off her fur coat and fur hat, revealing the fluffy blonde hair that gracefully scattered over her shoulders. She ordered a cup of coffee and, amid the cigarette smoke, thought about Lawrence. She would drive to the airport that afternoon to pick him up. Ah, Lawrence in his fine clothes and gentlemanly ways—during his two-week business trip in Italy, he must have hunted down at least half a dozen dark-haired Donnas.

She gazed at the parking lot outside the window with suspicion. How come there was this brown paper bag sitting on the top of her car? Oh hell, that damned cat! She had put it there just now when she was loading her shopping into the trunk. She had forgotten to dump it into the rubbish bin. As she was thinking these thoughts, she saw an old woman cutting through the parking lot. Her frizzy white hair was like dry grass, and she was all huddled up in a worn black overcoat. Marianne knew right away that the granny was from the slum in the inner city, the type that lived off welfare. When the old woman walked by Marianne's yellow car, she stopped and looked around stealthily. With the speed of lightning, she seized the brown paper bag and ran for the bus that was just pulling up to the stop. Marianne watched in amazement, slack-jawed. Gradually her lips curled into a mischievous smile. What a funny expression the old doll will have when she opens the bag!

After Mrs. Smith boarded the bus, she was so nervous she was panting. She sat down and put the bag beside her. God bless, her first try at theft had gone so smoothly! Couldn't blame her really! The paper bag had been sitting on a Mercedes-Benz. It was good stuff for sure. That was a luxurious brand for a car! The bag was small but weighed quite a bit. Probably an iron. Good, the one at home had been broken for four months! How she longed to open the bag and find out what was inside. But she was seated beside an old man, and the driver was right in front of her. Had better wait till she got off the bus to take a look. So she started feeling the bag with her hand. Hard and irregular in shape. Ah, she got it! A piece of first-rate beef steak! Since the old man was crippled the year before, the two of them had not eaten a single steak!

Thanks to the snow and the slippery road, the bus was moving extremely slowly. Mrs. Smith could not hold back any longer. She opened the bag and saw a pair of yellow eyes staring at her eerily. What? It was a black cat, stone dead and stiff. She was so scared she screamed. The bus was negotiating a turn, and the driver, frightened by her scream, lost grip of the steering wheel. The bus skidded off the road and rolled down a hill.

The bus rolled over and landed at the bottom of the slope. As it lay on its side, the dead cat was flung out through the door that had been smashed open. It landed on the slope, cushioned by the soft snow. All the dozen or so passengers were injured. Mrs. Smith lay face down on the floor of the bus, her leg cut by the glass. She was bleeding, but her cheeks blossomed into a silly smile. Now all her problems were solved. The bus company would surely pay her compensation for the rest of her life. Their lives, hers and the old man's, would definitely change for the better!

The ambulance was gone. The curious people had dispersed. No one had noticed the black cat that had caused the trouble. In the dazzling sun, the snow melted, and there was water everywhere. The snow under the little black cat had melted, too, revealing a black rock. The black of the rock and the black of the cat took in a generous amount of the sun's rays. The cat's limbs were not stiff anymore.

Two yellow-skinned boys came down the slope through the snow. They stashed their schoolbags and pitched snowballs at each other. One landed on the black rock, and they discovered a black furry ball. They ran over to check it out.

"It's a kitten. It's dead!"

"No, Brother. Look, its nose is still wet."

"Oh, yeah. There's even steam coming out of its nose! Let's take it home!"

"Great! Our cat died last week, so now if we bring it back, Linda will really be happy!"

The little black cat woke up in a toasty room. A huge fire was blazing in the hole on the opposite wall, where two big logs were burning. The cat had been sleeping on an old cushion, on which was sewn a long worm that looked like a snake. It even had legs and horns, a strange creature. There were lots of books on the floor. Wow, it could sharpen its claws here. From the inside room came three human voices, two of which were children's. The cat remembered these voices. It had a vague recollection that it was the masters of these voices who had saved its life. Early that morning it was so hungry and cold it finally collapsed in the snow and lost its cat-consciousness. Ever since it had learned to walk, it had roamed and begged for food all alone. Domestic cats were so lucky. Would this family keep it?

Suddenly the little black cat felt its hair stand on end. There was a dog here! It could smell the dog! When the cat turned its head, it saw a big German shepherd entering the living room and running toward it, the blood-red mouth opened wide! Little black cat was so shocked its heart almost stopped beating. It was too weak even to move, not to say run. It could only close its eyes and wait for its life to end. One bite from those sharp teeth and it would be cut into two halves, a mess of bloody flesh. But little black cat felt someone caressing its back. It felt wet and warm. Opening its eyes, the cat saw the German shepherd gently licking its body! A little boy's voice was saying, "Come and look, Mom. Linda likes it!"

1981

Short-short stories have both the captivating readability of popular literature and the profound substance of serious literature.

Bai Xuchu

IX. Sharing | *Howard Goldblatt*

Wham!

"Wow, did you see that? That big bird took that little goldfinch right off the thistle sock. What was it?"

"Here's a picture of a Cooper's Hawk. That must have been it. The book says they'll attack birds at feeder stations."

"Tell me about it! Hey, look at the white pine, where those cardinals are perched, casing the area. They're like bright red Christmas tree ornaments. I'm surprised the hawk didn't scare 'em off. The squirrels sure aren't showing their faces."

"It's long gone—mealtime. Isn't that a downy woodpecker having at that chunk of suet?"

"Oops, here comes the black assassin, our *favorite* feral cat. It's been a week or more since it nailed a mourning dove, if we can believe the trail of feathers. Meanwhile, the chipmunks are sleeping away the winter . . ."

"Hey, where are you going?"

"To refill the feeders. No food, no show."

Division | *Zhou Rui*

Translated by Howard Goldblatt

The room held one man and twelve mosquitoes.

All twelve mosquitoes bit the one man.

$12 \div 1 = 12$

The man couldn't stand it.

So he went looking for someone to come share the room.

Twelve mosquitoes bit two men. They had split into two forces.

$12 \div 2 = 6$

The man felt better than he had at first.

But things could always be better.

So the two of them went out and found a third man.

$12 \div 3 = 4$

Great! Let's go find number four.

$12 \div 4 = 3$

A fifth man came running over.

$12 \div 5 = ?$

They told number five to stay outside, since it would be hard to divvy up the mosquitoes.

But number five was determined to enter. *Whack! Whack!* Number five swatted two mosquitoes.

$10 \div 5 = 2$

OK, that did it.

Everyone was happy. But then: *Whack! Whack!* Number five swatted two more mosquitoes.

$8 \div 5 = ?$

No way to divvy up again.

Seeing how number five was messing things up, the others got together and drove him out of the room.

1992

Postcards | *Ye Si*

Translated by Julie Chiu

Time and again he received a postcard from her, crammed with small letters the size of ants, scurrying on their tiny feet conveying who knows what. Gentle, full of passion, and very seductive, her postcards were simply irresistible. But she was always on the road, always changing her address and shifting her routes. Now and then, on a gloomy evening or a sleepless night, she would send a postcard.

The postcard sat in his pigeonhole, sandwiched between a set of notes of meetings and some memoranda. Back in the office, he carefully sorted the papers out and began to read her words. Sometimes, when he looked up past the heaps and piles of documents, he thought he could see the corner of a colorful street; sometimes, white clouds drifted in to wash the four walls and dye them the colors of a morning in spring. He turned back to his trivial office routine, answering clients' phone calls and drafting a budget proposal for the next year, trying to meet deadlines he seemed never able to meet. He worked till late at night. As he was leaving, standing at the door reaching for the light switch, he turned back and saw, sitting on his desk, a tinge of flaming red. He switched the light off, and all went dark.

In his bachelor apartment spring nights seemed particularly cold and gloomy. He felt as if he were a blind fish hiding in the depths of the sea, cut off from the world. Sometimes he thought about those shapes and images from afar, those messages sent from across the oceans. But threads of cold rain were spun and woven into a hard cocoon. He felt that he was a soaked carpet, waiting for the next sunny day to be spread on the rooftop to dry. The next day was cold and gloomy, as always.

Every once in a while he received a postcard from her, sitting openly in his pigeonhole. He envied her openness in expressing herself. There was a feeling of surety in the way she loved, something he had lost in his trivial reality. He did not know how to respond to her monologues. Courteous remarks would only sound hypocritical. Her solo tune carried affection in every note and beat. If he intervened with his words, the rhythm would be interrupted, he feared. He could not find the words for a reply. He picked up the postcards one by one, each looking so thin and brittle they could be lost any moment in the ocean of documents.

Gradually the postcards decreased in number. Then, one day, he saw her at a cocktail party. She had returned. She was standing right in front of him talking to someone. They were like total strangers. He recalled that, except for the written communications, they had never once had a good, long conversation. He walked toward her. It seemed somehow she had chosen that moment to move toward someone else. He drew closer, raised his hand, and found the cold, glassy touch of a mirror. Wine spilled from his glass. Faces reflected in the glass tabletop became fragments of watery shadows. He looked up, and she was gone.

He heard that she had left again. A month later, he began to receive postcards from her once more. Sent from every important city, where important events occurred. Again the monologues, directed toward a certain him that was not necessarily him.

1990

Reading a good short-short . . . satisfies the modern man's need to read, a man who is busy and slothful, and whose blood is cold and nerves numbed. Undoubtedly it also serves to massage the soul and restore its health.

Chen Xinghui

The Cycle | *Ah Cheng*

Translated by Julie Chiu

Yuyin, an important city in the Zhonghuai region of Xinan Province, has a population of a million-plus and covers an area several times an arrow's range. In the city, eating and drinking go on from morning till night. What cannot be put into the mouth gets dumped in heaps and piles. Yuyin also boasts industries of all sorts. Scrap materials made redundant in the manufacturing process stack up like hills. And there are new ways of spending invented abroad or within the country, which the city picks up somehow. They bring people new thrills but also create an assortment of trash. All in all, Yuyin's trash output nears a hundred tons per day.

Yuyin is a city of many rocky hills, where trees are few and grass is scarce. Like a man living among poor, naked folk, Yuyin has long since been embarrassed. Luckily, among its myriad trades and doings, Yuyin excels in trash disposal: it may be poor but strives not to be filthy.

By greater luck still, some thirty miles from Yuyin there lies a piece of odd terrain, a fascinating sight indeed: in the multitude of hills and peaks, a few conjoin to form a stone bucket of a few hundred yards in depth and ten miles in diameter. These hills are devoid of running streams and, being rich in quartz, cannot store water like a reservoir. Yet their valley is as deep as a seaport, in which ten thousand tons of trash can be anchored.

And so trash is transported here every day.

Before daybreak, loud rumblings are heard in the streets of Yuyin. Dozens of dump trucks set off in turn and join an impressive march. Ever since the local garbage trucks were replaced by these imported "quarry-hill" dump trucks, many citizens of Yuyin have not needed their alarm clocks. When the fleet of trucks speeds past with an earth-shaking grandeur, wheels sucking up debris along the way, people part with their beds and rise. Some go on to brush their teeth and wash their faces. Some pull themselves together and get set for their morning *taichi* or grocery shopping, basket in hand. Like a man just out of bed, Yuyin rubs its cheeks and scratches its itch, and gradually wakes up to activities. Children still in bed are scolded and called lazy bugs by the adults. Now they finally get up, and a few of them start mouthing their syllables, singing:

> Lovely big trucks, wonders of the city,
> Thunderous rumbling rattles my ceiling.
> Big trucks take the trash out of the city,
> And bring us cash for clothes and earrings.

Negotiating one bend after another, overcoming countless slopes, the trucks go left and right, up and down the hills. No one knows how many times the gears are shifted, or the accelerators released and depressed, as the steering wheels turn like windmills. Dogs and chickens, startled, leap up and take off. When shadows of the mountain people are cast on the road by the trucks' headlights, they take hint and hop aside. They let themselves be wrapped in dust and smog for ten minutes or so, cough a few coughs, and continue on their way to the morning bazaar.

The trucks have now reached a pass that opens into the valley. The sky has turned bright. Mist stirs in midair, about to rise but not quite.

The accelerators bellow out slow, long roars, and the trucks line the top of the valley in single file, their rear ends turned toward the big hole. Without warning, the world falls into total silence.

A ray of golden light jacks up the disc of a sun, which, by chance, finds itself on a mountain pass. Suddenly numerous golden rays cut through the starry mist and fall on the line of trucks. As if on fire, the orange paint on the trucks now glows with a blinding glare. A sudden wave of heat spreads in the trucks, and with a deafening blast, dozens of truck beds start to move, their front ends rising slowly to 45 degrees. As if expecting what is to come, the mountain birds, hundreds of them, make a cry in unison and soar up to the sky like puffs of smoke.

With low moans like distant thunder, a hundred tons of trash begins to stir. Gradually the stirring picks up speed. Once out of the trucks, the trash plunges straight down the slopes like a waterfall. Now and then, broken by protruding rocks, the stream of trash splatters and sprays like water, and part of Yuyin's secrets is disassembled. The sun's rays invigorate the stream of trash and gild the slopes with shimmering colors. Smog and dust swirl and dance, trailing tails of red, violet, green, and pink, forming a cloud of multicolored mist in the hills.

After rendering their salute, the truck beds slowly return to their original position. The trucks are moving again.

As the beds are lowered, they give out another round of clangs. This clanging is the siren of the many hills. All at once another waterfall streams down, triggering a symphony of shouts and cries.

More than a thousand people have been waiting on the hills. When the dumping of trash is done, they put their baskets on their backs, grab their two-tine forks, and joyously run down into the valley. The birds are much slower in responding, so when they, too, plunge to the bottom, they are immediately chased back up by the people. Again, they soar to the sky like smoke, and again they make another plunge and get chased back up, until eventually they disperse and fly off in every direction.

When the truck drivers hear the shouts and uproar from below, they laugh, they curse. Again they make their bends and climb their slopes, their steering wheels turning like windmills. The grand march is on again, heading for Yuyin city.

At the bottom of the big hole, people sort the trash with meticulous care and hurriedly chuck the desired items into baskets they will carry on their backs. When the sun is halfway up the sky, the earth of the sloping hills can be seen again, blotched with sweat and food debris—

the birds' turn now to sort it out. The people have already made it to the road on top of the slopes, where they are taking a rest.

The sun shines warmly on their bodies. Even the trash in their baskets is relaxed, whispering notes that mingle with the human voices. Some of the people now pull out those items of trash they find fascinating, and show them to the others. They theorize about their original uses. They imagine the comfort and convenience these items must have brought. The speculations become knowledge, confirmed by the nodding crowd. Now and then a dispute emerges and is usually arbitrated by a young person—there are too many trends and inventions that the old folks can't figure out. Occasionally someone displays a torn-up love letter taken from the hole, but often, when the pieces are put together, the letter has no ending. Most likely it is a failed attempt by the lover; the successful one must be carefully kept in a certain corner in the city. The resting ground becomes a market, with people recommending or swapping trash they do or do not need. And so the trash gets sorted into further and clearer categories. The metal scraps, the most valuable items, are always prized and will not be swapped.

It finally becomes unpleasantly hot in the hills. The rocks start to make people dizzy. People grab their baskets and head for the road the trucks had traveled. They trail along the winding road in the hills like a stream. Back in the city, the waste-collection buying stations are not busy yet. They know that the trash is still on its way and won't reach the city until afternoon. That's when the hard work begins.

Trash is lucky. Coming or going, it doesn't have to toil or worry. On the return journey, in particular, it sits in a sedan chair like a wealthy man. Nor does it get lonely, for all along the way there are songs in the air.

All the hills listen to the songs. Their trash on their backs, the mountain people are extremely happy. The road is long and so, raising their many and varied voices, they sing:

Sun up in the east,
Sun down in the west.
Mighty good!
Rocks burning my feet,
I climb the blasted peak.
Mighty high!

Go cut your firewood in the mountains,
Go fetch your water jug at home.
Mighty hard!
Let me dig a golden egg,
Let me go home to my lady.
Mighty fast!
A-hei-hei!

1988

Black Umbrella | *Yi Ruofen*

Translated by Julie Chiu

In this world there are many black umbrellas.

Each black umbrella is a roof. We carry our black roofs with us so we can block out the weeping face of the sky.

When we go indoors, we have a solid roof above us. We fold up the black roof and set it aside, leaving it to shed its residual tears.

Black umbrellas often look alike. Some people take away others' umbrellas without realizing it; others lose their umbrellas and can never find them again. Perhaps few can remember the exact details of their own umbrellas. Black umbrellas, that is.

If you, too, use a black umbrella, you may want to listen to the following story.

A man and a woman were eating at the same table in a restaurant. I said a man and a woman, not a couple, so obviously they were not related in any way.

The man finished his meal first. He grabbed the black umbrella standing at the foot of the table and made for the cashier. The woman called him back, saying, "That's my umbrella."

"It's yours?" asked the man.

"Yes, it's mine," the woman said with conviction.

"Then where's my umbrella?" The man looked under the table but found nothing.

"Did you bring one?" The woman helped with the search, but there was only one pool of water on the floor, meaning there could only have been one umbrella.

"What's the color of your umbrella?"

"Black, like this one." The man showed the woman the umbrella.

"Your memory could have failed you."

"But I must have brought an umbrella with me, or how could I have stayed dry in this downpour?"

The woman turned to look outside the window. Sure enough, it was still raining hard. She simply had not been aware of it with all the noise and talking in the restaurant. "All right, then," said the woman. "I'll walk with you wherever you're going."

So, shoulder-to-shoulder, they walked into the rain. Together, owning a movable black roof, they walked, till, together, they owned a solid, concrete roof.

Even now, they have no idea whose umbrella it was. But it doesn't matter. What matters is that, ever since they met, they have gone through the wind and rain together, blocking for each other the gloomy clouds.

If you, too, use a black umbrella and do not have a particularly good memory, may the same good luck fall upon you.

1990

Writing a full-length novel is like playing a chef who, all by himself, prepares a big meal that is the equivalent of a state banquet. . . . Writing a very short story, however, is like cutting out fruit slices and turning them into a joyous platter of colorful display.

Zhong Ling

Small-Hands Chen | *Wang Zengqi*

Translated by Howard Goldblatt

In the old days there were never very many obstetricians where I come from. Most of the people hired midwives when it was time to have their babies, and each family used the same midwife every time one of their babies was due. The "little gentlemen" and "little ladies" born to Eldest Mistress, Second Eldest Mistress, Third Eldest Mistress, and however many others there were in the family would all have been delivered by the same midwife. Certainly it would never do to have a stranger in the house at a time like that. The regular midwife knew her families so well—including which of the old maidservants could be counted on to assist her—that there was no need to go looking for a special "waist holder." Not only that, most of the people had a superstitious belief that everything would be fine as long as their "lucky" midwife was in attendance. Since these midwives offered up prayers to the Matriarch of Sons and burned incense every day, what respectable family would ever think of asking a male doctor to deliver one of their babies?

The real doctors in our region were all men—except for the daughter of Pock-Faced Li, that is. Having taken over for her father, she was the only woman doctor in town. But she was a specialist in internal medicine, not someone trained to deliver babies, and, besides, she was an old maid. Certainly no self-respecting male who planned to go into medicine would ever become an obstetrician. The men all shunned it as a disgraceful calling with no future. That's not to say there were no exceptions. Small-Hands Chen, in fact, was a renowned male obstetrician.

Small-Hands Chen's reputation rested on the fact that his hands were so small—smaller than those of a woman, not to mention softer and more delicate. Specializing in difficult deliveries, he was particularly adept at sideways births and breech births (naturally he was aided in his efforts by medications and medical equipment). People said his hands were so small and his movements so precise that he was able to lessen his patients' labor pains a great deal. No upper-class family would ever have considered engaging him except under the most extreme circumstances. But since middle- and lower-class families were encumbered with far fewer taboos, whenever one of their women was having a difficult labor, the midwife would acknowledge her inadequate skills and say, "You'd better go get Small-Hands Chen."

Naturally Small-Hands Chen had a large following, but he was still known everywhere as Small-Hands Chen.

In the business of delivering a baby there can be no delay, for two lives hang in the balance. Small-Hands Chen had a horse, a pure white steed the color of snow, that was born to run. People who knew horses said that this animal exhibited the high-stepping gait known as "pheasant willow"—fast, sure-footed, and straight. There are so many lakes and rivers in our region that horses were a rarity. So whenever armies with mounted troops came through the area, the inhabitants all flocked to the banks of the canal to marvel over the "cavalry." Since Small-Hands Chen was often seen riding his white horse across the countryside on his way somewhere to deliver a baby, the people began to lump him and his horse together: White Horse Small-Hands Chen, they said.

Other doctors, internists and surgeons alike, all looked down on Small-Hands Chen, saying that instead of being a real doctor, he was nothing more than a male midwife. But this didn't bother Small-Hands Chen, who would leap onto his white horse and be off like the wind whenever anyone requested his services. The moment a woman in labor heard the comforting sound of the bells on his horse's bridle, her moaning stopped. A while (sometimes a long while) after he had dismounted and gone into the delivery room, the cry of a newborn baby would signal another successful delivery. Small-Hands Chen, his face bathed in sweat, would emerge from the room and greet the head of the household respectfully: "Congratulations! Mother and child are doing fine." The father, his face wreathed in smiles, would hand over the red envelope in which he had placed the fee, which Small-Hands Chen would stuff into his pocket without looking inside. Then he would go wash his hands, drink a glass of hot tea, and say, "I hope I haven't offended you," before walking outside, mounting his horse, and riding off, the bridle bells jangling noisily.

A lot of people owed their very existence to Small-Hands Chen.

One year the Allied Forces came. For several years that place of ours was the scene of constant warfare between two opposing forces—the National Revolutionary Army, which we called the "Government Forces," and the troops under the command of Sun Chuan-fang, who referred to himself as "Commandant of the Allied Forces of Five Provinces." These Allied Forces made their headquarters in the local Buddhist monastery, which housed an entire regiment. The commandant's wife (she might have been his real wife, but she also might have been his concubine) was in labor, but the baby would not come. Several midwives had been summoned, but they were powerless to help this woman who was screaming like a pig in a slaughterhouse, so the commandant finally sent for Small-Hands Chen. When Small-Hands Chen entered the monastery, the commandant was pacing back and forth in front of the delivery room. He welcomed Small-Hands Chen by saying, "I'm placing both lives in your hands, Sir. If you don't save them, I'll have your head! Now you may go in." The woman had rolls of fat, making Small-Hands Chen's work particularly difficult. But his efforts paid off, and the baby was born, even though delivering the fat woman's child had exhausted him. Almost totally spent, he stumbled out of the delivery room and made his sign of respect to the regiment commandant.

"Congratulations, Commandant, it's a boy. You have a son."

"I've put you to a great deal of trouble," the commandant said with a broad smile on his face. "This way, please."

Food and drink had been set up for him, with the commandant's adjutant serving as host. After Small-Hands Chen had finished two cups of wine, the commandant handed him twenty gold pieces.

"This is for you. I hope it's not too little."

"You are too generous, much too generous."

Having drunk the wine and pocketed his twenty gold pieces, Small-Hands Chen rose to take his leave. "I hope I haven't offended you."

"You can find your own way out, I trust."

Small-Hands Chen walked out of the monastery and mounted his horse.

The commandant, who was standing behind him, took out his pistol and shot him dead.

"I couldn't let him get away with putting his filthy hands all over my woman. Her body belongs to one man, and that's me. Who does he think he is, trying to do me like that. Screw him!"

The regiment commandant was feeling greatly wronged.

1983

It Was the Pumpkin That Brought Me Here | *Luo Feng*

Translated by Julie Chiu

It was the pumpkin that brought me here—can you believe that? In City A, where I live, they celebrate Halloween between October and November every year, when the market is stocked with pumpkins of all sizes. It took me a long time to pick out this particular one, which I rode on to come to you, to get in front of you and behind you, to find that you were still thin, quite unlike the pumpkin, and shy.

The pumpkin told me we hadn't seen each other for 351 days, during which time I had my hair cut seven times and wore out four pairs of shoes but did not gain an inch in height! The pumpkin told me, too, that in these 351 days you fell sick twelve times, your blood pressure went up twenty points, and your beard grew an inch longer. I know that it was all because we were dealing with a different sun and a different moon. Every time I was sound asleep you would still be seated by the window working on your portrait of a pumpkin. And every time you were struggling with yourself in a dream I would be eating an ice cream at the other end of the world. Perhaps our daily routines had gone upside-down, so much so that they fell out of the Galaxy's tracks. Which was why you were still so thin, not like the pumpkin.

It was the pumpkin that brought me here, but it did not tip me off how much you had changed. You were not wearing your blacks and dark blues anymore, having switched to gray, a hesitant, indeterminate color. You no longer enjoyed ice cream but went drinking instead. You drank all night, and you drank in the middle of the road. You seldom cracked any jokes now but put into effect the aesthetics of "silence." Yes, when the pumpkin brought me back, it had not prepared me for all these changes in you. And so, holding my pumpkin, I sat there stupefied, hesitating over whether I should simply cut the pumpkin in two.

In this City H, where you live, summer is edging in. The flame of the forest is in full bloom, and its reddish orange flowers have taken over the green branches, looking quite aggressive. When I walked under the tree, it sprinkled angry petals all over my body, as if challenging me, telling me to stay away and never think of settling down in City H. I have come on a pumpkin and must return to City A, where the pumpkin originated. But the tree does not understand my history. I used to live in City H, too. It was only by chance that I was taken away by the pumpkin. But I know the flame of the forest does not welcome the pumpkin, because the pumpkin's silence and patience are threats to its charm and ferocity.

On the eleventh night after my return, finally you told me a fairy tale. You said there was this boy who had the face of Cupid but was shy. This year his mother fell sick, and his grandpa died. He also lost the pair of wooden clogs that Big Sister Fairy had given him on his twelfth birthday. And so he did not know his way and got lost in the wilderness. On this eleventh night I turned myself into a pumpkin, not babbling anymore. Your passionate words brought the pumpkin to ripeness, although you were still thin, still shy.

In the remaining eleven days and nights I often came to see you with my pumpkin. You started to talk more, and your blood pressure fell back to normal. You began to talk about your wishes. You said you wanted to go to a place abundant in butterflies. You would collect their colorful wings and make paint out of them so you could rewrite your personal and City H's ancient history. I held the pumpkin to my bosom, quietly listening to you and trying not to interrupt your thoughts. Gradually I noticed that you were no longer thin and shy. Then we ate together. We did not eat the pumpkin, of course, for a pumpkin is not made for eating. We ate a mermaid and a pigeon, our greatest favorites. The mermaid symbolizes happiness, and the pigeon, peace. And so we had put peace and happiness into our stomachs.

The night before I returned to City A, you took me to Country C to buy fairy tales. It was drizzling that day, and everything was bleak and gloomy, like our steps that sank deep into the muddy road. I loved walking behind you, watching your back. It was big, but it didn't look like the pumpkin. Rather, it looked like a wall, sometimes providing shelter from witches and winds and thunderbolts, sometimes becoming one of the four iron walls of a fortified castle. It made me feel safe and steady, but it also gave me a feeling of indifference and frustration. Anyway, the silhouette of your back was fine looking. It was like an incomplete brushstroke in an ever changing landscape painting, full of obscurities. We bought many fairy tales in Country C: *Cinderella*, *The Little Mermaid*, *The Prince and the Pauper*. We also bought *A Midsummer Night's Dream*, *The Adventures of Pinocchio*, and *Alice in Wonderland*. It was a fruitful trip, and we even had a delicious meal of happiness and peace! But on this day I had forgotten to take my pumpkin with me and could not go home. So you gave me a copper coin and, pushing the heavy books, walked me home. The way home was short, but it was as if we had walked for twelve centuries. It was drizzling all the way. I was not hiding behind your back anymore. I walked beside you, listening to you recount the story of Cinderella— Once upon a time, there was a girl who was always dressed in humble clothes. She stayed home all day cleaning out the fireplace. She was forever covered in gray cinders. One day she bought a pumpkin and took it home. It suddenly changed into a fairy, who put a beautiful dress on her. The fairy also turned a pumpkin into a carriage and gave it to her, so she could happily take part in the prince's ball. But the fairy told her she must return home before midnight or the carriage would turn back into a pumpkin, and her glamorous dress with its shiny jewels would once again become a plain dress. Then what? I asked. You said you could not remember. I felt a little sad. When we begin to forget how a fairy tale ends, we know we have to accept the restrictions that imposes on us.

The way home was very short, but you and I had walked for twelve centuries—twelve centuries ago, you still had curly hair, your eyes were like the buttons on Prince Sapphire's sleeves, and you were still running up and down the hill barefoot; twelve centuries later your hair had grown longer, you had become nearsighted, and you couldn't stay awake, always in a dream, fighting or quarreling with yourself. Twelve centuries ago I had my hair tied into two plaits that flanked my apple-red cheeks, and I loved to sing; twelve centuries later I let my hair fall loose but still it could not cover up my pale cheeks and speechless lips. Twelve centuries ago we did not know each other; twelve centuries later we bid each other farewell. . . .

It was the pumpkin that brought me here—can you believe that? I must return before the pumpkin resumes its original shape, or . . . or what? I don't really know. And 351 days later, will the pumpkin still bring me back? Will we be able to walk through another twelve centuries? The fact is, we are just people banished by the fairy tales and cannot foretell how the story of the pumpkin will end.

1994

In-Law | *Cao Naiqian*

Translated by Howard Goldblatt

The early-morning stillness is broken by the braying of a donkey.

Blackie says, "That damn in-law has come for you."

The woman says, "Stall him while I put on my pants."

"Shit," Blackie says, "what difference does it make?"

The woman blushes. "Just say I'm sick and I can't go. It's that time of the month anyway."

"I can't do that," Blackie says. "Chinese don't go back on their word."

Blackie walks outside to greet his in-law, who is tethering his donkey at the gate. Blackie turns and shouts into the cave, "Go fetch a chicken. I'll get some liquor from the commune."

"In-Law," Blackie's counterpart says, "I brought a bottle, since we always drink yours."

"When did we start worrying about what's yours and what's mine, anyway?"

Blackie's woman walks into the yard and, without a glance at either man, heads for the chicken coop.

"No need, no need for that. A cow fell and died last night at our village," the in-law says to Blackie's woman. "I borrowed this donkey from the brigade leader, and the son of a bitch was cooking a pot of beef." He takes a leather bag from around the donkey's neck. "Here, take it. You might need to cook it a bit longer."

Head lowered, Blackie's woman takes the bag and goes into the cave without a glance at either man.

While they are drinking, Blackie says, "It's that time of the month. Day before yesterday. Want to wait till it's past?"

"Fine with me."

"On the other hand, the brigade leader might deduct work points for keeping his donkey. You can take her now. Just wait till she's finished before she does it."

"Fine with me."

"Bring her back next month. I can't borrow a donkey."

"Fine with me."

After they finish drinking, Blackie says to his woman, "Put on those clean clothes. I don't want people in the other village laughing at me."

"No need. The commune's on the way. I'll buy her a jacket and trousers there."

Blackie sees his woman and the in-law on their way, across one ravine after another and over a series of ridges.

"Go on back," the in-law says. "Here's the mountain."

Blackie says, "You go on up the mountain. I'll head back." He hesitates, then turns back. The in-law smacks the donkey's rump with his large fist; the animal starts clip-clopping down the road.

Shit. Go on, go ahead. A thousand yuan less would be the same as handing me his own daughter. Shit. Go on, go ahead. It's only one month a year. And Chinese don't go back on their word. These are his thoughts as he walks.

Blackie takes another look behind him and sees his woman's turnip-like feet dangling alongside the donkey's haunches, swinging back and forth.

Blackie's heart, too, is swinging back and forth.

1988

X. (In)Fidelities | *Howard Goldblatt*

"So, who is she?"

"Who's who?"

"Her! The half-naked woman in this photograph."

"Where'd you get that?"

"Now you know why a man should never leave his wallet on the dresser."

"Ah, I see."

"You see? See what? Quit stalling, and tell me who she is."

"I don't know."

"Bullshit! Nobody keeps a picture of a stranger—with or without clothes—in his wallet."

"I agree."

"What? Do you think I'm stupid? You agree what?"

"That nobody keeps a stranger's picture in his wallet."

"Meaning?"

"The wallet. I picked it out of a guy's pocket on the subway."

"Whew, what a relief!"

Elope | *Fu Aimao*

Translated by Aili Mu

Ah Jian decided to elope with Yu'er. For one last time Yu'er asked her lover: Ah Jian, are you sure you want to do this?

Yes, Ah Jian answered.

You won't back out before you leave the house?

No.

Yu'er still wasn't sure: You really want to leave your wife?

I don't love her anymore.

Can you really part with your son?

I'll send child support.

Yu'er thought for a moment and added: Ah Jian, will you really be at the railway station at eight sharp on December 28? (Note: December 28 was Yu'er's birthday, and they had planned to elope by train at eight that night.)

Yes, Ah Jian replied.

What will you do if your wife comes home when you're ready to leave?

I'll tell her I'm going on a business trip.

What if your son grabs your hands and says, Please Daddy, don't leave, I'm scared to be home alone.

I'll tell him not to be scared, that his mom will be home soon.

Yu'er lowered her head, deep in thought for a while before she asked: What if it starts to rain?

I'll put up an umbrella.

What if it's not rain but hard, icy hailstones?

I'll put on a helmet.

Yu'er was relentless: What if the sky falls, the earth crumbles, the river floods, and the bridge collapses the moment you're leaving?

Ah Jian answered resolutely: I'll rush over, no matter what, and wrap my arms around you. We'll live or die together.

After a long silence, Yu'er asked for the thousand and first time: Ah Jian, do you really love me?

Ah Jian answered: I love you so much I'm willing to give up everything, including my own life, to be with you day and night till the end of time.

Having asked all that she needed to ask, Yu'er felt reassured and left for home. She had to pack and get ready.

At eight on the night of December 28 Yu'er made it to the station exhausted, but Ah Jian wasn't there as promised. Yu'er waited patiently till daybreak, Ah Jian never showed up. All that night Yu'er tried but failed to figure out what could have kept Ah Jian. She picked up her heavy suitcase and went home alone. Yu'er never saw Ah Jian after that.

Maybe eight, maybe ten, God knows how many years passed before Yu'er ran into Ah Jian. At first she was going to leave without saying anything to him, but her curiosity got the better of her. She wanted to know what had kept him from sticking to his promise that night. She had convinced herself that it must have been a huge, insurmountable obstacle. Calmly she asked him: What happened that night?

Ah Jian answered earnestly: Nothing, really. When he was ready to leave, his wife hadn't tried to stop him; his son hadn't grabbed his hands or cried; the weather had been fine, no rain or hail. The sky, of course, wasn't falling, the earth wasn't crumbling, the river wasn't rising, and the bridge wasn't crumbling. He was all packed and ready to go, with money, clothing, a flashlight, candles, a knife, books, his phonebook, fluoride, and flu capsules, everything he could think of. All was in place, as the popular saying goes, except the last crucial act. Ten minutes before leaving he discovered that the lock on his suitcase was broken. He spent an hour trying to fix it but couldn't. Ah Jian paused at this point, and then, seeing no alternative, continued as honestly as he knew how: Yu'er, you know me. I know nothing about mechanical things like locks, and I couldn't go wandering the world with an unlocked, broken suitcase, could I?

At long last she learned that a stupid suitcase lock had ruined her great love.

2002

Frenchie | *Ai Ya*

Translated by Julie Chiu

He told me he loved France.

"The Arc de Triomphe and its grandeur, the bas-reliefs on its walls . . . everything is mind-blowing! And the sturdy frame of the Eiffel Tower simply fills your heart with awe! From big cities to little towns, from avenues to alleys, everywhere you look you see beautiful flowers and romantic cafés. Men are clean and polite, women are slim and charming . . ."

I had never been to France, but he had.

Still I said in protest, "Which country doesn't have its handsome, magnificent buildings? Which city doesn't have its unique charm? Take Rome, the city of art, or Tokyo, with its bustle. Take New York, with its inexhaustible museums, or Nepal, a paradise on earth. And what about the Netherlands, where there are more flowers than in France . . . ?"

He pondered my words for a while, and finally said, "But the French—they tolerate the keeping of a mistress." He looked at me and went on, "And the woman can keep a lover, too. It's a long-standing tradition, and society approves of it. A country as romantic as that—how can one not love it?"

My, my, there we go! This man who repeatedly told me he loved me, this man who had only been married to me for three years—he could view the idea of a "mistress" with such envy.

Of course I was sad and angry, but that did not erase the obsession from his mind. He seemed totally enchanted. Time and again he invoked the fun he had had during his French trip; he even tried to implant the concept of "mistress" in my head.

"If a Frenchman comes home to find his wife's bedroom door shut and a pair of men's shoes by the front door, he'll simply steal out and take a good long walk. Then he'll come home again and have supper with his wife as if nothing had happened . . ."

My, such a fellow!

Soon, I began to dub him "Frenchie."

One day, quite out of the blue, my younger brother came to visit me from Tainan. Like all young men, he had loads of surprises for me. He even arrived on a motorbike, his body covered in dirt and dust. I told him to go take a shower before he and I went out for dinner. My husband was engaged in some business and would not eat with us.

Just when I had locked the bedroom door from inside and started to change clothes, the door was suddenly flung open. A ring of keys in one hand and a club in the other, his furious eyes shooting fire, my Frenchman stood facing me, halfway through my changing—underpants, naked thighs, unbuttoned blouse. In a split second, he grabbed me by the hair, dragged me out of the bedroom, and threw me into the bathroom doorway.

The remaining details—I don't think I need to give. All I know is: "Frenchie comes home, Frenchie sees a pair of men's shoes by the front stairs, Frenchie finds his wife's bedroom door shut, so Frenchie . . ."

Ah yes, only a man can be a Frenchman.

1987

A writer of very short stories usually gets two kinds of reader response: one of marvel, the other of lament. Those who marvel say: A story of so many twists and surprises! Deeply touching! And in so short a text! Awesome! Those who lament say: So great a subject blown away in so small a handful of lines. What a waste!

Ai Ya

Hickey | *Ku Ling*

Translated by Lin Li-chun

There was a hickey on his neck, in plain view.

I started to regret coming to dinner at the Fang's. Although Little Fang and I have been colleagues for years, and his family and mine are quite close, it still wasn't worth the trouble for my wife and me to be part of this absurd situation, especially since things were just calming down between us.

I secretly observed Fang's wife; she was actually quite composed, still her old graceful and gracious self, cordially inviting us to sit. Little Fang, on the other hand, was doing his best to stay calm but unable to mask his nervousness. The hickey on his neck must be what did it. Leaving "ironclad evidence" behind after a little hanky-panky on the side, of course he'd die "an ugly death."

Problem is, I might not get away scot-free either: Fang's neck was still "virgin territory" when we got off work yesterday. Then a bunch of us buddies went to a pub, where he didn't seem to have transgressed except for flirting with a few older women. Who'd have known that, after heading out of the pub at two in the morning, he still had the energy for a "date"? Obviously his cover was that he'd been drinking with us.

Trouble is, we didn't get our stories straight beforehand, so dangerous missteps could easily happen during a "cross-examination." It was now Saturday; had it been any other day, I would have seen his "crime scene evidence" when he got to work in the morning and could have made up an outlandish story to help pacify Mrs. Fang. Now all was lost. Chewing on the food without even tasting it, I racked my brain for an answer in case she asked, "When did you leave the bar last night?" Fang would be dead meat if I told the truth; but if I didn't, my wife would know I was covering for Fang, which would ruin Fang's and my credibility. Fuck! That stupid Fang. Why couldn't he tell his foxy mistress to control her passion? Why did she have to "do" it on the neck?

I finished the after-dinner fruit in dread and apprehension. Mrs. Fang was still chatting away about this and that, her words echoed by Fang. Knowing it was to my advantage not to stick around the battlefield too long, I made up an excuse about having to go home to help with the kids' homework. They didn't insist we stay, and fortunately my wife didn't object either, so I walked out of their house feeling like a lucky criminal who's just been acquitted. I turned around, only to see a pleading look on Fang's face and traces of smug satisfaction on the face of his "prison guard."

"What time did you leave the bar last night?" The question came from my wife when we were in the car. I cleared my throat and collected my thoughts, keenly aware that this battle had to be fought carefully if I wasn't to suffer "collateral damage." "Just after one in the morning. Didn't I get home a little after two? We were at the same old pub. You've been there before. We just had some drinks, shot the breeze, nothing—"

"Did you see the bruise on Little Fang's neck?" Another sneak attack.

"Bruise? Oh, yeah, I think I did. Wonder how he got that. Maybe Mrs. Fang was so fired up with passion, ha ha ha . . ."

My wife turned and gave me a look, which effectively shut me up. What kind of old married couple leaves a hickey on the spouse's neck? I was going overboard trying to cover up for my friend. Better to keep quiet and subject myself to her tirade against all the worthless men in the world. Earlier the two women had spent a lot of time whispering in the kitchen, so maybe they'd already figured things out.

"You're right, it was his wife." I jammed on the brakes so hard my head almost slammed into the windshield. "But he didn't know," she added. Again I jammed on the brakes, this time followed by the squealing of brakes behind me, as well as a string of curses. But lucky for me, no rear-ender.

Barely recovered from the shock, I pulled over to the side of the road so she could tell me the whole story:

It turned out that Mrs. Fang was pissed that she had to stay home alone while her husband was out drinking late into the night. Then, when he finally got home, he was so drunk that "his ability couldn't match his desire," and nothing happened no matter how hard she tried to arouse him. Staring at her dead drunk husband on the bed, she was hit by a stroke of genius. She sucked on his neck long and hard until she saw a bruise, before going gleefully to sleep. Little Fang saw the hickey this morning and panicked; his face drained of color as he hemmed and hawed, trying to explain but not knowing how to begin. Mrs. Fang said nothing and asked no questions; instead, she treated him with all the tenderness of a good mother and a virtuous wife. Filled with fear and trepidation, Little Fang doted on his wife cautiously, as if walking on thin ice; he not only threw himself wholeheartedly into household chores but didn't even dare raise his voice. Mrs. Fang was very pleased with herself, certain that Little Fang was still in a fog as to how he got the hickey and had no choice but to "remain guilty without having his day in court." He really couldn't explain himself; if the judge doesn't start the trial, who can the accused tell his story to?

When my wife finished her story, she was laughing so hard that her whole body shook, as if she had been Mrs. Fang's accomplice. It was all I could do to stay calm and keep mum. I wondered whether to tell Little Fang the truth, when to rescue him, and whether it would turn him against his wife, when my wife wrapped her arms around me and planted a big kiss on my neck.

1997

Horse Talk | *Mo Yan*

Translated by Aili Mu

It was like a big, thick, bristly brush whisking across my face, waking me from my dream. A lofty shadow swayed before my eyes like a massive black wall. A familiar smell made my heart pound. I suddenly came to my senses. The backdrop of modern life behind me quietly withdrew; the sun shown brightly over that dingy yellow earthen wall.

On top of the wall, withered grass rustled; a brightly feathered rooster stretched its neck and crowed heartily. A haystack in front of the wall was crumbling. A flock of hens was digging for food in the scattered hay. There were also several oxen tethered to posts along the wall, all bending their heads and chewing their cud, as if deep in thought. The crooked wooden posts were coated in ox hair, the dirt wall covered with ox dung. I was sitting in front of the haystack. I could reach out and touch the hens; leaning over a little, I could also stroke the oxen. But I didn't touch the hens or stroke the oxen. I looked up at her—my close friend—that old mare, black, worry-laden, with "Z99" branded on her flank, blind, reportedly retired from a field army, currently the wheel horse for our production team, known throughout town for her limit-less strength and "all-work, no-complaints" attitude.

"Horse, it's you!" I jumped up from the haystack and wrapped my arms around her, embracing her strong, thick neck. The warmth and powerful smell of grease from her neck brought a surge of emotions and hot tears that rolled around on her smooth skin. The horse straight-ened her ears, which looked like whittled bamboo, and said, in a tone of experience and wisdom: "Don't cry, young man, don't cry. I don't like crying. There's no need to cry. Sit up and listen to me." As the horse flicked her neck, I was lifted from the ground like a feather and then landed on my backside by the haystack. I could reach out and touch the hens; leaning over a little I could stroke the oxen.

I studied this old friend I hadn't seen for more than thirty years. She hadn't changed: enormous head, tall and strong body, slender limbs, azure-colored hoofs, downy tail, and tightly closed eyes that for unknown reasons had become blind. Images of the past flashed before my eyes.

I had often plucked hairs from her tail to make bows, and she'd just stood there, silent as a wall. I had often sat on her broad, smooth back reading picture storybooks, and she'd remained motionless as a stranded ship. I had often whisked away the flies and gadflies that were sucking her blood, and she'd remained cold and unfeeling as a stone statue, without any expression of thanks. I had often showed her off to kids in neighboring villages, telling stories about her glorious past and boasting how she had charged into battle with a regiment commander on her back, distinguishing herself under fire, and, like a piece of cold steel, she would utter no sound. I had often asked the village elders about her past, especially how she had become blind, but no one would tell me. I had often tried to guess; caressing her neck, I'd implore:

"Horse, horse, dear horse, please tell me how your eyes were blinded. Were they hit by shrapnel, was it a result of an eye disease, or were they pecked out by a hawk?" But even though I asked you thousands of times, you would never answer.

"I'll answer you now," said the horse. When she spoke her soft lips flapped clumsily from time to time, showing snow-white teeth, worn down by grain and straw. The odor of rotting grass from her mouth nearly knocked me over. Her voice was very low, as if emerging from a long winding tunnel. The voice captivated me, intoxicated me, frightened me. It was as if I was hearing the sound of nature. I dared not but listen closely.

The horse said: "You should know that in the country of Japan there is a famous story about eyes. When Chunqin, a female *Qin* performer, was disfigured and blinded, her disciple Zuozhu, who was also her lover, poked out her own eyes. And another ancient story relates how Oedipus, upon learning that he had killed his father and married his mother, poked out his own eyes out of remorse and shame. And there was Ma Wencai from your village, who could not bear parting from his new wife. To avoid the draft, he blinded himself by rubbing lime in his eyes. All these tales show that, in the world, there is a category of blind people who willingly blind themselves to escape, to possess, to achieve perfection, or to punish themselves. I know, of course, that you are not interested in them. What you really want to know," the horse muttered, "is why I became blind." The subject obviously had evoked extremely bitter memories. I waited. I knew that at this moment words were unnecessary.

The horse said: "A few decades ago I was, in fact, an army horse. The brand on my flank is proof. The pain of being branded with a red-hot iron is fresh in my mind, even today. My master was a gallant officer. Not only was he talented and handsome, but he was also a skillful military strategist. I was passionately devoted to him, like a lover. One day, to my surprise, he allowed a woman, emitting the offensive odor of rouge and powder, to ride on my back. I was infuriated, became distracted, and ran into a tree as I was passing through the woods; it knocked the woman to the ground. The officer beat me with his leather whip and cursed: 'You damned blind horse!' At that moment, I decided never to open my eyes again. . . ."

"So, you are only pretending to be blind." I leaped to my feet from beside the haystack.

"No, I am blind. . . ." With this, the horse turned and walked unhesitatingly down the endless dark road.

1990

I believe that to have thought is to experience something in a special way—a way that far exceeds any other way. Many things in the world become "real" because they were conjured up in thought. And to think from different perspectives gives birth to different stories. To think, therefore, is to create.

Bai Xiaoyi

A Family Catastrophe | *Ku Ling*

Translated by Howard Goldblatt

"Where's your mother?" Father asked as he came running downstairs. But he didn't even give me a chance to answer (I'd just walked in after getting off work) before heading back upstairs. I wanted to say something as I watched him hobble up the stairs, but before I could open my mouth, he was already back downstairs. "Have you seen your mother?" He looked into the kitchen, then opened the bathroom door.

Finally he sat down, exhausted. For a moment Father seemed to have suddenly aged a great deal, and even his voice seemed old and raspy. "Your mother sneaked a look at the letter I wrote to my daughter . . . that would be your stepsister, who lives on the mainland . . . she saw the letter . . ." As I looked at Father's wrinkled face, I recalled hearing Mother on the phone that morning, complaining angrily: "He put it right there on the table to make sure I'd see it. Him and his 'My dear daughter, Yuqin.' He's kept it from me for more than thirty years . . . a grown daughter, and he's kept it from me for . . ."

"What's there to argue about? Her mother's been dead all these many years, and all she left behind was this daughter. She's suffered so much on the mainland . . . ai!" Father's eyes turned gloomy. "So what's there to argue about?"

"I always wondered why he never wanted me to have a daughter," Mother had said. Her indignation came over the telephone, loud and clear. "After I had you and your brother, I said I wanted a girl, but your father said no, he didn't want any more. He said stuff about family planning, but the reason he wouldn't let me have a little girl was that he had a daughter on the mainland all along!"

"How was I to know she'd find a way to get in touch with me?" Father defended himself, giving me an anxious look as I sat quietly. "After all those years without a word, I thought sure she'd been eliminated by the Communists. How was I to know she was still alive? After all, she is my own flesh and blood. Am I supposed to ignore her?" As I looked at my graying father, Mother's words rang in my ear: "All that talk about how he hadn't met his obligations as a father for more than thirty years and how it's his responsibility to send money. Like hell! I've worked like a slave all these years, without a penny of my own to show for it, and now he's talking about sending some of our money to her on the mainland. How dare he?"

It was getting late, and Father was beginning to blend in with the settling darkness. With sadness in his voice, he said: "After so many years of marriage, how can she just up and leave? Her purse is gone, her shoes are gone, just like that. And for what? It's our daughter, after all. Even if we brought her over, we'd still be one family. Besides . . ." His head was so low it was nearly resting on his chest. "No, I guess not," he sobbed.

Toward the end of the phone call that morning, Mother was weeping so much her voice was barely audible. "Everyone in my family opposed my marriage to your father, forbidding me from marrying a mainlander, but I wouldn't listen. Your grandfather wouldn't even give me away at the wedding. I've had plenty to complain about, but I never imagined it would come to this. I never thought I'd be the wife of someone who had been married before and who had a daughter. I can't accept that, I just can't. . . ."

I was growing more and more concerned, but now that things had reached this point, I didn't know whether to try to comfort Father, who was showing his age as never before, or sympathize with Mother, who had left the house in anger. Just as I was trying to find a way out of my predicament, the door opened and Mother walked in. Father's head snapped up, and there was a gleam of light in his eyes. "Where have you been, Mom?" I asked. She was surprised by the tone of my voice.

"I went out to buy your father some cigarettes," she said, holding up the pack to show me. "Where do you think I've been?"

1985

Hatred | *Ah Cheng*

Translated by Aili Mu

Lao Zhang and Lao Li were friends of many years. Many years, some people said, meant they'd been friends since childhood.

Lao Zhang disagreed.

Lao Zhang said, Lao Li and I didn't meet—he lived in Fujian and I lived in Shanxi—until we were in the same class in college.

Lao Li explained, Lao Zhang and I both loved literature and often talked about it. My family was better off at the time, so sometimes I took him out for some snacks that went well with wine—boiled peanuts, salted soy beans, or—

Lao Zhang cut in, Or sauerkraut. Lao Li is from Fujian, but he likes sour food. Right, Lao Li?

Lao Li answered, That's right. I guess I developed a taste for sour food around then. I think sour food enhances a discussion of literature, which is hard to talk about. Sour food generates a lot of saliva and forces you to talk. You can't avoid it. Wine, on the other hand, only gives you the courage to talk.

Lao Zhang said, That's strange, how come I didn't know you were like that?

Lao Li replied, Because I never told you.

Lao Zhang said, We've been friends all these years, and there are still things you haven't told me.

Lao Li said, That's right.

Lao Zhang asked, Is that how a friend should act? Friends ought to tell each other everything. Otherwise, how can they call themselves friends? Lao Li, we've known each other a lot of years, and I don't think you've been all that good a friend.

Lao Li replied, Friends are people who have things to talk about. Haven't we had a lot to talk about all these years? There should be no pressure among friends. I don't want you to pressure me.

Lao Zhang said, What a shame, after all these years! Now you tell me what you can talk about and what you can't. To be your friend, there are some things I need to consider.

Lao Li replied, This is a dilemma, a true dilemma. We've talked about dilemmas. You want me to say what I don't want to say. Do you still remember the campaign in which a person was supposed to open his heart to his partner for mutual thought remolding?

Lao Zhang said, That's irrelevant.

Lao Li said, When a person's attitude toward the campaign was interpreted as his attitude toward the Revolution, the Revolution became an ethical burden. The pressure from friends is the same sort of burden.

Lao Zhang said, I wouldn't have a hang-up if you hadn't brought this up. But since you did, I can't help turning it over in my mind. Come to think of it, we've exchanged so much talk over the years we can't even keep count. Now you tell me you've kept things from me. What a loss of face it will be if this gets out! People will say: Lao Zhang and Lao Li are friends who don't share their true thoughts and feelings.

Lao Li said, Is what I said really that big a deal?

Lao Zhang said, This isn't the sort of thing a friend would say. Let's just say I created a dilemma, trying to make you say what you don't want to say. Let's drop it there. Let's make it clear, here and now: Are we friends or aren't we?

Lao Li said, Yes, we're friends. We're friends who have a lot to talk about.

Lao Zhang said, Since we're friends who have a lot to talk about, please show some respect for my feelings, and tell me what you think of me.

Lao Li said, I've hated you all these years. But this has nothing to do with you. It's something I have to deal with. Goethe said—we talked about Goethe, didn't we?—Goethe said, suppose I love you, what does that have to do with you?

1998

Confession of a Photographer | *Ku Ling*

Translated by Lin Li-chun

I'm a professional photographer.

By professional, I'm not talking about the quality of my work but about the way I make a living. As to why I can call myself a photographer, not a shutterbug, that's because my photographic style is unique, unrivaled by those taking wedding photos or young women's studio portraits. It's no exaggeration to say I'm in a class by myself.

I only take pictures of women, which is not that different from most photographers who do portraits; but they usually do it for the "look." People line up to sign on whenever some organization invites models to pose outdoors. If it's nudes, then the place will be jam-packed, although more use their eyes than their lenses. Some don't even load the film, just use the crowd as a cover and drool like idiots.

In contrast, I take pictures of women of all ages, no matter how they look. I don't need to adjust the lighting in a studio or find the right pose out in the mountains or by the rivers. Mostly I hang around street corners or alleyways; sometimes I snatch my shots in places off the beaten path. But you're totally wrong if you think I'm a social-realist photographer. In my line of work, I never have to worry about light, speed, or lenses. All I have is an automatic camera with a flash, with which I rush up to snap a picture of my target and *click*! my work is done. And, I'm embarrassed to say, I've never failed, not once.

What do I do with the photos? Of course I can't sell them to collectors; I'm not famous like Guo Yingsheng or Li Xiaojing. I don't send them in for contests either. In fact, my photographs aren't for people to see. It's not that I cherish them so much that I think I'm the only one who can appreciate them; it's just that their value lies precisely in the certainty that no one sees them.

How do I make a living if I don't show my photographs? That's easy. My target, caught off guard and under the blinding flash, will usually be dazed momentarily, followed by a panicky, suspicious, and fearful look, mixed with a tinge of anger. At that time, all I have to do is put my camera away, walk up to her and say, in a cryptic voice, "I know all about the two of you." And that's that!

You're right; the locations of my shoots are outside hotel entrances. The man usually comes out first; he'll look around and then walk off pretending nothing has happened. The woman follows in a few minutes; she'll act calm but can't hide her fear and worry. She loses it completely when my camera clicks after she's barely taken two steps out the door. I don't say much, for the more you say the more trouble you get yourself into; besides, I'm not the eloquent type. In any case, she has just barely recovered from the scare, so she simply opens her purse and gives me all her cash. Some try to give me necklaces, rings, and watches if they think they aren't carrying enough cash. A few of them have even offered me their credit cards. But to avoid complications, I only take cash. Most of them thank me over and over before hurrying away, and that is how I, like a breeze, accomplish my "task."

How much do I get? I can definitely get several thousand each time, but it's not unheard of to get 50 or 100,000 if I happen to snap nicely dressed and well-groomed women. The most I've ever gotten is 380,000. Cash, of course! I don't take checks. Once there was this rich lady who didn't have any cash on her, so she begged and pleaded for me to go with her to get money out of an ATM. That was the riskiest incident I've ever been involved in. Usually it's nice and easy. Women are more afraid of people knowing about them than men, and they don't get violent either. Actually most of them don't even ask for the negatives. You want to know something really funny? I've never met one who refused to pay up. In other words, they are either sleeping with other people's husbands or are married themselves, or both. Ai! How morally bankrupt our society has gotten lately. . . .

What? Did you say it's against the law for me to blackmail them? You're joking. There's no film in my camera. I don't know who these people are or what they've done. They're the ones who offer me the money, so what can I do? You can't call *that* a crime!

1997

Good short-shorts, like love, come by chance, not by seeking. Once you are in possession of keen observation, understanding, and the virtue of diligence, the most ordinary phenomenon—a meteor flashing across the summer sky, a tender sprout bursting from the spring earth, the loud cry of a newborn baby at dawn, or the silent smile of an elder at dusk—will disclose to you their very special worth.

Guo Xin

XI. Nourishment | *Howard Goldblatt*

Mmm, this is good.
Thank you.
What's the mystery meat?
Guess.
Ouch! Bit myself.
Here, let me see.
Is it bleeding?
Yes.
Mmm, interesting.
Why are you smiling? What are you doing? Stop that!

Good Wine | *Chen Hui*

Translated by Julie Chiu

Mellow Chiu remembered her first drink of wine.

She could no longer remember her first day at school, the first time she lost her way, her first bout of insomnia, or the first death she encountered . . . but she remembered her first drink of wine. It was a toast in honor of her elderly grandma. She raised her cup and parroted the adults: "To health and longevity," she said, and emptied the cup. She felt as if she had a long string of firecrackers crackling its way down her throat, red and fiery and loud. When she regained her composure, she saw that all the adults were beaming. It was just a homey meal they were having, but now it glowed with an aura of happiness. It was Mellow Chiu's first experience with being lavished with love. And she loved drinking from then on.

Mellow Chiu studied the pottery wine set carefully—the cups were smallish like those they used to drink from at home. When the Chius hosted a banquet, they would each have a wine cup set in front of them. Always a small cup, one swallow per cup, so everyone could play the hero by emptying the cup in one swig. The Chius never drank alone. In the family, no drinking was done without a toast—in honor of an older member, in honor of Heaven, in honor of Fate—To health and longevity! To harmony and prosperity! To peace and good fortune! To good luck in everything! And so on and so forth, simply humankind's most truthful longings and humblest wishes. Mellow Chiu also believed that out of each toast flew a never- ending stream of love. To drink a toast one would need, of course, to raise the cup first. Then one would drink another cup as the person honored drank his or her cup. After that, one would accept a toast in return. Day after day, the Chius drank a great deal; they could really drink, and the drinking was always done with joy and festivity.

Watching Mellow Chiu's eyes go blank as she stared at the wine cups, Smooth Chiu said, Let's just buy the set and take it home. . . . Mellow Chiu was shocked that Smooth Chiu had become so generous. Is this the calmness one shows when one has decided to risk everything? Now Mellow Chiu really panicked.

When Mellow followed Smooth back to the small hotel, she discovered that he had checked in using a fake name. The room was a mess, the bathtub still stained with his vomit from last night. Smooth tidied up the room a bit and told Mellow to take the bed while he would sleep on the floor. Mellow kept her eyes open, not daring to sleep. Smooth heaved a sigh: Didn't I promise not to alarm you? You just have a good sleep now. . . . Mellow asked him: Do you promise not to do anything that will sadden us? Smooth turned his face away.

. . . Before Mellow set off for the trip, her mother had handed her a cup of wine, and said hesitantly: To a safe trip. . . . The mouthful of wine stuck in Mellow's throat. For a long while she couldn't swallow it, and she knew she couldn't promise her mother she'd definitely bring Big Brother home. Right after the plane touched ground, Mellow hopped into a taxi and told the driver to make the rounds of bars and pubs in the city. To her surprise, she tracked him down in a few hours.

Mellow finally fell asleep. In the haze of her dream, she found Smooth drunk again at the door at home, not daring to go in. He was way too drunk, and vomited into the incense stand at the front door—was it a dream or a sliver of memory? Again Mellow heard a wine bottle break, and, as she turned around, she saw Smooth's hand dripping with blood, her mother screaming: My son, you mustn't drink bitter wine . . .

Smooth had not drawn the curtains the previous night, and the winter sun was glaring. Mellow woke up, dazed and sweaty, as the sun quietly cast shifting shadows in the room. Smooth was gone. Mellow was terrified, knowing there was no road ahead for Smooth.

Mellow dried her tears and scanned the room for Smooth's belongings. He'd left nothing behind. If he never returned, no one would know that a man called Smooth Chiu had once stayed in this room—it was as if he'd never existed—and even the large debt he owed could be wiped out just like that. . . . Suddenly the phone rang. Smooth told Mellow to come down to the restaurant to pay his bill.

Mellow strolled into the little restaurant in the hotel and found Smooth seated in a corner. There was half a plate of peanuts on the table, and the rice gruel had all been eaten. A bottle of cheap liquor— *erguotou*—was newly opened, but there was no telling how many more had been emptied before it. Smooth was drinking alone. Mellow wanted to ask, Brother, when did you start drinking bitter wine? But she didn't know how to begin. She remembered a girl called Sue. She was told that Sue had hurt Smooth to the quick. Smooth gradually became a child and sought the company of a group wherever he went. They kept him company as he drank. Maybe they were all like that. Whenever they felt troubled, they drank. Except they didn't drink toasts. Without a word, they poured the liquor down their throats. Mellow remembered that her father had once said, you must never drink without saying anything; if you do, the drink will rot your guts and you'll end up spoiling the liquor and ruining yourself. . . . Smooth hadn't taken it to heart. The more he drank, the sadder he became, fretting over the thought of how joyful it had once been when they drank. . . .

Then it was past lunchtime. Mellow quietly ate some noodles while Smooth kept drinking his cheap liquor, one bottle after another. *Erguotou*, cheap, brutal stuff. Didn't even need to be drunk with food. Best for drinking alone. An outcast's liquor. Every swig that Smooth took seemed like the last one. Mellow couldn't bear to look, her heart aching to think of him leaving.

The waiter came and asked Mellow if she wanted to order supper. They had beef and chicken. Mellow ordered a plate of stewed beef for Smooth to eat with his liquor. Smooth remained quiet. Mellow could only silently keep him company. Without thinking, she lifted her head and saw outside the window a big, round, silvery moon, coldly staring at the two of them. Mellow was sad and perplexed. The moon truly looks as if it has nothing to do with all this. It simply waxes and wanes through the long years. How much good liquor has been turned into poetry in its light? . . .

Mellow picked up the bottle and poured herself a cup, then lifted it and said to Smooth, Sister Mellow drinks a toast to Brother Smooth—to the fullness of moon and life. At this she tossed back her head and emptied the cup. This caught Smooth by surprise. Mellow filled his cup. Smooth raised his cup with difficulty and stared at Mellow, dumbstruck. Mellow poured another cupful for herself. To Mother's good health and happy heart. Mellow emptied her cup again. She drank a toast to everyone in the family, emptying one cup after another. Smooth's hand shook holding his cup; his eyes slowly welled up with tears. His voice trembling, Smooth said, To Mom's good health and happy heart . . . and then broke into loud sobs.

The next day Smooth and Mellow went to the airport, and in the little pub they ordered beer. Mellow raised her glass at Smooth: To a speedy clearance of the debts. Mellow and Smooth each emptied their glasses and boarded the plane for home.

2003

Chimney Smoke | *Ah Cheng*

Translated by Howard Goldblatt

I

Lao Zhang had himself a daughter. That's good, Lao Zhang said, so long as she doesn't look like me when she grows up. She'd never get married if she did. So he named his daughter Beauty, Beauty Zhang.

Lao Zhang's college classmates said, There's nothing wrong with naming her Beauty, except it's a little common. Lao Zhang, with an education like yours, couldn't you have come up with a more elegant name?

What's wrong with being common? Lao Zhang asked them. It can't hurt. In times like this what's most important? Durability.

Lao Zhang's classmates said, Durability? Then call her Iron Ore, or call her Aqueous Rock. Yes, why not Aqueous Rock? That's what people in our field study, durability. Lao Zhang had studied geology in college.

II

Lao Zhang doted on his daughter. Lao Zhang was a smoker. Lao Zhang's wife said, If you want a child, then stop smoking. I read somewhere that smoke has harmful effects on a baby's genes. Lao Zhang took the cigarette he was smoking out of his mouth, threw it on the floor, and ground it out with his foot. He quit smoking. After Beauty was born, Lao Zhang went out and bought a pack of cigarettes. Lao Zhang's wife said to him, Do you want Beauty to grow up with black lungs? Lao Zhang was crestfallen. Lao Zhang's wife said, Smoke if you want to, but not around Beauty.

Beauty was born in the fall. When spring came, Lao Zhang's wife carried Beauty outside for some sun. A wind came up, and Lao Zhang said, Can't you tell it's windy, why don't you go inside? Lao Zhang's wife said, If Beauty doesn't get some sun, she won't be able to absorb the calcium she needs. Lao Zhang said, Then take her inside and sit by the window to get some sun. Lao Zhang's wife said, Windows keep out the ultraviolet rays. Ultraviolet rays make it possible for people to absorb calcium. Sunbathing through a window is a waste of time. Then wait till the wind dies down, Lao Zhang said.

Lao Zhang was watching his wife nurse Beauty. Lao Zhang's wife had read quite a bit, too. When she noticed Lao Zhang staring at her, she said, Haven't you seen enough? It's not the first time you've seen them. Who's looking at you? Lao Zhang said. I'm afraid there isn't enough there for Beauty. They both laughed. Beauty stopped and took a breath. She laughed, too.

III

Fall arrived, and Beauty had grown a bit. She could point to things. She pointed to Mama, she pointed to Papa, she tugged her ear, she tugged Mama's hair, she tugged Papa's nose.

One day Lao Zhang's wife was holding Beauty while Lao Zhang stood beside them screwing up his face and playing with Beauty, who shrieked with laughter and waved her hands in delight. Lao Zhang's wife held Beauty up next to Lao Zhang's face. Beauty stuck her hand into Lao Zhang's mouth.

It takes longer to tell than it did to happen. Lao Zhang raised his hand and sent mother and daughter reeling with a resounding slap. Lao Zhang was in the geology brigade and was always pounding rocks with a pick and hammer. His hands were powerful. The slap caught Lao Zhang's wife by surprise, and she fell backward. Her maternal instincts took over, and as she hit the floor, she twisted herself enough to cushion Beauty in her bosom.

Beauty was screaming. Blood trickled from the back of her mother's head. She'd never cursed anyone before, but she was cursing now. Lao Zhang's wife was cursing Lao Zhang.

Lao Zhang was dumbstruck. He was shaking from head to toe, he couldn't breathe, sweat streamed down his neck and down under his collar.

Lao Zhang was taken to the hospital. He didn't utter a word for two days and a night.

IV

The famine came in 1960. People starved all over the country, except in Yunnan. I'd graduated that year and was on a field trip. I went into the mountains to do some prospecting.

I was lost in no time. I had a compass, but it did me no good. I'm hungry, I'm hungry! Panic, I began to panic, and the situation turned desperate. My mind was still clear at first, and I knew I was finished. Without enough to eat, I couldn't keep up my strength, and when the sugar in my kidneys was depleted, that would be it. I began to sweat, then even that stopped. I wouldn't allow myself to think about anything, since the loss of body heat was increased by brain activity. I lay down. The acid content of my stomach was so overpowering my teeth seemed to turn soft.

Then heat began to rise from my stomach, and the soles of my feet, my neck, the tips of my fingers, were getting overheated. Didn't Hans Christian Andersen write a tale about a little girl who sold kindling? That old Dane really knew what he was writing about. People begin to overheat when they're starving. When the heat dissipates, death takes over.

I didn't die. If I had, how could I have married you? How could I have had Beauty?

When I came to, I still couldn't see clearly for a while. Then off in the distance I saw chimney smoke. My only thought was: chimney smoke means cooking. Go, even if you have to crawl.

Let's not talk about how I got there, but I managed. It was a house. Save me, I pleaded in the doorway. Give me something to eat. No one heard me.

I know, my voice was too soft. I went inside.

A man was standing up against the stove. So skinny his teeth were protruding, a frightening glare in his eyes. Give me something to eat, I said. After a long pause he shook his head. Even if you're my granddad, my ancestor, you have to give me something to eat. He shook his head again. Are you saying you don't have anything? Then what's that you're cooking on the stove? A few sips of hot water will do. Tears streamed down his cheeks. Screw your old grannie in the ear. . . .

I was past caring. I lifted the lid off the pot. Steam filled the air. I saw what was cooking in the pot, it was a child's hand.

1989

O Café | *Ku Ling*

Translated by Julie Chiu

Have a seat, sir. Want a smoke? No? Mind if I do? Thanks.

Is this your first time here? Alone? So you've come with a friend then. Where is he? Downstairs—ah, certainly. Yes, that's the basement. What's the difference? Of course it's different. You get girls to keep you company downstairs. Me? I'm not keeping you company. I'm just asking if you want company. Not necessarily me. See the girl seated there on the other side? The one in a suit, with long hair, reading a book? Very innocent, isn't she? Looks exactly like a student. She can be your company, too.

You don't believe me? Why would I lie to you? Check the decor here. Does it look like a place for coffee? You don't want any female company? Don't tell me you've come for the coffee. Besides, we don't sell coffee at all. Look, here comes your tea. Sorry, but that will be fifty Taiwan dollars for this watery drink. But, hey, no one's here for it anyway. See those gentlemen coming in through the door? They're regulars. Come almost every day. Those girls in the front row? Yes, they all are. Pick one, and you can go downstairs and "have a ball."

Have you spotted someone you like? Don't sweat it. See, the one who's just come up—look at that figure. Take her downstairs and you can do whatever you'd like with her. Doesn't cost much—only 500 dollars an hour. These days, what good is 500 dollars? But to have such a pretty, graceful, innocent girl at your disposal. Nowhere else in Taipei can you get such a bargain. Or why do you think we do such a good business? Look, our three or four dozen girls will all be selected soon. If you don't hurry, you'll be left with no one and wind up with a case of blue balls.

You just want to talk? With me? What makes you think I've got time for that? You'll pay me? Sure. Pay me well, and we can talk. Pardon me, but I do love money. Tell you what, I don't really like sitting downstairs all day. Yes, the return's great. I get seven or eight rounds a day—that's for sure. The shop takes a 50 percent commission. Sometimes I do a "walk-out"—you understand what I mean? Oh, that's to go out with the client to . . . you know what. I make a sure fifty, sixty thousand a month. That's more than you make every month, I'll bet. But our money's hard-earned. You can't really compare the two of us, can you?

Why am I here? Oh, what should I say? After I graduated from a vocational high school I couldn't find a job. Worked as a little book-keeper a while and made six or seven thousand a month. But a decent dress would cost half my salary. It wasn't a job fit for a human being! Then I saw an ad in the newspaper for a waitress, and came to this "0 Café"—yes, "0" for zero. No idea why they call it that. Maybe it means no coffee. The boss told me that all the waitress jobs had been filled, but they did have an opening for a job with better pay. Which was to chat with the customers. Chatting seemed okay, I thought, so I went downstairs with an old guy. He turned out to be an old letch, running his hands all over me and scratching my breasts. I ran upstairs and told the boss. He said, yes, the old guy was no good. And all smiley he told me not to let it bother me. I said I quit, and he said, No problem, but think it over, maybe you'll want to come back.

I stayed home for two days, and my family wouldn't stop throwing sarcastic remarks at me. Said I just sat around feeding off them. Said what worthless creatures daughters are. It made me so mad I came back. The boss taught me how to protect myself and handle the custom-ers. After a while I got used to it.

Does my family know? Of course they don't! They'd beat me to death if they did! I told them I'm working in a Western restaurant. They're all right with me so long as I keep bringing money home. Now who'd dare shout at me? It's cool to have money in my pocket. I can buy all the clothes and jewelry I want. I'm saving up to have my . . . breasts enlarged. Shh! You don't know what advantage they have, the ones with big breasts. Like the one you just saw. She may not be good-looking, but she makes more than any of us.

Hey, you aren't listening! What're you looking at? What do those kids come in for? You call them kids? Don't be misled by their youth and immature bodies. Some of them have been in for a year or two already. How old? Who knows? Look like they've just graduated from primary school! Yes, they do. Some people just love those girls, what they call the "baby-teethed." They even walk the girls out. Who knows if they can do it. As long as there's money to make, who cares if they're kids or not? I have no idea if they have parents or if they're still in school. Nobody's keeping tabs on them, that's for sure. See how they laugh and joke with one another. They look happy, don't they? What? You call it ruining the seedlings of the race? Come on, don't make it sound so bad! Didn't you come in to ruin me, too? Ha ha . . .

You're angry with me? Hey, don't go. If you can't bear it, don't look. Let's go downstairs. No? All right, all right. You've paid the 500 dollars anyway. I'll go serve someone else then, uh? Bye-bye. Do come again—we're "0 Café."

1994

The inverse relationship between the length of a short-short and its capacity calls to mind the image of a well—a very small opening that leads to immeasurable depth.

Jin Renshun

The Bus Stop and Haws-sicles | *Zhou Rui*

Translated by Howard Goldblatt

DAY ONE

Morning. A roadside bus stop sign. A peddler of haws-sicles stands a dozen or so steps away from the sign.

A bus pulls up. The driver spots the haws-sicles and stops before he reaches the sign. He leans out, buys some haws-sicles, and roars off.

Commuters waiting by the sign are bowled over by what they've just seen.

DAY TWO

Morning. Bus stop. Haws-sicles.

A bus pulls up and, like the day before, stops next to the haws-sicle peddler. He buys some.

Some of the sharper-witted commuters, prepared for anything, run up to the bus. Several manage to board.

DAY THREE

Morning. Same place.

A line has formed behind the straw pole from which the haws-sicles hang. All the commuters are waiting there. The useless sign has been taken down.

The bus stops in front of the pole. The commuters happily board the bus.

DAY FOUR

Morning. Same place.

The haws-sicle peddler hasn't shown up.

The commuters don't know where to wait for the bus, since the sign is gone.

The bus pulls up. The driver slows down and leans out, looking for the . . .

And so, bewildered, the bus creeps along; and so, bewildered, the commuters jog along behind the bus. . . .

1987

The publication of a short-short is not the end of the creative process. The writer can continue thinking, so can the reader, together with the writer. Only through doing this will a reader find pleasure in both reading and thinking.

Wang Zengqi

Granny Drunkard | *Feng Jicai*

Translated by Julie Chiu

Drinking places, like many other things, can be ranked. Be it on a scale of 3, 6, or 9, the drinking house on Shou Shan Street belonged at the bottom. Outside, no flag was flown, no sign was hoisted. Inside, not a single chair was offered. You'd never find food at the counter. There was always just a vat of liquor. Those who came for the drink were rickshaw men, coolies, and the like—all laborers from the lowest class. Some came in with a piece of braised sausage in hand; others brought their own spiced peanuts in a pocket. They paid for two or three ounces of liquor, carried it over to the windowsill or to a corner of the wall, and drank alone. When the place got really crowded, some drinkers would take their bowls outside to stand under the tree. As the liquor entered the mouth in small sips—ah, how each taste bud wakes up and rejoices. What gratification!

The drinking house sold only one kind of liquor. Made from dried sweet potatoes, it was cheap stuff with a strong taste. On Shou Shan Street, no one had ever missed a cat, for however lost the cat might be, it could sniff its way back. The liquor had no aftertaste to speak of. It merely packed a wallop. Once inside the mouth it burned like acid and had to be swallowed fast, or it would set the tongue and teeth and throat aflame. When it hit the stomach, a force would gather immediately and—pow!—it would spurt up to the brain, knocking it off-kilter. It was a potent force. Think of the firecrackers they set off on New Year's Eve, the kind they call "Lampgun." When the firecrackers explode, they send red lamps shooting into the sky. Well, the liquor *was* called Lampgun. Good liquor is supposed to be thick and warm, its effect slow and steady. It never goes to the head. But for the poor devils who've made it through another hard day, their hearts filled with bitterness, their bones and muscles consumed by a soreness and fatigue—why bother if not for this inexpensive high, when the head swells and spins and the heart breaks free of all restraints?

In terms of being unrestrained, no one could outdo Granny Drunkard. Every afternoon this old woman would come to the small drinking house in her ragged, beggarly clothes. She had a dark complexion and her hair was a mess. No one could describe her face or tell you her name. But everyone knew she was the number-one drunkard of the drinking house, respectfully referred to as "Granny Drunkard." Every time she came through the door, she would pull out from her bosom a square cloth packet. She would remove the cloth wrapping and reveal another packet, wrapped in a page of that day's newspaper or a dated one. Under the newspaper would be a layer of oil paper, and you would think there would be an emerald brooch inside. But, in fact, under this final layer was nothing but twenty cents! Granny Drunkard would push the twenty cents across the counter, and, as usual, the shopkeeper would hand her half a bowl of Lampgun. She would put it up to her lips and, with a tilt of her chin and a tipping of the bowl, empty it into her stomach, as if it were a liquor barrel. By the time Granny made it out the door, her legs would be like two ink brushes, painting invisible calligraphy on the ground.

Her body reeling this way and that, she would head north. After a hundred steps or so, she'd make it to a busy intersection where accidents were all too common. But don't you worry for Granny. Dead drunk as she might have seemed, once she made it to this intersection, she would sober up in an instant. Then she'd safely cross the road, not showing any sign of drunkenness. She did this every day and never got into trouble. Folks on Shou Shan Street enjoyed watching the old doll's reeling drunken walk. Swaying above and shaking below, her body reeling left and right, she spun and turned with a joyous grace like a lotus leaf in the wind. On rainy days, when she was soaked to the skin, she was like a big umbrella that was slowly turning round and round. . . . But what was it about this intersection that knocked Granny Drunkard into sobriety every time she made it there? Was that all the strength Lampgun could boast? Or was Granny Drunkard such a super being she could switch between being drunk and being sober at will?

The secret of any drink lies in the barrel. The shopkeeper, a wicked fellow, cut the liquor with water. Those drinkers might not see the world they lived in very well, but they were crystal clear about the liquid they put into their stomachs. Still, no one was willing to bring the fact to light. Drink your drink, enjoy the buzz, and that's it. The shopkeeper did, however, pay for his lack of business ethics. He was almost sixty and still childless. Most likely he would die without progeny. But one day he discovered his wife craving sour and spicy food—she was pregnant! When the shopkeeper bowed and prayed to the Buddha, his conscience was awakened. He swore he'd be a decent man from then on. He would do his business honestly and would never put water in his liquor again.

On that very day, Granny Drunkard came to the drinking house again. As always, she took out her packet, undid the wrappings, bought her liquor, raised her hand and lifted her chin, and all the "rehabilitated" Lampgun was poured into her stomach. . . . Now real liquor had a real effect. This time Granny Drunkard started spinning before she made it out the door. And all along the way her reeling was most beautifully done, the upper part of her body swaying to the left, the lower part swaying to the right. Faster and faster her body turned. At first you might have taken her for a roc in the wind. Then finally you saw only a big black whirlpool! The onlookers on Shou Shan Street were stunned. But they were also worried. Before they could do anything about it, Granny Drunkard had come to the intersection. She didn't sober up, and for the first time ever, she spun and stepped onto the busy road. As for the tragic scene that followed—well, let's not talk about it. . . .

After that, Granny Drunkard disappeared from the street. Now and then, the drinkers in the drinking house would talk about her, missing her as a true alcoholic with character. She never took her drink with food and always finished it in one swallow. She didn't drink to satisfy the craving of her tongue. It was all for the buzz. She minded her business and wasted no breath on conversation. Once she finished her drink, she got going, and she never ran a tab. A genuine drinker she was, content with herself and with leaving people alone.

As the shopkeeper listened to the talk, a thought came to him. The day Granny Drunkard got into trouble—wasn't that the day he decided never again to cut the liquor with water? And so it was he who had caused the tragedy. This made him uneasy: What twisted logic it is that governs matters in the world! Was it wrong to cheat? Or was it wrong to be honest? Why was it that over the decades, when he cheated people with fake liquor, he had gotten by just fine, with everyone enjoying the drink, but once he started getting serious, he messed it all up?

2000

Tea Scum | *Ling Dingnian*

Translated by Julie Chiu

A tea drinker the better part of his life, Gramp Shi had developed an odd theory of his own: The essence of tea is to be found in its scum!

His *zisha* teapot, a classic from Yixing made of sandstone clay, was never washed. Yet the dark-purple teapot had an oily, glossy shine, having been rubbed and loved in his hands for years. When the lid was removed, one saw that the inside had turned a reddish brown. In fact, it looked a size smaller than it should, what with a fat layer of tea scum built up over the years.

Unbecoming, even filthy, in appearance, the teapot was Gramp Shi's favorite. No one was allowed to touch it, let alone drink from it.

The story had it that the teapot was passed down from an ancestor of the Shi family, one who had been handpicked by the emperor himself as the Number One Scholar. Another saying held that the teapot was extraordinary for two reasons. First, even in high summer, tea that was brewed in the teapot tasted the same the whole day, and even after a few days would not go stale. Second (and this was unique, too), with the solid layer of tea scum, even if you ran out of tea leaves in the house, you needn't have worried. Pour hot water into the pot, and you got a pot of tea all the same—it looked like tea, and it tasted like tea.

Gramp Shi once said, proudly, "See this thick layer of tea scum? It takes over a hundred years of accumulation to get a layer this rich. You might obtain a teapot like this for a thousand taels. But the tea scum? That you can't get, even at ten times the amount. What you see here is a teapot among teapots, treasure of treasures. . . ."

Gramp Shi liked to sit straight in his old-style armchair carved from red sandalwood. Eyes half closed, he would take a small sip of his tea and allow the bitter liquid with its hint of sweetness to moisten his mouth and slowly slip down his throat. Leisurely, he tasted his tea, as if savoring the beauty of the finest flavors passed down by his ancestors, transported into a world where mind and matter were one.

Last summer Gramp Shi's son, who was working in Shanghai, came to see him in Old Temple Town. His son's daughter, Qingqing, who was on summer vacation, came along.

Qingqing, a lovely girl with an artless charm, was in second grade. Overjoyed to see this angel of a granddaughter, Gramp Shi was ready to make an exception for her. He offered her a sip from his *zisha* teapot. But the filthy look of the teapot disgusted Qingqing, who pushed the teapot away and said, "Grandpa, you have no sense of hygiene at all! I'm not going to drink it."

"Well, I am." Gramp Shi helped himself to the tea, savoring every drop.

The next morning he got up early and, as usual, fetched his teapot to make his first cup of tea. But when he looked at the teapot, his eyes glazed over, his cheek-muscles twitched, and his jaw hung down in shock. The teapot had been washed inside and out, and the hundred-year tea scum was no more.

He stood there frozen for a long while. Then, in a heartrending voice, he let out a frightful scream: "Give me back my tea scum! Give me back . . ."

With that scream, blood raced to his head, and phlegm clotted in his throat. Gramp Shi fainted.

Qingqing was terrified. Feeling wronged, she could not stop crying.

After much to-do, Qingqing's father brewed a fresh pot of tea in the *zisha* teapot and gingerly brought it to Gramp Shi.

As if coming out of a trance, still catching his breath, Gramp Shi spotted the teapot. He clutched it like a drowning man, pressing it hard against his chest. After a long moment, tears filling his eyes, he took a sip from the teapot, and spit it out immediately, sputtering in every direction. The light in his eyes went out. His hand dropped and his face turned an ashen gray. Weakly he muttered, "It's not right! Isn't . . . the . . . right . . . taste . . . at . . . all . . ."

1988

XII. Weirdness | *Howard Goldblatt*

The guy sat there trying to make up a story, believe it or not. He was so used to working on other people's stuff, he felt like a word thief whenever he wrote a sentence, even a few words. He knew how to lie, no problem there, but lies aren't really stories, are they?

Since he couldn't figure out what to write about, he just started pounding away on the laptop keyboard, figuring that if his brain wasn't much help, he'd give his fingers a go at it. What's that bit about a bunch of monkeys with typewriters . . .

He stopped to look at what he'd written so far: nothing but some nonsense about how hard it is to make up a story. "Can't stop here, I'd look like an idiot! Now get off the stick and show what you can do!"

He tried a bit of dialogue—monologue, actually—but that didn't help. Maybe if he intoned the name of the Poetry Muse—"Erato, Erato, Erato!" His wife yelled back: "Who's that I hear, Lord Byron?" Okay, that's dialogue, but it still isn't a story—sarcasm, maybe, but no story. "Ah, to hell with it," he growled. "I've got better things to do with my time."

XII. Weakness

Disputatiasis | *Wang Meng*

Translated by Howard Goldblatt

A physician I know told me of an encounter he had at his clinic with a sufferer of disputatiasis.

"Please be seated," he had said to the patient.

"Why should I be seated?" the patient snapped back. "You're not trying to deprive me of my right to *not* be seated, are you?"

There was nothing the physician could do but pour a glass of water and say, "Hey, have some water."

"Now that's the sort of crap you hear from people who only see one side of an issue. Not all water is drinkable. If, for example, you had mixed cyanide in with this water, it sure wouldn't be drinkable."

"I didn't put any poison into this water," the physician replied. "Not to worry."

"Who said you put any poison in it?" the patient demanded. "Are you hinting that you're about to be formally charged by the Public Prosecutor's office for trying to poison me? I never said you were trying to poison me. You're the one who said that I said you're trying to poison me. That sort of poisonous slander is *worse* than trying to poison me."

The physician, sensing that defending himself would be useless, heaved a sigh and changed the subject: "Nice weather we're having, eh?"

"What a stupid thing to say!" the patient snarled. "Just because we're having nice weather here doesn't mean that they're having nice weather everywhere else in the world, you know. Take the North Pole, for instance. They're having rotten weather there at this very moment, what with strong winds, nights that are twenty-four hours long, icebergs crashing into each other . . ."

His patience exhausted, the physician cut him off abruptly: "This is *not* the North Pole!"

"That doesn't give you the right to deny the existence of the North Pole." The patient shot back. "If you do that, you're guilty of distorting the facts and covering up the truth to serve your own purposes."

"You'd better leave," the physician said.

"Where do you get off ordering me to leave?" the patient demanded. "This is a medical clinic, not a public security office. You don't have the authority to detain me, and you can't execute me."

. . . Following a thorough investigation, it was determined that the patient had participated in the collective writing clinic organized at Beijing universities during the Cultural Revolution, and was thought to be showing residual effects of his training.

1982

Concise yet substantial, intricate yet intelligible, refined yet unassuming, a short-short is short but good and good but short. Although tiny as the flower of Chinese chives, short-shorts blossom in the same fashion as the beautiful peony.

Yan Gang

The Features-Column Editor's Daydream | *Liu Yichang*

Translated by Julie Chiu

The real world goes like this:
Those on the eastern hemisphere stand this way.
Those on the western hemisphere stand this way.

Lift the dream curtain, stretch out the hands to hold the moon. Moonlight streams through the fingers. So beautiful. Frame it with fanciful borders and assign it this title: "The Wish of Li Po."

You smile, eyes narrowed into a line. You are standing on reality's side.

You and I are separated by a transparent curtain in the door, like on a stage. The General out, on one side, the Chief Minister in on the other. Outside is dreamland, inside is the real world. We are forever walking between reality and dream.

Now I've just entered the realm of dreams. In front of my desk is a row of windows, cleaned once years ago. Beyond the grayish dust the scenery outside is a bit obscure. A lot of boats are sailing on Victoria Harbor, some big, some small.

You're still smiling, eyes narrowed into slits.

—I hate this deadly monotonous editor's office, say I. I want to roam the calendar-less dreamland and find something fantastic and new.

In my dream I walk with long strides. The page of six-point type is like a window of misty rain. Four-point calligraphy makes one think of

Margot Fonteyn's tiny waist. A vertical line on the right, another one on the left. They stand like guardsmen Zhang Lung and Zhao Hu, and sandwiched between them is Magistrate Bao with fiery eyes. More and more, I move farther away from you.

You're still yelling:

—Come back.

I pretend I do not hear it.

Down the street paved with green cobblestones, I walk by the door of Elder Brother Wu. I lift my head and look. Through the low-hanging curtain, I don't see pretty, sexy Golden Lotus and I am surprised. Then I notice Brother Huan walking toward me on tiptoes. He says in a whisper:

—Ximen Qing and Golden Lotus are in Granny Wang's room, and the door is shut tight like an angry man's lips.

The rest I can only tell with ". . ." instead of "to be continued."

Below the fold D. H. Lawrence is roaring with laughter, but Lanling the Jester laughs even louder.

I can still hear your voice, though I have entered yet another realm. Joyce writes up his thoughts without punctuation. Saroyan's dialogues have no quotation marks. O'Neill piles up his ABCD into a heap and makes it a big forest, so he can fool the dark-skinned Emperor Jones into losing his way. . . .

Then suddenly I hear the sound of hurried footsteps.

I look around and see a group of writers marching in place in front of the camera.

Up ahead is the sea.

Woolf's waves cannot break winter's sundry old dream. Thomas Mann makes it across the sea on a sailboat. Nobody notices the sweat on his forehead as he steers the boat.

I can no longer hear your voice. I do not know if you are still calling my name from afar. The land of dreams has no boundaries, and nothing fits into a pattern. But to highlight Black Jade's feelings with a screamer is no different from draining fresh water into Victoria Harbor during times of water rationing. And to use little stars for decorating Li's big axe? Why, that is to put on a padded jacket in high summer.

In my dream, I begin to run.

Get a soundless trumpet and noodle hard and fast, and it'll be the subject of parody in "popular fiction." All devils love wearing colorful painted masks. No commodities can do without some fanciful packaging.

The mandarin ducks are still chasing each other in the water.

The paired butterflies are still dancing among the flowers.

Throw the words in the boiling pot and sprinkle in some salt—one handful, two handfuls—and you've got a cheap commodity to sell.

Even in a dream one gets tired from running. The realm of dreams is not the realm of divinities. When one's feet get tangled up in thorns, one sweats and sheds tears, too.

Why?

For this is a dream one dreams with eyes open.

A daydream is a dream, too, but quite unlike a dream dreamt with the eyes closed. It makes you laugh. It makes you cry. It makes you cry while laughing. It makes you laugh while crying.

The bell in the typesetting room goes off, and I come back from dreamland to reality. I walk over and look down on the square hole in the floor. I pull up the tattered basket and take out a big sheet of page proof for tomorrow's paper.

The big page proof is a milestone of the journey. Hidden in the dirty oily printout are innumerable satisfactions and moments of boredom.

I return to my seat with the big page proof, like an athlete who has just engaged in strenuous exercise, so exhausted I will not spare a look even at glamorous things.

I frown.

You smile.

—At the head of Repulse Bay a few lone flowers are swaying in the sea breeze, but still you've got to put caution over courage—do not be happy too soon, say you.

Lifting my head, I see the lights on Kowloon Peninsula glisten like sequins on black velvet.

The real world goes like this:

Those on the eastern hemisphere see the moon.

Those on the western hemisphere see the sun.

1987

The shortness of the "very short piece" must not be understood as "short" of content, "short" of depth, or "short" in life. It is not a word game that will last as long as a mayfly's life. The "very short piece" is a performance that is "short" and cool, "short" and frugal, "short" and sharp.

Zhang Chunrong

Death Dream | *Ku Ling*

Translated by Howard Goldblatt

A dark and silent night. Suddenly the dull, heavy thud of footsteps comes from down the long, long corridor, one after the other, trampling on my heart. My forehead is bathed in sweat, my fists are clenched so tightly that the fingernails dig deeply into my palms. The thick steel door creaks as it swings open, allowing a thread of dim light from the corridor to fall on the court verdict lying at my feet: "Penalty: Death." Only those two words, everything else is blurred. A powerful hand reaches out and grabs hold of my trembling shoulder.

I force myself to calm down and seek a rational explanation for how it came to this: To be sentenced to death I had to have been guilty of an unpardonable crime. Except that I have committed no crime; everyone knows that I am a blameless, upright youth. So if I have been found guilty, it is a miscarriage of justice; someday, somehow, justice will prevail, and the wrong will be righted. If this had all happened in a world where chaos reigned, then nothing more need be said; but in Hong Kong, a city of laws, this sort of thing cannot happen to an innocent person like me. Besides, I'm not ready to leave this world of beauty and warmth. That being the case, this sort of thing cannot be happening, which can only mean that it is not real.

I awake from my dream, drenched in sweat. The steel door is still securely locked, the corridor is silent except for the faint rumbling of a passing train way off in the distant night. The person next to me glowers at me briefly, then rolls over and goes back to sleep. I look around to discover that there are at least ten people here, maybe more, all sleeping on the wooden floor. The air is hot and dank; an ancient fan turns lethargically, sending lazy gusts of hot air and interminable low groans. The stench from the latrine in the corner is sickening. I'm surrounded by four gray, windowless walls; a gecko moves slowly across one of them, hissing its strange little laughing sounds. The tiny ventilator opening is momentarily illuminated by the beam from a powerful searchlight as it swings by.

Once again reason takes over. Clearly this is a prison, so what am I doing here? Since, as I concluded a moment ago, I am neither guilty of a crime nor a suspect in one, am, in fact, a good person who always speaks and acts with discretion, who never gets involved in disputes, and who is incapable of harming a fly, why then have I been put in this place? A mistake has been made somewhere. I rack my brains but to no avail, and so I must conclude that none of this is real.

Again I awake from my dream, shivering all over. I am struck by the realization that a moment before I was only dreaming that I had awakened from a dream, so no wonder I found myself locked up in prison even though I had managed to stay my execution. Terrible things like that could only happen to me in a dream. With the realization that I am capable of spotting the unreasonable nature of my own dreamscapes and of willing myself awake, I congratulate myself on my powers of reasoning, which have insured that I can continue to live a normal, quiet life. Looking around me, all I see is the stillness and darkness of night. From far off comes the faint crow of a rooster. It must be nearly dawn.

Suddenly the dull, heavy thud of footsteps comes from down the long, long corridor, then the thick steel door creaks as it swings open, allowing a thread of dim light from the corridor to fall on the court verdict lying at my feet: "Penalty: Death." Quickly I shut my eyes, hoping desperately to reenter my dream, as a powerful hand reaches out and grabs hold of my . . .

1985

Empty Seat | *Yuan Qiongqiong*

Translated by Howard Goldblatt

He heard somebody sobbing.

It was the woman sitting next to him.

At first he hadn't noticed. He'd simply spotted the empty seat when he boarded the bus and sat down. But once he was settled he heard a strange sound like an imperfection in a machine wheel. Click-click-click-click, rhythmic, constant. Hard to tell what it was, what with the bus noises and all, but after a while he identified it. The woman next to him was sobbing.

He turned just enough to sneak a look. She wasn't trying to cause a scene or anything, since she had buried her face in her hands to stifle the sound. But she couldn't hide the depth of her sorrow, no matter what she did. Her shoulders were heaving, and yet the way she was being bounced around by the bus made it look kind of silly.

What in the world could cause such unhappiness?

He faced forward and instinctively leaned away from the woman. He didn't want people to think he had anything to do with her. But he had to hold on to the seat in front to keep his balance, and even then he rocked a little.

He glanced at his fellow passengers. A college boy in the aisle nearby was staring at him but looked away when he realized he was being watched. Too obvious. No doubt what *he* was thinking.

He glared, wanting to catch his eye one more time to let him know he had absolutely nothing to do with the woman. But the college boy not only looked away nonchalantly, he even turned his back on him.

No one else paid him any attention.

She kept sobbing. Impossible to tell how long she'd been at it, but she'd begun long before he sat down. If anything it was worse now, and louder. The other passengers would have to be deaf not to hear it.

Some were already glancing his way.

The person in the seat in front turned to look, then quickly faced front again without showing any emotion.

He crinkled his brow to show how disgusted he was, yet even that didn't prove he had nothing to do with the woman. A couple of indecisive seconds later he slid over until he was more off the seat than on.

She was still sobbing. Nearly in convulsions by now. Why did she have to cry on a bus, of all places? He looked at her again. She was pouring her grief into her hands. You'd think she was the only person on the bus.

He returned one of the passenger's stares. The man shrank back. But he wasn't the only one. Strange how they were more interested in him than in her. He wasn't crying, why gawk at him?

Of course! He should have known there was something peculiar about an empty seat on a crowded bus. No wonder.

With a show of insouciance he got up and mingled with the passengers in the aisle, stopping in front of the college boy, who smiled, as if to say, I know what you mean. Of course! The college boy had vacated the seat before he got on.

The bus pulled up to a stop. He and the college boy watched one of the new passengers take the seat.

1988

Because of its length a short-short is easy to remember and easily spread among the people. Short-shorts, with their poetic appeal and richness, are the jueju* of short stories.

Zhang Xiaolin

Little, Little, Little, Little, Little . . . | *Wang Meng*

Translated by Howard Goldblatt

The local drama in "H" province has declined in recent years. Here's why:

About a hundred years ago a truly gifted performer appeared on the scene, an actress whose stage name was Fragrant-and-Red. She had mastered every aspect of her art—song, gesture, monologue, acrobatics—and was all the rage for quite a while. But the years took their toll on Fragrant-and-Red, who eventually was no longer able to perform. By then the people's choice had become Fragrant-and-Red's favorite disciple, Little Fragrant-and-Red. Not only was Little Fragrant-and-Red a carbon copy of her mentor where theatrical skills were concerned but she looked exactly like her, enjoyed the very same things, and displayed identical idiosyncrasies. Fragrant-and-Red had an oval face, and so did Little Fragrant-and-Red; Fragrant-and-Red smoked a water pipe, and so did Little Fragrant-and-Red; Fragrant-and-Red had a mole beneath her left eye, and so did Little Fragrant-and-Red; and so on and so forth. As the years overtook Little Fragrant-and-Red, domination of the stage passed to Little Little Fragrant-and-Red. Currently the mainstay of the "H" dramatic stage is Little Little Little Little Fragrant-and-Red.

Based on the principles of calculus, if this "Littling" process continues unimpeded, we will soon reach zero.

1982

---

*Jueju is a poem of four lines, each line containing five or seven characters, with a strict tonal pattern and rhyme scheme.

Strange Encounter | *Mo Yan*

Translated by Howard Goldblatt

In the fall of 1982 I returned to Northeast Gaomi from Baoding to visit my family. The train didn't arrive at the station until after nine that night, and there was only one bus a day to the township—at six in the morning. Seeing a half moon hanging in a clear sky, I decided not to spend the night in the city but instead take advantage of the bright moonlight and walk, partly to get home earlier and partly to breathe the fresh outdoor air.

I was traveling light—only a small bag—so after passing under the station bridge, instead of the asphalt road, which would take me out of my way, I headed home on an unpaved road that had fallen out of use years before, but was shorter, since it went directly to town. In recent years parts of the road had been dug up, so it was seldom used and was overgrown with weeds, except for a narrow footpath. The road was flanked by farmland where people grew sorghum, corn, sweet potatoes, and more. Moonlight on the stalks and leaves lent them a weak silvery glow. The leaves were perfectly still in the windless night, the chirping of crickets out in the fields loud and exceptionally clear, until it felt that the sound had penetrated my skin and bones. That lent an eerie silence to the night.

The fields grew increasingly dense as I walked, and I could no longer see the city lights. I needed to cover altogether a distance of more than forty li. Besides the crickets, I also heard an occasional bird or small animal call out from the fields. Suddenly I felt a chill on my neck, and my footsteps sounded louder and heavier than before. I began to regret walking home alone and at the same time sensed that many mysteries were hidden amid the crops around me, that countless eyes were observing me, even that something was following me; at that moment the moon blurred as it hid behind a cloud. Without meaning to, I picked up the pace. But the faster I walked, the greater the danger lurking behind me, or so it seemed. Finally, instinctively, I turned to look.

There was, of course, nothing there.

Just keep walking, I told myself, and as I walked I voiced my displeasure with myself: You're a materialist, and true materialists fear nothing. Are there ghosts? Are there evil spirits? No! Wild animals? No! It's the weak and the mediocre who create fear out of nothing . . . I remained teeth-chattering nervous all the same. As a child I'd been told plenty of ghost stories, and they had stuck in my mind: A man walking down the road hears the sound of a porter carrying a load up ahead. When he's close enough to get a good look, all he can see are two baskets and a pair of moving legs, no torso, nothing . . . A man encounters a smiling figure coming down the road. He looks close—it's a woman with a red mouth, and nothing else, a "faceless" ghost . . . A man walking down the road spots a bearded old man eating grass . . .

To my surprise, my clothes were drenched in a cold sweat.

I started singing—loudly: "Forward, forward, forward—kill—"

Needless to say, nothing at all happened. I reached my village at dawn, as the early morning sun turned the eastern sky red. Roosters crowed in the village, signaling peace and tranquility. I turned and looked back: there were fields and there was a road, and I had to laugh at myself for having harbored all those ridiculous fears.

At the village entrance I spotted an old man by a tree. It was our neighbor, Third Master Zhao. Dressed neatly, he was no more than five paces from me.

"Up early, I see, Third Master," I said.

"I got up to go into town, and since I knew you were coming home, I decided to wait."

We chatted about home for a few minutes, and I gave him a filtered cigarette.

He lit up. "I still owe your father five yuan, Number Three," he said. "My money's no good, so I'd like you to give him this cigarette holder to settle the debt."

"There's no need for that, Third Master," I said.

"You go on home now," he said. "Your parents are anxious to see you."

I took Third Master's cold, agate cigarette holder, said good-bye, and hurried into the village.

At home, my parents asked me about this and that, and chided me for walking home at night alone. What if something had happened? I just laughed and said, "I was hoping to meet up with a ghost, but the ghosts were afraid to meet up with me."

Mother said, "A youngster like you shouldn't say such things."

When my father lit a cigarette, I took the cigarette holder out of my pocket and said, "Dad, I ran into Third Master Zhao at the village entrance. He said he owes you five yuan and asked me to give you this to settle the debt."

"Who did you say?" Father was visibly shocked.

"Third Master Zhao."

"You must be mistaken," Father said.

"No way," I said. "We talked for a while, and I gave him a cigarette. And then there's this cigarette holder."

I held it out, but Father wouldn't take it.

"Third Master Zhao died a couple of mornings ago!" Mother said.

So I had run into a ghost, after all. At the time I hadn't realized it. They're not as scary as everyone says. He was quite genial, in fact, and wanted to settle a debt. Ghosts don't hurt people. People hurt people. They're much worse than ghosts any day!

1989

The short-short is a self-sufficient universe. Not flustered, not impoverished, it is blessed with all the necessary facilities. Humble by nature, it calls itself mini, it calls itself short-short.

Wang Meng

XIII. ? | *Howard Goldblatt*

I think," he said, "that a train whistle is about the loneliest, saddest sound in the world."

Someone drew the words "I like vanilla" in the balloon over the head of the girl with the glazed look in her cartoon character eyes.

Meanwhile, he was having increasing trouble reconciling the fact that Taipei 101 is the world's tallest building and yet cannot be seen from the moon (no one ever explained to him a little matter called verticality).

Over the loudspeaker, Beethoven's "Für Elise" continued to prove Napoleon's comment that music is the least annoying form of noise (managing a place slightly above fingernails on a blackboard, in the view of purists). On TV a guy with funny hair was yelling "You're tired!"

Understanding is seriously overrated, on which they (and pretty much everybody they knew) agreed. Feeling, if anything, is worse (read your early Kundera, he would say). So what's left? Intuition is unevenly distributed, enjoyment can go in too many directions, trusting your gut only works in places like Indiana. Ridicule works, as does condescension. But in the end, there's only . . .

An Explosion in the Living Room | *Bai Xiaoyi*

Translated by Aili Mu

Now that the tea was ready, the host set his guest's cup on the tea table and covered it with a lid. Naturally a sweetly crisp *clink* accompanied the action. Then, reminded of something he needed to do, he set the vacuum bottle down on the floor and ran into the kitchen from where the sounds of a cabinet opening and rummaging inside emerged.

His guest and his daughter were left waiting in the living room, the ten-year-old girl standing at the window looking at the flowers outside. Her father's fingers had just touched the delicate handle of the cup when, suddenly, there was a *pop*, followed by the hopeless sound of glass shattering.

The vacuum bottle had fallen over, alarming the little girl, who immediately looked over her shoulder to see what it was. A simple matter, really, but one step removed from miraculous: neither of them had touched the bottle. An indisputable fact. When the host had set the bottle down on the floor, it had wobbled a bit without falling over, at least not right away.

The explosion of the vacuum bottle brought the host running from the kitchen. He was holding a box of sugar cubes. Instinctively his eyes were drawn to the steaming puddle of water on the floor.

"That's okay," he blurted out. "Don't worry about it!"

The father was about to explain what had happened, but stopped himself.

"I'm really sorry," he said. "I accidentally knocked it over."

"That's okay," the host repeated to show it didn't matter.

Once they were outside, the girl asked her father, "Did you really knock it over, Dad?"

". . . I was closest to it," he said.

"But you didn't touch it. I saw your reflection in the window. You didn't even move."

Her father smiled. "What do you think I should have done?"

"It tipped over on its own, the floor was uneven. It was wobbling when Uncle Li set it on the floor, and it just tipped over. So why did you say you—"

"But Uncle Li couldn't see that's what happened."

"You could have told him."

"No, dear," her father said. "Saying I knocked it over sounds better, makes more sense. Sometimes, for reasons you simply can't understand, the more you insist on telling the truth, the more it sounds like a lie, and the harder it is to get people to believe you."

His daughter didn't say anything for a long moment. "Does it have to be like that?"

"That's just the way it is."

1985

I think short-shorts should be composed purely of narrative. Description is unnecessary and should be rejected. Pure narrative guarantees the capacity of short-shorts to present content and to command subject matter within a limited space. Thanks to the expanding capacity of narrative language, and its flexibility to switch back and forth, short-shorts are able to relate both small stories of fleeting moments and grand stories spanning years, dozens of years, or even longer.

Bai Xiaoyi

Going Home | *Ai Ya*

Translated by Julie Chiu

He wrote "twenty dollars" in the checkbook and, with natural ease and briskness, signed his name in English. Then he wrote a letter to his friend.

Please, my friend, please buy a hand-woven straw hat for me. And please, please buy a bus ticket to my hometown. Then at the corner of the bus stop, buy a bundle of litchi from the old man who is always in his faded Chinese jacket. It is now the season for litchis, that I know. Please, don't take the bus. Put on the straw hat and walk across the noisy outdoor food market that is always dirty with waste water covering the floor. Take a turn at Old Wang's noodle stall, the one that sells noodles with spicy stewed beef, and go to my house. There's no need to knock. Please shout out, "Uncle Ah Lang!" That's my father. Please give him the litchis and stay to drink a cup of tea with him. Then please go next door to see a young woman, a coarse woman in plain, humble clothes. She was my first love. See if she still wears a sweet, healthy smile. See if she's borne yet another son for her husband. Please, my friend, please do all these things for me. I am enclosing twenty U.S. dollars to cover your expenses. Thank you.

He put the letter and the check into an envelope, glued the flap down, and sealed it with tears and kisses, then stuck on an airmail stamp. He picked up his pen and entered in his checkbook:

June 18, bus fare and expenses for going home, twenty dollars.

1982

It Looks As If . . . | *Teng Gang*

Translated by Aili Mu

At daybreak Zhang San went to the Five Grass Pharmacy at the bridge-head to have a prescription made up for his father. The pharmacy hadn't opened yet when he arrived. He knocked; someone inside called out, "Coming, I'm coming." Just at that moment Zhang saw a band of imperial guards on horseback charging over from the far end of the street. He thought the mounted troops were heading somewhere to the west, but they unexpectedly stopped in front of the pharmacy. Zhang heard the person inside call out, "I'm coming. I'll be right there." He had no sooner recognized Ruan Yuanjia's voice than the imperial guards broke the gate down and shoved Zhang out into the courtyard. A guard asked, "Is this Ruan Yuanjia's home?" Ruan, who was helping Zhang to his feet, replied, "I'm Ruan Yuanjia." Zhang watched the head of the guards produce an imperial edict from inside one of his sleeves and read, "Search the house!" Some of the imperial guards quickly blocked all the entrances and exits, others took down a trunk filled with tools from the back of one of the horses. They took out the tools and stormed into Ruan's house. Zhang San, having been mistaken for a member of Ruan's family, witnessed for the first time in his life the ransacking of a home. After the imperial guards had left, Zhang fled homeward in a desperate hurry, from time to time glancing back in disbelief.

Zhang San cried out as he stepped inside his home, "Scary! Really scary! Nothing in the world is scarier than watching a home being ransacked. You can't imagine what it's like, but I've seen it all."

His father asked, "Did they find anything?"

"Of course," Zhang answered. "The way they go about it, how could they miss anything? They confiscated absolutely everything."

Zhang took a sweeping glance inside the house and declared, "This is a joke. Stowing stuff like this is just asking to have it all taken away. You wouldn't have left stuff around like this if you'd known how they search a house. Ruan Yuanjia was caught off guard. If he'd been prepared, he wouldn't have suffered such losses. I'll be on the lookout outside while you hide our things."

"Will they come to search our house?" Zhang's father asked.

"I asked Ruan Yuanjia. He said even now he had no idea why his home was searched. That means everybody's house is at risk. We need to hurry. They are very fast. I'd no sooner seen them ride up than they broke down Ruan's gate."

Zhang San climbed a tall tree in front of his gate and tied a wind chime to it. He then came down and put his ear to the stone surface of the road. That way he could hear the clatter of horse hoofs a mile away.

His father came out and said, "We're done. Come inside and take a look."

"I'll be right in," Zhang answered. He told his son to climb the tree. "Ring the bell if you see mounted troops or hear horses' hoofs," he instructed him.

Zhang went into the house. They all had proud, happy looks on their faces. The place looked different now that some of the things were out of sight.

Zhang grabbed a hammer and took aim at a vat in the kitchen. With a *crash* he smashed the vat to pieces, revealing all the items hidden at the bottom. Everyone in his family grew pale.

Zhang San said, "That's how they search. Hiding things your way is a waste of time. You need to know how they do their searches." Zhang picked up an iron rod and ran into his father's room. With a few swings, he shattered his father's large bed, revealing what was hidden in its frame. The faces of his family went white.

"I'll be on the lookout outside," Zhang San said. "Continue hiding our stuff. I've just shown you how they conduct their searches, so now you should know how to hide things so that they can't be found."

Zhang put his ear to the surface of the road in front of the gate.

Zhang's neighbor, Zhao San, put his ear up close and asked, "Have you heard how they searched Ruan Yuanjia's house?"

Zhang answered, "I was there."

"Whose house will be next?" Zhao asked.

Zhang replied, "Yours, mine, anybody's. Who knows?"

"When will it happen?"

"I'm listening to figure that out."

Zhao San stood up and ran home.

Zhang's father came out again and said, "We're done."

Zhang stood up, gestured to his son in the tree, and went inside.

Zhang picked up the hammer, took aim at the cupboard, and smashed it to pieces. Nothing was found.

Zhang picked up the iron rod and shattered a few vases. Nothing there either.

Zhang's father and the rest of the family smiled complacently.

Zhang then began to tap on the wall with the hammer and listened carefully to the echo. He started from the front door, and when he reached a wall in the west room he heard a hollow sound. He looked up at his family, who were nervously holding hands. Hammer in hand, Zhang took aim at the hollow wall and swung three times. A secret cabinet was revealed. Zhang took out all that was hidden inside. His family gasped.

Zhang San warned them, "That's how they search. Your way definitely doesn't work."

Zhang's father disagreed. "Well, they won't be able to find some of the stuff."

"Are you sure? Have you seen them at work?" Zhang took out a handsaw from behind the door. He then picked up a nearby bamboo chair and deftly sawed off the arm, revealing what was hidden inside. Then he turned to the legs of a table, which he neatly sawed off, again revealing what was hidden inside. Next Zhang brought over a ladder and climbed up to the rafters. He sawed open a beam and the stuff hidden inside dropped out. Again his family grew pale.

Zhang's father exclaimed, "We have no way out if they search like that."

They placed everything they wanted to hide in front of Zhang San.

Zhang's father said, "You've seen how they search, so you ought to know how to hide things."

Carrying the valuables in his arms, Zhang San made a few turns around the house before stopping at the kitchen stove. He placed the valuables in the belly of the stove, then placed the wok on top of it. After sizing it up carefully, he picked up his hammer and smashed the wok and stove, revealing all that was hidden in the belly. "No, that won't work," he said. Next he went out into the courtyard. He dug a hole, put the valuables inside, covered the hole up, and planted scallions on top of it.

Zhang's father asked, "Are you done?"

"Yes."

His father and the rest of the family came into the courtyard with rakes and hoes, dug open the hole, and threw the valuables around the opening like garbage.

Zhang's father asked, "Is that how they do it?"

Zhang San answered, "It looks as if we really have no way out. I guess we'll just have to wait for them to come and ransack our house, won't we?"

2003

Not Seen | *Yuan Qiongqiong*

Translated by Howard Goldblatt

Drenched when he walked into the house, he left a trail of water all the way to the kitchen as he went looking for Mama. She wasn't there, so he went into the bathroom to shower off. He had just come back from swimming.

He looked at himself in the bathroom mirror. His freckles were nearly popping out, and his hair looked like a clump of kelp stacked on his head. His face was white as a ghost, all except for his lips, which were purple. As he stared at his reflection he had the strange sensation that he was gazing at the face of a drowned person. The skin seemed gray, sort of translucent—almost metallic. Maybe it was all a result of psychological, not physiological, factors—in a word, fright.

He had nearly drowned in the swimming pool.

Having only recently learned how to swim, today was his first venture out to the deep end. The first two laps, using the Australian crawl, went off without a hitch. It was about six in the evening, and although there was still plenty of light, the sun's rays were weakening. The pool was crowded. Off to his left a young fellow was teaching his girlfriend how to swim, and to the right a kid was floating on his back, pad-dling back and forth along the edge of the pool. Three lifeguards sat up in their chairs; people poolside were talking among themselves. The shallow end was packed, mainly with families—parents and their children. Most of the people at the deep end were swimming alone, like him.

The buoyant water gently supported him as he held on to the trough at the edge of the pool. He felt very relaxed, and his success the first two times had filled him with confidence. He started his kick, took a breath, and put his head under the water. Then he began his stroke.

He could no longer recall what happened then—how the situation could have changed so fast puzzled him. All he knew was that he sud-denly needed air, but he didn't know how to float to the surface or sink to the bottom where he could push off—all around him nothing but water, like a wall closing in on him, no matter where he turned. It was a pliant, flowing wall: it yielded when he struck it with his hand or foot, yet it was still there in front of him. He kicked frantically—nothing but water. It assailed his nose and mouth—he swallowed some.

He opened his eyes. The water was transparent, with a trace of blue. He didn't know which way was up. He thrust his arms above his head and clawed at the water. When he sensed he had broken the surface he yelled HELP! but the sound died on his lips as he again slipped below the surface, leaving behind a trail of bubbles.

Was this how he was going to die? He was surprised to note how clear his head was at that moment. Glug glug, he swallowed more water. It was all so incredible: the kid floating on his back, the lifeguards, the fel-low who had brought his girlfriend to the pool—they were all so near, could they possibly not see him? He was suspended in the water directly facing them, his eyes wide open. His thrashing caused tiny waves on the surface of the water in front of him, like floating gossamer. Was this how he was going to die? It seemed so strange, so very strange. He was sinking to the bottom—he swallowed more water. Everyone said that drowning was a fast way to go—it only took a few moments. He sud-denly regretted not having worn his waterproof watch. But what if he had? What was he going to do, time himself?

Slowly he sank to the bottom.

When he touched the bottom his swimming ability was immediately restored. He pushed off with his legs and shot upward; as he broke the surface he gulped down the dry air. He was alive.

He looked at his face in the bathroom mirror. A while ago, while he was drowning, he hadn't been afraid—the thought hadn't occurred to him. But now he was quaking with fright. He had come that close to dying, it would have been so easy.

He heard a door open—it must be Mama. He heard it slam shut. Then the stern voice of his mother: "Now look what you've done!"

Tap tap tap, her footsteps stopped at the bathroom door. "When are you going to grow up? Do you know how much water you've tracked into the house?" Really loud. Normally she'd have jerked the door open and given him hell. Except now he was seventeen—a seventeen-year-old son in the bathroom. Four or five years earlier she wouldn't have thought twice about opening the door, but now he was, after all, seventeen.

"Ma," he called out. His heart was filled with the unspeakable terror of someone who has nearly died; he was afraid—truly, desperately afraid.

The very instant he broke the surface he discovered that the world hadn't changed at all. The lifeguards were still sitting in their chairs, the people poolside were still talking, the fellow off to his left was hugging his girlfriend—whatever he was teaching her made her giggle. The kid to the right was still paddling back and forth on his back, slowly, peacefully. The sun was weak, the sky was bright, the surface of the white water that seemed blue was smooth except for the occasional ripple caused by swimmers.

No one had even noticed him.

So close, right before their eyes, and not one of them had so much as noticed him.

He opened the bathroom door. "Ma."

Mama said: "You may be a big boy now, but all you know how to do is get into trouble." She glared at him, disgusted. "Look at that hideous face of yours!"

A scene from the past flashed into his mind: he had never learned how to ride a bike because he'd fallen on his first try and Mama had said that was it.

He swallowed. If he told her what just happened, he'd probably never swim again.

Mama slammed the bathroom door behind her, but not before one final comment: "I wonder if you'll ever grow up."

He turned back and looked in the mirror again.

With anxiety creeping into his heart, he thought back to the peaceful, happy scene at the pool: parents swimming with their children, the warm rays of the sun, the balmy breezes. He had been fighting for his very life, and no one had seen him.

What did he have to do to be seen?

As he reflected on the incident at the pool, he was suddenly struck by the realization that Mama was like all the others—she didn't see him either. Just because he was right in front of her didn't mean she saw him.

What did he have to do to be seen?

Drown, maybe.

1988

My Wife Finally Goes Camping | *Lin Ji*

Translated by Julie Chiu

With my knapsack on my back, I must have waited at least twenty minutes. No matter how I tried, I couldn't see my wife over the top of the hill in front.

So I lit a cigarette. Might as well sit down, and I did, thinking: If she doesn't show in another ten minutes, I'll retrace my steps and see what's held her up and kept me waiting. If she's kept me waiting all for nothing, at the very least I'll give her a good scolding. Why must she disappoint me before we even get started?

In fact, it took no more than fifteen minutes to get from the pier to this peak. A short walk past a few humble seafood shops and a couple of village houses scattered along the way, then circle round the old Tin Hau Temple, and that was it. The road wasn't tough going, either. The first half was paved, the second half a muddy slope. And all she was carrying was a tiny little airline bag. No reason why she should lag behind . . . I checked my watch and couldn't help getting furious. I threw away my cigarette butt, snatched the knapsack, and started jogging back up the muddy slope.

Before we were married, we went camping just about every holiday. Then we got married and had our first child, and she stopped going. At first I thought that didn't mean she'd stopped enjoying the activity anymore but simply that she was too busy being a new mother and had to put camping aside for the time being.

But soon the child was three and started kindergarten. Still she wouldn't go camping with me, not once.

Over the years I begged her again and again, and more than once she promised to go. But when it was time to set off, with all the preparations completed and all the gear in place, she'd find an excuse to back out. It might be that the child had a mild cough in the morning, and she was afraid it could turn serious when he was in Grandma's care that night. Or why spend such a wonderful holiday climbing up and down mountains instead of enjoying ourselves? And there'd be all that piled up housework to take care of afterward, plus the child to look after . . .

It was only yesterday, as we took our exhausted child away from the park, when we made the turn and walked into the busy center of town and came face to face with a group of young backpackers. I could tell they'd been camping. Their shoes and water bottles were all muddy, and I couldn't help thinking about the good old days.

"Let's take the kid with us just this once?"

She stared at me. "Are you mad? Out in the middle of nowhere, what if he had an accident?"

It didn't matter that she objected again. Night fell, and I still wouldn't give up. I dug up a pile of old photos taken on camping trips in the past. I felt like a rejected lover who was making one last effort to win back his beloved's heart. I handed her the photos.

But she wouldn't take them. She just glanced at them and continued busily with the bed sheet and pillow cases. I was sort of upset, watching her struggle with the never-ending housework, tending to one task after another. I recalled how, over the past few years, I'd humbled myself, begging her over and over but to no avail. The thought drove me nuts. Suddenly I stalked out of the bedroom and went straight to the washing machine in the kitchen, where I grabbed her shoulders and shouted like mad, "You have to go with me! You have to go at least once!" My bizarre behavior must have shocked her. She jumped and scattered dirty clothes all over the floor.

"You have to go with me! You have to go at least once!" I shouted, saying the same thing over and over, and I started to shake her like shaking a tree.

"Are . . . are you all right?" she asked in a panic, turning her head, her body shaking.

"You have to go with me! You have to go at least once!" I didn't stop shaking her. I shook and I shook like mad.

"You, you . . . help! Help!" she shouted, finally freeing herself from my grip. She slipped under my arm and shot into the bedroom. Before I caught up to her, she had the door shut and locked.

I banged on the door, shouting, "You have to go . . ."

As the quarrel went on, I heard our child crying in the bedroom, but I didn't care. I kept banging on the door and shouting, until I heard, through the door, a wailed promise.

As I set my eyes on the muddy road stretching downhill to the old temple, I was still angry. Except for a few kids playing by the side of the road and an old village woman coming uphill with an empty chicken cage, all the way down the paved road to the pier she was nowhere to be seen.

Could she have taken a wrong turn? I began to get worried. But the road to the right was the only one that branched off. It led to the narrow bay, whose cliff-like bank would stop anyone from going any farther. Could . . . could she be in danger? Oh, no! I thought. Forgetting about the weight of my heavy backpack, I lurched down the slope.

Before I'd run very far, I saw her coming out from behind the temple wall, holding something against her chest.

As she walked haltingly up to me, I was so mad I couldn't speak. Now I saw what it was: she was holding a bunch of old bed sheets and pillow cases; even her airline bag was stuffed with dirty clothes.

1986

Short-shorts should maintain a certain degree of ambiguity. Ambiguity is not a narrative device but a writer's state of consciousness, wherein the understanding is by no means transparent. "The truth is in here; but words fail the effort to clarify it."

Wang Zengqi

Contemplating Water | *Zhong Ling*

Translated by Julie Chiu

The soft light of dawn fell on the little monk's scarlet cheeks. As he swung the big broom to sweep dead leaves off the ground, the dark green mountain pond came back to mind. Only a month ago, he had been swimming in the pond, feeling cool and happy. But now his family had sent him to learn to be a monk, leading a life of strict discipline and monotony—chanting sutras, sweeping the ground, and sitting in the lotus position. Worse still, the abbot was cold and indifferent, never having much to say. As he was entertaining this thought, the little monk glanced over at the abbot's meditation room in a corner of the courtyard. He noticed a strange phenomenon.

The wooden frame of the opened window glittered with crystalline white lights, a bit like his pond at high noon. The little monk put his broom down, walked to the window on tiptoes, and popped his head in. In the little room—no more than fifteen square feet—his master was gone; even the meditation mat, the side table, and the n-shaped cloak stand were gone. Instead, the floor was immersed in a shallow pool of water, the surface level with the threshold. Watching the bright, limpid water, the little monk itched for a game of pebble skipping. His personal record was five skips!

He looked around and saw a thin bit of tile lying at the foot of the wall. He picked up the tile and, stretching his arm inside, pitched it. Pong! Pong!—the tile bounced off the water twice. He gave out a hearty laugh, but soon he began to worry. What would happen if the master caught him? He'd better run.

Master Light was seated on the meditation mat with his legs crossed. He had gone into a trance again. His eyes were closed and his thin face radiated an ineffable tranquility. He could clearly see the red liquid of his blood flow through big and small veins in different parts of his body. Tears formed in the tear gland, stored but not shed. From the gland under the tongue some moisturizing liquid flowed into the mouth. In the urinal duct a few drops of light yellow liquid were slowly moving toward the bladder. Many droplets carrying waste and toxins were released from the ends of the sweat glands. His closed eyes saw the infinite number of tiny water droplets in the air that the naked eye could not see. He saw streams and oceans and many other worlds, worlds ruled and protected by various Buddhas, worlds where the sea was transparent as crystal and fragrant with the smell of eaglewood.

Master Light came out of his trance. Suddenly he felt a sharp pain at a certain point on the right side of his chest. He drew in a deep breath and the pain lessened a bit. His reflections flashed at the speed of lightning: after going through so many lives, I've finally made it to the realm of an arhat. All my past karmas have been eliminated. My body should no longer be subjected to ailments or pain. Has my practice regressed and a new karma been created? Then he caught a glimpse of the little monk peeping from outside the window, his eyes opened wide.

"Come in," said the master.

The little monk pressed his hands together in front of his chest and bowed. His curious eyes were rolling this way and that as he scanned the floor around him.

"Master, where has the water gone? How could the floor dry up so quickly? Only a moment ago there was a foot of water on the floor, very clear water."

The long eyes of Master Light flashed a watery light. "What were you doing just now?"

The little monk flushed. "Master, I was wrong. I skipped a tile on the water just now."

Master Light felt two more cramps in his chest. He realized his problem now. There was still a distinction between inside and outside the body. Calmly he told his disciple, "Tomorrow morning, when you see the water again, come in to get the tile, and put it back where it was."

Early the next morning, the little monk came to the master's meditation room and looked in through the window. Sure enough, there was a foot of clear water on the floor, just like yesterday, and the furniture had gone who knew where. The bit of tile was lying in the water by the door, a spot of red in the cold, lucid water. He opened the door, stepped into the water and picked up the tile. He put it back at the foot of the wall outside.

When Master Light came out of his trance this time, his chest pain had disappeared.

One month later the little monk was sweeping the late-autumn yellow leaves that had fallen into the courtyard. Raising his head, he saw another strange phenomenon through the window of his master's meditation room. This time, the window frame did not glitter with the lights of water. Instead, the window was lit up, and he could see red balls of light and glowing green sticks inside the room. He put his broom down and tiptoed over to the window. Wow, Master was practicing his magic again! Through the window, he could see that the room was filled with water all the way to the ceiling. But it was as if a transparent wall had been installed in the window, and the water did not spill or pour out. In the water, a few little fish were swimming, their red bodies flashing gold. On the floor green weeds were swaying. The window was like the kind of glass they would use in an aquarium many karmas later, through which visitors could view the fish and shrimps. The little monk burned with a longing for the pond in the mountains. He used to dive in the refreshing water. He had seen weeds at the bottom and encountered fish with glittering scales. He could not hold back any longer. He took a deep breath and jumped in through the window.

The little monk found himself in a vast expanse of water, deeper and wider than his pond in the mountains. He looked down at the bottom and saw all kinds of strange, semi-transparent flowers blooming in the sand. All the flowers were of beautiful bright colors, gently dancing in the drifts of the current. Fish of all colors were swimming around him. Not far away, a fish as big as a hill was gliding by. It was all so fascinating! But he could not hold his breath any longer. He turned back toward the window, crashed through it and fell onto the ground. Things were really strange today. There were no drops of water on his hands or face. Even his robe was dry. He immediately raised his head and looked toward the window. Seated on the ground, he could see the upper half of the room inside. There was no water at all, and clear in his view was the master's robe hanging on the stand. He got to his feet and popped his head in through the window, and saw the master seated on his meditation mat with crossed legs. Had he been dreaming just now?

Master Light turned toward the little monk, wearing a warm smile on his long, thin face, with its fair skin. He said to the wide-eyed little disciple outside the window, "Don't you agree that the monastery is as much fun as the mountains?"

2002

XIV. Elegy | *Howard Goldblatt*

She could write letters that'd knock your socks off—funny, smart, the kind that made you wish e-mail had never been invented. I'd catch her in a spelling error from time to time (what does that say about me?), and that always elicited another letter, this one molded around words like "mortified" and expressions of self-ridicule. I hated that but only at first; after all, it generated another letter. Oh, and did I mention that she never "wrote," that she always "printed" (capital letters only)? Said she didn't like her penmanship, never felt comfortable flowing from one letter to the next.

She lived in a place where you had to take a plane to go just about anywhere. But she hardly *went* anywhere. That's what made the infrequent meetings so eagerly anticipated. When we weren't being serious, we were laughing our heads off. We got together with a mutual friend at one of those gatherings. We three were collaborating on something, and then he died. Boy, did that hit her hard. Now I know how that feels.

A few things made her angry; they were things that would outrage any sane person. They just made her angry. She got over it; sometimes I wished she hadn't. There were plenty of things that made her proud and made her happy. Running was one of them, though that came late. I saw her run once; she looked kind of awkward, all but the grin. Her cats (kittens, actually) were another. She loved her husband, her work (to be distinguished from her "job," which turned sour when people decided she was in their "space"), human contact, book covers, Manhattans. I know she considered me a good friend. We visited her once. Two wonderful meals and a great outing within view of a volcano. That's what sticks in my memory: the base of a mountain.

Father | *Yuan Qiongqiong*

Translated by Howard Goldblatt

Zhimei liked to sit by the window and look outside, in hopes of seeing the man in the gray jacket.

He was a tall man with lanky arms and legs, and had a crew cut, which he let grow unchecked until it looked more like a furry cap than a head of hair.

The man was her father.

Zhimei lost her father when she was four years old. In her mind these days, that was the last time she ever saw him. Was it a true memory or just her imagination? She couldn't say, but it was a lot like a scene in a movie: Her father lying on a hospital gurney, holding her tiny hand in his right hand. His head was so big; his face somewhat pale, like a movie star. He then bent over and kissed her forehead. That likely never happened, since it would have been uncharacteristic for Chinese. But then she was only four at the time, so he might have kissed her.

They then pushed his gurney into the operating theater, the wheels making a slight noise as they rolled through the double doors, each one swinging open and then closing behind him. The white-uniformed nurse was as big as a statue; the movement of her large buttocks filled the screen.

Most of this came straight from a movie.

The reality was, her father died on the operating table. Her mother sometimes talked to her about him. How, for instance, he'd carry her on his shoulders on Sundays, or how he'd bought her a set of children's literature before she even knew her alphabet.

There were pictures of her father in the house: a family photo, his ID photo, and snapshots taken here and there. He was quite a handsome man. In most of the pictures he was wearing a gray jacket; the jackets might have been other colors, but they were gray in the black-and-white photographs.

Sitting by the window and looking outside, in the hope of seeing the man in the gray jacket, gradually became a habit with Zhimei.

They lived in a second-story apartment. People on the street looked smaller from up there, but Zhimei still enjoyed sitting by the window and looking outside, taking note of passing men in gray jackets and thick crew cuts that looked more like caps than heads of hair.

Like the one down there now.

Zhimei had to smile as she watched him. If her father were alive, he'd look just like that, walking fast and dragging a roly-poly child in a hooded jacket by the hand. Finally running out of patience, it seems, the father stopped, squatted down, and put the child—no, not on his shoulders but on his back.

They couldn't be the same in every respect.

When father and child had nearly reached the corner, Zhimei ran downstairs, hoping she wouldn't be late getting to the front door. She arrived just in time to see the man in the gray jacket put the child down on the ground. The little boy stepped in through the door and cried out, "Grandma! Grandma!"

"Oh, good boy," Zhimei said, as she picked him up. Her son thrust his hands into his jacket pockets and smiled at the sight of Grandmother and Grandson.

1993

We can say that short-shorts are the art of the blank space. . . . "Creating blank space" means, simply put, to use as few words as possible. . . . Every single word counts. What is not written exists in the spaces "above, below, to the left and right" of each sentence. Because of the blank space, every sentence in a short-short is loaded with meaning; every short-short is pregnant with suggestions.

Wang Zengqi

A Knock at the Door | *Lin Jinlan*

Translated by Aili Mu

The retired poet drew the curtain and took off his clothes—just as he did before bed at night—to take a nap. For several days after he retired, he enthusiastically told people: "I'm going to nap all afternoon!"

Later on, he would look annoyed and grumble if there was a knock at the door in the afternoon. But he would respond loudly to keep the visitor from leaving. As he dressed quickly, his mind came alive.

"Who is it?" In a loud voice.

"It's me."

In a low voice: "Who is 'me'?" In a loud voice: "I'm coming." In a low voice: "Confucius said, Your body and your name are given by your parents . . ."

This day he had a dream: Long hair was immersed in a wash basin; long hair emerged from the water—it was a head . . . A common sight on TV, except that there the head would rise from a pond, a lake, or the sea. How big can a wash basin be? A real thrill to see a full-fledged head with long hair emerge from it! The face became visible, then the shoulders . . . It was his cousin. She appeared as a young girl. Drops of water and tears merged as they dripped from her face and body. Her eyes were fixed on him but saw nothing, wandering in the universe, recounting her dream, passion, and diminishing hope . . .

A knock at the door.

The poet woke up with a start: "Who is it?"

"It's me."

While he dressed, the poet grumbled: who is "me"? We Chinese won't announce our names unless we have to. As soon as a foreigner picks up a phone, he'll say, this is Stevenson's office. In Chinese opera, those who are required to announce themselves onstage are either subordinates or juniors. When announcing a name is required, ridicule and wily practices are intended. That's why it's awkward to ask a visitor's name. So let's be more roundabout and ask the name of the work unit. While buttoning up, the poet asked in a loud voice:

"Which work unit are you from?"

"It's me."

In a low voice: still "me." The names of our elders must be written with one stroke more or one stroke less, or using homophones to avoid being disrespectful. But foreigners address their fathers by their given names, their grandfathers by nicknames, saying that it's affectionate and genuine. But they don't take care of their elders, and they let their children become "independent" when they reach eighteen. What kind of affection or genuineness is that? What has become of the natural bonds and love of a big family? While zipping up, the poet shouted at the door: "I'm coming."

Chinese believe in consanguinity. There can be, even among bosom friends, clairvoyance . . . clairvoyance. Ah, in his mind's eye, there suddenly appeared a small wooden building by a pond. His cousin sat inside by the window. It was dark, but her look of diminishing hope penetrated the last glow of dusk. Her father had locked the door; her brother had nailed up the window. . . .

The retired poet shuffled to the door, pulled it open—no trace of a visitor outside, not a soul. There was, however, a puddle of water the size of a wash basin in the middle of the hallway . . . The poet stared at the water and saw himself in his youth. Waiting until dusk, he climbed up the small building by the pond. Through the tightly nailed window, he told his cousin not to lose heart, that there was always tomorrow. His cousin said not to worry. If worse came to worst, she would come to say good-bye. . . . His heart was broken. How had he forgotten this over the years? So she came to knock at the door today, to say good-bye. She must have left by water, an escape by water.

Chinese clairvoyance.

2001

Grandpa Pothook | *Cao Naiqian*

Translated by Howard Goldblatt

Grandpa Pothook was carried back from the graveyard again.

Grandpa Pothook was from another province and had no kin in the village, but everyone still called him Grandpa. When he got drunk, he became everyone's grandpa, young and old. That is exactly what everyone called him.

Pothook was the only individual who drank every day and could afford to do it. His younger brother, Panhook, a ranking official in their native province, sent him twenty or thirty yuan every month—he spent it on drink.

Pothook was not one to eat anything with his wine, which he drank warm. He had a unique method for warming his wine: he made a little pocket in the crotch of his pants, where he tucked away the wine bottle after every couple of swigs.

Pothook liked to share his wine. "Come on, take a goddamn swig for your grandpa here." He'd then suck in his breath, making a hollow in his wrinkled belly so he could reach down into his crotch to bring out the bottle. It would be nice and warm. Besides the smell of wine, the bottle carried other odors, rank enough that some refused the offer. But others, less fastidious, hoisted the bottle like a bugle and—*glug glug*—took a healthy swig. Pothook, his eyes crinkled in a smile, would cock his head to watch, his mouth opening and closing as if the liquid were pouring down his own throat.

As soon as Pothook was drunk, he staggered off toward the graveyard, muttering the same two lines from a folk song:

When I think of you in the daytime, I climb the wall to you;
When I think of you late at night, there's nothing I can do.

Once he reached the graveyard, he lay spread-eagled atop a large stone to sleep it off. Weather permitting, he would strip naked, exposing his skin to ants and an assortment of bugs.

"Go on, go down to the graveyard, and carry Grandpa Pothook back. We can't let him catch cold," one of the older generation would say to one of the younger ones, who would take four or five friends along.

When he had sobered up a bit, they would start teasing him: "Do the tiger hop for us, Grandpa Pothook!"

And he'd reply, "I'm too old for that sort of stuff."

"You're not too old," they would say, as they wove a tail out of tall grass.

Pothook would hold the rope in the crack of his ass and begin hopping all over the place. Instead of falling out, the tail would smack loudly against the scrawny thing hanging between his legs. That had everybody in stitches.

Now they were carrying him back once again, but this time Grandpa Pothook uttered only a single comment before passing out for the last time: "Bury me in Widow Three's grave."

Never expecting him to say something like that, everyone who heard him stared blankly into space.

1988

A short-short is too fine to have room for preaching, elaborating, decking out, plastering, or padding. A short-short tests most directly a writer's ability to experience life through art.

Wang Meng

Killer Well[*] | *Zhong Ling*

Translated by Julie Chiu

Frogs that live in this neighborhood are terribly afraid of my elder brother. Any frog spotted by my brother ends up on our dining table, stir fried with celery. This morning Brother's already caught seven, which are now jumping every which way inside my bamboo basket. Presently Brother stares at me with his bright, fiery eyes, and points ahead with his puckered lips. Wow, there under the tree is a huge, king-sized frog. Quietly Brother moves the sieve over its head. But it's as if the creature has eyes all over its body. It makes a sudden leap and bounces off a long way. It describes a few arcs in the air and hops its way toward Worm's Pond.

Brother stands at the irrigation well by the pond. He is looking down into its depths. Naughty King Frog must be hiding somewhere at the bottom of the well. By the time I hurry over to the well, Brother has already climbed into its circular opening. He climbs down the rungs of the iron ladder and, holding the sieve in one hand, looks up at me and smiles: "It's dead for sure."

The well is so deep, nearly five times my height. King Frog seems to have shrunk in size down there. It's spreading its green legs, gliding on the mud-yellow water. Suddenly, with a loud splash, Brother's sieve drops into the water. He is half-way down, lifting his head to look at me. How come Brother's eyes are so unfocused? Then he loses his grip and plunges straight down. Brother, why aren't you swimming properly? Why are you jerking your arms and legs wildly like that? God, even his head is underwater! Help! Help! I shout as I run home. Mom is standing by the door. When she hears that Brother is drowning, she runs to the well like a whirlwind. But she isn't strong enough and can't possibly drag Brother up. I rush in to wake up Dad, shaking him with all my might.

Dad runs ahead of me in his bare feet. Auntie and Uncle Xin, and Cousin Long and Uncle Mu, who happen to walk by, all follow me and run like crazy toward the well. Why isn't Mom by the well? Oh she must

[*]Author's note: On 7 August 1981 an irrigation well by Worm's Pond in the New Territories, Hong Kong, was found with swamp gas, which killed four people. "Killer Well" was inspired by this piece of news.

have gone down to rescue Brother. Dad bends over the well and shouts, his voice cracking: "Ah Zhen! Ping Zai!" Still shouting, he steps over the rim of the well and climbs in.

That's strange, why does the bottom of the well have a tai-chi pattern like one I saw in the temple? But it's not a tai-chi pattern at all! The black is Mom's silk top, the white is Brother's school uniform. They are in each other's arms, afloat in the water. Dad, get them up quick! When Dad makes it to where Brother is, he stops and stands still. He looks up and stretches his arm toward Uncle: "Ah Xin, grab my hand. . . ." Before he has finished his sentence, his eyes narrow and he plunges down. Uncle Xin hurries into the well. Quick, Uncle Xin, get them out of there! You saved three refugees from the sea last month—you can do it! What's going on? Why have you turned as limp as a rag doll and are sliding down? Oh, no, you're pushing Dad and Mom down to the muddy bottom! Oh, help! They're so noisy, the crush of people crowding around me. Someone shouts out Ah Xin's name with a shriek like the sound of scraping glass. It's Auntie. Many voices shout: You mustn't go down! It's Cousin Long and his father, who drag and force Auntie back. Another voice is shouting: Go get some rope! There's poisonous gas down there!

Uncle Xin's body isn't wriggling anymore. He curls like a shrimp and floats on the surface of the water. He is wrapped in a piece of blue cloth—Dad's pajamas. Look, the pajamas are moving! No, it's not Dad moving—it's King Frog hopping onto Dad's belly. Who cares what that is, Dad? Get on your feet now. The water's not deep, it's only up to your shoulders . . .

1981

Looking Back at Life at the Moment of Death | Cai Nan

Translated by Aili Mu

A yellow leaf blown aloft from the ground grew back onto the barren branch. The leaf became fresh and plump as the branch turned from yellow to green. The budding leaf burst into life after a spring rain squall—in this story, we assume that time flows backward.

Pierced by bullets, a life was snuffed out on the execution ground. Through the traces of blood, we saw Du's life, like that fallen yellow leaf, rise again. The blood that had seeped into the ground and congealed began to revive, reform, and return to his body. His bullet wound formed a scab. Du sat up straight, stood, and walked to the road by which he'd come.

Du broke away from two policemen, left the judgment pronouncement rally, and returned to the prison cell. A few thin threads of light squeezed in through the narrow window overhead. Chewing on one of the two pieces of cornbread that came twice a day, Du found it hard to swallow. The famous lyric by Chi Zhiqiang* came to mind: "I hold cornbread in my hand, but I can't hold the tears in my eyes." Tears then really came to Du's eyes.

What's the use of tears now? said the secretary of the county commission for discipline inspection, in a tone of anger softened by sympathy at Du's trial. You're so young!

Indeed, Du was very young. He was only thirty-one when he became the vice president of the county's Agricultural Bank, in charge of business operations. At thirty-one, life's golden age, he had high career ambitions. But the seductive power of this world was irresistible. It takes a man of extraordinary control and restraint to indulge in lofty career ambitions while enduring the absence of comforts. Du succumbed to the dizzying attractions of money, beautiful women, cars, and houses. It all started with the construction of the bank's office building. A construction firm's contractor knocked on Du's door and offered, as a gift, a lovely wall calendar. Even lovelier was the $50,000 yuan tucked away in the rolled-up calendar. Du, the person in charge of construction, did not sleep that night. Two Dus fought through the night, one wanting to return the money, the other refusing to let that happen. Du resolved the issue with a compromise of sorts—he deposited the money in a different bank under his wife's name. Before long, the construction contract went to that contractor. What came after that caused Du no loss of sleep. Business representatives invited him to dinner. After plying him with food and wine, they dragged him over to a sauna bath. When he was completely enervated, they thrust two cartons of cigarettes into his hands. Upon returning home, Du discovered that every "cigarette" was a 100-yuan bill. The next day, with a single stroke of his pen, Du granted the business a 3 million

---

*Chi Zhiqiang was a young movie actor in China during the 1980s. His crime, a sexual offense, and imprisonment made headlines in the mid 1980s.

yuan loan. After that, there was the Hong Kong businessman who came to President Du with a proposition to do some steel business. The businessman took Du to Hong Kong. At the end of a five-day visit, the key to a villa was in Du's hand. To repay the favor, he diverted 8 million yuan of savings deposits. What happened after that? Half the newly built office building collapsed, with three bank personnel buried beneath it. Following that, the loan could not be recovered, and the diverted savings deposits were nowhere to be found. And after that, Du was exposed, investigated by the commission for disciplinary inspection, transferred to the procuratorial branch, and sent to prison.

First to visit Du in prison was his middle school teacher. The teacher, now gray at the temples, didn't say a word. With trembling hands, he handed Du a piece of yellowing paper. Du opened it—it was his application for Youth League membership, the red stain in the bottom right hand corner still distinctly visible.

Du returned to the beautiful campus and began middle school. A diligent student, Du applied for membership in the Communist Youth League. When he heard that he was not on the list of the first group to be accepted, he applied again. He bit his middle finger, signed the application in blood, and delivered it to the Youth League secretary. At long last Du was able to wear the Communist Youth League badge. He was cited as a "role model" during the socialist ethics campaign of "Five Emphases and Four Beauties"** for returning to the owner 100 yuan he had found.

His parents came from the countryside, bringing along a big canvas bag of boiled corn and baked sweet potatoes. They said, Son, these are for you, your childhood favorites! Du dropped to his knees in front of his aging parents, his head touching the ground.

Du was walking with his parents, in a field in his hometown, going to work for the production team. He chased after his young pals when he saw them harvesting sweet potatoes and corn. The autumn was deep as an ocean. In the broad and mysterious field, a column of smoke was curling upward, and his pals were shouting and jumping for joy—they

---

**The "Five Emphases and Four Beauties" was the name given to, and the norms advocated in, the socialist ethics movement of the 1980s. The "Five Emphases" refer to an emphasis on civility, courtesy, sanitation, orderliness, and morality; the "Four Beauties" to soul, speech, behavior, and environment.

were cooking corn and sweet potatoes. Du, swallowing the saliva in his mouth, turned resolutely and ran back to the field where grownups were working and reported the theft to the team leader . . .

On a long, hot, stuffy summer night, Du sat in his father's lap, listening to him tell the story of 13th Sister Gallant, while his mother fanned mosquitoes away from them. Du fell asleep in the middle of the story. In his dream, he grew younger and younger: Du babbling, Du toddling, Du on all fours, Du crying for food. With a sharp pang of childbirth from his mother, Du came into this world.

It was the time when budding willow leafs burst into life after a spring rain squall.

1998

An Encounter with General Zhou | *Chi Zijian*

Translated by Julie Chiu

It was a night like any other night. My head pillowed on a reedy patch, I saw Zhou Yu, the dashing, spirited rider from the Three Kingdoms whose carefree gallops echoed over many lands.

The moon was pretty that night, and I was in the vast, open wildwood. It was late, but through the transparent air I recognized him right off. I was in a nightgown, white in color, my dark hair let down, my not-so-elegant feet bared. I was strolling on the riverbank with no destination in mind. Cool, moist air greeted me, carrying with it a hint of burned mugwort, and the sound of the drum and bugle. Leaving the riverbank, I traced the smell and the solemn notes until I came to a desolate spot filled with tents that shot up like mushrooms. Campfires had been lit in front of the tents. Their heads lowered, war horses leisurely grazed the nighttime field. Faint snores rose and fell over the vast land. Then and there, I saw Zhou Yu, standing alone in the wildwood.

I don't have the looks of the famous beauty Diao Chang. The only reason Zhou Yu spotted me was that ours were the only opened eyes. Everyone else was sound asleep. In the moonlight two people gazed at each other, and they were Zhou Yu and me.

Here was the one man I had longed to see. I was speechless, wearing an expression I always wear when I see someone intimate to me.

Zhou was in his suit of armor, eyebrows dashing like a pair of swords, eyes bright and piercing. Overwhelmed by his gallant spirit, I trembled.

"The war hasn't started yet. Why are you trembling?" asked Zhou.

I wanted to tell him why. I wanted to tell him that whenever I am with someone whose charm I cannot resist, I tremble. But I could not speak.

I did not know what battle—yet another one—was about to take place. The scale of the camp, with its many tents and extensive stockade, and the fact that Zhou Yu was staying up all night, all foretold an extraordinary battle. When the two sides fought at close range, all the polished swords would be stained with blood. Only when there is blood on the swords can a war be declared over. How many people's blood has stained and dried on the swords? How many bloody swords have been left in the yellow earth, dimmed by a thick layer of rust?

Zhou Yu paid little attention to my trembling. He threw a handful of mugwort into the campfire, and I realized where the smell had come from. But what about the drum and bugle?

When Zhou Yu turned and walked toward the tent, I spotted a drum set up on the ground. A bugle was hanging from the tent. He picked up a drumstick and struck a rhythmic beat. Then he reached for the bugle and began to blow. He was enjoying it immensely, drunk with the beauty of these notes of war, his armor glistening and glowing.

"That drum and bugle get on my nerves," I said.

He laughed. His laughter was like echoes off a snowy mountain. He set the bugle and drumstick down, and walked up to me. "What sounds do not get on your nerves?"

"The sound of flowing water, the sound of birds singing, the sound of children shouting and screaming, the sound of a woman washing clothes or a man drinking."

He laughed again, his teeth glinting in the moonlight.

"I don't like the suit of armor you are wearing. You would look much better in civilian clothes."

"What kind of a hero would I be without a suit of armor?" he asked.

"Without your armor, you would be a true hero."

We did not speak anymore. Slowly the moon glided westward as the campfire burned with a faint glow. The strong smell of mugwort weakened, and the war banner in front of the tent snapped and billowed in the wind. I sat down on the ground. Zhou sat down, too, his legs crossed.

We looked at each other.

"Where are you from?" he asked. "What brought you here before I set off on my conquest?"

"I am a village woman. I was strolling by the river after harvesting reeds. The mugwort and the drum and bugle brought me here. I did not know I was going to meet you."

"Did you not want to meet me?"

"Meeting you has been the greatest wish of my life."

"But wouldn't you rather meet Zhuge Liang instead?"

"No," I replied. "Zhuge is a god. I do not associate with gods, only with human beings."

"You call Zhuge Liang a god. You must be mocking me, seeing me as a short-lived hero." He was agitated.

"What is wrong with a short-lived hero? I like a hero whose spirit is transient, not a god who will never fall. A true hero falls."

Zhou Yu did not laugh anymore. He threw another handful of mugwort into the campfire. The moon now glowed with a tinge of white. Its milky light gave the wildwood an extra touch of gentleness and peace.

"I must go now," I said. "It will be dawn soon. My baby wants my milk, and the pigs and chickens need their feed."

Zhou Yu did not move. He only gazed at me.

I stood up and repeated what I had just said. Slowly I turned around and, already missing him, started to walk away. I winced—I always do when I am leaving someone intimate to me.

I walked for a long time, not daring to look back. I was afraid of seeing his figure under the moon again. As I was about to reach the riverbank I couldn't help it and turned my head. But, oh . . . Zhou Yu was no longer wearing his suit of armor. He wore a long white robe made of coarse linen and was driving a cold, shiny sword into the earth. Silvery moonlight danced on its blade. The horses were still grazing leisurely in the night. There were no more drum and bugle, only a faint smell of mugwort in the air. This figure that had lived for centuries, this figure of one who had captured my heart, was now burned in my deepest memory.

I reached out my womanly hands to try to catch his hand. But we were too far apart. I grasped only the wind that swept the empty wildwood.

It was a night like any other night. My head pillowed on a reedy patch, I saw Zhou Yu. That patch of reeds was now wet with my tears.

1995

XV. Looking Backward and Looking Ahead | *Howard Goldblatt*

It had been a terrible year, the worst in memory. If it had been a fish, they'd have thrown it back; a Broadway play, they'd have rung down the curtain; a Chinese dinner, they'd have canceled the fruit and fortune cookies.

So they loaded the trailer with their belongings, gassed up the car, and headed North. In the mirror the lines of traffic stretched all the way to the horizon.

The Look | *Li Zuchen*

Translated by Howard Goldblatt

Forsaken by love, she had never felt so wretched, so grief-stricken, and had just about given up on life itself.

She walked down the street, alone, aware of neither a gentle summer breeze nor the lovely flowers.

A handsome young man was walking toward her, his shining eyes glued to her. He was totally absorbed, absolutely infatuated. That merely added to her turmoil.

Startled by a sudden *thunk*, she spun around and saw that the young man had walked right into a telephone pole.

She smiled.

That night she slept like a baby.

1988

Notes

Introduction

1. "Quanmin xiezuo," as the slogan goes in Chinese. It became the title of two anthologies published by Lianjin Press in the mid-1990s.

2. Erya Press alone has a Very-short Pieces series of sixteen volumes, each devoted to a better-known writer in the genre. Crown Press, often associated with popular literature, has published several short-short collections with titles like *Infidelity Won't Hurt* (Wu Danru) and *Here's Where Love Stops* (Ku Ling).

3. Wang Xiaofeng, "The Current State of Short-shorts," in *The Theory of Short-shorts* (Zhengzhou: Garden of Flowers, 2004), 129.

4. Hou Deyun, "A Chat about Short-shorts," in *The Theory on Short-shorts*, 150.

5. Yin Di, "The Challenging Genre," in *The Aesthetics of the Short-short* (Taipei: Erya, 1992), 13–14.

6. Yang Xiaomin, "Survival Strategies for Literary Journals," in *The Theory of Short-shorts*, 187–90.

7. The same practice can be found in Hong Kong and Taiwan. In Hong Kong, for example, outstanding short-shorts are selected every year in writing competitions, including the Youth Literary Award and the Hong Kong Mini-short-story Writing Competition, launched in 2003. The genre has also been embraced by writers of children's literature and educators, and adopted in creative writing classes at secondary and tertiary levels.

8. According to Zhang Chunrong's select bibliography, at least twenty-five collections of foreign short-shorts in Chinese translation were published in Taiwan between 1975 and 2001. These collections include classical as well as contemporary short-shorts by writers from Japan, the United States, France, Italy, and Russia, among others. See Zhang's *Very-short Pieces by Prominent Writers: Guide to Pleasurable Reading* (Taipei: Wanjuan Lou, 2004). Besides various collections of foreign short-shorts, mainland China has also published anthologies composed of best works by both foreign and Chinese writers. Two eminent examples are the collections edited by Zhang Guangqin and Wang Hong (*An Anthology of Chinese and Foreign Short-shorts* [Beijing: Shehui kexue wenxian chubanshe, 1990]; and Jiang Zengpei and Zheng Yunqin (*The Best of World Short-shorts* [Nanchang: Baihuazhou wenyi chubanshe, 2001]). The latter is comprised of four volumes devoted, respectively, to Chinese, Asian (other than Chinese), American (both North and South), and European writers.

9. See Wang Meng's speech at the twentieth anniversary celebration of the *Journal of Selected Short-shorts* at http://lit.eastday.com/eastday/wxhg/wxdt/userobject1ai1034720.

10. We have also scanned online resources but gave up after coming to the same conclusion drawn by Yuan Qiongqiong about her failed attempt to "pan for gold" on the Internet: "It is not very likely one may discover good fiction online. . . . With net-fiction, there is the wipe-out effect of 'bad coins expelling good coins.'" See her preface to *Collected Short Stories 2002* (Taipei: Chiuko, 2003).

11. We borrow the idea from Rhonda Dahl Buchanan. See her "Literature's Rebellious Genre: The Short Short Story in Ana Maria Shua's *Cas De Geishas*," *Review of Inter-American Bibliography* 46, nos. 1–4 (1998): 181.

12. Wang Zengqi, "On Short-shorts," in *The Theory of Short-shorts*, 15.

13. Feng Jicai has an interesting idea about how the genre of short-shorts may serve writers of full-length novels. In his introduction to *Odd Characters from the Mundane World* (Beijing: Writers' Press, 2000), he confesses that the self-contained character sketches in the collection were, in fact, "leftovers" from his full-length novels, now turned into short-shorts reminiscent of classical Chinese short-pieces (see "Granny Drunkard" in this anthology).

14. See Janet Wilson, "Teaching the New Zealand Novel: Prose-Poetry and the Ideology of the 'Third Way,' " in Gordon Collier and Frank Schulze-Engler, eds., *Crabtracks: Progress and Process in Teaching the New Literature in English* (Amsterdam: Rodopi, 2000), 307–8.

15. In Hong Kong, Taiwan, and mainland China, short-shorts have found their way into Chinese writing classes for secondary school and university students. Since short-shorts are perceived as a great vehicle for acquiring and sharpening narrative techniques, some secondary schools in Hong Kong hold annual short-short competitions to encourage creative writing in the genre. The annual Writers' Forum for Short-shorts in mainland China often draws young practitioners under twenty.

16. An article in *The New York Times* expressed such a concern: a goal China failed to achieve in the 1950s is probably being achieved now. See "From Pest to Meal: A Leap Forward?" in *The New York Times*, April 3, 2002, A4.

Grooming

1. From a saying by Chairman Mao made famous during the Cultural Revolution: "Modesty helps one move forward, whereas conceit makes one lag behind."

Controversy

1. Liu Wencai was a landlord in Sichuan Province before the founding of the People's Republic of China. During the early years of Communist rule, the landlord was considered a stereotypical oppressor of poor people. Liu's story was taught in primary schools. He was said to have fed on a peasant woman's milk to gain extra nourishment.

Creatures

1. A kingdom during the Zhou dynasty (ca. eleventh century to 256 B.C.).

2. The Shang dynasty (ca. seventeenth to eleventh century B.C.).

About the Authors

Personal information on some of the authors is unavailable.

AH CHENG (b. 1949). Writer, Mainland China: "Cloth Shoes"; "Observe"; "Pets"; " The Cycle"; "Hatred"; "Chimney Smoke"

AI YA (b. 1945). Writer, Taiwan: "Frenchie"; "Going Home"

BAI XIAOYI (b. 1960). Writer/Editor, Mainland China: "Accidental Confidante"; "An Explosion in the Living Room"

BEI DAO (b. 1949). Poet, Mainland China.

CAI NAN (b. 1963). Worker for a Municipal Tax Bureau, Mainland China: "Self Murder"; "Looking Back at Life at the Moment of Death"

CAO NAIQIAN (b. 1949). Worker in the Public Security Bureau of Datong City, Mainland China: "In the Haystack"; "In-law"; "Grandpa Pothook"

CHANG GANG. Mainland China: "'Left' with No Chance"

CHE ZHENGXUAN (b. 1981). Hong Kong: "Last Stop, Mongkok"

CHEN HENGCHU. Mainland China: "Promotion Report"

CHEN HUI (b. 1960). Writer, Hong Kong: "Good Wine"

CHEN HUIYING (b. 1955). Professor, Hong Kong: "Tied Together by Fate"

CHEN KEHUA (b. 1961). Eye Specialist, Taiwan. "Mothballs", "Lover"

CHEN SHIXU (b. 1948). Writer, Mainland China: "What's Up, Lao Cao?"

CHI ZIJIAN (b. 1964). Writer, Mainland China: "An Encounter with General Zhou"

DENG HONGWEI (b. 1972). Bank Employee, Mainland China: "Gan Xiaocao's Bamboo Pole"

FENG JICAI (b. 1942). Writer, Mainland China: "Granny Drunkard"

FU AIMAO (b. 1966). Worker for a County Cultural Confederation, Mainland China: "Elope"

HE WEIPING (b. 1957). Deputy Mayor of Jiangshan City, Mainland China: "Returning Home on a Stormy Night"

JI DONGLIANG (b. 1963). Writer, Mainland China: "Black Hen, White Hen"

KU LING (b. 1955). Writer/Editor/Talk-show Host, Taiwan: "Jailbreak"; "Hickey"; "A Family Catastrophe"; "Confession of a Photographer"; "0 Café"; "Death Dream"

LI ZUCHEN. Mainland China: "The Look"

LIANG DAZHI (b. 1963). County Official, Mainland China: "The Crow and the Fox"

LIN JI. Hong Kong: "My Wife Finally Goes Camping"

LIN JINLAN (b. 1923). Writer, Mainland China: "A Knock on the Door"

LIN LI-CHUN (b. 1962). Professor, USA: "Sexual Harassment"

LING DINGNIAN (b. 1951). Member of Taichang Municipal Government, Mainland China: "Tea Scum"

LIU GUOFANG (b. 1957). Writer, Mainland China: "A Seat"

LIU JIANCHAO (b. 1960). Bank Employee, Mainland China: "General"

LIU JING (b. 1973) Regional TV Station Employee, Mainland China: "A Capable Man Can't Handle a Small Case"

LIU XINWU (b. 1942). Writer/Teacher/Editor, Mainland China: "The Beat"

LIU YICHANG (b. 1918). Editor/Writer, Hong Kong: "Wrong Number"; "The Features-Column Editor's Daydream"

LUO FENG (b. 1964). Poet/Cultural Critic, Hong Kong: "It Was the Pumpkin That Brought Me Here"

MO YAN (b. 1956). Writer, Mainland China: "Horse Talk"; "Strange Encounter"

QIN YONG (b. 1978). Journal Editor, Mainland China: "Here's How the Flu Spreads"

SI LI (b. 1948). Librarian, Taiwan: "Rendez-vous"

SUN XUEMIN. Department Head, Mainland China: "Ears"

TENG GANG (b. 1960s). Writer, Mainland China: "It Looks as If . . ."

WANG KUISHAN (b. 1946). Teacher, Mainland China: "Parting"

WANG MENG (b. 1934). Writer, Mainland China: "A Shaved Head"; "Learning to Talk"; "The Upholder of Unity"; "Right to the Heart of the Matter"; "Disputatiasis"; "Little, Little, Little, Little, Little . . ."

WANG YANYAN (b. 1972). Journal Editor, Mainland China: "Wait for a Windfall"

WANG ZENGQI (1920–1997). Writer, Mainland China: "A Tale"; "Small-Hands Chen"

WEI JINSHU (b. 1968). Business Manager, Mainland China: "Matching Sets"

WU YIMIN. Taiwan: "Number Eight"

XI XI (b. 1938). Writer, Hong Kong: "Sunday Morning"

XIU XIANGMING (b. 1958). Chef, Mainland China: "Home"

XU HAIWEI. Mainland China: "The Principle of Rebound"

XU SHIJIE (b. 1930s). Editor, Mainland China: "Purchase Request for a Kettle"

YE SI (b. 1948). Professor, Hong Kong: "Postcards"

YI MING. Mainland China: "My One Comment Too Many"

YI RUOFEN (b. 1964). Researcher, Taiwan: "Black Umbrella"

YUAN BINGFA (b. 1960). Journal Editor, Mainland China: "Confinement"

YUAN QIONGQIONG (b. 1950). Writer, Taiwan: "A Lover's Ear"; "Cat"; "Flies"; "Empty Seat"; "Not Seen"; "Father"

YU YINGMAO. Mainland China: "A Cup of Tea"

ZHAN JING (b. 1957). Writer, Mainland China: "The Busy Secretary"

ZHANG JISHU (b. 1951). Writer, Mainland China: "Wet the Bed"

ZHANG KANGKANG (b. 1950). Writer, Mainland China: "Sea Turtle"

ZHANG ZHENG. Mainland China: "Fad"

ZHONG JUFANG (?–2005). Hong Kong: "Losing the Feet"

ZHONG LING (b. 1945). Professor/Dean/Writer, Hong Kong: "Little Stray Cat"; "Contemplating Water"; "Killer Well"

ZHOU RUI (b. 1953). Editor, Mainland China: "Division"; "The Bus Stop and Haws-sicles"

THE
RETURN

A Tom Doherty Associates Book

New York

THE
RETURN

BUZZ ALDRIN
& JOHN BARNES

THE RETURN

Copyright © 2000 by Buzz Aldrin and John Barnes

This book is printed on acid-free paper.

Edited by Patrick Nielsen Hayden

A Forge Book
Published by Tom Doherty Associates, LLC
175 Fifth Avenue
New York, NY 10010

www.tor.com

Forge® is a registered trademark of Tom Doherty Associates, LLC.

Book design by Jane Adele Regina

ISBN 0-312-87424-3

First Edition: May 2000

Printed in the United States of America

0 9 8 7 6 5 4 3 2 1

ACKNOWLEDGMENTS

Special thanks are due, this time, to.

Andrew Aldrin, for excellent technical notes on a wide variety of problems.

John Blaha, for insights into the actual operation of the shuttle, and answering many dumb questions with patience and good humor.

Dan Tam, for enthusiastic reading and more ideas than would fit in 100 books.

Hu Davis, for the engineer's perspective, and for many amazing and useful ideas and insights.

Maureen Gaetano, for her keen eye for what's corny.

Dr. Geoffrey Landis, for some very helpful back-of-the-envelope computations.

The characters in this book really *are* fictional; there are plenty of people of their type in similar positions, but there is no way to match up an individual character to any existing person. And because institutions, finally, are the shadows of the people who staff them, the companies and agencies in this book are not always what they are in real life. So we have chosen to rename many of the key institutions in American and foreign space policy. NASA, of course, is real, but when they began privatizing most of their launch operations in the 1990s, the company they turned it over to was named USA (United Space Alliance), not ASU (American Space Universal), and USA is jointly owned by Boeing and Lockheed-Martin, not by our fictional Curtiss Aerospace and Republic Wright. In general, where we have created fictional companies, we have used names historically linked with the same field. Perhaps we should have carried this farther, so that Scott would drive a Nash and the federal agents in the book would work for the OSS, but in general we've adhered to this rule: where the fictional company is substantially different from its real counterpart, we have changed the name; where it's merely the brand name of something in the story, we have kept the name as it is in our real world. The one exception is our NASA, which is not really the present-day NASA; in that case, the name was too familiar not to use it.

THE
RETURN

CHAPTER ONE

SCOTT:

"So how are you planning to top this mission? Are you sending the Pope next time?"

All the reporters laughed. Of course the question wasn't serious, but it did give me a chance to work in a sound bite that my PR coach had suggested. "Eventually, we'll send everybody. But one step at a time, please."

Outside, it was seven in the morning on the kind of pleasant, clear Wednesday in October that makes you think of football, or a long drive someplace where the leaves are turning—the sort of day that whispers "too good to waste." Inside, the press conference room was just like its equivalent at any Washington hotel—plastic "crystalware," stiffbacked chairs, lots of room down front for cameras, a long table on folding platforms with all the legs concealed by fabric velcroed to the edges. I sat at one end of the long table, answering questions before the person the reporters wanted to talk to got here.

"Mr. Blackstone," the man from CBS asked, "we all know that you originally hoped to fly civilian tourist flights yourself, as pilot. Is there any chance that you'll be doing that any time in the next few Citizen Observer flights?"

"Of course I'd like to go," I said. "But it took some pretty generous offers to get ASU to let us put people into empty seats. My next spaceflight, pilot or passenger, is a few years away, I'm sure."

"Would you fly a shuttle again if ASU invited you to?" This reporter, for some reason, didn't seem to want to give the question up. "You've been very careful about keeping your qualification to fly a shuttle."

"I keep my pilot's license, too," I pointed out. "You really shouldn't read any more into it than that."

After that, the questions were less personal. I didn't mind the attention, particularly, but as CEO of ShareSpace, I'd rather it went to my company.

Then we went into the usual ritual questions—the reporters in the room already knew the answers, but their editors might need footage of someone saying those things.

"What kind of mission is this?"

"Like most of the ones *Columbia* flies nowadays. A general, mixed-bag deal—a little science, a little tech, a little business, a little promotion. You all know I can't talk about anything classified, but sometimes they do classified work, as well, for a defense or intelligence agency."

"Do you know what factors influenced Pegasus Corporation's decision about who to send?" It was the same guy from NBC who had needled me before.

"They wanted maximum publicity, I'd guess. Hard to find a more famous person who would get more attention and be better identified with their shoes. Or maybe the Pope wasn't available." That got a laugh; I had just time to wonder if I'd crossed over one of those invisible boundaries that my PR people were always warning me about, before the next question. The reporter from the *Times* had me explain that the seats ShareSpace was selling were available because the International Space Station (ISS) was behind schedule, and so some shuttle flights had been released to other projects.

Then the tall woman from MSNBC walked me through a detailed review of who the first two Citizen Observers had been, in case somehow anyone watching the news now, in October, had managed to miss all the news in the previous May, or October a year ago. That seemed especially silly because "well, the first one is in the room," I said. "Why don't you tell us all about it, Fred?"

Fred Gernsback had been anchor for the Federal Broadcasting Network for almost two decades, and due to his enthusiasm for the space program, his voice had become more identified with spaceflight than that of any broadcaster since Walter Cronkite. He looked around the room, smiling broadly, and I wondered if anyone ever gets tired of being made the center of attention. "Well, it's not complicated and it's not all that interesting. The way it works is that ShareSpace is a private business, like a travel agency, except that Scott Blackstone only sells two or three tickets a year. ASU operates spacecraft, like an airline operates airplanes, because NASA got out of direct operation, for the most part, a few years ago. ASU bought *Columbia* from the government, and most of the time they lease the other three shuttles. So what happened was that FBN bought my ticket from ShareSpace, which got me onto a flight on the *Columbia*, operated by ASU. No different from what happens when they buy me an airline ticket from Amex Travel Services to get me onto a 747 operated by United. Dull as dishwater."

Everyone groaned and laughed; Fred's irony was even more heavy-handed than usual. For ten days in October last year, millions of people had hurried home to catch Gernsback's evening broadcast from orbit. The American public's jaundiced perception of space travel—routine as airplanes and ancient as railroads—had been flipped right back over into wide-eyed wonder by Gernsback's babbling joy about everything connected with the mission.

Gernsback went on. "And so it's the same deal with this next Citizen Observer. Pegasus wanted publicity for their shoes, so they had to get publicity for their guy, so they went to Scott, Scott sold them a ticket, ASU is honoring the ticket, and tonight we're going to witness a new space record—the tallest man ever sent into orbit. Just an ordinary business deal."

"What does a company have to do to get someone on the shuttle, Mr. Blackstone?" a tall, slim black woman asked. "Officially for the record, and also because for all I know Pacific States Network might want to do that for me."

It took me a moment to realize who it was—Nikki Earl, radio correspondent for a little shoestring network that mostly ran very liberal commentary and covered social welfare issues. Normally they weren't big fans of the space program, so if she was here at all, it meant either they were gunning for us, or it was a slow news day. I answered, carefully, "I hope they can afford to send you, but for the moment it's pretty expensive. It starts with a corporation becoming one of ShareSpace's corporate partners, for one million dollars—or more, if you want to be near the top of the list.

"For your million you get a nice-looking plaque inside the shuttle, plus a turn at buying a ticket. When your turn comes up, we ask you for a five-million-dollar seat charge. Once you pay that, you can send anyone who can pass a medical exam and a security clearance. Your five million dollars does include meals and clothes for the trip." There were a few chuckles at that. "There's also a required commitment to devote at least eight million dollars to publicity—primarily about the sponsor itself, of course, but it also has to be clearly tied to Share-Space and the orbital flight. So the real price of the cheapest ticket is about fourteen million, at the moment. We hope that within a decade we can be down under a million."

Nikki Earl nodded. "So why does any corporation buy a ticket? I can understand why it was worthwhile for Fred—someone else bought his ticket, and he had a good time, and I'd go, myself, in a *minute*, if PSN would pick up the tab—but how can that fourteen-million-dollar ticket be worthwhile for any of the corporate sponsors?"

Her tone was reasonable and friendly, so I thought chances were that she was just here because it was a slow news day, and not because PSN was out to do a hatchet job on ShareSpace. She had asked a question I'd have loved to devote a whole interview to, but she needed something a minute long at most.

I started off with the obvious. "Well, it *is* private money, and they have to answer to their stockholders, so mostly I can just assume they want it and let it go at that. After all, the baker doesn't care what you want his bread for, only that you'll buy it, and so far we've got eighteen buyers lined up, so we must be selling what they want.

"But if I were speculating . . . I guess the sponsors must figure that kids love space. Being associated with space is the best publicity there is for companies like Pegasus and Avery that are so strongly oriented toward the youth market. And just now things connected with space seem to be more popular than at any time since the late sixties, so the sponsors probably see being associated with space as a good investment in publicity, period, not just with kids. The best way to find out might be to ask them."

She nodded. "I have, and they said what you said. How about a follow-up?"

"Sure."

"As the parent of a ten-year-old, I can hardly miss that space is suddenly popular again. Why do you think that is?"

"Uh, I'm the parent of a ten-year-old boy myself, and I don't know that I understand it any better than you do. I can make some guesses: the millennium. The anniversaries of so many space events. The new private ventures. The new pictures from the new generation of telescopes. A couple of big realistic movies, where they got the special effects right, after all those years of pure fantasy movies. Take your pick. How does that sound?"

"Like a baker who doesn't know why he's selling more bread, but is real happy that he's selling it," Nikki Earl said, and grinned at me— *not* one of those media-fake smiles for the camera. Mentally I marked her down as a possible ally and someone to float a story to sometime soon. ShareSpace was riding high on a wave of good publicity right now, driven by our sending the third most recognizable name in America (after Jesus and Santa) on this mission. But I didn't want to neglect Nikki Earl—talking to her could be a chance to reach people we hadn't reached yet, and nobody in the public eye ever has enough friends or knows when they might need one more.

So far, ShareSpace had plenty of friends. We were riding the crest of a two-year wave of popularity. Fred Gernsback had just been the beginning for us; he had barely returned to Earth when we took our next step. Avery Filmworks, the dominating giant in family entertainment, had gotten their turn at a ShareSpace slot on a *Columbia* flight for the following May, and they'd come up with an ingenious way to use it: they had launched *Pyramid to Space*, a competitive quiz show on the Avery Channel. The show was in the form of a tournament of space knowledge (or space trivia—I wasn't sure how much an astronaut really needed to know how much the makers of Tang paid to have it included in the early space rations). During the winter holidays, fascination with the competition grew, for the winner—if physically fit enough—would be the next Citizen Observer.

In mid-January, *Pyramid to Space* was won by David Calderon, a garage mechanic from Brownsville, Texas. He had gone into orbit aboard *Columbia* last May, and if anything, he had done us even more good than Fred Gernsback had.

David could hardly have been better if Avery had created him from Central Casting—he was a good-looking twenty-five-year-old, muscular, slim, in perfect shape, a nonsmoker who drank rarely, and poised and confident as he revealed an encyclopedic knowledge of space and astronautics. When he won *Pyramid*, he was bombarded by congratulatory emails, phone calls, and letters, and not a few marriage proposals.

Between his victory, the MTV series that followed him through training, and his flight, he had been endlessly on camera for about six months, and during that whole time, he always enthusiastically boosted the launch, Avery Filmworks, *Pyramid to Space*, ShareSpace, the space program, and life in general. He had a knack for communicating, in ordinary language, his deep and broad knowledge of everything connected with space, astronomy, planetary science, and astronautics—a knowledge he had acquired from years of reading science magazines and watching space documentaries, sources available to anyone, so that even in that regard he seemed to have the common touch. He charmed Barbara Walters, and was so popular that Larry King brought him back on the show twice; for a few weeks he was on every talk show that could possibly book him.

He was especially a hit on radio and TV call-in programs, and all the calls for David Calderon were very much alike: people who just wanted to tell him that they too had applied to compete in *Pyramid to Space*, that family and friends had made fun of them, and now they felt vindicated. "You proved that ordinary people *will* go to space," they would say, or "This is what it's all about, that space is the future of the whole human race." Lots of people wished him luck and many suggested that if he had something else to do at the last minute, they'd be willing to take his place. He was good-humored and friendly through all of it, and every time David Calderon went on the air, we picked up more approval points, and another sponsor or two came banging on ShareSpace's door, wanting to get in on the adventure.

On his flight, Dave was enthusiastic, happy, quotable, and still a brilliant commercial for the idea that space was going to be for everyone. We had put him on the payroll, and now he was out touring the country, visiting with corporate heads where we needed to sell a sponsorship, stopping off to talk to grade school classes and civic groups, speaking at high school commencements and Scout jamborees, and generally producing about as much good will as anyone possibly could.

But although Gernsback and Calderon had been wonderful, what was about to happen would trump every bit of past publicity

ShareSpace had gotten, and make all our past triumphs mere prologue. Now that I had teased the room enough, "I think the time has come to meet the crew." I nodded toward the door, and Naomi, my secretary, nodded back and pushed it open.

Seven people came into the room and joined me on the dais, but for all practical purposes, there was only one person in the room—Michael James, or M J, as pretty much the whole planet called him.

He was over seven feet tall, and graceful, which would have been impressive even if he had been just a random stranger. Knowing his accomplishments, you felt awe—he had presence enough for some ancient king or legendary hero.

Two years earlier, when M J had retired after more than a dozen years as the top center in the NBA, every newsmagazine had put him on the cover, and *Time* had found an excuse to feature him twice.

After the success of the journalist in space, since we had the second Citizen Observer contract already nailed down, it was time to reach for something even bigger. I put all my effort into hustling a contact with M J, and to persuade Pegasus—maker of the most famous athletic shoes in the world, which were the most famous largely thanks to the autograph "M J Michael James" stamped on the side of every one—to sponsor him as the the third Citizen Observer.

He was perfect for more reasons than just his fame, or his immediate recognition. M J was a widely admired role model for American kids, known for his polite good sportsmanship and his advocacy of excellence in all fields. He was bright, articulate, spontaneously funny, but also thoughtful and serious when the occasion called for it. Best of all he was a space enthusiast, and had been ever since he was small. (We had some wonderful footage of his mother, AnnaBeth James, reminiscing about when "Mikey" was ten, and unhappy because he was already too tall to be an astronaut by the NASA rules of the day.)

ShareSpace had announced M J's selection nine days after David Calderon returned from orbit. Ever since, everything M J had done had shown us that the idea was even more brilliant than we had thought. In the last four months, his appearances on kids' shows and news and talk shows had been the best of all possible publicity for everyone—himself, Pegasus, ShareSpace, ASU, NASA—and for that matter, me.

It was an extra hassle to fly the crew up from Canaveral the evening before, then back to Kennedy Space Center for an evening launch today, but that was another public relations maneuver that I felt was paying off pretty well. If you hold your big events at or near KSC, you get a mix of second-string reporters and older ones who want a quick trip to somewhere warm. But if you hold the same events in one of the cities where the media's first string is located, that's who covers you—and those cities, basically, are New York, Washington, or Los Angeles. Washington was the shortest flight to Florida, ShareSpace corporate headquarters was here, and best of all, Washington was the major media city with the most predictable schedule— in NY or LA you could be pushed right out of the evening news slot by any freak local story, but in DC only a war or a sex scandal could steal your coverage.

M J made a few introductory remarks, and everyone relaxed and settled in as if the press conference had just become a group of friends sitting around the living room. "Let me introduce the rest of the crew," M J said, spreading his arms as if to embrace all of them. "This man to my far right, next to Scott Blackstone, is Billy Kingston, the commander. During the mission, he's the guy who we all have to listen to. And if any kids are watching this—"

"They better be," said Samantha Carter, who headed the special team for Nickelodeon, and everyone laughed.

"—like I said, if there's any kids watching out there, something for you to pay attention to—Billy knows what he's doing and knows how the ship works and everything else, a hundred times more than I do. He has all the knowledge and experience. Just like your mom and dad and your teachers know more than you do. So when he says to do something, I do it, and I don't give him backtalk and I do it right away. When we're up in space, my ten thousand field goals are just ten thousand of nothing compared to his knowledge and skill and experience. Listening to him and respecting his authority is part of keeping me safe and out of trouble, because there's all kinds of trouble that can happen up there. Even M J has to do what people who know more tell him to do. It was the same way when I was little and Mama wanted me to do something."

In his deep Gulf Coast drawl, Kingston said, "In that case, your mission commander says to get the rest of the introductions done so we can get back to KSC."

"Yes, *sir!*—you see how I did that?—now, next to Major Kingston is Wes Packard, from West Virginia by way of West Point. He's the pilot, the one who actually flies *Columbia*, and the father of Kati and Mary Lou, who are watching this morning, I bet. This guy next to me is Josh Pritkin, mission specialist in electronics—" he gestured to the tall, thin man, who nodded to the cameras "—and he also plays pretty good ragtime piano, or at least he's good enough to fool a basketball player. Lorena Charette here—" he gestured to a short, stocky black woman on his left "—is from Baltimore, is a medical doctor, is an Air Force major, and has had a much more exciting and interesting life than any professional athlete ever did, and if you media folks had any sense you'd be interviewing her instead of me."

Actually, thanks to M J's quiet pressure, there had been a number of interviews with and features about Lorena, and she was on her way to becoming something of a celebrity in her own right.

"Now, the nervous-looking dude to Lorena's left, who is wondering what embarrassing personal facts I'm going to bring up, is Marc Clement, astronomy mission specialist and my roommate during training." M J winked and said, "But with a nice, good-looking guy like that, all I have to do is ask what his mother would have asked—'why is he still single?' " Clement blushed, everyone laughed, and M J added, "I've done all I can, man, now it's up to you. And, finally, not at all least, all the way to the left, our military payload specialist and our poker wizard, Damian Agustino—" he nodded to the short, square-built man "—my fellow Texan on the flight, so you know with two Texans on board, ain't nothin' to worry about."

M J was from Dallas, a fact that you couldn't help knowing within ten minutes of meeting him. There wasn't much about him you didn't know pretty quickly. We'd vetted him thoroughly. As far as we could tell his biggest personal vice was a liking for mystery novels and his biggest problem was the difficulty of meeting women who might think about him as a serious romantic possibility, rather than as a trophy. He really *was* as nice as he seemed on TV—it drove the detectives crazy.

The first question was from a short, balding man, way in the back. "I just wondered if you'd like to comment on the fact that while you're doing very well, and people will spend fourteen million dollars to send you to orbit, just this morning the House chopped twenty million out of the US Department of Education."

My heart stopped. Michael was a world-class nice guy, but he had a temper, and he wasn't used to being challenged about much of anything; I'd had a run-in or three with him over various things.

He stared at the man. "Well," M J said, finally, "you know, I'm sure, that Pegasus will spend the money to send me to orbit, but they also give around a hundred million a year to schools around the country. They *have* to, in a country that's too damn cheap to take care of its own schoolchildren."

Great, I thought to myself, *we just lost ten more friends in the House.*

"And of course I'm going to go if I get the chance. Any human being with a soul would want to, you know. That's part of why questions like yours . . ." He looked down and shook his head. "Dude, where do you come up with something that dumb? You think I don't know that we need more and better education, and hospitals, and food for the hungry and shelter for the homeless? You think that's a surprise to your viewers? You think, maybe, you're going to make me ashamed of where I came from, or ashamed to be rich from my success? I'll tell you this. I know very well that I am a very lucky man. I know that I didn't 'deserve' my chances in life. But I also tell you this. I got those chances, I took them, I'm taking them, and that's the way it is. And more than that—because I do what people dream about, I give other people the power and the right to dream. And children—and grownups—all human beings need those dreams, the way they need oxygen and food and shelter. You tell me some people are poor? That's a damn shame and I'm sorry, but I gave more to charity last year than you make in ten. You tell me my country, the best place on Earth, is robbing its own children? I'll remember that when I vote. You tell me I ought to hang my head and feel bad about the greatest moment of my life? Chump, you can go to hell."

One part of me wanted to hug him, and another part wanted to run out and issue a denial that he'd ever been in the room. Balanced between the urges, I stood there for a second, before Naomi loudly said, "Hey, he isn't wearing a press badge!"

Hotel security closed in on the little man, who rushed out the door and down the hallway. I never heard whether they caught him or not.

After that, the questioning was a lot more routine. MJ deflected more than half of the questions directed at him to the rest of the crew, making sure that people understood that this was a team effort, and giving most of the credit to the regular astronauts. He kept the media focused on the nature of the mission and the vision of where it led in the great scheme of space exploration. "If we could afford him," I muttered to Naomi, who was handing up some papers to add to my swollen briefcase, "we'd put him on the payroll with Calderon. The two of them would get us a Mars mission set up and funded in no time."

"He might be willing to do that free, you know," she pointed out. "After he gets back, maybe you should ask."

"—and another person you should all be watching—the person

who saw that there was a need for all kinds of people, and not just specialists, in space," M J said, "Scott Blackstone. I owe a lot to his company—metaphorically speaking. Pegasus owes the money."

I waved at the reporters. M J's re-introducing me was my cue to say that everyone needed to get back down to Florida. The seven of them posed for last-minute shots for the prescribed three minutes, and then I got them out the door while Naomi handed out thick press packets that insured that even the most un-awake reporter would have something accurate to start from.

"That's *sure* easier than the press conferences I used to have to do for the team," M J commented, as we settled into the bus that would take us to the charter plane at Washington Reagan. "You go to one of those conferences and they only let you say two things, over and over: you think the team's going to win and you're here to play basketball. And you have to find ways to keep saying that for an hour. Here, it was only twenty minutes, and there was something to talk about." He leaned back and said, "Damn, though, that first clown— the one that wasn't even a reporter—he pissed me off."

"I wasn't happy with him myself," I observed. "I'm sorry he got through security; we're going to have to check on that and find out how he did it."

"You do that. I'd like to see a report. Because if a rude little chump can get through that easy, how do you know the next guy won't have a gun? Makes me mad, and makes me scared, and this is one day when I didn't need to be upset."

Marc Clement was turned around, looking for a way to get a word in edgewise; the two of them had really bonded, which was good for the mission, and maybe better for M J. Now Clement said softly, "That's the problem with hotels."

"That's why you needed to hire your own," M J said, still talking to me. "And you didn't."

"No," I said, "we didn't bring our own security, and that was a mistake. I'm sorry."

M J blinked for a couple of moments, then extended his hand and shook mine. "It's okay, Scott. Really. I'm letting myself get more upset than it's worth. Sorry." He moved forward and sat down to talk with Marc Clement. That was Michael James for you; the terrible temper faded in seconds, as if it had never been there.

I stretched out in the back seat that I'd commandeered for myself, pulled out my cell phone, and made a call. It should be half an hour at least before Amos was due to leave for school. On the second ring, I heard, "Hello?"

"Hello, Thalia, it's Scott. Does Amos have a minute to say hello?"

My ex hesitated a moment, which told me she'd been expecting my call and wasn't happy about it. "As long as it's just a minute. I have to drop him at school early this morning, so you can't talk to him long. But he didn't want to go without getting a call from you. You could have called earlier."

"Not really," I said.

"We'll have to go soon," she said. "I can't afford to be late today. I only have an hour to get things done before I have to get on a plane."

I felt like asking her how it felt to be always running for a plane, and maybe even quoting some of the things she'd said to me about not putting my family first, but fighting with Thalia would cause her to hang up, and I really wanted to talk to Amos this morning. So I just said, "I'm sorry. I didn't have much choice in the matter, but it was inconsiderate of me."

I heard her breath hiss over the mouthpiece and thought she was going to find one more way to get on my case, but then I heard Amos, in the background, saying, "Come on, Mom, let me talk to Dad, I've been waiting." The rustle and thud of the phone being handed over was followed by the *clat-clat* of her heels walking away from the phone, and then at last Amos said, "Dad?"

I swallowed hard and made my voice upbeat. "Hi, Amos! We're

on our way out to the airport to get these guys into orbit, and I just wanted to squeeze in a second and say hello. How are things going?"

"School's fine, I'm going to do peewee wrestling this winter, and I got that program I was playing with to work on the computer," he said, covering all the usual bases of conversation in one sentence. "Mom works too hard and isn't home enough, and I'm looking forward to seeing you the weekend after this."

"Hmmm," I said. "You're stealing all my lines."

"Well, we do have to go soon . . ." he said, sounding much too mature and responsible for a ten-year-old.

Maybe it was just that tone that made me feel like I had to offer something special to him. "Why don't we spend the weekend after next at the cabin?"

"In the *fall*?" He sounded like he thought I was crazy. "Is there anything to do? Won't it be too cold?"

"In the fall," I said, emphatically. "The cabin has a woodstove, remember? We can fire that up and be warm and comfortable. The only summer things we can't do are swim and buy cheap souvenirs. It will be sort of like camping out, but more comfortable. Probably it will be just you and me—nobody else on the beach. We can hang around and talk, you can beat me at chess, and we can build driftwood fires at night and tell ghost stories till we're both too scared to sleep. It's a nice time of year." Desperate to sell him on the idea, I pulled out a reference to one of his heroes, and to a time of life he was already fascinated with. "Back when we were in high school and college, your uncle Nick and I used to go down there in the fall a *lot*, just to hang out and do guy stuff."

That clinched the deal. "Sweet, Dad. Let's do it."

"Weekend after this. What're you up to this weekend?"

"Mom'll be getting back from California late on Friday, and then she says she's going to spend the whole weekend staring at the ceiling. I don't know, probably just play with my friends and catch a movie."

"Well, let her know that if she gets trapped in California, and Mrs. Talbert can't take you on short notice, you can come over to my place. I have some boring stuff I have to do, meetings and appearances and things, but I don't plan to be away this weekend."

"Okay, I'll tell her."

"I love you, Amos."

"I love you too, Dad." I was about to say "bye" when MJ plopped down beside me. "If your son's still there, let me talk to him."

"Amos?" I said. "Hey, Amos—"

"Dad?"

"Somebody here wants to talk to you." I handed the phone to MJ.

A few weeks before, MJ had come by my house late on a Friday to sign some papers. He arrived in a van, floating in a cloud of lawyers and assistants. The business had gotten concluded quickly, but just as MJ had been loading his entourage back into his van, Thalia had come by to drop off Amos for the weekend. While my ex and I had a nearly civil short conversation about clothing that was getting outgrown and persistent low grades in handwriting, the NBA's highest-paid player taught my son the basics of the layup and the jump shot. Afterwards, Amos was walking on air for days.

Now MJ was teasing him on the phone. "After all that work we did improving you in your b-ball, you gonna *wrestle?* . . . Oh, well, you just have to go and be the best wrestler you can, then, don't you? Listen, just make sure you do what your coach tells you, and you always do everything one hundred per cent, 'cause that's how you get somewhere. If your dad tells me you've been slacking off, I might have to come and dribble you around that driveway a few times before I slam you through that hoop, all right? . . . Yeah . . . now, you know, in every sport, there's fundamentals, and you make sure you know them and you're good at them. First two years in any sport, make sure you get the fundamentals, try to be the best at those. Never try to get fancy till you're perfect as you can be at the basics. . . . All right, you do that. . . . What? No, I'm not scared. Maybe a little bit. But not any more than your dad was when he flew into space. This is gonna be more fun than anything I ever did before. . . . Yeah! . . . All right, Amos, talk to you later."

He clicked off and handed my phone back to me. "That's a really nice son you have."

"Thank you," I said. "You just made his year."

M J suddenly gave me the famous big toothy grin, full of mischief. "Hey, do you know anything about wrestling?"

"Not a thing," I admitted.

"Me neither. Couldn't think of a thing to tell him to work on! That's why I said that stuff about fundamentals."

I laughed. "You could've told him anything in the world and he'd be happy. Guess I have to bone up on wrestling, so I can at least have a faint idea what my son's talking about."

M J smiled. "I'd call that a fundamental in parenting."

The van took one of the corporate entrances into Reagan. I shook hands with the whole crew and thanked them all again. They got on the charter jet.

Back at the van, I looked at my watch; it was only nine A.M., and their liftoff was at 9:30 P.M. I had much to do in the next few hours, but I felt great. I sat back in the van and let the driver take me to the ShareSpace offices, up in Silver Spring.

It had been a long journey to this point in my life—the brink of total success—and I'd paid quite a toll for it. In a sense, my family had been paying it for decades before I was born. My great-grandfather, Peter Blackstone, the oldest of six brothers, had been a banker who loaned money to both the Wright brothers and the Curtiss family, and put some of his own money into stock with both fledgling companies. His kid brother, Henry, flew mail over the Appalachians in a Curtiss JNE, back when the best way to avoid too close a federal inspection was to be, literally, a fly-by-night operator; his three-airplane operation eventually ended up as the nucleus of the first airline on the same route.

Henry's oldest son Stephen escaped from Stanford and paid his own way to became a mechanical engineer, holding several patents on the earliest jet engines, and was a founding stockholder in Republic, which went on to buy out the Wrights and created the powerful Republic Wright aircraft company for which my older brother Nick would eventually work. His youngest brother, George, whom I remembered as Grandpa Blackstone, ran away from home before his parents could pressure him into going to Yale, thus depriving them of their other chance for a lawyer or politician in the family. Instead, George joined the Army Air Corps in the 1920s, worked as a liaison training the Nationalist Chinese Air Force in the 1930s, flew with the AVG (the Flying Tigers) during the Second World War, and finished his career as an Air Force colonel supervising training in the military test pilot program. Because that was where so many of the first generation of astronauts came from, Grandpa Blackstone used to brag that he had bawled out, insulted, and screamed at more future astronauts than any other living person.

When Dad, the older of Grandpa Blackstone's two sons, struck off on his own, he'd wanted nothing more than a quiet, settled life, one that didn't involve moving every couple of years, plane crashes, or shouting. He had found his place in the world building models for wind tunnels at Curtiss Aircraft, which was about to become Curtiss Aerospace. When I was four, his brother, my Uncle Ted, died in a T-38 crash, just after being selected for the astronaut corps.

Nick and I followed family tradition: one tycoon, one lunatic. Nick went off to engineering school, and then as fast as he could into management, and rapidly rose to corporate VP at Republic Wright. He used to enjoy telling Dad and me that he thought engineers and pilots were fine people, and he admired them so much that he wanted to own as many as he could.

I went from AFROTC to the Air Force to pilot training as fast as they'd let me, and from there into the astronaut corps. Along the way, I married Thalia Pendergast, whose family had been friendly with mine for decades. Thalia had finished her law degree during my first years in the Air Force, coping with moving every few months and getting most of her degree work completed on-line. She was four months pregnant with Amos on the day she got her invitation to serve as clerk to the Chief Justice of the Florida Supreme Court.

Life became more settled once I became an astronaut and we could buy a house in Orlando; from a family perspective, being an astronaut isn't so different from working for a company that requires lots of out-of-town trips. Thalia had a good position with the Florida Attorney General's Office, and though Amos spent most of his time at day care, he seemed pretty happy.

Common sense would have kept me in the astronaut corps for a long time, and might well have kept my family together, but that itchy need to be doing something different eventually won out. After I had flown three shuttle missions, I started to be bothered by a peculiar thought: we didn't really have a space *program* anymore.

Of course the United States had a presence in space, and we flew to Low Earth Orbit fairly often—I had been there three times myself. But no American—in fact, no human being—had gone farther than LEO since December 1972. We went to space for lots of things: commerce, navigation, communication, knowledge, military advantage. But a "program" would imply we were going somewhere, or had things to accomplish that we hadn't done yet, and I just felt that "going somewhere" was exactly what we weren't doing.

Any real space program would require getting many more people off the planet on a much more regular schedule than we had ever done before; the expression for it that emerged around 1985 was "airline-like operations." I decided I might as well learn what an airline operated like.

That entailed changing jobs and changing towns. At least Amos wasn't in school yet when we moved. Better still, since Global Airways, my new employer, was headquartered in DC, it was very little strain on Thalia—"You're moving me to lawyer heaven," she said, when I first brought the subject up.

I didn't plan to stay with Global, but it was a good place to get the knowledge and experience I needed. They were a charter airline that specialized in transporting high-income tourists to and from adventure experiences, and I was already fairly sure that high-cost adventure tourism would be the first major stepping-stone in the private-industry pathway to routine human space travel.

There was an obvious way for a highly experienced pilot to get some of the experience I needed, and that was what I applied for at Global. As a pilot, executive, and tour leader, I took planeloads of wealthy customers to Australia to snorkel the Great Barrier Reef, into and out of half the airports in East Africa and in the Cone of South America for safaris and climbing and fishing trips, and to South Pacific islands I could barely pronounce. I learned a great deal about pleasing tourists, even more about getting along with other companies (most flights were sponsored or paid for by some corporation), and far too much about international aviation law and coping with what we politely called "irregularities in the infrastructure."

You haven't really improvised until you're taking off from the boondocks of Bangladesh, you hit a water buffalo on the runway, and the plane veers into swampland and sinks to its belly—and you've got sixty Republic Wright execs, including your own hypercritical older brother, aboard, and they're all due home in forty-eight hours. I got them home, and stayed out of jail, and Global still made money— but it was a *very* long forty-eight hours.

Meanwhile I kept my shuttle rating. For four years I was a reserve Air Force officer, so that I could get in my monthly fifteen hours of jet time, and I got up early on many mornings so I could use the shuttle simulator at Langley AFB to do that part of maintaining qualification. As space gradually privatized throughout the nineties, and launch systems operations were moved out of NASA and turned over to the newly created private corporation ASU, Global had increasing hopes of being able to rent *Columbia* for a flight and have me take up a load of passengers.

On my fortieth birthday, I took stock of where I had been and what I was doing. By most people's standards, I had had four successful careers, as a military pilot, astronaut, airline pilot, and airline exec, but I felt I had just completed my training. I wanted to start doing something that actually got people into space, and I wanted to start right away.

Three days later the phone rang. The first-generation astronaut who had promoted ShareSpace into being was ready to step down. He wanted someone with more of a day-to-day business-and-management perspective to take over, because with seats opening on the shuttle, the job would move from promotion to operations. "And when we started looking for a person to replace me," he said, "you seemed to have spent your life creating the perfect résumé for it."

I said I would take the job.

Four days later, I moved into my office. Three weeks after that, it was official—ShareSpace would be able to buy some seats from ASU, and plaque space on *Columbia*. We were in real business, we had things to sell, and we needed to start selling them now.

I'm not proud of how I handled that at home. Thalia had just launched the Coalition for Effective Justice, a group to push her ideas for how to make the criminal justice and prison systems work more effectively, and she didn't have much time. I can't claim I didn't know it would be a hard time for her—we had discussed it for more than a year before she made her move. But instead of supplying any stability, I suddenly grabbed a new job that was just as demanding as her new job, and dumped a load of new problems, issues, and crises into her lap and expected her to help out with them.

Probably a more sensitive man—or even one who thought about human relations at all—would have realized that it wasn't a good

thing to do that without at least some discussion with my wife. Whatever the reason, I just presented all the big changes to her as a fait
accompli, and expected that she would just adapt as she always had
before.

With both of us launching new careers, the changes hit hard and
fast. I had whole months living on yogurt, microwave burritos, and
Big Macs, dashing out of the house early and getting home long after
Amos was in bed, missing any appointment that wasn't business, skipping any chance of a normal social life. Once, for nine straight days,
I got home past midnight and left the house again at six. I was living
on a round of flights and phone calls, trying to make sure nothing
derailed getting Fred Gernsback into orbit. Meanwhile, Thalia was
struggling to get foundation funding for the Coalition, and to manage
the house and be, at least, more of a mother than I was a father. I
think she did better than I did at almost everything, but I truly didn't
have the energy or attention to see it.

One reason why I was always so exhausted in those days was
politics. I don't know anybody who genuinely does anything for a
living, whether it's flying spacecraft or mopping floors, who has any
use for politicians, and my first year at ShareSpace didn't make me
like them any better. Probably a quarter of the Senate, and maybe as
much as a third of the House, were avowedly hostile to what we were
doing. I was over on Capitol Hill or at various agency headquarters
almost every day, trying to make sure that all the deals stayed done.
Over and over, Congressman Brian "Bingo" Rasmussen and his gang
were getting on C-SPAN with speeches that rang with phrases like
"completely irresponsible use of national resources," "putting civilians
onto a barely controlled bomb," "wasting the taxpayer's dollar on toys
for the rich," and so forth.

Like any set of lies, it was built around a core of truth. Space
travel *is* dangerous. It takes big quantities of energy to get to LEO
and that energy has to be released fairly fast, and it *can* get out of
control, as it did on *Challenger*. Space has hazards—vacuum, radia-

tion, orbital collision—that have no equivalent on Earth. If enough heat shielding tiles were to peel off during re-entry, the shuttle could go from a billion-dollar marvel of technology to a tumbling shattered meteor before the crew could do anything to save themselves. The shuttle slams down onto the runway at a steep angle, and hits the pavement rolling about as fast as the race cars at Indy, and it lands powerless, so it can't go around for another pass if something doesn't look right.

But millions of people run risks every year, as part of daily life or even purely for recreation, that are far greater than those run by the shuttle crews. Skydivers, skiers, stock car racers, surfers, rock climbers, even just people driving on the freeway—all run bigger risks, and do it more often. I wasn't kidnapping people onto the shuttle, nor were Citizen Observers taking seats away from any other, more important, purpose—those seats would have flown empty without ShareSpace.

The high price we charged for a seat, finally, was what won enough wavering congressmen and senators to our side, and made the Clinton/Gore administrators, who didn't much like or care for anything connected with space, grudgingly accept it. ASU would get a high-paying customer—ShareSpace—and that would allow it to charge its government customer, NASA, a little less. On the whole, it looked like the taxpayers would come out ahead, and that was what mattered in the waning years of the Clinton Administration.

One day, I came out of one meeting, on my way to another three meetings, and Thalia was waiting for me. I stared at her, unsure what she could be doing here, afraid that perhaps Amos had been hurt.

She handed me a thick stack of papers, and when I looked down, I saw that she was petitioning for divorce. I looked back up at her impassive face, and couldn't think of anything to say. I finally asked if she wanted to talk about anything, and she said she thought it would be better if we just let the lawyers handle everything.

I don't know if it was better, but since she didn't want to talk, that day or later, I didn't see too many other options. I told the lawyer from Gordon and Gordon, the Blackstone family firm, to be generous and quibble about nothing. In turn, Thalia wasn't asking for much except to get this too-busy stranger out of her house, so that her life could be less chaotic.

Of course I was miserable, but the same lack of time and space in my life that led to the divorce also gave me a way to get through the bad time. ShareSpace always needed something done, all the time. A growing company isn't as warm and supportive as a family, but like a family it can consume nearly unlimited energy and much more time than you have. They say that being a workaholic is a hard addiction to shake because it's the only addiction that improves your life, and that was certainly true in my case for many months. The only time I relaxed was during my visitation times with Amos, when I more or less forced myself to park the phone somewhere else and get away completely. At least it made me look forward to visitations.

After a while, Thalia and I started speaking to each other again, almost always about Amos, and usually not very kindly or happily. It was better than the terse, sullen way we'd communicated just after I moved out, but not much better.

As the van rolled into Silver Spring, and I yawned and stretched and wondered what it was like to go to bed without setting an alarm, I realized that no matter how things went, my workaholic days were going to be numbered, and that I was coming to the end of that grimly determined part of my life. In the business community, and particularly in aerospace, ShareSpace was no longer regarded as a goofy start-up project doomed to failure, but as a serious venture with a known path of expansion. We would be staffing up substantially over the next few months, and there were now routine procedures for things that, a year ago, we'd still been making up case-by-case.

Every single step was not going to require the CEO's intervention, and some time and regularity would come back into my life. I knew I wanted to spend more time with Amos, but beyond that I wasn't sure what to do with a more conventional life. Maybe I should take a long vacation, or start a hobby, or try dating someone more seriously . . . perhaps I'd get some thinking done while I was down at the cabin with Amos, on the beach, ten days from now. Meanwhile, there was plenty to do. I picked up my cell phone, dialed my voice mail, and was rewarded with the phrase "Nineteen new messages. You last picked up messages at 10:50 P.M." With a sigh for the clear, crisp sunny fall day rolling past the van's windows, I got to work again.

CHAPTER TWO

SCOTT:

My third time through a ShareSpace Citizen Observer launch, I had the drill down cold. When I got to the office, I signed what had to be signed right then, looked at everything vital, and then sat down on the couch in the office, with the phone, and told Naomi I was in to all press and media calls. By the time I did that she had them stacked about ten deep, and after that I was on the phone, continually, with only brief breaks, for seven hours. I answered the same simple questions over and over, did my best to sound as if the question were a pleasant surprise each time, and kept firmly in mind that you never know when you're going out live from some big-transmitter station in the middle of the country, so you can't afford to sound like a jerk to anybody.

At 7:30, about two hours before launch time, I ducked into the small shower in the building, got clean and changed clothes, and went down to our press buffet, where we had set up a row of big-screen TVs and an array of food for the reporters who would be covering the event from our headquarters. I circulated around, shaking hands and talking to each of them.

A reporter is either eating from your hand, or eating you alive.

For the moment, our diligent PR campaign and our cultivation of the press was paying off, and the media people were acting like I was doing them a favor, instead of vice versa.

The TV reporters were all sort of half-there, with one eye on the screen, lost in the audio feed from their earpieces; they mostly kept an eye on their own organization's coverage, so that, if they were suddenly called to speak to the viewing audience, they would know their context.

The screen that drew the newspaper reporters was tuned to the feed from inside the shuttle, which let you watch MJ lick his lips, squirm to get more comfortable, and occasionally answer a question, probably from someone running through a checklist. I was glad he was smiling frequently, and still looked more excited than bored or frustrated; I didn't need another display of that temper today. (Naomi had been monitoring the news coverage, and it looked like Michael's dressing down of the gatecrasher with the rude question had not made it onto any major network news by that evening—which meant it probably never would.) That last hour of countdown was never my favorite part—everything was either dull, or trouble.

We had a "capture" button for the press, so that they could record a still off the video whenever they liked. When MJ looked at the camera and grinned at the same moment, one reporter slapped the capture button. "Got it," he said. "Page one everywhere tomorrow, eh?"

"Right under the big slug headline, unless something big breaks between now and one A.M.," the woman beside him agreed. "Great smile, with lots of hardware in the background."

Nodding at the still shot still hanging there on the monitor, with MJ beaming like a kid at Christmas, Naomi said to me, "That's been missing from space for a long time—that feeling that this is something *great* to do."

"Maybe it's been missing from everything for a while," I said.

"Just the idea of doing something because it's beautiful and fun and hard. How's the food holding up?"

"The reporters are nibbling and the crews are pounding it down, same as ever," Naomi said. "We'll be fine, Mr. Blackstone. The press reception is going just fine."

I kept circulating. Reporters kept soaking up free food and watching their own channels. The countdown crept downward. It was a publicity-perfect night launch, with a chance for some terrific photos.

Now all the screens showed *Columbia* in the harsh glare of the artificial lights, clouds of cold vapor rising around it. The gantry pulled back. The white glare burst from underneath the rocket as it began, slowly, to climb.

It never got old for me, and it never got completely comfortable, either. Having made three liftoffs myself, and seen more than I could easily remember, I stood there making sure I was grinning confidently, in case of any cameras pointed my way, but privately checking off each place where something could go wrong.

Nothing did. They stayed on trajectory. They rolled over on time. The solid boosters separated properly. All three SSME's, the main engines, kept running at the appropriate 104 percent power, carrying them right through each abort point. Finally, as they reached orbit, the SSME's shut down on the dot. It was a perfect launch. I didn't have to fake the grin anymore.

I became aware of a noise in the background—clapping and cheering. I accepted handshakes and pats on the back just as if I'd flown the shuttle myself, and made sure that everyone got as much champagne as they'd take.

The media had wanted to book every second of M J's time from liftoff to landing. ShareSpace and Pegasus had often had to remind the more aggressive ones that ASU and ShareSpace were private companies and therefore there was no "public right to know" involved. If they wanted some of Mr. James's time while he was in orbit, and he wanted to give it to them or sell it to them, he could do so, but even if we could compel him to provide them with endless free footage, we wouldn't.

M J declared that for his first orbit, he would not talk to the media; he said he was going to spend as much of that time as possible looking out the window. In retrospect, I've always been glad he did. Billy Kingston said he'd never seen anyone more excited and happy in all his life, or anyone who took to weightlessness more easily.

Meanwhile, down on Earth, I was keeping the press amused with as jolly a party as the budget of a small company allows. We had a teleconferencing uplink arranged so that M J could talk to all these people at once, but that wasn't scheduled till 11:30 P.M., still almost two hours away—time enough for him to have his first orbit, compose himself for the conference, and even get started on his official mission duty, taking photographs.

Our first two Citizen Observers had demonstrated that if a person shoots enough pictures, a few of them are bound to be interesting, and those few can then be sold as posters, rented to advertisers, distributed to the press, and so forth. A picture taken by Michael James, with his signature printed on the poster, should sell well, making us all some money, and a good set of slides could give him things to talk about, back on Earth, for decades of lectures.

You can't just shoot photographs through the window of the shuttle with a Wal-Mart disposable camera and expect to get much. The special glass is extremely thick, so that anything not directly in line with the camera lens appears distorted; glare is severe; contrasts between bright and dark are far greater than anything on Earth. Most of all, it's hard to know what you're seeing—one tall snow-peaked mountain, one blue winding river in a deep green plain, one shimmering white-brown desert streaked with shadows by the sunset, tends to look very much like another.

Thus we'd had to commission one piece of new technology, the only one so far that ShareSpace had had to develop for itself. The

"CO camera" was a small miracle of self-correcting lens trains, adjusting polarizers, GPS and IR receivers, and gyrocompasses, plus a dedicated microprocessor that constantly knew the position of the camera in space, and the direction it was pointing, so that as the shutter clicked, the camera wrote a slugline at the bottom: time; altitude, latitude, and longitude of the shuttle; and latitude and longitude of the center of the picture. The camera always knew and recorded what you had photographed, from where, and when.

During the second orbit, before his conference with the reporters, MJ was supposed to use the CO camera to take two practice shots through the front window, so that the first shots on the roll would be dramatic. Then Marc Clement was supposed to take two pictures of MJ floating by each corporate plaque inside the shuttle, so that the sponsors got what they had paid for.

A modest complication was added while I was at the reception—Perry Lager, my customer-service guy, called me and said that he'd had a request from many of the sponsors for the very first picture on the roll to be a shot of MJ floating beside the wall of plaques, instead. At the rate they were paying, some of them were anxious to make sure that their logo got the full treatment, and it was no problem to do it.

I went into the bathroom, where I hoped no one would notice I had a phone contact going on with MJ, and called the patch-through number at Houston. In a minute, I had Michael on the line, and I relayed the request.

"No problem, man, no problem at all." His voice was full of pure glee; if there were a drug that could get you as high as he sounded, we'd all be addicts.

"Are you having a good time, Michael?"

"The best. The absolute best. I love it up here and I love all of you. Thanks for calling—we'll get you that shot."

"Thank you, MJ," I said, and we hung up.

As I came out of the stall, a short, balding dark-haired man in a blue suit emerged from the next stall. "I bet you came in here so that we wouldn't all jump at your phone and shout questions."

"That's right."

"Well, I didn't. But I *did* eavesdrop. Would you mind telling me what he said when you asked if he was having a good time?"

"He said he was bored stiff, he wanted to come home, and that kids everywhere in America should stop drinking milk, sass their parents, and take buckets of drugs."

The guy laughed out loud. "Serves me right." He stuck out his hand. "I'm Ken Elgin. *USReport*. I'll behave and save my questions for the press conference."

I thanked him. We went back out into the reception area and got sandwiches. He knew space issues well, so we ended up doing a little impromptu interview. Most of the other reporters were still busy eating, drinking, and watching the screens, but Nikki Earl came over and taped parts of what I said, too. I was just explaining how a "space hotel"—basically a one-launch space station that was set up to cater to tourists—could easily be a prototype for the living quarters of a ship that could go to Mars, when the room fell terribly silent.

Naomi ran forward and turned up the volume on FBN. Fred Gernsback was just saying, "We are guessing, from the last minute of radio traffic, that something has gone seriously wrong on the space shuttle *Columbia*." For half an hour afterwards, except for Gernsback booming through the TV monitor, there was nothing but silence as the terrible news poured in.

SOMETIMES I STILL have nightmares about it. Probably I always will. I went over the evidence and the recordings more times than I can count. I knew what the cockpit and crew area of *Columbia* looked like. I knew all the crew well. It's hard for me to remember that I wasn't actually there myself—it feels like I was there and like I remember every moment.

The crew had gotten into coveralls and was settling into its normal work routine. The big payload bay doors were open, and the automated experiments in the bay were up and running. Billy Kingston called everyone to the mid deck, where they floated in a small group, hanging on to seats as needed. The commander read off the checklist of tasks.

Most astronauts, most of the time, are not only scientists and pilots, but also medical test animals. The environment of space is still new, and it's still customary to do a whole battery of medical tests on every member of every crew, building up a collection of data for space medicine. Usually one of the first jobs in orbit is to draw each other's blood samples and record vital signs.

Marc Clement and MJ went first, drawing each other's blood and taking each other's temperatures and blood pressures. Josh Pritkin and Damian Agustino were scheduled to go next, and sat waiting their turn and teasing the other two. Meanwhile, Billy Kingston was slated to be a test subject for some experiments Lorena Charette was running in the LBNP—"lower body negative pressure"—device, a gadget disliked by many astronauts, that reduces air pressure on the lower part of your body and thus redistributes blood and other fluids for some experiments on the effects of weightlessness.

The only person concerned directly with shuttle operations was Wes Packard, who, as primary pilot for the mission, had the first watch in the pilot's chair. Normally, on a shuttle mission, that job is dull—while the shuttle is orbiting and not under power, there's very little "steering" or "flying" to do, and the pilot's seat can be left unattended for minutes at a time. Wes sipped at a bulb of coffee and watched the Earth roll by underneath.

"Well, according to all this, we're both still alive, so I guess we have to keep working," Marc Clement said, swimming back forward with MJ behind him. "Your turn, guys."

Pritkin and Agustino glanced at each other, shrugged, and began to take their own measurements.

MJ got the camera out of the locker, switched it on, and looked over the indicator lights. Everything was green. "Looks like we're ready for the pictures."

"Can you keep an eye on the pilot's chair while you're doing that, Marc?" Wes asked.

"Sure."

Wes unbuckled. "Then just a second, let me get past you. My coffee's coming through." Wes swam back to the head and closed the door.

"All clear," M J said. "Okay, let me get in front of those plaques— or I guess more to the side, I'm probably not supposed to hide any of them—all right, show time."

He passed the camera in a gentle toss to Marc, who caught it easily.

Marc positioned himself, bumping with his hands to get the right angle, before pointing the camera. "Hang on a second . . . real good."

"Let me get stopped," M J said. He was now slowly rotating. "I want this shot *perfect*."

He brought himself to a stop in the new position. Marc said, "Okay, your position is perfect and you're still. I've got all the plaques in the frame. Looking good. Give me your biggest smile."

"That'll be easy because—"

A *crack-boom!* reverberated through the ship. Billy Kingston and Lorena Charette both said it sounded more like a small cannon than a big rifle; in the tiny confined space of the shuttle, it was deafening.

The klaxon for pressure loss was going off. Kingston pushed out of the LBNP and scrambled forward, bellowing "What's going on?" Charette followed. They arrived in the forward area as Wes came out of the toilet and bounced to the pilot's seat.

Marc Clement was tumbling end over end, his head wobbling at a sickening angle; his face was crushed as if he had been rammed into a wall at great speed. M J floated against one wall, eyes and mouth wide open, blood drifting out of his mouth and a hole in his chest. His eyes were distended and bloodshot, sinking back to normal size even as they first saw him. Spheres of his blood bobbed around the cabin.

Kingston swam to him and felt his neck for a pulse; as he did, he saw there was a much larger hole between the big man's shoulder blades. Whatever had happened had killed him at once. Blood had splashed across the wall of plaques, and in the middle of the smear, sucking blood out into space, was a hole about a quarter inch in diameter. Kingston rammed his baseball cap into the hole, poking it in with a pen from his pocket until he could stuff it no further.

A moment later the klaxon turned off, and then the terrible silence was broken by Josh Pritkin saying, "Jesus, what happened?"

Lorena Charette snapped, "Over here, Josh, Damy. Marc's got a broken neck but he's alive. I'm trying to hold his spinal cord in line here. Josh, get me my kit. Damy, come here and help me support him."

Wes Packard said, "Pressure breach. We lost about three hundred pounds of air in less than two minutes, and we've still got a slow leak, with pressure dropping. We're yawing a little, no pitch or roll—basically we're in a slow flat spin."

"Wait till I have Marc stabilized before you correct," Lorena said.

"Roger."

"I've got at least one leak here," Kingston said, "with my hat stuffed into it. How's cabin pressure?"

"About a third of an atmosphere," Packard said.

Charette grunted with irritation. "We've got to get that higher, soon. The only reason we don't have anybody passed out is that we're all hyperventilating."

"Everyone who isn't helping with Marc, get into pressure suits, ASAP," Kingston said. "Trade off as soon as you're suited up." He climbed up on the mid deck to get his own from the rack. A moment later, Packard and Pritkin were suiting up beside him. "Is there anything we can do for Marc? M J is dead—no pulse and something went right through him."

"Just a sec," Charette said. A moment later, Charette and Agustino were suiting up. "We've got Marc secured into a bunk with his head tied down to keep his neck straight. He's in a bad way but it's hard to tell how bad. I'll do a trake on him, right now, because his breathing isn't good and I think there's a crushing injury to the neck. Damy, you be nurse."

"Tie M J down somewhere," Kingston said, quietly, to Pritkin, and then moved forward to the copilot's chair. "Okay, I'd better give them the bad news. Wes, get working on where we can do an emergency landing. No water ditch, and no rough country, even if we have to stay up a few extra minutes."

The shuttle doesn't float, and it lands too fast and hard to put down on water, or on any land that isn't a paved runway, without breaking up. Standard procedure for an emergency is for the crew to bail out once they are low and slow enough. With a crew member with a broken neck, they couldn't evacuate the shuttle; they would have to land it, somehow.

Packard pulled a laptop computer from its slot beside his chair, and began to work on the problem. Distantly, Kingston heard Lorena Charette saying, "Okay, here goes, get that suction in close." He took a deep breath, made sure he was on secure channel, and spoke into the radio. "Houston, we have an emergency situation here, hull breach, other unknown damage, one crew member dead, one severely injured. We're going for an emergency deorbit and a landing at the nearest emergency field—"

"Easter Island," Packard whispered. "Start burn in nine minutes."

"Nearest emergency field is Easter Island. Request all the emergency help you can get there, ASAP. Injured crew member has spinal cord injury. We're starting deorbit burn in—" he looked at the laptop Wes held up "—eight minutes ten seconds."

"Roger, *Columbia*, you are go. Be advised weather at Easter Island is clear. We're praying for you."

*　　*　　*

I HAD MORE chairs brought in. The caterer called out an emergency order of food and coffee. Our conference room had plenty of data links, and we allocated them to the reporters as evenly as we could. But after we made things as comfortable for the press and media as we could, we still could do nothing about what they needed most: some idea about what was going on.

Every news division had gone to live coverage at once. Since there was no information, they filled airtime by reviewing everything every couple of minutes, and called every possible field reporter over and over to confirm that nothing was happening in the field as well. Television reporters at ShareSpace's now suddenly somber press reception took turns standing in front of the ShareSpace corporate logo to recite, again, that no one here had any idea, sometimes adding that Scott Blackstone was right here and had promised to pass on information the moment he had it.

"HIS NECK IS broken, the front of his skull is crushed, and I don't see any way he can have missed spinal cord damage, but he's breathing on his own now that we have an oxygen tube going in through the tracheotomy," Lorena Charette said. "We have him immobilized as best we can, but even a perfect landing will probably kill him. You might as well start your maneuvers."

"Do it," Kingston said.

Without a word, or a glance at his crewmates, Wes Packard set his hands on the controls and applied the reaction control thrusters to stop the yaw and bring the shuttle into position for deorbit burn, with its tail pointed in the direction they were orbiting. "Burn starts in seven minutes. Get the payload doors closed and get strapped into those seats quick, people."

Everyone hurried to strap in. Pritkin and Agustino stopped going over the plaque wall, where they had been gathering up and bagging the blood droplets, stray bits of metal and flesh, and other shattered objects in the compartment, and started the automated sequence to shut down the experiments and close the big doors.

"What's our damage situation?" Kingston asked, over his shoulder.

"We were still working on it," Agustino said, "but it looks like damage was just that hole in the hull, the camera, and two crew members. It's lucky the hole is over the wing, not on the underside. We'd be in a real mess if we'd had a big hole in the tiles."

Kingston grunted. "I hate the idea of Easter Island but the next place after it would be most of an hour, and it's just an old bomber runway in western Siberia—we *know* that one hasn't been maintained, and there'd be nobody there to meet us or help Marc. At least people *say* they've maintained the strip on Easter Island."

An orbiting shuttle doesn't have much choice about where it goes. The enormous load of fuel that it takes off with is almost entirely burned in getting to orbit, and, for safety, what remains is jettisoned shortly after. Because the shuttle orbit is tipped at an angle to Earth's equator, in addition to going around the Earth it swings north and south of the equator by hundreds or thousands of miles. During the time it takes to make an orbit, the Earth turns through anywhere from 20 to 30 degrees of longitude, so that every orbit shifts to the west of the one that preceded it, drawing a kind of giant sine wave across the map of the Earth. A shuttle that passes over Chattanooga on this orbit will pass over Albuquerque on the next orbit, and won't pass over Chattanooga again for twenty-four hours. The Orbital Maneuvering System thrusters are small, and the Reaction Control System thrusters are even smaller. The shuttle can alter its trajectory only very slightly, and so it can land only on fields that are very close to its orbital path. Furthermore, since the shuttle lands as a glider, without thrust for a go-around, everything has to work right the first time.

There is a system of landing fields for the shuttle all around the world, in case of emergency, but not all are equally good. The main landing fields at Edwards Air Force Base in California and KSC in Florida are well-maintained and their crews are experienced. The field at Zaragosa, Spain, is nearly as good. But those were all out of reach.

Easter Island is something else again: a small dot on the map of the South Pacific, owned by Chile, one of the few Pacific islands on a regular flight path with room enough for a long, wide runway, but without much else. It was hardly the ideal place to come down with a damaged ship and a badly injured crewman.

"What do you think it was?" Damian asked. He was strapping into his seat; there were still seventy-five seconds left till time to begin the burn.

Packard shrugged. "Looks like the classic profile for a micrometeoroid, doesn't it? All the damage is in a straight line, and whatever it was hit with enough force to pass through the hull, right through M J's chest, into the camera, and drive the last bits of the camera into Marc's head so hard it broke his neck. That looks like a very high velocity impact to me."

"Micrometeoroid or space junk," Pritkin added, as he rechecked his suit.

ASU Mission Control called then to ask for definitive information before making a press announcement, and Billy Kingston relayed their speculation about what had hit them, along with the news that Michael James was dead and Marc Clement very seriously injured.

WITHIN A COUPLE of minutes, an ASU executive was talking to the James family, and ASU had notified me privately. Ten minutes later, the whole planet knew, and world phone traffic set new records. I stood in front of the reporters and had to keep saying, "All I know is what Mission Control tells me, and what they are telling me is that Michael James was killed in an accident, Marc Clement was seriously injured and his survival remains in doubt, the shuttle was damaged, and they are going to try to land on the emergency field on Easter Island. That's all they've told me. ShareSpace is not in the chain of command for the mission, and this is all need-to-know information. I'll share everything they give me, but right now they are not giving me any more than that."

Nikki Earl waved a hand. "The crew is speculating that it may have been a micrometeoroid or a piece of space debris. For our listeners, could you just explain what those are and how they might be dangerous?"

It was a relief to have the chance to say something other than what I had been repeating for several minutes. "Micrometeoroids are meteors too small for radar to see—anywhere from the size of a pea down to the size of grain of sand. They're moving at very high velocities—twenty or more times the speed of a bullet—and so they hit with tremendous force. There aren't very many of them relative to all the empty space, and there's never been a known accident caused by one, but sooner or later something was bound to be hit.

"Space debris is stuff that got left up there from past space missions— bits and pieces of everything, broken-off bolts and screws and chips of paint, tools that escaped from building ISS, dead rocket upper stages, lots of other things. It's not usually moving as fast as a micrometeoroid, but it's still several times bullet speed, and most of it's bigger, and there's more of it. People have talked for decades about the need to clear that out, but no one's ever really done much more than think about the problem. Anyway, if the *Columbia* ran into either a micrometeoroid or a piece of debris, it probably went right through the skin of the ship—and anything else in its path—and that could certainly kill someone and damage the ship. Billy Kingston and his crew are there, and I'm not, and if their guess is that it's an impact accident, then that's probably the best guess that we're going to have for a while."

Nikki nodded and gestured to indicate that she had something coming in through her earpiece.

A couple of the cable networks kept asking me how I felt, and all

I could do was keep telling them that like everyone else on Earth I felt overwhelming grief at the loss of Michael James, but having known him for several months as a friend, that it was hard to believe he was gone, and that I would miss him terribly. By making me repeat it, they got me more and more bothered, so that after a while I was blinking back tears. Perhaps that's what they really wanted, anyway.

The long minutes crawled by; finally it was time for the landing on Easter Island. Luckily for the American networks, a Chilean TV crew was there on another story, and they'd hurried to the emergency landing field and patched into satellite feed.

Easter Island is on Pacific Coast Time, minus a half hour, so it was about an hour after sunset when *Columbia* made her attempt. The runway was bright from the landing lights, the sky pitch black above it. The TV camera watched from near the end of the runway, where the shuttle would come to rest if the landing succeeded. We had managed to patch into their audio, but since I didn't speak Spanish, I had no idea what they were talking about.

For a moment it looked like the other shuttle night landings—a flash of white as the shuttle slid into the lights, a graceful suspended instant as it glided in and touched down. The ship leveled off and began to roll down the runway.

The nose wheel slammed into a pothole on top of a soft pocket, and the landing gear twisted sideways and collapsed. Still moving forward at a hundred miles an hour, the shuttle nosed down, the broken landing gear tipping it to one side. Then the nose bit into the crumbling pavement, and her tail bucked far up into the air as she slid down the runway, sparks flying and trailing tiles and bits of fuselage. The tail slammed back down, lifting the nose for a moment, and the shuttle skidded sideways out of control before the right-side landing gear buckled. *Columbia* slumped sideways, spinning another quarter turn before coming to a rest on the crumpled mess that had been the nose, with one wing broken against the ground, and one badly bent landing gear holding up the other side. Sirens wailed in the background as we watched the image of the shattered *Columbia* bounce around and grow larger; the Chilean camera crew, on the back of a pickup truck, was driving toward it.

The hatch on the side fell open. Slowly, painfully, the five survivors climbed out, pulling off their helmets. They just stood there, a few feet from the wreckage, staring at their smashed and battered spacecraft.

A minute later, medics rushed into the shuttle, and shortly afterwards they confirmed that Marc Clement had died during the re-entry or the crash.

The networks endlessly reran that crash, between reporters talking in front of an image of poor, broken *Columbia* lying in the glare of the sodium lights. I spent the next hour expressing my regrets and saying that the whole thing was terrible, so many times that I was afraid I would slur or rush it or sound like I didn't mean it. Finally the reporters left, and the caterer's staff were allowed to clean the place up. As we half-stumbled out, I noticed that Naomi's face was red from crying.

I had nowhere else to go, so I just drove back to the drab, lonely house that I had gotten after the divorce. All the art and the newer furniture had stayed at the house with Thalia and Amos. I had a scattered collection of used furniture between bare white walls. It had never looked more empty.

I poured a diet Coke, sat down on my couch, and pulled out a video called *M J! Grace Flies High!*—a collection of clips of his amazing ball handling and shooting. I watched him, the way he would laugh and smile when another one went in, the way he flowed through opposing players to get at the ball, "the most physically sublime athlete of our age," as Jorge Wimme had called him in a famous essay. Tears ran down my face. I didn't bother to brush them off.

At 2:30 or so I took a shower, as hot as it would go, and went to bed. I fell right asleep, but when the alarm went off and I sat up in the gray pre-dawn, I felt like I hadn't slept at all.

CHAPTER THREE

SCOTT:

I'd have to meet with the board, who would not be happy. In my head, on the drive over to the office, I outlined what I would have to say to them, so that I could dictate it that morning and be ready to deliver it that afternoon. We would have to tough this one out and spend more than we ever planned on PR, marketing, and advertising, and we'd have to manage much longer than we'd planned on without the big revenues of selling tickets into space. But the only way we were likely to lose everything would be to give up now. Those seemed to be the important points.

By the time I was turning the car into the ShareSpace parking lot, I had worked out what I would say to reassure all the staff from the secretaries and custodians right on up through my three VP's. They were all good people, anyway, not prone to panic. Probably by midmorning we could have everyone thoroughly on task for the difficult days ahead.

When I arrived at 7:30, half an hour earlier than usual, Naomi, who was crying and wouldn't look me in the eye, told me that the Board was already in the conference room holding a meeting.

I walked in on them. They seemed to be dripping with embarrassment. My first thought on seeing their wide stares and hasty turning away was that they had voted for something stupid and panicky, were already regretting it, and wanted me to talk them into reversing it.

A moment later, Norm Aquinas, my VP for finance—and now the CEO of ShareSpace—told me. There had been a unanimous vote to fire me and put Norm in my place.

Well, it was their circus, and they could fire any clown they wanted to. I had nothing to say, so I got out of there.

In my office, the security guards, being as nice about it as they could, were piling all the stuff from the desk into "personal" and "company." They also had a pile they wanted me to sort for them.

That took about half an hour. It's weird to sit in a chair and at a desk that aren't yours anymore, while a bunch of people who used to work for you make sure you don't steal any pieces of what used to be your life.

When I was finished, Gerry Richland, whom I'd hired personally and who had been with ShareSpace for three years, said, "They told me to check to make sure you're not taking any company documents. I ain't gonna do it. Damn, I'm sorry about all this, Mr. Blackstone."

"Me too. What time did they get in?"

"I guess there were three outside people they wanted to meet with, and those guys said they wanted to meet at six in the morning, so that's when the Board got here."

"Outside people?" I asked, not really curious.

"I don't know who they were, Mr. Blackstone, most guys in suits look alike to me—they look like trouble."

"Well, this time you were right," I said. They might have been PR consultants, or lawyers—almost anybody with some sense about publicity or law might have told them that getting rid of me would help save ShareSpace. Objectively speaking, they might be right.

Three boxes held four years of my life. Gerry, the other guard, and I each carried a box down to the parking lot. I put them in the trunk of the BMW, shook hands with the two guards and wished them well, got behind the wheel, and, having nothing else to do, went home, taking side streets and going slow. I wasn't eager to get back to the place where I slept and kept the television and fridge. Amos would be on his way to school by now, so I couldn't call him at Mrs. Talbert's. I could try my brother Nick, but he and I didn't talk much anymore. Besides, on any given day I didn't know whether to call him at his satellite office in DC, at the main Republic Wright Aircraft office in San Diego, or via the private line into RW's Advanced Projects Facility. Wherever he was, he'd probably be too busy to talk anyway.

I even thought about seeing if Thalia would talk to me; we often fought about petty things, but she was probably the person who understood me best, and maybe Thalia would be willing to listen, or say "I'm sorry," or suggest something or other that I could do. But Thalia was in California, on Coalition business, and wouldn't be back till late this afternoon. We had each other's cell phone numbers, but those were strictly for emergencies involving Amos. Maybe I'd try calling her on Saturday or Sunday, at some convenient time—Amos had said she'd be home—if I still felt so raw and miserable.

Thinking of my son had made me think about that last phone conversation with MJ, and that had brought the whole terrible mess home to me again. I couldn't quite figure out what to do with myself just yet. Maybe I'd go to a movie or something. It looked like I was going to have time on my hands.

When I pulled into my driveway, I found a small mob of media types on my lawn. Ken Elgin and Nikki Earl were the only people I recognized. Even this early in the morning, the camera crews still had enough energy to run in and out of the flower beds and shrubs, trampling everything flat.

As I got out of the car, the NBC guy led off with "Congressman Rasmussen has issued a statement—if I may read you a brief part of it—and I thought you might care to comment. He says, 'It is not the job of civilians to get killed in space. Furthermore, since a civilian with very little training was given important responsibilities on this mission, it is clear that this accident could have been prevented.' Any comment, Mr. Blackstone?"

I cleared my throat. "I don't know, yet, what caused the accident," I said, "and neither does Congressman Rasmussen. But everything sounds like they ran into something, probably space debris, maybe a micrometeoroid. Neither the ground crews nor the shuttle crew themselves could have seen that coming. It would have happened no matter who was on board the shuttle or what they were doing."

Nikki Earl asked, "You said last night that at those speeds even a paint chip or a loose washer is dangerous?"

"*Very* dangerous," I said. "At orbital speeds, even a tiny object hits with many, many times the energy of a bullet from a gun. With an object the size of a pea in an orbit that's tens of thousands of miles long, traveling at several miles per second, you really can't keep track of it well enough to duck it every time. All you can do is hope you won't meet up with it, and that's all anyone has ever been able to do. Sooner or later our luck was bound to run out. It was absolutely unpreventable, and I think it's a disgrace that Congressman Rasmussen chooses to blame M J, or any of the regular crew, for the accident. It could have happened on any flight, to any crew, any time. It's terrible that it happened this time."

One advantage to losing my job, I realized, was that I could say what I was thinking, so after a pause, I added something. "It's especially appalling that Congressman Rasmussen, who has no facts about the case, and wouldn't be able to understand them if he did, has rushed to judgment and blamed the dead." I felt better for having said that.

"Can we quote you on that?" the CNN reporter asked, pushing her hair back from her face.

"I hope you put it on the six o'clock news, right after you run Bingo's statement," I said. "This was a terrible tragedy. Space is dangerous and will always be dangerous. That's why we make people sign so many waivers."

"What are the odds that anyone will ever be able to identify the object that did the damage?" Ken Elgin asked.

"Pretty poor," I said. "Parts of it will have vaporized, and the impact scattered a lot of other material around the cabin—bits of shuttle wall and of everything it went through." I realized I had just implied "bits of M J" and hurried on, hoping no one would notice. "And the shuttle wrecked on landing, so very likely some gravel and small junk got loose in the cabin during that, making it harder to pick out which object is the one that did it. I assume right now that NASA's investigators are looking into all the possibilities, but we'll have to wait till there are more facts. Not being a congressman, I don't proceed further than the facts will take me."

The first questions had gone pretty well, I thought, but I still didn't like the look of this crowd—apprentices and B-teamers, very few business reporters, no science reporters—their surest road to advancement would be to really nail somebody, anybody—me.

Well, all the same, if you didn't tell the complete truth as you knew it, you were in ten times worse trouble. So, though what I really felt like doing was going inside, getting under the covers, and not coming out till Christmas, I looked around and said, "I'll be happy to answer questions after I get my personal stuff moved into my garage. For that matter you can talk to me while I carry these boxes in. It won't take long. Do you all know that I've been fired as CEO of ShareSpace?"

There was a startled silence, and then Nikki Earl stepped forward, holding out her recorder, and said, "Uh, no, Mr. Blackstone, I don't think any of us had any idea. Did they give a reason?"

"Good of the organization," I said, "the same reason anyone is given when they're fired. They didn't tell *me* anything other than to clear out my desk and go."

"Well, *that's* tacky," Ken Elgin muttered.

"Any other questions?" I asked.

They all looked at each other, and finally Nikki Earl shrugged and said, "I think if you already knew what we came here about, you'd have brought the subject up yourself, so I guess I'm elected to tell you this. Mr. Blackstone, the family of Michael James announced, this morning, that they will be suing you, ShareSpace, ASU, Curtiss Aerospace, Republic Wright, and NASA, for a just over a billion dollars. That's what they say he would have earned with his endorsements and appearances in the rest of his life."

My guts dropped a foot. I felt cold all over. All I could do was stare, for a long breath, before I finally I managed to say, "I know nothing about it as yet. You'll have to ask the James family what their intentions are. If I am being sued, I'll need to talk to an attorney before I say anything else."

"Then you haven't heard or seen AnnaBeth James's statement to the press this morning?"

"No, I haven't. I don't think I should talk till I do. That wouldn't do either me or the James family any good."

"Why are you worried about what will do you good? Why aren't you worried about what happened in the accident?" the man who shouted the question at me came up very close; he was making sure we'd both be in the video frame.

"I don't think the investigation will be helped if I start commenting on things I haven't seen or heard for myself. To my knowledge today, no one was even careless, let alone malicious. I'll tell you whatever I can whenever I learn it, but since I've been fired, my access to information is no better than yours."

"Sir! You were responsible for the completely unprecedented event of a global celebrity going on the space shuttle as a paying passenger, and that was followed immediately by an actual collision in orbit, the first one!" The aggressive way he delivered that made me wonder if he thought I had insulted him with my answer to his previous question.

"If you'll phrase that as a question," I said, walking back to my car, opening my trunk, and getting out the first box, "I'll answer it."

"Sir, it's a simple yes or no question."

"I don't know what yes or no would mean in response to the statement you just made," I persisted. I carried the box to the garage door, clicked the automatic opener, and carried it in to put it on a worktable.

I had closed my trunk; when I got back to the car several of them had cameras and faces pressed up against the car windows. One guy was working a screwdriver under my trunk lid. "Don't damage the paint, all right?" I said, coming up on him quickly so that he'd be visible in a couple of the TV camera views. Not that they would air it.

"Sir, are you going to answer the question?"

"When you phrase it as a question, so that I know what you're asking."

"Isn't it obvious that there *must* be a connection between the unprecedented decision to fly a major celebrity into space, and the unprecedented loss of a shuttle due to an accident in orbit?"

For an instant I wondered how Fred Gernsback or Senator Glenn would feel about being classed as "not major celebrities," but that didn't seem like a good response to the question. I unlocked the trunk, got out the second box, and slammed the trunk lid down quickly enough that a couple of people had to yank their heads and cameras back quickly. "Well, no, there doesn't have to be a connection. The only thing that Michael James going to orbit, and the orbital accident, had in common was that they were unprecedented events on the same flight, as far as anyone knows. More investigation is needed, but this has all the signs of just being a terrible accident, which would have happened no matter who was on board *Columbia*."

"Mr. Blackstone," Nikki Earl asked, "with one shuttle gone, are there going to be any more seats for space tourism?"

I carried the second box into the garage. "Probably not until some private passenger spacecraft enters the market."

"Do you think it was worth it?" someone shouted, from behind me.

"Having been there three times myself, I can say that I'd have run that risk to have that experience, myself. Ask Fred Gernsback or David Calderon, for that matter." I set the box down on the worktable and turned around to face the mob that had poured in behind me; I was certainly glad I'd never been the type to have pinups in the garage. The cameras kept running, pointed at two oil-change kits, a cluttered workbench, and a box of fishing gear I hadn't touched in ten years. I almost felt sorry for how hard they were working to get so little.

When they had backed through the door, I closed it and got the last box from the car.

"So you don't feel that there is any responsibility or blame for you in the death of a man who was loved by millions?" one woman demanded, holding the microphone up to my face as she walked backwards in front of me.

"I didn't say that. Like everyone else, I want to know how this happened. When we know that, we'll know who, if anyone, to blame."

"Will ShareSpace be issuing any statements?"

"I'm sure they'll have to, but I no longer work for them and they no longer tell me anything. Look," I said, "give me your business cards. I will either call you individually, or set up a press conference, as soon as I have any information or a public statement. You will be first in line for anything I have."

It was odd how few of them looked me in the eye as they handed me their cards. By the time I had rubber-banded the stack of cards together and dropped it into my coat pocket, they were loading up vans and cars and leaving. Ken and Nikki, since he worked for a news magazine and she worked for a radio network, had no big crew to take with them, so they hung back until the others had gone, and then took a moment to express some sympathy. I smiled slightly and said, "I may be in more of a hurry to call either of you than the rest of the press."

"It's what we call developing a contact," Nikki said. "Lord, they trampled your yard. Hope your gardener likes a challenge."

Ken sighed. "Put a TV camera on anyone's shoulder and they immediately feel free to go anywhere and do anything."

After they left, I lay down on the couch and tried to nap. I couldn't, so I mostly just stared at the ceiling and tried to think of what, if anything, I could have done differently. After a while I wasn't thinking about Michael, but about Thalia, and Amos, and all the friends I'd lost track of. That didn't help my mood either.

The doorbell rang. I lurched off the couch, running a hand over my hair, and opened the door.

It was the papers for the James family's suit. I saw numbers that were even bigger than the billion dollars I had expected. Killing a celebrity, even by accident, is not cheap.

The James family had hired Jasper Haverford. I rarely follow crime stories or celebrity news, but *I* had heard of Jasper Haverford. I leaned back in the chair, sighed, tried to think of what to do. I'd have to get a lawyer.

Probably it could wait an hour. I turned on the television for distraction, but the first thing I clicked to was AnnaBeth James's press conference.

She looked just as terrible as I'd imagined. I doubted she had slept in the time between the accident and the press conference eighteen hours later. Michael's three sisters, beside her, looked no better, all of them crying.

AnnaBeth James read her statement from a typewritten page, stopping now and then to regain control of her feelings. "Our family always supported Michael in whatever he did. My husband Allen never missed a single game of Michael's, up to the day he died. His sisters and I have always stood behind whatever Michael wanted to do. And we knew how much space always meant to him. So when he told us he wanted to go into space for Pegasus, we were so happy for him. But we have learned that neither he nor we were properly informed of the dangers. There was negligence on the part of ShareSpace in selling the tickets, especially on the part of Scott Blackstone, the president and CEO of ShareSpace. He, and ShareSpace, and every other organization named in our suit should have taken steps to make sure we were aware of the danger. Lack of information, and outright misinformation, directly affected Michael's decision to fly on the *Columbia*.

"These individuals and organizations created an atmosphere in which what was actually an extremely dangerous, high-risk activity was portrayed as reasonable and safe for anyone.

"Furthermore, the whole activity of sending civilians into space was portrayed to us individually and to the public in general as a positive, desirable project. We know now it was a commercial boondoggle whose only purpose was to enrich Scott Blackstone and the ShareSpace investors, to get favorable publicity for a government agency and the major aerospace contractors, and to provide the media with an exciting story.

"My son died in a deadly mix of shortsighted greed, reckless disregard for safety, media hype, and outright lying, amplified by private corporate deception and a government cover-up. I have no further comments at this time." She walked away; Jasper Haverford draped his coat around her shoulders, and the camera zoomed in to get a shot of his perfect staging of the grieving mother and of the strong man supporting her.

"Well," one of the commentators said, "that was heartbreaking. It clearly points up the terrible, terrible disaster this is, and how much the American people need to know, right away, that those responsible for this will pay."

My heart sank. I clicked the remote and shut off the TV. I looked down into my lap, at the papers I had been served a few minutes before. I wanted to phone AnnaBeth James, but it was too late emotionally, and probably a bad idea legally.

I sat there for a long time, facing the blank television. It wasn't even noon yet.

At least I could try to find a lawyer. I left a message on the family law firm's machine, made a sandwich, and ate it without tasting it. The crunching sound from my food seemed terribly loud in the very empty house. I wished I'd either kept a couple of paintings, or maybe bought some new ones.

About twenty minutes after I had left the message, the phone rang. It was Harry Gordon, who mostly handled things like deeds, property transfers, wills, administering trust funds, and so forth for the Blackstone family. "To tell you the truth," he said, "I don't think much of our trial lawyers here; mostly we write documents to keep people out of court. We aren't the right ones for your situation. And I'm not sure I know who the right ones would be. I'll ask around and get back to you."

"Thanks for doing that for me, Harry."

"It's what you pay a retainer for. I'll see what I can turn up. How's Nick? Has he checked in with you?"

"Uh, not yet," I said. "We don't see much of each other anymore."

"Ah, that's a shame," Harry said. "Times like this, you need relatives and friends. And it seems really strange to me that you're not in touch; remember when I had the beach cabin not too far from your dad's? You and Nick and Thalia and—what was that other kid's name?"

"Eddie Killeret," I said, automatically. "Yeah, we were all pretty close, back then. But it was a long time ago, Harry," I said.

"Well, yeah. Funny how it's kids who make friends so easily, and adults who need them so badly," Harry said. "Anyway, I will do my best to find the right guy to take your case, and I'll try to move fast on it. I'll at least give you a progress report by end of day today."

While I waited for Harry to call back, I leaned back in my chair and let myself just think. Me, Nick, Thalia, and Eddie. Inseparables, for a few summers as kids. Dad had referred to us as "the club," and we had called ourselves the Mars Four, but the Mars Four was not exactly a club. I don't think we ever even tried to figure out what it was. It had just been something we talked about, something we identified ourselves as. . . .

My mind drifted back, and if longing or wishing could make a thing so, I'd have stepped right onto that Virginia beach again, back when life was so much simpler and so much less complicated.

WHEN WE KIDS had formed the Mars Four, we had known each other as long as we could remember. Our parents' summer cabins on the Virginia beach were within a hundred yards of each other, and the families had started coming to the beach before I was born; Nick and Eddie, the oldest of the Mars Four, could each just barely remember that there had been a first summer and that they had met then. For Thalia and me, the summer cabins had always been there.

The Mars Four idea probably hit me harder than any of the others. We came up with it in the summer when I turned eleven, which was about as old as anyone can be and take something like Mars Four seriously.

It had been a complicated summer, emotionally. Thalia had been thirteen and already mooning around about Wade Gordon, the sixteen-year-old down the block, son of Harry Gordon, and eventually a real-estate salesman in Vail.

Wade had never been one of our group, and I think his major ability, at sixteen and for that matter at fifty, was looking good in a bathing suit. For most of the summer, Thalia never managed to exchange two sentences with him, but he gave her something to talk about nearly constantly. Meanwhile, I had a hopeless crush on Thalia.

Nick and Eddie were fifteen, just coming into their strength, without an ounce of fat on their bodies or fatigue in their spirits, constantly running, swimming, building things, playing chess, arguing, reading things to have more ideas what to argue about, getting into trouble, lying their way out of trouble, and making Mom and Mrs. Killeret wonder what it was going to be every time the phone rang. Mom always said that if the phone rang and it was a lifeguard, telling her that Nick had been in a shark attack, she'd have asked if the shark was all right.

Nick and Eddie fascinated me, and I tagged along when I could. I was only sporadically welcome around them, but sporadically is better than nothing.

It was 1969—to me, a great time. Campus riots, Vietnam, ghetto riots, wars and repression around the world, and the first big news stories about pollution, were mostly the incomprehensible noise that came on at the beginning of the TV news and made my parents mutter and complain. I learned what had been going on much later, from history books. The country's troubles, to an eleven-year-old boy, were mere backdrop. I was right in the middle of the exciting couple of years when you're a big kid and can do things—swim, play sports, go places by yourself, and all the other things that are fun at the beach in the summer—while still being a kid, and therefore wanting to do them. I had a great time, most of the time, and many casual friends everywhere on the beach and in town.

Still, compared to previous summers, it was often lonely. Eddie Killeret and Nick were off in the world of their own intense competition, and Nick was really closer to Eddie than he was to me. Thally, my friend, mentor, and guide to getting out of trouble, whose sidekick I had been for several summers, was going through her own peculiar experiments in growing up, and though I saw more of her than I did of my brother and his friend, it wasn't a very satisfying experience. Every other day or so, Thally and I would sit on the beach and she'd talk endlessly about who she liked, who she didn't, what she wore, what she'd never wear, and so forth, always returning to the eternal fascination of Wade Gordon. I'd have sat next to her while she read the dictionary aloud, just to be there.

Usually, though, Thalia was off with girls her own age, hanging around the concession stands on the boardwalk and having fits of giggles about whatever it was they talked about.

Yet the excitement of finally being a big kid myself outweighed all that. I was everywhere, all the time, as if I were afraid that they might roll up the beach and take it away, so on the whole, 1969 would have been a grand year, just being on the beach with my energy and newfound big kid status, without anything else at all.

What made it perfect was that men were landing on the moon. All the kids were moon-mad by July 20, the landing date, but some of us had been crazy for years before. My brother had had space program fever first, because he had been seven years old, and able to follow what was going on, when Alan Shepard flew. He and Eddie had been enthusiasts for every flight after that; they could still name everyone, American and Russian, who had ever been to space. By the later Gemini flights, I was big enough to be as hooked as they were.

Even kids who had never been space-crazed before were space-crazed that July. All of us could find the Sea of Tranquility on the face of the moon, and knew all the major maneuvers and steps that would have to be accomplished to get to and from the moon. We knew all the abbreviations—LM and CM and EVA and so forth. Almost any afternoon you could see model rocket launches, the thin white streaks arcing up over the beach, and the occasional kid swimming out frantically to try to retrieve his rocket.

In the first week we had been at the cabin, Nick had built the big Estes flying model of the Saturn V, three feet tall with miles of glued-on plastic detail, which never flew very well but looked impressive taking off. Nick stopped flying it after its sixth flight, when it came down in the ocean. Eddie swam out and rescued it, but a dunking in seawater is not good for cardboard and balsa. Nick carefully sanded and repainted it, but if you knew where to look you could see it was slightly bent. Now it hung, like a trophy, from the rafters of the cabin's big attic room where Nick and I slept.

The Mars Four started as a conversation on the beach, just after Armstrong, Collins, and Aldrin had departed lunar orbit and started the long fall back to Earth. Space fever was fading in the kid community already. They all seemed to think it was over, even though three astronauts were still far from Earth.

Since the families had all gone to the movies and then to the seafood shack together, it had been natural for us to drift out the door, away from the adults playing cards in the Killeret cabin. We wandered along the beach for a short distance and sat down near the top on the sea side of a big dune, to look at the stars. Nick and Eddie sat close together, so that if one of them thought of something dirty they could whisper it to each other and giggle; Thalia and I sat in front of them. I felt awkward and strange sitting next to her, but very happy; she was wearing a pink dress, the sleeveless tube-shaped sort of thing that was popular then, and white sandals with slight, clunky heels. To me she looked practically adult.

The sea was calm, and it was just late enough so that there weren't many people out; a few older teenagers had a bonfire about half a mile south of us, and we could occasionally hear snatches of the Beatles or the Doors drifting up toward us, but mostly it was just us, the birds, and the soft crash of waves onto the shore. I watched waves roll in, and stole very discreet sideways glances at Thalia, and was happy just to be there with everyone. After a while Nick and Eddie began to discuss the one subject about which either of them could talk forever: what they wanted to do when they grew up.

"I can't believe you're both planning that far ahead," Thalia said, after the two of them had been going on for a while. "I mean, I don't even know what I'm going to do next week. Not literally, I mean we'll still be here at the cabin and all, but you know what I mean. It just doesn't seem real to me that you could already be planning what to study in college."

"If I don't plan," Nick said, "I might not take the right stuff in high school."

"It's pretty competitive, getting into the kind of programs we want to," Eddie said, "and we can't all rely on our natural brilliance and good looks."

Thalia stuck her tongue out at him.

I thought about Nick and that Saturn V rocket model. I remembered that before he took it out of its box to start assembling it, he had to make sure that he had every tool on the "required" list laid out on the workbench in perfect order, and all the glue and the Q-Tips to apply it with. Nick probably did have the rest of his life planned.

I'd been drifting away mentally, starting to fall asleep. Nick said, "You know what Dad said; we could probably have had a man in orbit in 1950 if we'd really had to do it, like if there'd been no atomic bomb and the war had gone on that long or something. He says the real miracle is that there was ever any people or money to go to space with at all. Even now, they aren't sure how many flights there will be after this one."

I had heard Dad saying that too, but I hadn't thought about it. People would just go to the moon once, then stop?

"Well, I'm going to find a way to keep it going," Eddie said, firmly.

"Me too. Did I say I wasn't?" Nick replied.

Thalia said, very seriously, "I don't know what I'm going to do about space, but I know why I'm going to do it."

"Explicate for us, oh Lady of Mysteries," Eddie said.

I wasn't sure what "explicate" meant but Eddie was always pulling out big words to intimidate us younger kids with, and I figured it probably meant "keep talking." Either Thalia knew what it meant, or she made the same guess I did.

"Well, I'm not good at the science stuff, but the whole space and moon thing just seems so beautiful to me. You know the way some pieces of art are so beautiful that you can't imagine how the world could have existed before they were there? Or some things, like a cathedral, you look at them and you say, a whole century went by, with people getting born and growing up and dying and everything, and all that human time was worth it because they made that one thing? Well, that's kind of what I feel about going to the moon. Do I sound really stupid?"

"Not to me," I said, loyally.

"It's so . . . *grand* that I just like being in a world where it happens." Then, maybe because it was all getting so serious, she said, "Of course, Scott just wants to fly, right?"

"Rocket Boy is ready to go any minute," Nick agreed. "If we had five hundred Estes engines, we could strap them on him and that poor idiot child would be ready to go this minute."

"There's nothing wrong with wanting to fly," Eddie Killeret said, instantly becoming my hero. "If we're going to go there, somebody's got to fly."

It got darker. Waves rumbled gently, slowly onto the beach. Maybe the conversation was over for the night.

Around the older kids, I tried not to call too much attention to myself. I didn't want to be treated as Nick's little brother.

Maybe everyone was going to just sit there for a while and then go home to bed. We had done that many evenings before. A cool breeze began to blow in off the sea, rustling the spots of long grass, and the waves picked up slightly, but it was still warm and still quiet. I felt my eyes drifting shut.

When Thalia spoke I almost jumped. "Wouldn't it be really, really cool," she said, "if fifty years from now—that would only be 2019—we could all come back to the beach?"

"I'll just be retiring," Nick said.

"Yeah, well, if we all came back to the cabin, and we were celebrating the first baby born on Mars?" Thalia persisted.

I was confused, and asked, "The first baby born on Mars?"

"I get it," Eddie said. "Thally's right. A baby on Mars would be the real sign that people had gotten serious about space. Because if a baby is born there, it's going to be because people have gone there to settle for good. By that time there'll probably be ten big cities on the moon."

"That's where I want to live," I said, immediately.

Nick made a funny noise, and said, "Jeez, this is hard to believe, but it's true. You probably *will* live on the moon someday, Scott. If you want to be a pilot you'll probably be flying a regular route between the moon and a space station in orbit around the Earth. Like in that movie, *2001*, you know? The PanAm Space Clipper. You can bring me back from a business trip up there, and then we'll both fly down to Earth to get to the reunion down here on the beach."

"It's still going to be a big job," Eddie said. "All the rest of our lives."

Nick's tone was surprisingly serious. "A big job is not the same thing as an impossible job."

"Wouldn't it be cool," Thalia said, "if we all promised, right now, that we were going to help it happen, and be a part of making the first settlement on Mars? Maybe even one of us would fly there, or live there, but not necessarily—just, like, help it any way we can. And in 2019 we'll have a big party here to celebrate however far we've gotten. You know, Scott won't even retire till 2023. None of us will even be seventy yet. Maybe we can all go on a trip just to see the settlement on Mars. We might even have *grandchildren* there."

When Thalia mentioned grandchildren, I was amazed to realize what a long time it would take.

"Tickets are going to be expensive," Nick said.

"Well, then, maybe we should start saving now," she said, teasing him. It was just like Nick to worry about something like that when we were talking about going to Mars fifty years in the future.

"All right, if we can afford a ticket, and they're selling them, we'll go," Nick said.

Eddie snorted. "Try and stop any of us from buying one, no matter what they cost."

"You have to promise to work to make it happen," Thalia said, "otherwise, it's just wishing."

" 'I promise to work to get people to Mars in the next fifty years'?" Nick asked. "Is that all we have to say?"

"That should do nicely," Thalia said. "I'll start off if you like. I promise to work to get people to Mars in the next fifty years. And I promise to come back here to celebrate in 2019. Your turn."

I repeated what she had said, then Eddie repeated it, and finally Nick did. We all sat quietly till it began to get chilly. I don't know what the others were doing, but I was trying to figure out if we had really done anything.

About the time I was starting to shiver, Mom called for Nick and me. The group broke up in a quick little chorus of good-nights and see-you-tomorrows and so forth. Nick and I walked back up the beach, sand crunching under our feet, toward the bright yellow square of the cabin light, and I remember him resting a hand on my shoulder for just a second. Maybe he was just steadying himself from a bad step in the sand.

That evening, in the upstairs room, Nick fell asleep instantly, as he always did, but I lay awake a little while. The dust motes danced in the moonlight from the window, surrounding the Saturn model that hung on fishline from the ceiling. It glowed ghostly white, and in the dim light the glue spots, and the traces of re-sanding and repainting, vanished, and it seemed to hang there just as if, somehow, the whole big rocket were really in space. The dust motes seemed like distant twinkling stars, obscured and revealed by the Saturn and its shadow as it slowly turned. The nozzles (painted silver—in the dark you couldn't see that they were lumpy over the slightly charred parts) would swing into the brighter light, and back out; a while later, the escape tower, CM, and third stage, all painted stark white with black detailing, would swoop into the bright light for just a moment. I watched it turn around one more time, and then I was asleep, too.

WHEN I LOOKED at the clock, I realized I must have been daydreaming for an hour; that was probably the longest I'd spent just sitting in a chair, truly doing nothing, since my first year in the Air Force. I wondered how long it was going to take Harry Gordon to find me a lawyer, and if maybe I should start looking for one on my own. As involved in business as I was, and with a certain amount of time on the social circuit, I knew plenty of lawyers, and I had a nagging feeling that I knew someone who would be perfect.

It was a bitter joke when I realized it was Thalia. Beginning a year and a half before the divorce, she'd been running her small prisoner's-and-victim's-rights group (I had never quite understood how those two fit together). Much of it was lobbying and testifying in Congress and the state legislatures, but she also fought cases in court, helping victims sue the criminal and helping criminals sue the state. At least she had litigated plenty of civil cases, very much in the public eye, which was more than could be said for anyone Gordon was likely to find, and she might have a good idea who I should talk to. Though we weren't exactly friends since the divorce, my ex was a thoroughly honest person and I could trust whatever she recommended.

Just the same, I thought I'd wait a while to call her and ask; maybe if I didn't have anyone by end of day Monday, which seemed improbable. I didn't want to create unnecessary times in which to quarrel, and it bothered me to feel as if I were asking for free legal advice. I picked up the Yellow Pages.

What you can find there, unfortunately, is mostly "We'll make them pay" ads, or phone numbers with no information, but after spending the better part of an hour reading through the fine print, I found four names that I recognized, people I knew socially who seemed to be senior partners or proprietors of firms that might handle this kind of thing. I tried the first one, using my personal connection to get past the secretaries.

He talked with me for about ten minutes about a charity board we were both on. Then, before I could tell him my business, he told me that his firm couldn't take on any additional cases at this time. Strange that a business would turn away business, especially a big case with a lot of publicity value, but I didn't know much about law.

The next firm told me they had an unspecified conflict of interest. The guy I knew at the third firm, an old Air Force buddy, called me back after half an hour. "I hate to say this, Scott, but I just can't." He didn't give a reason and I didn't ask for one. The fourth and last one told me she couldn't afford to handle "such a sensitive case" at this time.

Sunlight was slanting east across the rug now, and the air conditioner had come on to cope with the late-afternoon heat of Indian summer. I wondered what to do next. As I was putting in a load of laundry, the phone rang.

It was Harry Gordon. He'd been calling around. Nobody wanted the case. I asked, but we hadn't called any of the same firms. Gordon would keep trying but wasn't hopeful.

"If we can't find anyone else, do you have somebody around in your firm who could handle it for me? Any lawyer is better than not having one."

Harry hemmed, hawed, and backpedaled pretty hard.

"Look," I said. "You obviously have some reason or other not to take the case. I bet it's the same reason why the other firms don't want it. And it might help me if I knew what that reason is. Why don't you just tell me? I've known you all my life; you're the family lawyer; you could at least tell me what the hell is going on."

Suddenly he had to take another call, and then his secretary called to say he'd get back to me.

It looked like I'd have to renew my quest for a lawyer in the morning. Tomorrow would be Friday, though, and I wondered how many lawyers would be around town to talk to me.

When you're up to your neck in bad publicity, you need to stay inside the news cycle, so I drafted a press release that expressed my admiration for Michael James and for Marc Clement, my sorrow at their deaths, my feeling of empathy for AnnaBeth James, and my belief that it would be shown that I was not at fault. All of that was true, so it wasn't that hard to organize it; coming up with words that couldn't possibly be misread as trite, dismissive, callous, or duplicitous took longer. I wrote it out carefully and then began calling my way through the deck of reporters' cards.

Since she'd been so helpful, I called Nikki Earl first. She recorded the statement in my voice, and then added, "I'll copy this and give one to Ken Elgin, so you don't have to call him. We're going to dinner tonight," she said. "I probably ought to thank you for that."

"Huh," I said, mildly surprised. "You work for the most liberal network, and he writes for the most conservative newsmagazine—"

"Yeah, but he's cute, for a Republican. And at least we understand each other's jobs, which is more than our exes did, and besides, he said the magic words that go right to any single mother's heart— 'I'll pay for a sitter.'" Her voice got more serious. "Something Ken and I have both been noticing, Scott, that we thought maybe you should know about. PSN and *USReport* are both so small that we have just one reporter on the job, and you know we know you and we're sympathetic. The bigger outfits seem to be putting all their attack dogs on you. We don't know why, but it doesn't look good. You be careful."

"I will. And I know where I can go to get accurately quoted."

She chuckled. "I knew you'd see my point. Good luck. If I were you, I wouldn't watch television news for a while." We rang off. At least I had two friends in the media.

I left several messages on answering machines before Bryn Pogwell picked up the phone for CBS. She recorded my statement and then said, "I really appreciate your calling back with that statement." Then, after a long pause, she said, "I really don't like the editing they're doing. I think you were candid and fair with reporters this morning, and I don't think CBS is going to be fair with you."

"Should I watch CBS tonight?" I asked, my heart sinking.

"Evening news. Probably very early in the broadcast. I'm really sorry. I was overruled. I think you'll be pretty angry. I just wanted to say that it wasn't my idea, even if you don't believe me."

"I'll try to believe you," I said.

"Thanks." She hung up.

I got three more answering machines before I hit the reporter from NBC News, who was having dinner at his desk. After he realized that I was just calling with a follow-up statement, he seemed to relax and said, "Okay, I'll relay it to Brown. It's his story now."

"They've moved it to another desk already?" I asked.

"Yeah, I had a disagreement with management about how to use the material, and they took me off it and gave it to Brown. I'll see that he gets your statement. Of course he'll do whatever he wants with it. Thanks for calling." He hung up.

I set the phone down. The evening news was an hour and a half away; till then there must be something I could do. I thought about calling Nick, but we'd really drifted a long way apart. Nick was a big success at Republic Wright, their youngest corporate VP. People who are succeeding rarely have time for failures.

I tried to take a nap while I waited for the evening news. I still couldn't sleep.

Just before six, I set the phone to not ring, and the answering machine to pick up automatically, because I knew from bitter experience that if it was really a hatchet job, they'd be calling me while it was on the air, hoping to catch me while I was still mad and get an over-the-top reaction. I set the VCR to tape NBC while I watched CBS.

They didn't air any of my expressions of sympathy, or any of my definite statements. They did include every time I said that things weren't known yet, that I couldn't answer until I talked to a lawyer, and so forth. In between they interjected shouted questions that I was pretty sure I hadn't been asked at all. If I had been casually watching this on the evening news, I would be saying to myself, "This guy is a crook."

When I played the tape from NBC News, it was even worse.

I went to the answering machine, re-read my statement into the outgoing message, and left the ringer turned off on the phone. Maybe some local radio station would call up, get that message, tape it, and play it.

For an hour, as it got dark outside, I just drifted around the house looking for any old thing to amuse me. My earlier attack of nostalgia led me to my copy of the family photo albums. If I had stared any harder I might have fallen forward through the photo onto the warm summer beach itself. Right then I'd have loved to.

THAT NIGHT, WHEN we made the promise on the beach, was the beginning of the Mars Four. I think maybe we got the idea for a name like that from the Chicago Seven trial that had just happened, or maybe from the Mercury Seven astronauts. I'm pretty sure we didn't dub ourselves the Mars Four that night; it must have been some time the following day, or even a few days later. But anyway, for the rest of the summer, it was both a joke we used on anyone who seemed to be too serious, and at the same time a unique, special thing that was just ours. Like most kids, we were pretty shy about the things that were most serious to us, and it was easiest to speak of them as a joke.

. If somebody got an extra scoop of ice cream, we'd say "Shouldn't you be saving that money for your ticket to Mars?" Or if someone did something hazardous, we'd say "Don't get killed before we go to Mars." Late in the summer, Mrs. Pendergast caught Thalia kissing Wade Gordon behind the Pendergasts' cabin, and grounded her for three days. (Incidentally, she broke my heart into a thousand pieces.) After she "got out on parole," as Nick and Eddie called it, Nick said, "I'm afraid you are just not living up to the standards we expect of the Mars Four."

Gradually I came to think that I was the only person who still took it seriously, and that I'd been too young to realize that they were just kidding. The Mars Four jokes stopped when we all got home and started school again. I don't remember any Mars Four jokes the next summer, though probably there were some. I kept quiet about it anyway, and made myself forget it as much as I could—though that was surprisingly hard. Young boys aren't the most rational people in the world about flying in space, or going to Mars, or keeping promises no matter what.

I WAS HUNGRY, and the photo album was only further depressing me. I could hear the answering machine clicking in the background, over and over, as it sent the outgoing message to who knew how many callers. I closed the album, got up, and got dinner: a diet Coke, some Doritos, and a thin ham sandwich, all I had the appetite for. The answering machine was still telling everyone in the universe that I was sorry for everyone's pain but confident that I would be completely exonerated. It must have fielded fifty calls in two hours.

I finished the meal, such as it was, thought about microwaving a breakfast burrito, and decided that I'd rather go to bed. The phone wasn't ringing quite so often anymore, so maybe they'd found someone else to bother, or maybe everyone who needed a copy of my message had one. I got up, stretched, put the dishes into the sink, and wondered whether I'd be able to get to sleep tonight.

The doorbell rang. Well, perhaps it would be Ken Elgin, or even Fred Gernsback—someone sympathetic, anyway.

I opened the door and found my brother Nick standing there with a pizza. "Is mushroom and roasted garlic still your favorite?" he asked, and walked in past me, setting it down on my table. "Have you eaten nothing at all, or just a sandwich and a handful of chips?"

I closed the door. His pricey Italian suit was unwrinkled and perfectly in place, his shoes practically glowed, and his neat mustache and close-cropped hair looked fresh from the barber. He'd have looked like that after swimming away from a shipwreck; Mom had always sworn that he'd been born fully dressed with his shoes shined. "You look good. When did you become psychic?"

"About the time I decided to take a second job in pizza delivery," he said. "If there are two clean glasses and two clean plates in here, I'll be pleasantly surprised, and we can have a family dinner and I can tell you about what's going on."

I grabbed the required stuff from the dishwasher, and pulled out a big bottle of diet Coke from the fridge. While I did, the phone answering machine activated twice more.

Nick said, "By now that outgoing message of yours must be on every channel except the Cartoon Network."

"I figured I couldn't improve matters by talking to them," I said.

"Probably you're right, for tonight." He served the pizza and I realized I was starving. With an amused little smile, he watched me wolf two pieces while he ate a few bites of his, carefully, with a knife and fork. "I thought you'd probably need the food. When you're upset, you don't eat. If you're ready to discuss business, I do have some comforting news, but I'm afraid it starts with some additional bad news."

I took a sip of the diet Coke and said, "You still look as good as ever; how do you do it?"

"An outward mark of inner superiority," he said, smiling. It was an old joke between us. "How is Amos?"

"Pretty much a normal kid. He's doing peewee wrestling, so I'll have to learn something about wrestling. His sitter says he was heart-broken about M J. He and I are going down to the cabin to spend some time next weekend."

Nick nodded. "This is the best time of year there, really, unless you insist on swimming. The tourists are gone and the beach is perfect for walking."

"Yeah," I said, putting down some more pizza. How had I ever thought I wasn't hungry?

For the next twenty minutes or so, between bites, I talked about Amos, mostly, and Thalia a little. Nick filled me in on what he was allowed to say about what was going in his life—which wasn't much. He had never married, he couldn't discuss much about work, and his life was nearly as busy as mine. Nick worked for Republic Wright, where he was the youngest vice-president at the company. He held the plum job there, the one he had probably wanted ever since he was ten years old—he ran their "black shop," the secret projects de-velopment facility. I'd gotten used to Nick not talking about work, and he barely had a personal life. As usual, he said he was busy, that there was some interesting new hardware that would go public within a few years, and that he spent ridiculous amounts of time commuting by corporate jet between DC, San Diego, and Scorpion Shack. "It's the only time I have to do any paperwork," he said cheerfully. "If they ever leave me in one city for an entire week, the administration of Scorpion Shack will collapse." He set aside the crust from his single piece of pizza—I noted how perfect the arc he had cut with his knife was. "Have I given you enough food and brotherly support to prepare you to face the world again?"

I took another sip of the diet Coke, looked at the remains of the pizza, and nodded. "Yes, thanks. I'll nibble some more while you talk. Jeez. I needed somebody to take care of me just then."

"Well, we *are* family," he said, a little uncomfortably. Nick doesn't like people to remember when he does them favors; it makes him self-conscious. He's always been that way.

He made a precise little tent with his fingers and said, "This is a surprise, I expect, and not a pleasant one. Curtiss Aerospace is selling you, and everybody else, down the river, just as fast as they can. Furthermore, since they are the majority stockholder in ASU, ASU will also be settling. All of that will prejudice the case against the remaining defendants, which includes you, ShareSpace, and RW."

"Why?"

He shrugged. "They've got by far the deepest pockets in the business. If there's a big financial settlement, Curtiss will be the one that pays the most. So by settling early and making it easier for Haverford, they limit how much comes out of their pockets, and they make it very likely that Republic Wright will lose enough to go bankrupt or have to sell out. Curtiss has aspired to be the one and only aerospace company for a long time, and this might be their final step.

"Then, too, every player in the aerospace industry knows that space is privatizing sooner or later. The communications companies need reliable space transport for communications satellites, the shuttles are getting old, and the federal government doesn't have much of a commitment to space anymore. But government, for the moment, is still the biggest single customer for launch services, and most of the government's business is currently going to Curtiss. That helps to keep us permanently in second place.

"Now, that would change if we had a more competitive launcher—and we're about to."

"I've heard about the Starcraft series," I said.

He nodded. "We try to keep that hushed up, of course, but a project that size can't be concealed. It's a miracle that *Aviation Week* hasn't already done a cover story about it. Yes, the first group of the Starcraft series is very close to flight test. Igor Jagavitz thinks this is what will make us a 'storefront space agency'—that's his expression for the kind of convenient, efficient service we could provide, with a reliable operations schedule and standardized pricing. My best guess is that Curtiss is a few years behind us in everything—they've maintained a commitment to their established products and services, because those were dominating the market. Therefore, in a year or two, Curtiss's launcher business can expect a serious, across-the-board market challenge from RW's Starcraft—unless something happens to RW in the interim. If something serious *enough* happens, Curtiss might own Republic Wright, six months from now, and reap the profits themselves. I'd imagine they're thinking that settling one large lawsuit is nothing compared to maintaining their dominance of the market. I don't need to tell you there are plenty of people in Washington who sympathize with Curtiss's view that there really ought to be just one big aerospace company—and just who it ought to be.

"So this is about RW's survival, which is why I'm going to spend a good part of tomorrow making sure that everyone else at the company sees it that way. We'll have to fight this with everything we have. But we do have plenty of resources, and we also have something the other side doesn't have—a real case in law and logic. And that's your good news. You're not alone. You're a long way from being alone. Now, no despair, no self pity, and don't get sentimental and thank me, because that will embarrass us both. Besides, I have perfectly good business reasons for doing this for you, reasons that would be good even if I didn't know you from Adam. Is that all right?"

"Okay. Thanks, Nick." I felt my shoulders relaxing, my attention increasing, a calm awareness of everything; tennis had been my high school and college sport, and this was how it felt to be psyched before walking out onto the court. It was a million times better than the way I had been feeling an hour and a half ago.

After more small talk, mostly about things decades in the past, he left, and I tossed the empty pizza box and soda bottle into the wastebasket. Maybe due to his lingering influence, I got the clean dishes out of the dishwasher, and loaded the dirty ones in, while I listened to a music station on the radio; I even hummed along when an old

Beatles song, "Get Back," came on. That had been all over the air during one of the best of those old summers. Not that there had been any bad ones . . .

I tried to remember if I ever *had* had any place, other than the dishwasher, for my coffee cups. Eventually I just picked a vacant stretch of cupboard shelf—there were plenty of those. This had been my house for more than two years, and I was finally moving in.

At one in the morning, tired but finally relaxed, knowing Nick would be on the job, I sank into my bed, and slept soundly.

CHAPTER FOUR

NICK:

Whenever I had been away for a few days, walking into my office in Washington always led directly into a series of unpleasant discoveries. My office at Scorpion Shack, down on the Texas Gulf Coast, was a workplace, a friendly, comfortable home base. Republic Wright maintained an office for me at corporate HQ in San Diego, but I was there so rarely that it held almost nothing of mine. The DC office was different—it was the place where problems came in, and where I decided what to do about them. In Washington, the inbox was always bursting with new crises, the outbox was always primed with notes to send accountants, engineers, and scientists scurrying in circles, and the phone rang all the time.

The first thing I did that morning was to give Roger Przeworski a call; he was an in-house Republic Wright lawyer, the legal consultant for the Starcraft project. In putting him on this case, I would have to be careful to use him only on issues that had a direct impact on Starcraft. If nothing else, I would get the benefit of his shrewd, impartial judgment.

I asked him to prepare an assessment of the impact of the James lawsuit on the space tourism business, and the effect of that on the eventual market for the StarBird I, which was far into its prototype stage. I further asked him to assess our probability of securing a favorable outcome (for us) from the James family case, depending on various strategies that ranged from outright surrender to fighting to the last ditch.

Roger said he could give me an oral report by end of day. I cleared him and his two assistants to get whatever information they needed from anywhere within Scorpion Shack, had my secretary send out the memo, and moved on.

Even for me, the last few months had been frenetic. Republic Wright needed nothing short of a miracle, but the Starcraft project *was* a miracle, very nearly ready to go. Now it was a race between my shop and disaster for my company. So far my shop was coming in ahead, but it was still a race; the best new technology in the world does you no good if it arrives a week after you're out of money and credit.

The case against Scott and the aerospace companies added one more ball to be juggled. I had to make sure that Starcraft survived as a viable commercial project. If the James family could sue space tourism out of existence, the market we needed for the middle phase of the Starcraft program would be lost. RW had a vital interest in winning this case, and it was certainly winnable. I had to make absolutely sure that that was clear to the rest of management, before I could put my full time and attention on Starcraft.

I should have known better. By midmorning I had a sinking feeling that this was spinning out of control. Few of my fellow executives could see how much of Republic Wright's future was tied up in this. I had found only one ally—Caitlin Delamartin, the VP for Market Development. Given what was expected of us, if Starcraft failed as a commercial project, the first heads to roll would be Caitlin's and mine, probably within a few months, but they would be far from the last and in a few years there would be nothing left of RW's current management.

Unfortunately, no one wanted to look more than a few months into the future. The finance people told us that settling would have a fixed price tag, and however much we might make eventually, by not settling, the gains were indefinite. Community Relations worried about appearing to be too tough on a grieving mother. Flight Ops was more worried about losing positions within ASU to Curtiss than they were about whether there would be anything to fly. Production profoundly didn't care; they just built whatever they were told to.

By the time I met Caitlin for lunch to plan strategy, we were both very discouraged. "I don't like to say this," she said, "but it seems to me that many of these people have already given up, or maybe they gave up a while ago, when we lost the last big bid on ISS or when Curtiss got the commitment from the Air Force for a bunch of Delta launches. A majority of our senior management seems to have decided that we're doomed to be another Curtiss brand name, like Douglas and Chance-Vought and Convair and all the others who were swallowed up before us. So they look at this situation and they say, 'Oh, let's just do whatever the Puget Sound big boys want to do, we don't want to have done anything they didn't like when we go under and they buy us out.' "

"I'm sure that's part of it," I said. "And besides, many of our people spent their whole lives in an environment where the federal government was our only customer, and we were one of a handful of suppliers. If all this ends with us as a branch of the Curtiss Aerospace Monopoly, many of our older executives will be much more comfortable than they would out in the world of real free enterprise, where Jagavitz is trying to lead us."

"But they won't *get* that security they're looking for," Caitlin said, sighing, and pouring herself more coffee from the pot on the table. "If Curtiss wins this, we're *all* doomed. Our production capacity is redundant to theirs; they'll just shut most of Republic Wright down, take over Starcraft, and cherry-pick our talent." She gulped her coffee. "We're in a grow-or-die situation; we have to get ourselves a growth path for new sales, and privatization is the only one that Curtiss isn't sitting square in the middle of already." She pushed her red hair back from her face and pulled out a small pad. "Let's see what we can figure out. I contacted all the people you asked me to talk to, and none of them is any better than neutral. How did you do?"

"The only person in the top leadership we haven't talked to so far is Jagavitz." Igor Jagavitz was CEO of Republic Wright, a crusty old engineer who'd come up through airframe design. Neither of us had any doubt that he'd be on our side, but a corporate CEO governs by consent. He could do little if the rest of management opposed him. "We have a meeting with him, and whichever other executives are also in Washington today, at one-thirty."

"Who else is in town?" she asked, scribbling a note.

"Barbara Quentin, who we should be able to persuade," I said, "and Riscaveau, unfortunately."

Caitlin made a face; that's what most people did when they heard Riscaveau's name, these days. Also like everyone else, she said, "Well, you can't argue with his results; he's caught more industrial spies and intercepted more stolen information than anyone else I've ever heard of. I suppose it's the way he insists on being thorough."

"I guess," I said. "He's certainly thorough about checking out everyone for *my* operation. And he's never vetted someone and then had to come back and tell me he screwed up and the guy shouldn't be working for me. I've never seen anyone manage *that* before—normally every system has a leak or two."

Caitlin nodded and turned back to her notes. "Well, we can't uninvite him, anyway, irritating as he is. Now, it happens I have a meeting on an unrelated matter with Jagavitz, at 12:45, before our meeting. I'll try to squeeze in a few minutes to brief him on what you and I are up to. I have a pretty good rapport with the guy. That's our first resource . . ." she made a note on the pad. ". . . Jagavitz will back us." She drew a line, dividing her notebook page into two columns, which she labeled RESOURCES/US and VULNERABILITIES/ THEM.

"Now, resource two—we head up two of the more dynamic divisions of RW. So we have employees who we can count on to work late and do extra stuff for us during the campaign. I can't picture any of the bean counters in finance staying late to work on selling out the company and losing their jobs."

I nodded; it was a good point.

"Three, there's the prestige of your division; you're still the king of the status heap around here, Nick, and you know it."

I could have tried to demur, but it would have rung hollow; what she said was the simple truth. Aerospace hasn't really lost the mystique of super-science that it picked up during the Second World War. Much of my power and influence within Republic Wright derives from my connection to our secret city of five thousand people in Kennedy County, Texas, with its five major labs—aerodynamics/ supercomputing, metallurgy/materials science, fuels chemistry, avionics, and what we call "fundamental physics" to try not to give too much away of what we're doing. A world-of-tomorrow magic clings to our having the world's best design supercomputers, and our own machinists' shops, crucible-metals plant, and ceramics shop—not to mention three runways, each of which could handle a loaded B-52, and two launchpads—all where most maps show a big empty space on the Gulf Coast. Anybody who goes into aerospace has at least a touch of the romantic and a little feel for history, and therefore can't help being impressed by the kind of operation I head up.

Caitlin quickly enumerated the other places in the company where we had leverage, and the places where we didn't, and it looked to us as if we probably could secure a razor-thin agreement to fight the case out in the way we wanted.

BARBARA QUENTIN, THE head of Issues Management, smiled when I came into the meeting. She might or might not be on my side already, but I thought she would listen. Andrew Riscaveau, the security chief, didn't bother to look up from doodling on his pad. He would never be on my side; each of us had grudges against the other, dating back to well before we'd attained our present positions. It was unfortunate to have him here, but as head of a major section, he had his rights.

After Jagavitz arrived, Caitlin and I made our case that RW needed to fight the *Columbia* lawsuit, using the basic points we'd thrashed out at lunch. I was encouraged that Barbara Quentin nodded at most of the key points, and unsurprised that Riscaveau sat with his arms folded across his chest and a smug little smile.

When we finished and Jagavitz asked for comments, Riscaveau spoke at once. "The first thing I want to say is that we've got more or less carte blanche, from a security standpoint. I've done a lot of research and of course we're doing constant checkups. Lots of people know we have a project called Starcraft, and a few of them have heard of one or two components of the thing—the StarBooster, usually, and sometimes the StarBird—but not always very accurately. And we've kept most real information out of the trade press. So if we cancel it, no one will have any idea that we were close to success, and if we go ahead with it, our hand isn't tipped very much. Word would get out eventually, of course, but basically we can do whatever we want without any major reaction in the outside world. And even though he doesn't like all the hoops I make him jump through, a lot of the credit for the successful security goes to Nick Blackstone, who has been a big help." He nodded at me politely.

"Now," he went on, "the question is really whether we should fight this suit to keep our options open with regard to Starcraft. Nick says that if we win the suit—no matter what it costs us—we save Starcraft, and that way Starcraft can save the company. But let's seriously consider—is Starcraft a good idea? You're talking about killing expendable launchers, which have been a highly profitable bread and butter business for us for thirty years. Starcraft could easily trigger cutthroat competition that might completely destroy both our expendables business *and* Curtiss's.

"Besides, we've got access into the Chinese, Indian, Brazilian, and Korean markets by agreeing to subcontract so many of the systems on our expendables to facilities in their countries. We've moved thirty thousand jobs overseas in the last ten years, just to get market access. If we destroy the jobs that we gave them, you think the rising markets won't retaliate? They'll shut us out of their markets, *and* get serious about building a competing launch business."

Jagavitz raised his hand off the table, and nodded at both me and Riscaveau. "There is something that we have to think about here. First of all—bear with me on this, Nick—there's no magic about Starcraft—except that we've got it *now*. If we can make it work, so can someone in Beijing, or Rio, or probably anywhere eventually. So there will, will, will be a collapse in launch prices. We can either *make* that price collapse happen, and reap the profits—or we can keep hoping it won't, and jump into the pool with the other sharks once it does. I have to say, I'd rather drive than ride.

"In my gut, I feel, we've got to have Starcraft. We traded away first-rate American jobs for overseas markets, and as part of the trade we gave them a lot of our technology. Now, if Starcraft kills the expendables business . . . we'll have made everything we gave them *worthless*. We'll have those sharp-trading bastards over a barrel, and do what we want to them, and I have to admit I'd enjoy the hell out of *that*." He grinned in a way that always made me want to shudder; it was an expression that wouldn't have looked out of place on General Patton—or on Al Capone.

"*You'd* enjoy it?" Barbara Quentin said, grinning. Jagavitz started, but gestured for her to go ahead.

She leaned back in her chair and lightly ticked her points off with her fingers. "Do you realize what it would mean from an Issues Management standpoint? Just to begin with, the IAM and every other union would adore us. So would both political parties and the stock market. We'd be apple pie and mother to a hundred million Americans for five years afterwards. We'd have the kind of rep that AT&T got for operating communications during the Second World War— as golden as the glory days at Apple, Xerox, Ford, or General Dynamics. I know people here are always saying we mustn't make technical decisions based on PR considerations, but I can tell you, if you go this route, we'll be the most popular company in America inside three months."

Jagavitz nodded. "It's a consideration. All right, then, one more thing I'm thinking: yes, Starcraft kills our expendables business. But that just loses us a division that wasn't making money. Starcraft also kills *Curtiss's* expendables business—if we're aggressive about getting StarCore II and StarBird flying, it also kills off their new expendable heavy lift, and cuts into their shuttle. And then we *clobber* them the way they did us. Payback time. It's a big play for all the marbles— and I didn't get into this business to be number two."

Riscaveau said, "May I raise just one more point? We have no idea how big, or how small, the market for launch services and general space transportation may really be. Maybe with the price cut we'll get it all back in volume—from tourism, from DBS media systems, from being able to do repairs in geosynchronous orbit for the first time, from government contracts to go up there and knock down all those old top stages that are hazards to astrogation. It could happen. I gotta admit that. But maybe the market for space transportation is actually only what it is now. Maybe the truth is that the few people who really, really have to go to space will pay whatever they have to pay, and nobody else will pay a dime. And in that case what we're doing is grabbing up all the business, sure, but we're also reducing what we can charge for it. We could wind up a hundred percent of a barely profitable market, instead of fifteen percent of a super-lucrative one, which is what we are now. I just wanted to point out that that's a problem."

Jagavitz nodded a couple of times and said, "This is a problem, possibly, something we should think about, eh? I see it is in our interests in the long term to continue Starcraft. But as Mr. Riscaveau and Barbara both made very clear before the meeting, the costs of fighting this lawsuit may run very high. So *for the moment*, we will play to win, big. We'll try to get a precedent in our favor. But if the bet starts to look worse, we'll reverse, quick. And along with the policy," he added, looking straight at me with a slight twinkle in his eye, "I would point out that one of us is heavily involved due to a family connection . . . and if that relative were to take a more aggressive stance . . . it might influence my decision in the future. Does one of us have the personal funds needed, eh?"

It was as much as an order to back Scott with my own money, but an order I was happy to receive. Jagavitz wasn't willing to declare for our side, yet, but he was practicing a very tilted neutrality.

"I think everything can be made to work out," I said.

From the way Riscaveau glared at me, and straightened his tie and vest, I knew we had done well.

Caitlin and I agreed, over a quick cup of coffee after the meeting, that Jagavitz had gone as far as he could go today; he wouldn't let RW settle out of court right away, but getting the Board to wade in and supply the deep pockets would be our problem. After shaking hands on our success, I went back to my office, thinking it would only take me a few minutes to find Scott a lawyer, given what I was prepared to pay.

By about three o'clock that afternoon, I had determined that obtaining any top-drawer lawyer who knew anything about space or aviation law was going to be more than tough. It had all the marks of the fix being in; the four firms at the top of my list all had been put on retainer by Curtiss, supposedly to supply "advice" to Jasper Haverford, probably just to make them unavailable. It was good that Republic Wright was going to play to win, because Curtiss certainly was.

The phone rang. "Mr. Blackstone, I have Edgar Killeret, from Curtiss Aerospace, on the line. He wouldn't say what it was about."

"Put him through," I said.

Eddie Killeret and I had been friends, rivals, comrades, opponents, or allies, in everything, since we could speak. The Blackstone summer cabin was two doors down and one across from the Killeret cabin, and our families both went so far back in the tight, intertwined world of aviation that Eddie's father had flown as a test pilot under my grandfather's skeptical eye. From the age of three we'd raced each other, competed at every game, spent hours together arguing and bickering, watched each other's backs against bullies. In college we'd played lacrosse for rival teams, dated some of the same girls, and sometimes called each other for hours at a time just to talk. But since we had become each other's counterparts at RW and Curtiss—he ran their black shop in southeast Utah, known as "Ghost Town"—we hadn't communicated much.

As always, Eddie cut right to business. "Nick, I'm calling because I imagine you will be involved in all the sound and fury about the *Columbia* accident."

"You're right. I'm up to my neck in it."

"Well, I thought you ought to know about something. You know that Curtiss is planning to settle with the James family out of court, and they'll probably vote their shares so that ASU does the same, leaving Scott, ShareSpace, RW, and whoever in the lurch?"

"I'd heard."

"The decision is *not* unanimous here at Curtiss. Some of us think it would be utterly stupid to destroy space tourism and the private market for a temporary advantage like this. Unfortunately, we've lost every vote so far."

"Do you mean there's a chance that decision might be reversed?"

I could see him, in my mind's eye, sitting at a desk in an office not unlike mine, looking out across the desert from his windows; just as he had when we were boys together, and he had to tell me something that he figured I wouldn't want to hear, he'd be looking up at the ceiling, lips pressed together. Sure enough, a moment later he gave his characteristic little sigh and said, "Well, no, I don't think the decision will be reversed." He sighed. "To tell you the truth, this is nearly a purely social call. I was worried about Scott, and I hated the idea of my company being on the wrong side of this thing, and of personally being on the losing side. I just wanted to tell somebody—and who else could I tell?"

"I really appreciate your calling—I'll relay the word to Scott."

Eddie said, "Thank you for listening. Nobody over here will. I wish I were calling with support. The accident is a bad thing all around for the business, but it will be a much worse thing if it sets back the future, the way *Challenger* did."

"I agree," I said, "and I'm sure Scott does, and I'll pass along your message."

"Have you—uh, been having trouble finding counsel?"

"Is there a reason to think that I will?"

"There's every stone wall Curtiss can put in your path," Killeret said. "It's disgraceful. My company is behaving as if we were the plaintiffs, and I don't understand it at all. No doubt you've run into our little 'retainer' program, to lock up most law firms with expertise in aerospace."

"I have," I admitted.

The pause stretched on, and I realized that Killeret probably didn't feel he could say anything any more critical about his own corporation, but he certainly wanted to. Finally, I said, "I'll pass your concern and sympathy along to Scott. He's feeling very alone."

"I bet. Did you catch CNN or any of the network coverage?"

"No."

"Well, from what I've seen, I think they're building up for a real hatchet job on Scott, on the evening news. It sounds like they will really play up ShareSpace's having fired him. You know and I know that nothing Scott could have done would have changed the outcome, but I'm afraid the media has already found for the plaintiff."

"Well," I said, "I guess I'll have to watch some of the coverage. And on Scott's behalf, I really appreciate the support. It means a lot at the moment, and he'll be glad to hear from an old friend." I realized what a long time it had been, and asked, "Did you even know he and Thalia were divorced?"

"I think that's the last time I heard from either of them—just a short note from Thalia. I was really sorry to hear about it. Their son must be—what, five, now?"

"Ten."

He sighed. "Where does the time go? Anyway, I'm working on doing more for Scott than a friendly phone call, but I don't think I can say more about it until I know more. Meanwhile, does he have a private line I can call, just to offer support?"

I told him the number, and thanked him again. We spoke awkwardly for a few minutes about how little time we both had, how hard we both worked, and the general frustrations of fast-track career life; so much was confidential, or supposed to be, that it was hard to have anything like a normal conversation between old friends. Besides, both Eddie and I had always been rather reserved and formal, and neither of us was going to be the first to say "I miss you" or "Let's take a vacation and do something together," even though either of us would have been delighted if the other one had spoken first. So the conversation dwindled down to my thanking him for calling again, and promising to be in touch. Just before we said "goodbye," as I was thanking him for the third unnecessary time, he said, "Oh, don't mention it. Mars Four forever, you know?"

I laughed and said, "Mars Four. That's right." Then we hung up. I sat back in my chair, and though my eyes drifted to the window and the view across the brightly colored park—the leaves were just at their prime—I saw neither office nor park. Instead, it seemed I could hear Thalia's eleven-year-old voice saying, "Hey, couldn't you two *just* be friends, just once?," and the memory made me smile, and brought back several summers that, truth to tell, might have been the best in my life so far. In those days, I could probably have lived without oxygen more easily than without Eddie; now, we had a hard time even talking about making time to see each other.

IN THE SUMMER of 1969, I was caught between a hundred rocks and a thousand hard places. At my school, if you were fifteen, you had to have hair down to your shoulders and believe in peace and love and all that. If you knew the right songs and phrases you could usually pass, but it just wasn't cool to be enthusiastic about the moon landing—even though it made my heart want to jump out of my chest. I knew already, though, that you've got to maintain your network of peers, even if they're idiots—maybe *especially* if they're idiots. So I was supposed to either be very coldly cynical about the moon landing, or to deplore the waste of resources, or to see it as one big military stunt. I did my best to give the impression that those were my feelings.

It was so different with my beach friends. Eddie Killeret was the only other person my age who saw space the way I did. Thally and Scott at least didn't treat me like I was insane.

Dad's job should have been a source of comfort, but it was a mixed blessing. When I listened to my father, an engineer at Curtiss in the long-range development office, talking about projects and policy, I realized that it wasn't just my peers who were turning their backs on the new frontier. Politicians and businessmen needed the first landing to happen, but after that, now that we had beaten the Russians, most people with any power would be very happy if space just went away.

The space program, into which I wanted to pour my heart, soul, brains, and guts, looked like it was about to be over. Dad was already starting to look for some military project—he didn't even think they'd ever build the space shuttle that was then under discussion.

So when Thalia suggested that promise, in her very serious way, it felt like there were three more people in the world who understood, and I didn't feel so all alone. I'd have promised anything at all to my friends at the time, just because they were people who cared about what I cared about. As much as I tried to hide it under my teenage cynicism for the rest of the summer, there was no getting around it; a part of me had quite seriously made its commitment to the Mars Four. After a while I realized that Eddie was as serious as I was, and we got to be even closer buddies, if that was possible.

It was so strange that once we both began to work on real space projects, we had lost touch. We had expended more of our friendship, of our mutual words and love and attention, on that old, toy Saturn V that I had assembled and he had rescued from the sea, than we had on our real drives into space. It seemed terribly unfair.

When Eddie and I had been in second grade together, we'd read and re-read a picture book called *You Will Go to the Moon*. It had shown a very different way of getting there—winged rockets flying up to a donut-shaped space station, and specialized moon ships leaving the station to go to the lunar surface, and a permanent lunar base—all sorts of things that had never really happened. Yet one part of it had stuck with me . . . the realization that you don't ever go to space with just one thing, that besides the rocket itself, there's so much else that needs to be built.

And as I had come to be a businessman, I'd understood the real magic, the thing that made it all possible: paying as you went. If every gadget you needed began to pay for itself the moment you deployed it, then you had a chance. No one was going to build a dozen separate systems, none of which was profitable without the others, and try to set up everything all at once.

That was why Starcraft had appealed to me, from the moment

that it had come to us from a team of older engineers and aerospace business people who—because they had no funding and nothing to lose—had asked a question that hadn't been asked in a long time: "What's the best way to *expand* American space operations? Not just to serve existing needs, or serving one additional new need in isolation, but to move from where we are to somewhere better?"

Unlike other such groups, they didn't disdain the successes of the shuttle and the expendable rockets; rather, they concentrated on how things could be done step-by-step, with each step paying for itself, and each step expanding our capabilities. No part of the Starcraft series was a "miracle machine," but collectively they could change everything.

First-generation Starcraft vehicles would close some of the holes into which money had been pouring for decades. The first stage of a big rocket is an immensely complicated piece of machinery, expensive to build and operate. In the expendable rockets that carried most satellites aloft, we used them for a few minutes during launch, and then just let them fall into the sea. For the shuttle, we reused them in a terribly expensive way—we let the solid rocket boosters parachute back into the ocean, pulled them out of the seawater with a ship, hauled them back to land, put them on railcars, and shipped them to Utah to be completely rebuilt. So the quickest way to cut costs, the Starcraft people told us, would be to bring boosters back for reuse.

StarBooster 200 was a cheap, pilotless airplane that enclosed an Atlas III first stage—the Starcraft people were so dedicated to doing things in small steps that they didn't even propose a new engine, or a new way to mount it. It was "StarBooster 200" because it carried about 200 tons of fuel; there were possible StarBooster 350's and 700's in the future, using other well-established engines, but the StarBooster 200 should be enough for several years.

Attach two Starbooster 200's to a cheap Athena II launcher—something our company already made, which was why the Starcraft group approached us first—and Athena went from launching small scientific packages to competing in the big communication satellite and defense markets. It was as if they'd turned a Volkswagen Minivan into a semi-truck.

When the StarBoosters separated from the Athena, they turned around, switched on an autopilot, and flew themselves back to a landing field near the launchpad. Crews could pull out the engines for overhaul and reconditioning, slap in new ones, and have the booster ready to use again within a matter of a day or two.

The StarBooster 200 was a graceful-looking ship, roughly the size of a 737, with an elongated lifting body, a short thick wing at the back, and a canard wing at the front. It didn't *fly* gracefully, but it didn't have to—just by bringing itself home for repair and re-use, it would allow us to beat the price of every expendable, except perhaps the French Ariane and the new heavy-lift Curtiss expendable rocket.

Logically, the next step in the process would be to replace the Athena with an upper stage big enough to surpass the Ariane. This was also nearly ready to go; StarCore I was just the first two stages of an Athena mated to the high-energy Centaur upper stage. With that, we'd have the lowest priced heavy-lift rocket on Earth.

StarBooster 200/StarCore I would put us on top of the industry for the next decade, but there were five more possible vehicles in the Starcraft series, and some of them were already in prototype; it might mean that RW would dominate spaceflight out to the 2040s or beyond. StarCore II, with a space shuttle main engine (SSME) inside a parachute-recovered pod, with two throwaway hydrogen fuel tanks, would be able to put heavier loads higher than anything else flying—giant communication satellites and modules for ISS, just to begin with; things nobody had ever thought of putting up there before.

Nor had we neglected crewed missions. We had a simple crew recovery vehicle, a lifting body that was roughly intermediate between a capsule and a glider, called StarRescue, which we hoped to sell to

NASA as the ISS lifeboat. It had been designed to be Starcraft-compatible, and if we used it with the propulsion system of a StarCore II, we had StarBird I—a spacecraft that could take ten people, but no cargo, to low Earth orbit, and compete with the shuttle for many missions.

Just on the drawing board and in the concept stage, there was a StarCore III/StarBooster 700 combination that might loft a whole space hotel into orbit at one shot, and a StarBird II that could take eighty to one hundred passengers per flight up to the hotel. The Starcraft family, if it all were built, would include every vehicle we would need, right out till we were routinely flying to Mars.

And yet each of the seven steps along the road was individually profitable; each craft would pay for itself, and create the conditions that would make its successor pay for itself.

It was all the wonders of *You Will Go to the Moon*, but with a timetable and a plan. It was the unbroken path from a cardboard Saturn V to being able to buy a ticket on the PanAm Space Clipper. It was the road to the stars we had dreamed of when we'd been the Mars Four, back on that Virginia beach so long ago.

In some ways I couldn't wait for Starcraft to go public. I wondered if Scott and Eddie and Thalia remembered, and if they would see the connection before I pointed it out to them. I wanted to tell someone, *See? Same old dream, just with real rockets and real money this time*, but a VP for black projects is not supposed to be that kind of a romantic; I thought my old friends might tolerate, or even welcome, my childishness a little better. I wanted them to know that, whatever had become of everyone else, for me, the dream of those summer nights had never ended.

I especially wanted to be able to tell Scott the whole thing, and to tell him what it meant to me. It might give him a chance to laugh at his sentimental older brother, and I thought anything that could make him laugh would be good right now.

*   *   *

I SHRUGGED OFF the reverie and turned on the television. CNN Headline, and the teasers for the network nightly news, really, really didn't look good for our side. Killeret was absolutely right. Everything they were doing with the story looked like a setup before they jumped on Scott.

The intercom buzzed and the secretary let me know that Roger Przeworski, the Scorpion Shack house attorney that I'd put on the job of preparing an impact evaluation, was here to give his report.

Roger said hello, declined coffee, sat down, pulled out his notepad, folded his arms across his chest, looked at me intently, and went straight to the bad news. "Mr. Blackstone, it's always gambling when you get in front of a jury, but taking this case—and pouring Republic Wright money into it—would be a big gamble. No major firm will touch the defendant's case, the media's against you, Congress is in on the other side—not just from that clown Rasmussen. Name any big player and they're against us. And so far our side isn't even shooting back." He plainly had been chewing over many thoughts, none happy.

"Do you recommend we settle?"

"No. In our present position, Republic Wright would lose nearly everything. We *have* to play it out. But there's no point in playing if you don't play to win, and given the resources being poured into the other side, we need to start fighting, and we need to do it right away and with all the resources we can command. I'm not sure that the Board will stick their necks as far out as they would have to."

"The politicking is my problem," I pointed out. "I've made that Board see reason many times before. What's essential is that you do agree it's what we have to do."

He nodded once, emphatically. "It is. But the legal battle is going to be *big*. I think you're on the right track, Mr. Blackstone, but I can't really claim to be optimistic."

I thanked him for his candor and saw him to the door, then went back to sit, look out the window, and ransack my memory, running through all my personal contacts and friendships—there weren't many of those, Scorpion Shack and Republic Wright having been my life for a long time. I tried to think of any trial lawyer I knew, with any knowledge of civil procedure, in any connection at all, who might help.

The phone rang. I picked it up. The secretary said it was Andrew Riscaveau. I stared out the window for a moment while I tried to figure out a way to not have the conversation, but when you run a secret facility, you have to talk to security people. "Put him through." Probably he'd found out some trivial thing about a staff member and was going to present it to me triumphantly; he tended to see spies and conflicts of interest wherever he looked.

"Good afternoon, Mr. Blackstone. This is Andrew Riscaveau, Security." (He always began that way, as if I might not remember him from the last time.) "I've got two pieces of news for you, one good and one weird. The good news is that we vetted the three Chinese engineers you wanted—the one from Hong Kong and the two from Taiwan—and they're all clean as can be. Human Resources already has the clearance, so you can start them as soon as they can do the paperwork."

That was a fuels chemist and two metallurgists that I'd desperately wanted. "That news was more than good," I said, "that was wonderful. And a week early."

"Sometimes I get lucky. Now, on the other thing, I've got something kinda weird going on and you might be able to help me with it. Three of your employees from your Washington office, Meg Barlow, Roger Przeworski, and Percy MacKay, have requested extremely classified material in the last few hours."

"Yes," I said, wondering where the copy of my authorization had gotten lost to, "that was at my request. If you didn't get a copy of my authorization, I can have one forwarded to you; meanwhile, I'd appreciate it if you could just clear them to continue."

"But this isn't stuff they need to know," he said.

"They need to know it for the project I put them on," I said. Everything always had to be explained to Riscaveau more than once, though he was no fool. It must be his way of getting more than one version of the story, so he could compare the two and look for lies. "I did send out the authorization. I'll send it again if need be."

"I got the authorization. Why do you believe the company should be digging your brother out of his mess?"

"I don't believe that," I said. "I believe that the *Columbia* disaster is going to have major impacts on the space tourism business, and space tourism is the likely first market for StarBird. I authorized our attorneys for an impact study to figure out what the lawsuits arising from the accident will do to space tourism—and to suggest possible interventions to help things move in a direction favorable to us."

"Marketing and politics are not your territory and you shouldn't be messing in them. Plus you're authorizing people with no need to know to go prying into classified matters. And think about how it all looks. If Republic Wright gets seriously involved, it's going to call attention to you, because you're his brother, and there would be press accusations."

"Republic Wright already is involved—we're a defendant. And there are press accusations of every damned thing in the world," I said, trying to keep my temper.

"Well, exactly. There will be accusations, and that means attention will be called to you, and once attention is called to you, what happens to the secrecy around the Scorpion Shack? If you get involved in a highly publicized case, they'll make the connection, start looking into you, and before you know it, the cover's blown on Scorpion Shack."

"There's hardly any cover left," I pointed out. "We've been around for seventy-one years. You can find 'Scorpion Shack' in the index of almost any history of aviation. There are aviation buffs with binoculars out in boats in the Gulf for half our test flights. And I'm sure that every foreign embassy in the United States already knows who I am, and probably has my home phone number. The secrecy is more of a convenience for the company than anything else." I thought of Eddie, and it seemed to me sillier than ever that we had to pretend that Ghost Town and Scorpion Shack didn't exist, when we both knew almost everything about each other's operations. "And besides, I'll admit to being worried about my brother, but I'm not endangering Scorpion Shack—or threatening your security concerns—in any way. The hypothetical security issues you're raising seem to be motivated by a dislike of the business policies I support. You've made no secret of your dislike for Starcraft, but decisions about it are not made at your level. I'm a vice-president; you're a section head. Are you so sure you're within your own bounds?"

After a long pause he said, "Should you mention that project on the phone?"

"Should you call the head of Scorpion Shack from a line whose security you don't trust?"

He slammed down the receiver. I let myself gloat for a moment before reminding myself that I had let my temper get the better of me and that as likely as not the whole affair would turn around and bite me. Riscaveau had a bad temper and once he lost it at someone he would find ways to cause trouble for months afterwards. I wouldn't be getting any more early, easy security clearances for a while—that was certain.

Perhaps I'd have to come up with something in the way of a peace offering, or maybe the time had finally come to crowd that annoying, petty man out of my company—I had the influence to do it, but I hadn't felt, until that moment, that it might be worthwhile.

I let my thoughts drift away from my clash with Riscaveau, and back to the problem of getting Scott a lawyer. Just before Riscaveau had called, I had had a thought on the tip of the brain, some idea that would work . . . I couldn't remember what that half-formed thought had been.

I jumped when the phone rang; it was the secretary letting me know that she was going home. I thanked her, wished her a good weekend, hung up, and realized I did know one Washington lawyer with a powerful reputation, who was good at difficult and desperate causes, and not afraid of anyone. Furthermore, she was an old friend.

A few minutes later I was driving north, toward Georgetown, in a much better frame of mind. No doubt this would be quite the sales job, but since she'd been seven years old and I'd been nine, I'd usually been able to get Thalia to see things my way. Even if she couldn't represent Scott, herself, she could find the right person.

Besides, no fight that Thalia got into was ever hopeless for her side. My ex-sister-in-law was probably the toughest and most tenacious person I knew.

I thought that I shouldn't just knock on her door after several months of not even saying hello, so I dialed her on the cell phone. In ten minutes I had persuaded her to let me stop by to explain things; Thalia and Scott didn't know it yet, but in a short time she was going to be his lawyer. I rang Scott, passed on Killeret's good wishes and the news that RW was moving toward getting serious about the legal fight, and told him I was very close to having a first-rate attorney for him.

"Is it going to be someone I've heard of?" he asked.

"I'm nearly certain you have." I hung up the cell phone and enjoyed the drive in the fine fall weather.

CHAPTER FIVE

THALIA:

I had been getting bits and pieces of the story of the shuttle crash every few hours as I went through my too-busy days. Just after checking into the hotel in Sacramento, I'd caught the launch on television. I was annoyed with myself; two years after the divorce, I still had the habit of seeing how my ex's business was doing. As far as I could tell, he'd made a clean break and only thought of me in connection with Amos; I still kept waking up in the night and wondering where he was and when he was coming home.

After turning off the television in annoyance, I'd gone out for a quick bite, and then to bed early. When I got up Thursday, an hour before dawn, the networks were fully into their macabre repetition of the footage of the crash on Easter Island.

Remembering how much MJ had meant to Amos, I called Mrs. Talbert. She said Amos had already heard, and had seemed very sad, and that the teacher was doing a special session about MJ's death. I didn't have any easy way to get hold of Amos at school, and besides it wasn't really the kind of emergency for which I could have him summoned to the phone.

While I ate room service breakfast, showered, made up, and

dressed, I left the television on. I caught a glimpse of Scott surrounded by shouting reporters, just before I had to go testify. He really looked like hell, of course.

I was kept waiting all day (something that happens every time you go to Sacramento), until finally I got to give my testimony at 4:45 in the afternoon. By that time the cameras and microphones were all gone. Half the seats for the committee itself were empty. The only person in the audience was a guy waiting to testify after me, somebody from a parolees' organization that I wasn't familiar with.

Dutifully, I put in my hour of talking to bored legislators, explaining why the Coalition was concerned with prisoners, with victims, and with parolees, and why any policy that dealt with just one group without thinking about the other two was bound to fail. I testified that it was stupid to release dangerous people, and stupid to lock up people who were no danger to anyone, and perfectly possible to avoid doing either. Maybe it all did some good. Sometimes you testify just so that, later on, they can't pretend that they didn't know.

I had been able to get a red-eye flight to DC from San Francisco for the next morning, and I've gotten good at sleeping on planes. At Dulles, as I gulped some plastic-wrapped preservative-ridden pastry and stale burned coffee, I was able to hear twenty minutes or so of news from the snack bar TV. It really looked like they were out to get Scott. Most of it was sympathetic coverage of the James family's planned lawsuit.

I also saw Jasper Haverford, perfectly groomed and completely corrupt as always, at a press conference. I was worried about Scott, in the abstract, perhaps, but given the weakness of the case, any good lawyer should be able to chew Haverford up and spit him out.

I had to testify on Capitol Hill late that afternoon, but I was supposed to attend a parole hearing as an expert witness in Richmond at ten A.M., and with luck, in between those obligations, I'd be able to shower and change clothes. For now, I just washed my face and redid my makeup in the airport bathroom. I checked myself once more in the mirror before going. I looked tired. There wasn't much I could do about that.

The parole board kept me around for an hour, trying to decide whether they needed to hear from me that this prisoner was a bad candidate for parole because he had made a number of threats against victims who had testified against him, and violent offenders often do carry out such threats.

About the time I was thoroughly wilted and almost falling asleep in my chair, and my stomach was rumbling, the parole board noticed they didn't need to hear from me after all, since the prisoner had committed a violent crime while in prison, and therefore they couldn't grant parole anyway.

I drove back north and had time to dash into my house, pour bottled Italian dressing onto a bag of ready-to-go salad and devour that, heat and devour an entire frozen pizza (that and the salad had been most of what was left in the fridge, except for some bread, milk, and lunch meat), get a shower, redo my hair and makeup, put on clean clothes, and catch a twenty-minute catnap in my favorite armchair. I got out the door eleven minutes ahead of schedule, with my composure nearly intact. I even got to the hearing on the Hill early, and they were happy for the chance to start right on time.

As it turned out, the hearing was a show staged by three senators who had invited me so that they could be videotaped berating me, probably for campaign footage in their states. I didn't get to say much—the purpose of this hearing was to have me on camera, while the senators accused me of being soft on crime and of subverting the Constitution.

After forty minutes, I was allowed to read my testimony aloud, while the senators got up and walked around. There were no questions at the end. At last I was free.

I drove by Mrs. Talbert's and Amos was sitting in the chair nearest the door, his overnight bag, already packed, in his lap. He had most of his homework already done, except the math—if he'd had that already done, I'd have thought Mrs. Talbert must be giving me back the wrong child. Amos liked school, as much as any normal kid can, and did most of his homework without prodding, but making himself do math was not yet in his power.

Amos wasn't hungry and we both just wanted to get home. I talked with Amos about the trip, but I'm afraid it probably bored him; adult frustration and stress usually did.

When we got home, while I sorted out mail, email, voice mail, and all the other stuff that piles up any time I go out of town, and drafted some quick memos for Monday morning, Amos had some milk and cookies, and started his math homework—or rather, he drew airplanes and rockets all around the margins. I suggested that he ought to do a few problems. I wished this were Scott's weekend with him, because Scott seemed to have a knack for getting him to tolerate math.

For that matter, every so often, Scott, who was often lonely and bored, would take both of us out to dinner before departing with Amos. The idea of not having to do anything about dinner was very appealing right now, even though when Scott did that, as often as not, he and I ended up barely speaking before the meal was over, sniping at each other while Amos stared down at his plate and all of us wanted to be somewhere else.

I was disgusted with myself—wishing my ex would take care of me because I was tired. All the same, it would have been nice . . .

To banish the thought from my head, I reminded myself that Scott had gotten Amos into the idiotic idea of going to a beach cabin in the fall. I knew that the Blackstones frequently did that, but my side of the family had more sense. Just once, the year before we got married, Scott had talked me into doing that. It rained all weekend, we both got colds, and the power went out so that neither of us got anything that we were supposed to do done. The woodstove was too hard to light and neither of us was good at cooking on it, so we ate at Burger King, the nearest open restaurant. Scott spent half of Saturday afternoon splitting wood and ignoring me, took the first hot bath because his muscles were sore, and then wanted a back rub afterward, instead of letting me get *my* hot bath.

I couldn't quite believe I was letting myself get angry about a fight we'd had before even getting married, especially since Scott need not ever trouble my life again, but I hold grudges a long time, and this was one I'd probably hold till my dying day. Even today, with everything so different, just thinking about that cold, miserable weekend makes me furious.

And now he was trying to get Amos into it.

A therapist I had once, before I got too busy to make it to appointments, told me that when people are tired or have too much to do, they sometimes deliberately make themselves angry, just to get the adrenaline to attack the next problem. Maybe that's what I was doing, because after sitting there and stewing myself into a half-fury for a few minutes, I took a deep breath, sat down next to Amos, and made sure he was doing all the problems, especially the fractions and decimals he hated. I extorted a promise to work until he was done, stuck the kettle on the stove, and started getting things ready for my standard decompression routine.

When the kettle whistled five minutes later, Amos was still making his way through the worksheets. Usually that meant he had made a real commitment to getting his math done, and could be trusted to keep going. I poured the boiling water into the pot with the tea ball and carried the tray down to the bathroom. It was time to apply the process that usually humanized me: it started with putting on an Art Tatum CD, and pouring the first wonderful cup of Imperial Gunpowder. Then I took a long, extra-hot shower, to get the feel of airports and legislative chambers off. I dried with a couple of my favorite big, soft towels, and slipped into T-shirt, sweatpants, and fuzzy slippers, and sat down and read a chapter of one of Lawrence Block's "burglar" novels, sitting right there on the toilet, where I couldn't hear a ringing phone or be aware of anything other than the book in front of me, Art Tatum's swinging piano, and the perfect taste of the extra-strong tea.

Forty-five minutes after heading into the bathroom, I was most of the way back to human, though still tired. When I came out to the dining room, Amos had done his math, and was working on getting ahead for next week, reading an excruciatingly dull article about pioneers moving across the Appalachians. I settled onto the couch to drink the last cup from the pot and consider whether I should order a pizza, or Chinese, or just make up some sandwiches. I'd just eat and go to bed; Amos always thought it was funny that on the weekends we had the same bedtime. Tomorrow I had nothing in the morning, so I could look forward to a long night's sleep, until Amos would wake me up with his cartoons.

I finished the cup of tea, sighed with contentment, and set it down on the end table. "Kid, what would you like to eat tonight?"

"Anything except pizza, Chinese, or sandwiches."

"Got the homework about done?"

"Yeah. Mom, is the Cumberland Gap that place up in the mountains that we went to, that Saturday last month?"

"Yep."

"There's a thing in my social studies book about it. It says it was a vittle pass through the mountains."

"Vital."

"Whatever. Did we go there because it was vital?"

"Vital means life-and-death, Amos. Latin 'vita,' meaning life. Like vitamin and vitality. So they mean that the whole movement to go west and settle the frontier would have died out without it; if you didn't have the Cumberland Gap, you couldn't settle the West. But the Cumberland Gap isn't vital to you and me. *We* went there because it was close and cheap."

"Whatever." He flopped down on the couch next to me.

"Are you hungry?" I asked. "I'm not, yet."

"Naw. Mrs. Talbert gave me some soup and a sandwich and a

piece of pie just before you picked me up, cause she said that you might not feel like getting dinner right away. We can have a late dinner tonight, as long as it's not pizza, Chinese, or sandwiches."

Clearly my son was not going to negotiate on that issue. "There's a Mexican place that delivers. I'll call them in a while," I offered.

"Excellent. Can we watch a video together tonight?"

For once I didn't have work to do at home, so of course I said yes. It was only 5:45 and I could still probably get to bed by nine, sleep right through till 7:00 the next morning, and still have the full day to spend with Amos.

Agreeing to watch a video was the easy part. Amos was ten years old, and his favorite movies were the ones that involved the maximum possible number of explosions. We finally agreed to some suspense movie in which there wouldn't be too much shooting—maybe an older mystery—and started to look through the shelves of videos (I'm a movie nut and I have a couple of hundred).

Naturally the phone rang. As I got it, out of the corner of my eye, I could see Amos shrug and turn the TV on, already sure the evening with his mother would vanish. I had disappointed him again. Worse yet, he was used to it.

"Thally, it's Nick." Nick is the only person who still calls me "Thally." "How are you?"

"I'm all right," I said. I couldn't remember when I had last spoken to my ex-brother-in-law—probably close to a year.

"Well, I imagine you've seen the news."

"Not in the last few hours. I know MJ was killed, the shuttle crashed on Easter Island, and the James family is going to sue Scott about it."

"Here's the additional news, then. Curtiss Aerospace is going to settle out of court in a way that leaves Republic Wright, Share-Space—and Scott, as an individual—in a very bad position. Curtiss will walk away with minor damage and everyone else will be devastated."

"I see that this is terrible news for Scott, but is there something that you think I can do about it?"

Nick's voice broke up for a second and I had to ask him to repeat it.

"All right, can you hear me now?"

"Yes."

"Curtiss Aerospace, and Haverford, and maybe some other parties, are putting very heavy-handed pressure on the big firms not to take Scott's case. And for some reason I don't know, the pressure seems to be working. So I had hoped to get some advice about where we can find a good defense attorney who can take the pressure. I'll pay whatever I have to, but I want a Clarence Darrow or a Bill Kunstler or an F. Lee Bailey on this—someone that will fight to win, not find a nice friendly compromise to take a big share of."

"Well, I know plenty of people with the personality, but most of them are more acquainted with criminal law than civil, and more up to date on breaking-and-entering than on space law. This is a terrible break for Scott, to be caught in the middle of something like this. Does the other side have any genuine grounds for the suit?"

"Well, it's my opinion that the poor idiot child didn't do anything wrong, but that is just my opinion."

Nick is only four years older than Scott, but I suppose that when Scott is 80, and Nick is 84, he'll still be calling his younger brother "the poor idiot child."

Amos had come creeping in to see what was up; I mouthed "Uncle Nick" at him. His eyes got wide, and he went back to the room with the TV. Scott was Amos's hero, of course, but his Uncle Nick was sort of a mythic demigod, partly because Amos had seen him so rarely in the last few years.

"Anyway," Nick said, "it happens that business is taking me through your part of the city, and I've got a while before I've got to go to a late dinner. I was wondering if I could come by and just get some of your thoughts. This isn't something I should discuss over the phone, especially not over an unsecured cell phone. It has some delicate points about it. And there's some complexity."

" 'Some complexity,' " I said, laughing. "You almost had me fooled into the whole deal for a second there, Nick." I wasn't angry at all. It was all too familiar. Ever since I'd been six years old, and Nick and Eddie had been my eight-year-old heroes at the beach, I knew that when Nick said "there's some complexity" what he meant was "I've got several angles of my own that I don't intend to tell you about" or "Please don't ask me about the way I'm shading the truth"—usually both. Whether the question involved a chilled watermelon stolen from a neighbor's porch, or a kite that happened to be blown apart with illegal fireworks within sight of the township constable, or the question of how Scott had happened to be dyed that funny color all over with cranberries, one of the first things out of Nick's mouth was always "Well, there's some complexity."

Nick laughed too. "Okay, you caught me. But it so happens that getting Scott out of this mess would do me good, and that's turning out to be much harder than I'd ever have guessed. And I do need a far better defense lawyer than I seem to be able to find on my own. That much is absolute truth." He paused. "May I come by, to talk? It wouldn't take more than half an hour."

"Aw, Nick, I flew back from California real early, and it's been a real long day. I look like hell, I'm incredibly tired, and Amos and I were going to watch a video and go to bed. My calendar's pretty open tomorrow; couldn't it keep till sometime tomorrow morning?" I couldn't imagine letting my super-neat ex-brother-in-law see how I lived.

Nick said, "Oh, well, I had hoped to get something put together so I could tell Scott about it. I'd rather he didn't go through another night of worrying."

I had caught him, but that hadn't made Nick stop working angles. He knew that though living with each other had proved to be impossible, Scott and I were still friends, deep down, going back too far to remember. And Nick was right. Scott would worry and brood until some kind of help arrived.

I decided. "You win. Come over, and we'll talk. Call Scott and tell him I'll try to find him a tough lawyer that can get him out of this."

"Will do. I'll see you in a few minutes. And thanks, Thally."

"Hey, the Mars Four stick together," I said.

"Amen." He chuckled and hung up; I was smiling myself. Funny how memories of our childhood club came back, even now.

WHEN MY MIND ranged back to the summer of 1969, I remembered the way I kept veering all summer between dressing up, putting on makeup, and going out to do girl stuff, or hanging around with Scott, Nick, and Eddie and still being one of the guys. It wasn't an easy decision to make. I suppose such things never are.

Favoring "stay one of the guys for another year," there was adventure, creativity, and peers I could punch in the nose when they deserved it. Favoring "get girlish," if I managed to have a summer romance I'd be the envy of the rest of the girls in eighth grade, next fall.

The idea of the Mars promise had come to me because I'd gone through a phase, the year before, of reading the kind of bad biographies of great achievers that are written for schoolkids. Usually there was a scene where the great-man-to-be (there were just starting to be a few books about great women in 1969) vows to do the thing for which he will become famous. I more or less borrowed the whole idea from those books.

I guess I needed to feel like I had a *real* future. Even then I knew that the silly girlish period of adolescence wouldn't last forever. In me, it didn't even make it all the way through eighth grade. After a short period of trying to live for boys, clothes, and makeup, I found out that it was just easier to stop hiding my brains and behave like a person.

Somehow, having made the Mars promise helped that happen sooner and faster. Back there on that sand dune in July 1969, I realized it was a world where people could go to the moon if they decided to, and four kids promising each other might start a journey that ended on Mars. I needed to feel that the world really was that big and open.

Many years later, I thought that a human voyage to Mars would probably never happen. I knew politics and law and public policy, and I knew how difficult it would be to put it together; I had spent years trying to put some rationality into a basic government function like criminal justice, with almost no success.

For a while, I had thought I might contribute indirectly to the human future in space, by keeping Scott functional, but I came to see that that had to be Scott's job.

Maybe, when I had extracted that promise by the Atlantic, more than thirty years before, I had pledged us all to a cause that we were all doomed to give up on. Yet, back then, it had done wonders for me, inside. The feeling that I *could* contribute, or be somebody apart from what I wore and who sat next to me on the bus, stayed with me. Just having said *I am a person who can decide to go to Mars*—no matter how impossible it had turned out by the time I was forty—made being thirteen and fourteen slightly less miserable.

AMOS HAD TUNED to CNN and was solemnly watching the who-knew-how-many-times rerun of the crash, which kept intercutting with pictures of his father answering questions. He had it muted, but I didn't like the look of the visual—when they start showing big dramatic scary moments, and follow them up with pictures of a guy talking calmly, it's usually a way to make the guy who is talking calmly look like either a fool or a liar.

When the commercials came on, Amos killed the screen, still without ever having turned up the volume, and asked me, "Is Dad going to go to jail? They don't think he murdered MJ, do they? They were *friends*."

"It's not a murder case—it's a wrongful-death suit. He's not at risk of jail, but life is going to be pretty tough on your father for a while." I tried to explain the difference between civil and criminal negligence, but he was more interested in the question of what the shuttle had run into. A hole in a spaceship is an easier concept for a ten-year-old than "liability" or "tort."

"So what did Uncle Nick want?"

"He's trying to help your dad out by finding a good lawyer, and it's not going very well, so he's asking me to help him. He'll be coming over here tonight to talk about who he can try to get to represent your father."

Amos's eyes widened. "Wow."

"Wow?"

"You're a lawyer. You could defend Dad in court."

"Most good lawyers keep things out of court, Amos, if they can. But yes, if I had to, I could do it. Right now Nick and I are just going to try to figure out what would be best for Scott. If we're lucky that won't even involve going to court."

"Why, if you're lucky?"

"Because, kid, as you have heard me say so many times before, you never know what a judge or a jury will do. Better to settle it where everyone can make a deal together than to have a bunch of strangers decide what's fair."

"But you still could defend him in court. I mean if you wanted to, and he wanted you to, you could defend Dad. Like lawyers on TV."

"Yes, I might."

"Wow."

I could have tried to clarify things, but this was really the first time I'd ever impressed my son. If he wanted to imagine me in the style of the television trial lawyers, maybe I could let him.

CNN showed a replay of AnnaBeth James making her speech. It was even worse, for Scott's case, than the footage of the wreck.

"Mom? Why did M J die?"

Amos's eyes were serious, but also trusting; he was about as old as you can be and still think your parents might have all the answers.

"Well," I said, "everybody dies, Amos. Someday I will, someday you will. People who do dangerous things—even if they're very, very careful, like your dad—sometimes they have to depend on luck, and sometimes the luck just isn't with them. But even people who never take any chances die sooner or later. So I guess there's not really a why about it."

"It doesn't seem fair."

"No, it docsn't."

"He was really cool. He taught me all that basketball stuff, and he remembered my name. He even talked to me on the phone, that morning when he flew."

"Yes," I said, not sure where Amos was going with it, and just letting him find his own way.

"And now nobody's ever going to believe me."

"Your dad and I will."

"I meant my friends."

"But you know it's true."

"Yeah."

He was quiet for a while, so I slipped my arm around his bony shoulders. He cuddled against me, in a way he hadn't in some years. I could see tears running quietly down his face. "He was really cool," Amos repeated.

I stroked his hair, gently, and handed him a tissue when he snuffled, but my eye was quickly drawn back to the TV screen. The more I saw of AnnaBeth James and the presentations that Jasper Haverford was having her make, the more I thought—I could beat this. I could win this case for Scott.

It was an interesting set of problems, not so much in law as in

PR. You'd have to handle the whole case so carefully—a mother wanting justice for her dead son, the reality that it had just happened and it hadn't been anyone's fault, the need to isolate her from too much jury sympathy while always respecting her grief—entirely apart from my concern for my old friend and the father of my child, this was one *interesting* case.

Normally any good trial lawyer could have won this one hands down, but with so much money and expertise on the other side, plus their huge PR advantage, the very simplicity of the case would work against you. You'd have to keep the idea simple and clear while a huge PR blitz and dozens of high-paid lawyers tried to make it complex enough to argue for liability.

It was a great case; high stakes and high challenge. What Nick needed to find was somebody sharp but new, out to make a reputation, with the right kind of passion. I knew a few attorneys, going hungry on too much pro bono work, who might enjoy a challenge like this, and would love the money.

Just as CNN went to sports news, the doorbell rang. I opened it, and there was Nick, carrying a small briefcase as always. If I hadn't known him as a kid, I'd have thought he'd been born in a dark suit.

He said hi to Amos, accepted the offer of instant coffee, and sat down on my couch. I went out to brew up two cups.

Through the kitchen door, I could hear Amos talking and Nick answering questions. I knew that the blank pad of drawing paper had come out of Nick's briefcase, and he was sketching things about orbits and physics. I wished we saw more of him—though no longer exactly family to me, he was an old close friend, after all, and still Amos's uncle.

I stuck the cups of water and coffee powder into the microwave, and drifted mentally back to the Mars Four and all the things that had happened since those happy days.

The microwave dinged and I got out the coffee, stirred it a couple of times, and carried it out to the living room. "Okay," I said, "now tell me what could be so important that you'd risk the sight of me in my fuzzy slippers to tell me about it."

Nick chuckled. "If you had put it that way, perhaps I *would* have waited for tomorrow. Er, Amos, your mother and I will have to do that unpleasant adult thing of sending you to some other part of the house."

"This is to help Dad, right?"

"You bet."

"Okay." He went off to his room. Because he was so often a latchkey kid I'd broken down and let him have a TV and VCR in there; in a few moments I heard blaring music followed by multiple explosions.

"Well," Nick said, as we sat down at my dinette table, and he carefully squared up his pad to align with the edge of the table, "the facts *are* pretty much what you hear on the news. The accident looks like a collision with a micrometeoroid or orbiting debris.

"Now, here's why I'm so involved, aside from my interest in Scott. There is a big project that this impacts, at the Scorpion Shack, because the project will depend on space tourism to become profitable. Right now it's in that gray area where we haven't actually rolled it out in public yet, but it's very much an open secret in the industry. I think Curtiss may be hoping to strangle our project, and preserve their position, by throwing this suit—at our expense, and NASA's, and Scott's. It's the only explanation that makes any sense of their behavior. Furthermore, there seems to be a fix in, dedicated to keeping us from getting any decent legal representation."

Nick told me about all of it in some detail, and ran far over the half hour we had agreed on, but by now I was fascinated—there was something so clearly wrong here.

Normally plenty of firms would have taken Scott's case just for the connections and the publicity. That's how a law firm accumulates clout. Scott's phone should have been ringing off the hook with offers of representation. Surely the James family wasn't frightening them away, and though Curtiss might buy up some of the available talent, there was no way in which they could buy all of it.

"There has to be another player in the game," I said. "One that neither you, nor RW's legal staff, nor Scott, know anything about. That's who's putting in most of the fix, though they're obviously getting help from Curtiss."

He stared at me. "You really think so?"

"Curtiss wouldn't spend so much money, or use so much influence, just to *lose* a lawsuit. Sure, they don't much care if they don't win. Sure, they benefit from *you* losing. Nevertheless, they're still parties to the suit, and could still lose a lot. And the James family doesn't have the money—they're rich but not *that* kind of rich—or the influence. So Curtiss wouldn't, the Jameses can't, and yet it's clearly being done. Therefore there's at least one more adversary than you know about."

"Who could it possibly be?" Nick asked.

"I have no idea. I was hoping you'd snap your fingers and tell me who you thought it must be. But I can tell you this—sponsoring a suit without acknowledging it in public is *not* the behavior of honest people with honest gains in mind. Depending on what they're doing and how far they're going, it could even be highly illegal. So they're risking millions in something covert. . . . I think you're up against a very big, tough opponent, and whoever you hire as a lawyer will have his or her hands full."

"It seems to me that some lawyers *like* a good, difficult fight," Nick said. "Is there anyone who'd be attracted to a case like this?"

I sighed and admitted the truth. "If Scott will have me, I'm beginning to think of taking this case myself. If I were in private practice, and didn't know Scott, I'd take it in heartbeat. It doesn't belong in court in the first place. There's no way that it's reasonable to hold him liable. That's something their lawyer must have pointed out to them. I would bet that's why they brought in Jasper Haverford, as a hired gun, because their own lawyer, who was probably more prudent, wouldn't touch it. There's nothing about Scott's case that any smart law student couldn't win, hands down, as long as the case is on the up and up—so I don't think it is. And whoever the forces behind it are, they act as if they are very afraid of exposure. That tells me everything I need to know—there's some bastard out there that I can beat, and I'd like to beat." By that time I had the pad out and had been scrawling notes to myself for a while. I don't know whether I have a good memory or not, because I've been a note taker since the minute I could write. I do know that I never feel like I'll remember anything unless I write it down.

I scanned over the notes. "I *could* get a leave of absence and handle the case myself if I wanted to, and I'm beginning to want to." I hadn't tackled anything as interesting as Scott's case in a long time. If the politics around it were really as bad as they looked . . . well, Scott wouldn't get a better lawyer, my life had gotten dull, and the thought of doing anything other than Coalition work for a while had some charm.

Besides, I was intrigued by the question of who was really behind this and what they were after. Not to mention that I had really liked the expression on Amos's face when he realized I might be the one to defend Scott. "If you can provide the funding, I'll take the case. If we're lucky they'll file in New York State—that's the place where it's easiest to win a claim for damages—and it so happens I'm still admitted to the New York bar. If we have to cope with California law, I'll need to find someone to serve as my partner out there."

"I'll get you whatever you need. Money won't be a problem," Nick said. "Well, now that we've solved Scott's problems, how do we let him know they're solved? I would bet that he's at home, but he has his ringer turned off and his automatic answerer on."

"He only lives fifteen minutes from here," I pointed out. "Let's go knock on his door. Just let me tell Amos what's up."

I leaned into the room, where Amos was watching actors run away from an exploding building, and said, "Nick and I are going over to

Dad's house for a few minutes. We'll get him and then come back here. Is there anything you need?"

"We need supper, sooner or later, Mom," he said. "You haven't had any either."

"Well, neither have I," Nick said behind me. "We'll get something on the way back and all eat together."

"Sweet," Amos said.

"He wants something sweet?" Nick asked.

I shook my head. "It means what you or I would mean if we said 'cool.' " I nodded at Amos and said, "Don't open the door for people who aren't us."

As we got into Nick's car, I suddenly thought of something. "Didn't you have a dinner engagement? Can you afford to cancel it?"

"Uh, I kind of figured we'd end up doing this," Nick explained. "So I just figured my dinner was already scheduled, for later at night, so I said—"

"Not exactly the truth, was it?"

"There was some complexity." He backed quickly out of my driveway, as if afraid I might get out of the car and tell him to go find another lawyer.

CHAPTER SIX

SCOTT.

The doorbell rang. Maybe it would be somebody friendly, like
Nikki Earl or Ken Elgin, or even Fred Gernsback. It might be Nick.

Nick and Thalia were standing there. "Here's your attorney,"
Nick said, "I happen to know she's very good. And I seriously doubt
the other side can buy her off."

"But—the Coalition—"

Thalia shrugged and gave me that great smile of hers that I
hadn't seen in so many years. "I needed a break from it, anyway.
And the more I heard from Nick, the more I realized that you were
in real trouble. Besides, Amos thinks I'm going to come to your
rescue, personally catch the bad guys, and generally fix the whole
world, like a movie lawyer. How often do *I* get to be the hero in the
family?"

I had a funny tight feeling in my chest. "That's . . . How are you
getting paid?"

"I'm paying her," Nick said. "At least until I get my employer to
do the right thing."

"Thank you. Thank you a lot. All right, I have a lawyer. Now
what?"

"Come on, you're coming to dinner at my house," Thalia added. "And then we're going to talk about getting you out of this mess you're in."

My eyes were swimming with tears. I hugged Nick, which startled the hell out of my poor old stiff plank of a brother, and Thalia, who hugged back. "Hey, you're welcome," Thalia said. "Let's go. This dump is no place to be when you're depressed."

Once I was out of the empty, echoing house, I felt much better. Inexplicably, a few blocks later, we stopped at a grocery store. Nick jumped out, said we'd just slow him down if we tried to come along, and went in. Thalia and I sat in the car. I think we were both afraid to talk. I was worried that we might start to fight and that I'd lose my lawyer.

In less than fifteen minutes, Nick came back, pushing a cart with three big sacks of groceries. "We're going to be up late tonight," he said, "and we haven't been together as a family since three Christmases ago."

"Well, we're not exactly a family anymore—" Thalia pointed out.

"Nonsense. You're the mother of my nephew and of Scott's son. We've got ten more years of being family ahead of us, whether we like it or not. So, we're going to have a meal together. I'm doing the cooking, and Scott's cleaning the kitchen, and Thalia is supplying the place."

"This is what's called a take-charge leadership style, right?" Thalia asked, winking at me.

"If you're his employer," I responded. "His little brother always called it something else."

"Absolutely," Nick said. "Somebody has to take charge. If there are no further questions, let's get going."

We drove back to Thalia's place and I helped Nick carry the groceries in. It would be hard to explain how much better I was already feeling; part of it, I'm sure, is that at least I wasn't feeling nearly so *alone* anymore, and part of it was sheer familiarity. Nick and

Thalia had rescued me from so many situations when I was younger . . .

After the groceries were in, I spent a few minutes talking to Amos, and going over his math homework with him—he had covered the margins with airplanes and rockets, but he'd solved most of the problems. He was still having some trouble with decimals.

Meanwhile, Nick made all sorts of noise and clatter in the kitchen, punctuated by Thalia's answers to questions about where things were. They were laughing a lot. I heard Thalia say, "No kidding, you're really going to do that, aren't you?"

Amos and I exchanged glances. We went to the kitchen together, to see what was going on.

Nick was laying out an array of food on the kitchen table. I saw it at once. "Friday nights!"

"Well, it *is* Friday night," Nick said, with a twinkle in his eye.

"What's Friday night?" Amos demanded, looking at the kitchen table that had probably never held anything like that before.

"Baked beans, tomato and lettuce salad with French dressing, tater tots, and sloppy joes," I said. "I bet there's vanilla ice cream for dessert."

"But of course," Nick said.

Amos gave me the dirty look you get from a kid who isn't being let in on a joke.

Thalia grinned and put her arm around him. "Well, back when all the families had cabins near each other, down at the beach, we had a shared cooking system. Saturday nights, when the fathers were all down from the city, all the families went out to dinner, usually to the big seafood shack, which was still open then—you know, that burned-out building we go by on our way to the beach. The other nights, we'd feed all three families at one cabin, because making a big meal every third night is much easier than making a middle-sized one every night, and besides that way we all got to spend the time together and help each other with cleanup.

"So Mom—your Grandma Pendergast, Amos, she died before you were born—had Tuesdays and Fridays, Grandma Blackstone had Wednesdays and Sundays, and Mrs. Killeret had Mondays and Thursdays, you see? Now you might remember how we used to go to Grandma Blackstone's for Thanksgiving, before she died, when you were really little, and if you do you probably remember that your Grandma Blackstone was a pretty good cook. Eddie Killeret's mother was even better, nearly a genius in the kitchen. But then there was my mom. She was a great mother but not much of a cook. She had two very simple meals she made, one for Tuesday and one for Friday, every week, every summer, for I don't know how many years. So tonight, evil Uncle Nick is teasing your dad and me by making the Friday night meal—which, I'd have to say, it looks like he's done much better than Mom ever did."

"They kept right on doing it even after the kids were grown, and not coming to the beach anymore," I said, remembering. "Those three women just really liked each other's company, and it was an excuse to enjoy it all summer long. How many years *do* you think they did that?"

Nick looked up at the ceiling. "I think Mrs. Pendergast and Mrs. Killeret were trading off meals for a couple of years before our folks bought our cabin, Scott. And I think they had Mom in the rotation . . . oh, probably within a month of the first summer we were there, because I remember it pretty well. So it would have been—hmm. 1958. The summer Mom was pregnant with you."

"Right," Thalia said, "and the last time they really did the rotation was the summer before my mother died—I was home for the summer, as a sophomore from college, and at the cabin for several weeks. All three of them were still doing it. 1976, remember all the Bicentennial traffic? Anyway, it was around twenty summers of the same thing every Tuesday and Friday, and what Uncle Nick has laid out here is an absolutely perfect copy of the Friday night meal."

"We only got down to the cabin two times last summer," Amos said sadly.

Nick said, "It *is* kind of a shame that we don't get the use out of it we once did."

Amos looked sideways at me, obviously asking a question, and I said, "Well, Amos and I are going to go down there next weekend. Matter of fact, it's a surer thing than it was before, Amos, because at the moment I don't have a job or anywhere else I have to be."

"Fall's great down there," Nick said, and a faraway look came into his eyes.

"If you like cold and rain," Thalia added.

I decided not to have the old fight with her. "Well, let's eat," I said.

Carrying dinner out to the dining room table was almost a ceremony. Nick had copied Friday night dinner so well that my mind kept wandering off into all those summers in the past, and the dreams and hopes we'd held, and the way that the future had seemed to open in front of us like a vast, untouched country, bursting with adventure and achievement for the taking.

I felt sad, as you do about a good thing that's past, but it would have been hard to feel depressed. I felt like I was really home and really where I belonged.

NICK:

I manage people for a living, and management mostly is a matter of getting people to work together when it doesn't come naturally to them. I had thought we'd better get back together emotionally before we tried to take action together. Something as intimate and "family" as a meal had seemed like a good bet.

Oddly, as I was mixing the sloppy joes, it really touched *me*. Almost, I could hear the waves and taste the salt in the air; almost, I could feel the night chill and the cold damp breeze blowing off the ocean, the comfort of curling up by the fire with a magazine on a day with nasty weather. I hadn't made enough time for these people I cared about, in much too long a time. As feelings and senses poured back to me, I realized that whether or not I had made *them* feel like a team, I had made myself feel that way.

While everyone ate, and later over coffee, we all got into telling Amos stories about life on the beach. It occurred to me that this was something of a dirty trick on Thalia, because he would lobby all the harder for the summer cabin for the next year. I might very well like to spend some time there myself—maybe I could spell Thalia and Scott with Amos, so that neither of them would have to try to get the whole summer off? At least if I was down there, Amos would get a decent meal now and then. He looked thin to me.

Amos seemed to like the tales of life at the cabin, anyway, though really they were no more than everyday funny occurrences, and things we'd done like building and flying model rockets, or reading our way through all of the *Mutiny on the Bounty* books in one long week, or that kind of thing.

The meal was a hit, and even the coffee afterwards came in for some praise. (I had discreetly cleaned the coffeemaker, since neither my ex-sister-in-law nor my brother ever does, and I'm not partial to the flavor you get from months of coffee tar.) I'd forgotten how much more fun it is to cook for more people than just me.

After a while, Amos seemed to be tired, and happy enough to go back quietly to his room. Thalia made a pot of fresh coffee, and pulled out one of her notepads. "This will take a while," she said, "but I don't think any of us was going to do anything else tonight, were we? All right, what does everyone know? Let's start with Scott."

He told his story for about half an hour, and her pad got fuller and fuller. Finally, she said, "Do you guys realize that you are playing for the soul of the space program here? Not just its future, but its soul?" She looked at both of us and shrugged. "Serious question. Do you realize how much is at stake?"

THALIA:

I'd enjoyed wallowing in the nostalgia, but at the same time the power of the memories alarmed me. What I remembered more than anything else about summers at the cabin was the way we'd all been bursting with life; every day we got up knowing that something interesting was bound to happen today.

Even as I took notes on what Scott told me, part of my mind wandered off into questions about what the deep issues were here, what kinds of values and ideas were at stake. I had that habit from working on reforming the criminal code—because it's not just about one criminal or one victim, but about getting the system to pay attention to what is just, effective, merciful, and compassionate for *all* the cases, *all* the people that might become criminals, *all* the victims that there might be in the future.

Thus when Scott finished his account, I was struck by the depth of the issues at stake.

"Thally, I still don't see it," Nick said, after a considerable pause. "Without space tourism it's going to be a much slower road to the stars, to be sure, and we won't travel nearly as far down that road in our lifetimes. I understand that. But what do you mean, 'the soul'?"

"I mean this is the case that settles whether space exploration finally becomes what we all hoped it would be when we were kids. The dream was always that people would fly in space—real people, ordinary people, people with kids and mortgages and jobs. Sure, it would be a very small elite that would blaze the trail. Everyone understood that the first people to go up would be highly trained military test pilots, natural athletes with PhD's in science, and other unusual, dedicated people. But the frontier was *supposed* to be opening up to all of us. We hoped that in our lifetimes we would get past one guy in a cramped cockpit who was mainly concerned with getting the spacecraft to fly, and move forward to a whole crew with places to go and things to accomplish, and from there, maybe, to thousands of settlers at a time, spreading out from Earth across the solar system, and maybe even eventually on to the stars, as dreams could reach . . . and *everybody* being part of it."

I looked at the two brothers and couldn't read their expressions. "Remember, guys? We were going to grow up and *live in the space age*. Not just in a period when trained specialists would go above the atmosphere, but the age when the frontier of space would open out in front of us. The final frontier, you know?

"Well, so far, space is settling into being just another industry, no more special than telephones or steel or electricity—everybody knows you need it, and it keeps on going, but there's no spark, no excitement any more.

"And that was the moment when you did something that was just beautiful, Scott. Fred Gernsback's mission reminded people what space used to be about. It showed us the open door to the frontier. Then David Calderon showed that an ordinary person from Anywhere, USA, can go out there and make a contribution. Before the accident you were so *close*. The dream was alive again and growing and spreading.

"Millions of people watching on television were rooting and cheering—remember David Calderon on the Larry King show? How many people sounded like they wanted to go? Don't you both see it? People who had barely looked at the sky in ten years were alive and awake to the possibilities—and they still are.

"If we lose the lawsuit, in the eyes of everyone who shapes opinion, it proves that the whole dream was foolish, and space is for professionals the way that coal mines and operating rooms are for professionals, too dangerous to send people who don't absolutely have to go, just another industry with a not-great safety record.

"*But if we win*—people can start to think about living in the space age, again, about a time when you don't even have to be lucky or rich . . ."

My ex and his brother were staring at me intently.

"Okay, have I run off at the mouth here? Do you think I've had too much coffee or something?"

Scott shook his head. "Thalia, I just wish you'd been writing ad copy for me a year ago."

My god, I had impressed my ex. When was the last time that had happened? To cover my confused feelings, I got back to work. "Okay, now I need whatever you can give me, Nick."

"Let me see," he said. "Officially I'm breaching all kinds of corporate and national security. Since I'm paying you, would what I say be covered by attorney-client privilege?"

"Yep," I said. "And what Scott says to me is also covered. On the other hand, what Scott hears from you isn't covered."

Nick shrugged, nodded, and told us the whole story of Starcraft. He explained why anything that killed space tourism would kill StarBird, and dead-end the Starcraft program, and might well bankrupt Republic Wright itself.

I looked at my notes again and said, "Well, this clinches it. The stakes are more than big enough. There's a fix in, all right, and it can't be anybody that we know about. Mrs. James is a sweet old lady—but all she is, is the mother of a dead athlete. And Curtiss isn't going to come out of this badly, win or lose—so they couldn't possibly have the level of commitment that would be required to go out there and twist so many arms so hard. We're up against someone with incredibly deep pockets and more drive than I think any American corporation has, and we don't know who they are. Finding out is going to be one of my first priorities. Can you guys give me fifteen minutes to just think while I look at my notes?" I like to do that before I tell a client anything. I had already arrived at a conclusion, but I wanted to check my own thinking.

The two of them went out on the couch to talk aerospace industry gossip.

I sat down and checked over my notes. I had no doubt. Not only was there a big, powerful silent partner on the other side, but for some reason they were specifically trying to scapegoat Scott and ShareSpace. It didn't look like personal revenge—hardly anyone taking revenge can resist telling their victim what is going on. Scott had no business competitors, so the most likely objective was to make Starcraft fail.

I called them in, summed up, and said, "Therefore, our first job is to find out who we're really fighting, so that we know what the stakes are, what the other side might do, and most of all what we have to offer them in the way of compromises or threats."

"I can't believe you're convinced there's a conspiracy agsint me in this. That just sounds so paranoid to me," Scott complained.

"There's an old saying among lawyers that even paranoids have enemies," I said. "And don't knock paranoia—in moderation, it's a survival trait. The interesting question is, *who?* Bingo Rasmussen hates your guts, because besides being a shortsighted hick who plays to his most ignorant constituents' prejudices, he's also petty and vengeful. But he wouldn't have the pull to do all this, and though I'm sure he hopes you lose the suit, he also wouldn't have the imagination to see it as anything more than a way of harassing one space business, one time, into bankruptcy. This is more like a subtle way of redirecting American space policy, and guys like Rasmussen aren't subtle. There must be far more money or power at stake than I can see here."

"What about Curtiss?" Nick asked. "Is there a way they could get money out of losing the suit, or having it all land on Scott?"

"I don't see how. They've already got more than fifty percent of shuttle operations and they're the prime contractor for the space station. An expanding private market might inconvenience some old execs there who are set in their ways, but I can't believe the company as a whole could resist the reward of having their market expand enormously."

"That sounds right to me," Nick said. "So do you want me to ask around, try to find out who this could be?" He sat back, straightened his tie—I just realized that he had cooked all of dinner in his three-piece suit and hadn't gotten a spot on him, which was perfectly Nick. For that matter, so was being in a coat and tie, visiting family at eleven at night.

"That might be helpful," I said. "But I can't imagine that there's much in the US aerospace industry you haven't already heard about. So it must be somebody who's not even part of the US aerospace industry, and that makes no sense at all." I yawned and stretched. "I'm probably about ready to pull this together into a plan, after which we can all get some sleep. Would you guys like to switch over to beer?"

Scott and Nick both shook their heads; those two brothers had always been kind of straight-arrow. "Diet Coke?" I asked, and they nodded.

I got a beer for me and diet Coke for them, opened them all up, and carried them back from the kitchen on a tray. As I served them out, I held up my can of beer and said, "Spirit of the Mars Four. I kind of wish Eddie was here."

Nick chuckled—I had been sure he'd remember and probably think it was sort of childish, which I guess it had been. Scott, on the other hand, gaped at me as if I'd really startled him. We clinked our cans together, smiling at each other.

I explained. "The only way we will get anywhere is to fight it out, head-on, and force our real opponents to disclose themselves. Until we do know who's behind this, we play this out like any ridiculous lawsuit by someone going after the deep pockets for an accident that wasn't anybody's fault. The grounds for that are overwhelming, anyway. So if we push hard, sooner or later, whoever they are, they're going to have to show themselves."

The phone rang. I picked it up. "Hello?"

"Thalia Blackstone?"

"Yes?"

"We know what you're talking about with the Blackstone brothers, and we want you to stop. If we see any evidence at all that you are continuing with this, you'll be sorry." There was a click and a dial tone.

I hung up the phone and told the guys, "See, there they are now."

After I told Nick and Scott about it, they were both determined to stay there and protect me and Amos. That was really silly, and I said so. "Do you know how many calls I get every month from people who think that what the Coalition does is wrong? And how many of those threaten me? This is routine for anybody in any kind of political activism. The world is full of people who can't be bothered to have a coherent opinion or try to solve a problem, but who have unlimited time to make anonymous threats. It's part of the cost of accomplishing anything. You *know* that, Scott. We got harassing phone calls a couple of times a week after I set up the Coalition; you used to get furious about them."

"Well, I'm still furious about them. And it used to be just people calling up and being rude. This was a direct threat."

"Oh, I get those too, nowadays," I pointed out. "You can't let them run your life, really."

"How often do people act on those threats?" Scott asked.

I shrugged. "Depends on what you mean by 'act on the threats.' Now, come on, we all have a lot to do tomorrow."

Nick said, "Not so fast. You're avoiding the question."

"You could at least call me when something like that happens," Scott added.

"How often do you stand next to machinery that could kill you? And how often do *you* call *me* about that?"

"You're evading again, Thally," Nick said.

"Right. I'm a lawyer. I can evade all night if I have to. But I want to get to bed, and I don't want you guys camping on my floor tonight. This one didn't sound nearly as serious as some of the others I've had. If there are more threats, I'll hire a bodyguard. Why don't you both go home and get some sleep, so that tomorrow we are not all exhausted, with frayed nerves?"

I had to repeat that argument, pretty much exactly the same way, three times before they left. Finally they did, making me promise to call them if anything even slightly out of the ordinary happened. I did check the locks, but otherwise I just went to bed.

CHAPTER SEVEN

Thalia:

The next morning, Saturday, I phoned all the board members of the Coalition and told them I would be taking a few months off to handle a private case. They weren't happy, but they were all well aware that the Coalition had been my creation from the start and that I had more than trained the staff to keep it running. By the time I was finished with Scott's case, either the Board would be eager to have me come back again, or more likely they would find out that the people I had trained were as good as they needed to be, and I would have to go start another job for myself elsewhere. There are always enough things wrong for a reform-minded lawyer to be able to create some work.

After that, I made sure Amos had the rest of his homework done, and spent most of the day running necessary errands and setting up an office, plus deliveries and appointments. Amos went out and played with his friends; it was probably the first "weekend off" he'd had since the divorce, and he came in tired out and happy.

On Sunday, Scott took Amos to the Air and Space Museum, while I made up an extensive set of "to do" lists.

On Monday morning, I was finally able to get to work on my

side of the problem, and I was up early to do it, eager to get started, which told me, more than anything else, that electing to defend Scott had been the right choice. I hadn't had a big, high-publicity case in a long time, and I'd forgotten how much you "get up" for them.

I was officially out of the office at the Coalition by noon, leaving things in the hands of Maggie and Craig, my two assistants, who had been practically running everything for the last couple of years anyway. That afternoon I looked at four offices, picked one, signed a by-the-month agreement on it, and made some more calls. Late in the afternoon, I recorded a couple hours of an interview with Scott, and talked to Nick on the phone, to make sure I had absolutely anything that they knew or could think of in connection with the case.

Scott ran through everything once again: He had been interested in getting space tourism going as a profit-making venture for a long time. He had sold tickets on the single most reliable method of getting human beings into orbit ever invented. He had been scrupulous in every aspect of his dealings. There was no reason apart from sheer bad luck for him to be in the dock.

Nick supplied a few more details of background: Republic Wright had to win this or be bought out, and there seemed to be some people within the company who thought that getting bought out would be a good thing.

Despite all my re-emphasizing that they were to tell me everything, no matter how trivial or how unimportant it might seem, neither of them could remember anything very different from what they had come up with on Friday night. I hadn't really expected them to, but you always have to try.

Tuesday morning went into setting up some rented furniture in the by-the-month office—I refuse to work out of my home, since I'm convinced it's the shortest road to utter madness for anyone who has to be both a lawyer and a mother. I called Jasper Haverford's office, along with ShareSpace, Curtiss, Republic Wright, and the NASA investigators, to let them know that I was Scott's attorney and where I was accepting mail.

During the afternoon I had a temp agency send over a bunch of people and interviewed them. By dinnertime I had a staff of one secretary, a researcher, and a paralegal, and a good private detective whom I'd worked with a couple of times before. I called Nick and told him how expensive it would be. He laughed and said he'd thought about spending more than that on a private jet last year.

Early Wednesday morning, the FedEx guy brought in a book-sized red and blue cardboard box, stuffed with all the documents Haverford had filed with the court and all the responses he had received so far. Haverford was corrupt, hyper-aggressive, and as near a crook as he could legally be, but he was a pro (or at least one of his junior attorneys was) and it was exactly what he was required to give me.

The first page contained the best news, as far as I was concerned—we would be in the New York courts, which meant a jury that was friendly to the plaintiff, but smart. Since the alternatives were Florida (friendly to the plaintiff and maybe not so smart) or California (friendly to every flaky argument in the world and, worse yet, creative) I was pleased. "In a New York court, even if we get no more breaks," I told Scott on the phone, "we stand a good chance of getting the jury to see the law and the evidence the way we do, and if we do, we win. When you have a strong team, you want a good ref."

The first part of winning a celebrity lawsuit is pure PR, because just as it's possible to have a client convicted in the media, it's also possible to have a client acquitted there. It's hard to say how much influence public opinion has on the verdict, but there is no question at all that it affects the size of settlements and what kind of life your client will have once the case fades from the headlines.

I set up interviews with reporters who I knew would be sympathetic to Scott, like Nikki Earl and Fred Gernsback, and worked on getting placement in syndicated columns and feature stories. I lined up as many appearances, press conferences, and public communications of all kinds as I could, which is what you do when your guy is not only innocent, but obviously and sympathetically innocent. I declined anything that would put Scott on the same stage with any member of the James family—when you're doing a public appearance, you just can't win if you're bluntly telling an obviously suffering victim that they aren't entitled to a settlement. If you want people to think your client is the "real victim in all of this," you'd better not have them sitting too near to anyone who looks like a better candidate.

I got two of the lower-rung cable channels interested in doing stories about the dangers of space with a promise of getting Scott, plus a bunch of people that Nick would set up for me, for their interviews. Within a few weeks, they'd be doing something tied to Michael James and space travel anyway, and if our side didn't have input, then the other side would go unanswered. This way we could probably steer coverage toward the challenge and adventure—and the general feeling that tourist space flights were a positive thing with relatively little risk—and make it sound as if the big question were "Are we going to let one grief-maddened family, having fallen under the sway of a sleazeball lawyer, shut every American out of space just to gratify their feelings of remorse?"

On the other hand, if I let those same producers run along on their own, without providing them with anything from our side, no doubt the issue would have been presented as something like "Are we going to let greedy businessmen steal spacecraft that the taxpayer paid for, specifically to use to kill the celebrities who are most loved by children?"

Neither question really had much to do with the merits of the case, in fact or law, but whichever one of them was in the public mind by the day the verdict came back would determine the course of our whole next generation in space. It was a silly way to run anything, but, at least in the near future, my job was to win the case, not fix the system.

I had told Scott early on that even if there had not been an issue of truth, it made little sense to try to claim that space *wasn't* dangerous; manifestly some people had died in space, getting to space, and coming back from space, and any points made about the relative odds compared with other destinations and transportation would be perceived as technically picky, word games, or beside the point. It made more sense to claim that the dangers had nothing to do with having a civilian travel in space, and that the accident had resulted from bad luck, not negligence and certainly not malice. If we could get that claim out in dozens of different print and media channels, then pretty soon people would be repeating it as if they had thought of it themselves, and our spin on the subject would become part of the "climate of opinion" or the "conventional wisdom." In a highly public case, that means that if the client loses, the public reaction is "Don't those people have any commmon sense?" and if the client wins, it's "Well, of course, what else could the jury do?"

Sooner or later there would be some real evidence, of course, and I'd be able to get to work on the case to be presented in court—but for right now, understandably enough, NASA was keeping all the evidence under wraps while they performed their own investigation, and so I kept right on working on the public-relations/issues-management side of the problem. Time enough to do other things, when there were other things to do.

The most unpleasant part of the whole business was that to win in the court of public opinion, we would have to isolate AnnaBeth James from much of the sympathy and support she had been receiving, and get people to begin saying out loud that, sorry as they felt for M J's mother, her emotional need for "closure" was far outweighed by the greater social need for progress and opportunity. We would have to encourage people to see her as unreasonable, obsessive, even a little crazy.

It was a cruel sort of face to paint on a woman who had lost a son like Michael James. I couldn't imagine the pain that she and M J's sisters must have been feeling. All the same, I was out to win our case, not the James family's, and their lawsuit, however emotionally cathartic it might be, had little equity or justice about it. I couldn't let it prevail in the public mind. Ultimately the goal had to be not just to win, and not just to have people believe we deserved to win, but to have people think that suing us had been a ridiculous thing to do; that was what would free Scott and ShareSpace, and the whole community of space activists and entrepreneurs, to push ahead in the years to come.

During those first few weeks, at least every other day, the lawyers for ShareSpace, Curtiss, and ASU would call. They always urged me to settle out of court, even before the NASA report gave us any facts to go on. They kept edging closer and closer to offering to pay any judgment against Scott, which was nice of them, but not the issue that interested us.

Every time they would call with another offer, I'd get on the phone and try to reinstall the spines in the attorneys working for Republic Wright, and then call up Nick's house lawyer, Roger Przeworski, and have him call them too. The RW attorneys were Boucher, Baker & Chandler, a huge New York firm, and it seemed that when I called them, I never spoke to the same person twice. Przeworski was having much the same experience, and we were both becoming convinced that this was one of those law firms that was used to handling things "professionally," meaning that they never did anything that could be construed as a failure to act correctly, but they were much more interested in being correct—and racking up fees—than in winning.

My problem, and Przeworski's, was to try to get them to make some kind of commitment to doing what it took to win the case; from their viewpoint, that was much more risky than just jumping through all the right hoops, having RW pay an out-of-court settlement, and sending in a bill. They kept calling me about ways that perhaps we could get Curtiss, ASU, and ShareSpace to pay more of the settlement deal, even though we'd emphatically said we had no desire to settle at all.

After the third such call from Boucher, Baker & Chandler within a week, Nick suggested that I have a talk with Eddie Killeret, and gave me his home number. "Just like the rest of us," he said, "Eddie's been too busy for family, and so he's divorced and mainly living out of his company apartment at Ghost Town."

"What became of his wife?" I asked.

"No idea. She came and went while I was out of touch with Eddie. You never knew her either, did you?"

"No. I think he invited Scott and me to the wedding, and I think we scribbled him a note to say we couldn't make it, and that was probably the last contact we had. Other than that, it's been what? . . . wow, probably fifteen years since I saw him or spoke to him," I said. "It's strange how time and people slip away."

Since Nick said that Ghost Town was on Mountain Time, I waited till about nine that evening to phone Eddie, figuring I'd give him time to get home from a late meeting and get some dinner. When I did call, I was amazed at how glad I was to hear him speak, and at the obvious pleasure in his voice. "Thally! Nick said you were going to call."

"And he was right. It sounds like you two are talking much more these days; doesn't that make your companies nervous?"

"It makes my director of security nervous, and it makes the guy at Nick's shop, a jerk named Andrew Riscaveau, completely screaming over-the-top-and-down-again paranoid. But, you know, if you work in a development facility of any kind, security guys are never going to be your friends; guys like Nick and me want our engineers to talk to each other—and security wants them to talk to nobody. Yeah, it's been nice to talk to Nick again; there aren't too many people in the world, besides us, who understand us. And now I get to talk to you again; I guess some good came of this whole mess. You ought to have Scott call me, too, for that matter. Don't forget, it's less than twenty years till the Mars Four have our reunion." It was more words than I'd ever heard Eddie utter at once before; he must really be lonely.

"Not looking so good for getting to Mars, though, is it?" I said.

"You never know. Things happen. But, yes, objectively speaking, I'd have to agree with you." He sighed. "The thing Nick wanted me to tell you about is that the politics of this case are looking worse and worse within Curtiss. I'm about out of allies here. These idiots are still cozying up to the James family instead of trying to win the case. I'm not at all sure what's up. At first I thought they were just out to strangle the tourist business, hoping to bankrupt RW, but it's looking much more like the whole company is changing direction. I'm alarmed at how many of our more talented guys are leaving, and the way that our no-vision bottom-liners seem to be finding all the allies and support in Congress.

"Used to be you couldn't get Bingo Rasmussen out to any of our facilities on a bet; he and a bunch of his cronies have been to corporate headquarters a couple of times this month. There's a big change of policy going on, and I don't think I'm going to like it. So the bad news is that you can expect even more pressure to settle. And I don't think you're going to see any turnaround or get any help from Curtiss."

"Well, it's not *unexpected* bad news," I pointed out.

"I wish I could be more definite about this, but there's something else going on as well," Killeret added. "It's like there's another hand at work in the company, or a force that I can't quite put my finger on. People I've known for years seem uncomfortable and unwilling to talk to me—and there's been quite a turnover in middle and upper management; every couple of days an old face disappears and a new one comes in. It just seems as if this isn't the Curtiss I used to work for. I've been through some corporate transitions before, but this is by far the biggest, accompanied by the least information. That's just

... well, it's weird. I don't know that it proves anything, but it is certainly weird, and I don't quite know what to make of it."

"Any idea who these new people coming in are?"

"Many of them are out of think tanks and they seem to be much more political than the people they are replacing—they're either strongly Democrats or strongly Republicans, and they come from places that have 'Public Policy' in the name, or out of government agencies, especially the finance and budget ones. But they don't all seem to be from the same place—it doesn't exactly feel like the kind of corporate mafia you see after some takeovers. And on the other hand, it might just be my paranoia. Most of upper management is still in place; there just seems to be something new going on, underneath and around them."

I asked a few more questions, but Eddie had told me about as much as he knew; the thing he was most worried about was painfully vague. Then we got to talking about all the intervening years, and what we'd done with our lives, and by the end of that conversation, it was half-past midnight my time, and Eddie was apologizing, and I was thanking him for spending so long talking, and we'd agreed that we'd have to be in touch again, even after this case was settled.

THE WEEKS WENT by while I waited for NASA to get around to releasing its report, and our case stayed somewhere near the top of the hour on the television news while November came, and the calendar crawled down toward Thanksgiving; I was beginning to really hope for a major scandal to erupt, because in a few weeks the national government would virtually shut down for the holidays, and if nothing took public attention away from our case, we'd be stuck as the lead story for another six weeks.

Besides coping with all of the PR aspects, and responding to a huge volume of correspondence and then adding to it myself (every civil case begins with lawyers demanding information from each others' clients), and a certain amount of legal strategizing and intelligence gathering, there was also the task of getting my team to function together as a team, to understand what we were about to do, and how we were going to do it.

Still, if the case was moving slowly, at least my home life was better than it had been in a few years. I almost always got home on time for dinner, and if I didn't, Scott, having little to do, was happy to pick up Amos from school and take him somewhere to eat, often stopping on the way to pick me up as well. Amos and I saw more than I'd ever planned to of Chuck E. Cheese's and Red Robin, and much more of Scott; it was good for Amos to see so much of his father, and I really didn't mind, since we were getting along better. I hadn't quite realized how lonely I had been after the divorce, and now that he wasn't nursing a fledgling company through a series of crises, and had time to relax and think and be with his son, Scott was surprisingly good company.

Nick checked in daily, occasionally by having lunch with me when he was in Washington, more often calling from Scorpion Shack, and though he wasn't happy with how slowly Republic Wright was moving towards supporting us, he seemed to think they might eventually. At least RW would not throw themselves all the way over to the other side, as Curtiss had done. About once a week Eddie Killeret would call, and though his news was usually that the change in personnel and the anti-new-development policy at Curtiss were continuing, at least things there didn't seem to be much worse.

By the second week of November, we were getting some traction. Several television news stories and newspaper pieces had pushed our point of view. Spot polls showed that we were reaching the public with our message, and we were also pulling ahead in the support of those who said that they were getting tired of the Michael James case. As the OJ case had demonstrated and the Monica Lewinsky affair had confirmed, some of the best support you could get was from people who said, loudly, "Oh not that again" and "Isn't that over *yet*?" every time the story ran on the evening news.

On the Wednesday two weeks before Thanksgiving, I was going over a report from my researcher on the number of occasions, and their exact times, when MJ or a member of his family had been briefed on the dangers of the flight. There was perhaps a ten percent chance that we would need to use it in court, but just in case, I had to know everything about it. Still, it was absolutely dull. I was drifting off every few minutes as I prepared some notes for my secretary.

The phone rang—a woman from the NASA investigation who wanted to know if I could be in Houston the next morning for a private presentation of the commission's findings, prior to the public presentation later in the afternoon. I said of course and got a time and a location. They wanted only attorneys present, so I wouldn't be able to bring Scott or Nick along. I thanked her, hung up the phone, and got busy, getting a plane ticket, making sure that Scott would be able to take Amos for the day, and letting Nick know what was going on.

"Cross your fingers," I told him. "Three things could happen here. The least probable, I think, is that they're going to turn up some crew error, or some mechanical problem, on the shuttle, that contributed to MJ's death. If they do that, we're screwed, especially if it's anything Scott could have known about—nowadays juries tend to say if you could have, you should have. Most likely of all it will turn out to be just what Billy Kingston and the crew thought in the first place, and it won't affect a thing. But I suppose there's just a chance—because there always is—that they'll have turned up something that kicks a big hole in Haverford's case. If that happens, it might be all over before the holidays. So cross those fingers *hard*."

"I'll do that," Nick said. "By any chance, would you like to take Roger Przeworski along? One more lawyer on the side of the angels?"

"Sure."

It took just a minute to arrange to meet Przeworski for breakfast in Houston—we were both going to be staying at the Airport Sheraton—and that was that. I'd fly out tonight, be back late afternoon tomorrow, and at least get a breath of warm air and sunshine before returning to cold, rainy DC.

THE NEXT MORNING , in the hotel room in Houston, came too early. I hadn't been able to get to bed until past midnight. Just the same, I was up and ready, showered, made up, and dressed, with the briefcase in perfect order, half an hour before I was due to meet Przeworski. I decided to go down to the café; I could have coffee until he got there, and I was too nervous, pacing around the room all by myself. I tossed the key into the return box, put the overnight bag into my rental car, and went into the café, still twenty minutes early.

Roger Przeworski, hair and suit in perfect order, was sitting there having coffee and looking nervous. We realized we'd had the same kind of morning—too excited to wait—and rather than fight it any longer, we just ordered breakfast and started to speculate about what we were going to hear. "It's strange how long it's taken," Przeworski pointed out. "You'd think if they were hit by a meteorite, all they'd have to do is confirm that, and then decide whether Kingston did a good job of landing it or not."

"But if it was anything other than what we think, it doesn't seem like they'd have had time to establish what else it was. So maybe the time was awfully short." I buttered a roll and glanced down; Przeworski wore a wedding ring. Well, he was kind of tall for my tastes, anyway.

"So it seems like it was either too long or too short . . ." Przeworski said, letting it trail off. "Well, I guess those are all the alternatives there could be, aren't they? This is really theorizing in the absence of data. And I suppose another possibility, while we're at it, is that they're just announcing one especially interesting partial result. Maybe they found out that MJ died of some cause other than the obvious, or that somebody should have identified the piece of space junk that got them, and the rest of the investigation will continue."

"As you say, it's all theory in the absence of data," I pointed out. "We'll know at nine-thirty, for sure. How long till then?"

"An hour. Plenty of time for some more irresponsible speculation."

"Let me get another cup of coffee first."

Finally it was time to get over to Johnson Space Center and get however much of the truth there was supposed to be. The drive was uneventful, and the room could have been any room for a press conference or a public announcment anywhere; so much of the business of government happens in places that are completely anonymous.

The team from BB&C, the Republic Wright lawyers, came over and sat with us, and we made the usual small talk, mostly establishing that we all knew someone in common. In the opposite front corner, the Curtiss and the ShareSpace lawyers huddled together and whispered, obviously locked in some kind of strategy conference. I wondered if they had gotten an early tipoff, and if they had, how I could get in on it. Just before the meeting began, Jasper Haverford swept in, flanked by two junior lawyers, said hello to everyone by name, and shook all our hands, just as if he had called the meeting himself.

He was a handsome man, but handsome in a way that obviously required plenty of expensive maintenance. He had silver hair, fine-boned features, a deep tan, and dark eyes, teeth that were straighter and whiter than occurred in nature, and a way of grinning that looked absolutely sincere; this was a man who could look you right in the eye and ask for your trust while rifling through your purse. The fact that he was looking so cheerful this morning was a mixed sign; either he was working hard to keep up appearances, or he had an inside line. From what I knew of Jasper Haverford, it could be either.

The NASA investigating committee came in and did the usual round of introductions. As was traditional, there were two astronauts on the team, since it was assumed that they knew something more about space operations than most people. Colonel Pete Slendwick, the senior of the two astronauts, who had commanded two missions, was the chair of the inquiry; Victor Carlson, a four-time shuttle pilot, was the other active astronaut. There were also two senior engineers, one each from Curtiss and Republic Wright; a couple of experienced coroners, one of whom had been the doctor on a shuttle flight ten years before; and a nearly expressionless FBI agent.

Aside from the actual investigators, it was necessary to have some celebrities, because Americans wouldn't trust a report from a commission that didn't include people they knew, so they had gotten Sally Ride to sit on this commission, as she had on the *Challenger* investigation. They had also gotten one of the old Apollo astronauts, to supply prestige and experience, and the physicist who had hosted the popular *Beyond Micro* series on PBS. *At least none of them seems likely to do any harm*, I thought.

The official report was delivered by Colonel Slendwick, who looked nervous. He had a habit of sucking on his lower lip between sentences, as if wondering which sentence would cause the room to go up in an uproar. "Thank you for coming," he said. "We felt that this information was so directly important to you, as the involved attorneys, and had so much bearing on the case, that you should know it before we release it to the media later this afternoon." He paused and looked around the room. "I emphasize that although this is a preliminary report, our conclusions are firm. Our full report will come after the first of the year, but only two parts are unfinished at this date—the minute-by-minute chronology of what happened from the moment of the explosion, and the review of the security breaches believed to have occurred."

Heads whipped around as we all looked at each other—the mentions of "explosion" and "security breach" had been enough to change everything. Whatever had happened up there, the commission didn't think it was a micrometeoroid impact.

Slendwick seemed to give us all a moment to absorb all that and get ready for what he was going to say. "Here's what we have determined. After careful investigation, including reconstruction of the surface through which the object exited, and of the camera, and studies of the injuries to Michael Tyree James and Marc Akira Clement, we have found that the event is absolutely inconsistent with any scenario involving an impact with an external object, either orbiting the Earth or from interplanetary space. We have found instead—"

"I have an injunction here," Jasper Haverford said, "which prohibits your going on with this, as prejudicial to an ongoing court case."

Colonel Slendwick looked stunned. Haverford rose and triumphantly handed out copies of the injunction; in a room full of lawyers, that immediately created a storm of shouting. I was part of that storm myself.

Haverford's injunction was written in such a way that it might very well allow Haverford to suppress *any* report that didn't support his client's case, until the trial was over. It was also from a New York State court, which meant that they didn't have jurisdiction here anyway.

Naturally the NASA bureaucrats in the room wanted to hold the report back and make sure everything was all right before going on. The engineers, scientists, and astronauts on the commission wanted to just bull ahead with the report. Przeworski, BB&C, and I thought the injunction was invalid. To no one's surprise, the lawyers from Curtiss, ASU, and ShareSpace lined up with Haverford. Presumably that was what they'd been whispering about before the meeting.

Luckily for the good guys, Przeworski was a better improviser than the rest of us. He whispered what he was up to in my ear and said "Just make sure nobody leaves for an hour or so." While I argued, objected, and leaned on the NASA people, Przeworski sat down, hand-scribbled a plea, slipped out the side door, walked across the road to a Kinko's, and faxed it to a federal district judge who was an old buddy of his from law school. Forty minutes after Haverford's rolling his bombshell onto the carpet, while everyone was still quarreling, and after Jasper Haverford had called me a number of names that I was more accustomed to hear from people doing life without parole, and threatened to call the police to have the meeting broken up, Roger Przeworski walked in with a fax of a federal order, voiding the injunction.

There was a stunned silence once Przeworski had managed to make it clear what he had. After a long moment, Haverford said, "All right, I'm forced to concede that you win this one. And I admit I'm curious."

Slendwick looked about as irritated as I've ever seen anyone look. Everyone sat down again. After a pause, Slendwick resumed. "The results are consistent with an explosive device which was inside a very exact replica of the CO camera. The device appears to have been made up of about half a pound of Semtex sealed inside a ten-centimeter length of tapering steel pipe, designed to fire a tungsten projectile about a centimeter in diameter by three centimeters long.

"The projectile had a hole in its base to cause it to seal against the walls of the tube, exactly like a bullet in a conventional rifle, and a hollow nose and series of grooves around the outside to cause it to break up when it hit the forward window—where it was supposed to be pointed for the first photograph. The steel tube, out of which the projectile was fired, was tapered to produce greater compression and a much higher muzzle velocity, very much like the barrel of a modern anti-armor cannon. Probably by design, the explosion fragmented the camera case and destroyed most of the device. The device appears to have been rigged to be fired by the first pull of the shutter."

Slendwick looked around the room once and said, "We believe that we can reconstruct the intentions of whoever planted this device, because plans were changed at the last minute, as the testimony of Mr. Scott Blackstone and of Mr. Perry Lager clearly shows, and which is corroborated from several other sources. The original plan would have had Mr. James attempting to take the initial photograph through the forward cabin window.

"Our reconstruction of the projectile indicates that it was intended to hit at very high velocity and deform on impact. If it had hit its intended target, the projectile would have shattered most of the forward window, resulting in explosive decompression of the crew cabin and the almost instant deaths of the entire crew. We would have had no idea what had happened; *Columbia* would simply have been slowly tumbling along in orbit, apparently dead, with telemetry indicating that cabin pressure was zero. Given the extra care we would have had to take in preparing a mission to investigate, and the difficulty of a rendezvous with *Columbia*, and the fact that the most incriminating objects might well have gone out the shattered window to be lost forever, it would have been months, perhaps years, before we had any idea that this was a deliberate attack. It is quite probable that we would have concluded what the crew first thought, that the loss of *Columbia* was caused by a micrometeoroid impact. Had things gone according to plan, this could have been a nearly perfect crime, and one that would have grounded the American shuttle fleet for months or years."

He looked around the room. "We were lucky enough to learn the truth. The death of Michael James almost certainly saved the lives of most of his crewmates, because the projectile lost a great deal of force as it broke through his sternum, chest cavity, and spinal column. The collision with the bone caused the projectile to break up prematurely, leaving several pieces embedded in his chest cavity. Only a part of it continued on, at much reduced speed, to make a half-centimeter-wide hole in the hull.

"The broken neck that killed Marc Clement was caused by the explosion, directly in front of his face, of a block of Semtex, fracturing the front of his skull as well as whipping his head back hard enough to break his neck. Given that the skull damage would have been consistent with a massive cerebral hemmorhage, Dr. Clement could not have been expected to survive in any case. He probably died during the strong, varying accelerations he experienced during re-entry, but in any case could not have survived more than a few hours, even if he had been on the ground and state-of-the-art care had been available immediately.

"Two members of the packing crew left the United States within less than an hour of *Columbia*'s liftoff, and one of them was in fact responsible for the CO camera. The FBI believes that they are now either underground with a terrorist organization, or concealed in some hostile foreign nation.

"Those are the essentials of our results; you'll find much more detail in the report. As I stated before, after the first of the year, we'll release some additional supporting documentation, but our conclusion stands."

"Is there any indication at all as to who planted the camera-bomb?" I asked. "Not the packing crew members, but the people who paid them to plant it?"

"That investigation is continuing," the FBI agent said, quietly. "We have not narrowed it down to any particular outside terrorist organization or hostile foreign power. Naturally we do find some nations and groups more suspicious than others, but we have no reason to point the finger at any one of them just yet."

There was as much uproar as a dozen lawyers can make. NASA had been wise enough to have full packets of photocopies, covering all the major reports about the evidence, for each of us, and that helped us formulate questions, but within a few minutes, Przeworski and I were nodding vigorously, and in a mood to celebrate. The evidence was as strong we could have hoped for—ballistics, autopsy, chemical traces, reconstruction of the explosive device, even a decent match between the chunk missing from the tungsten slug and the hole in the hull. "If this were evidence *against* my client, I'd settle," Roger said cheerfully.

"Me too."

The beauty of this, from our standpoint, was that if this were an international terrorist incident or an attack by a hostile foreign power,

legally it would be an act of war, and you can't sue the US government for enemy actions. Doubtless that explained why so much of
the yelling and objecting was coming from Haverford and his staff.
They held that this whole report had to be suppressed, that the facts
were impinging on Mrs. James's rights to win a judgment, and that
there could be no public disclosure of this report since it was clearly
prejudicial. The committee, as an administrative body and a purely
fact-finding one, included no lawyers and did not make any decisions
by itself on what to release and when, so Haverford couldn't have
any real effect on them, but either it was taking some time for him
to understand that, or he hoped to intimidate them with sheer presence, or he was trying to build up evidence that they had not taken
his client's rights into account. Whatever it was, he was making himself annoying.

When we were sure it was over—when you're dealing with characters like Haverford, you don't let them be the last to leave a meeting—Roger Przeworski and I went to a quick lunch, agreed that this
might well mean the whole case would be dropped within a few days,
and called Nick and Scott to let them know the good news.

Scott seemed pleased but distracted, as if he had something else
on his mind. I finally asked him why, almost having to shout over the
noise of the dining room behind me.

"Uh, it's your car," he said. "Someone set it on fire at the airport
parking garage. The airport cops left a message on your answering
machine. When I talked to them, they said it looked like someone
just stuck a Molotov cocktail under the front end, lit it, and walked
away. I'm afraid, from what they tell me, it's totaled."

"That's what I buy insurance for," I said, relieved to realize nothing of any importance had been in the car. "I guess I'll need a ride
at the airport."

"You don't seem to be taking this seriously."

"We've just about already won the case," I pointed out. "Really,
we couldn't lose it now if we wanted to. So if this is someone trying

to threaten us, they probably didn't know that they'd already lost at the time that they torched my car. Most likely they'll dry up and blow away once they do know. Or, you know, it always could be just some bored kid vandalizing a pricey car for thrills."

He wasn't pleased with my attitude, but I managed to get him to focus his attention on picking me up at the airport, and on the good news that the other side's case had just gone to pieces.

After I hung up, said goodbye to Roger Przeworski, drove to the airport, turned in the rental car, and got on the plane, I leaned back in my seat, stared out the window, and allowed myself to be quietly scared out of my mind. This was by far the closest anyone had ever come to carrying out a threat, and I was worried sick. You just can't allow the client to see that kind of thing, and I'd need to have my game face back on by the time I saw Scott.

CHAPTER EIGHT

THALIA:

When I checked my voice mail at the office, somebody had used a computer-speech program to call my office number and leave the phrase "Drop this case now" repeating for five minutes. My guess was that even if a phone trace had been available, it would turn out to lead only to some pay phone.

I did *not* win the argument with Scott that night; he stayed on the couch in the house. I though it must be pretty weird and depressing to be back in his old house, but not in the bedroom, but he actually seemed to cheer up. The next morning I awoke to the smell of breakfast cooking and came out to find Amos getting through his second helping of French toast. "Hey, remember, I don't have a job anymore," Scott said, apologetically. "I guess I could see if NASA or Global would take me back—I've kept up my training flight time and my time on the simulator—but for the moment my best prospect is to find some nice woman to support me, so I'm practicing my domestic skills. I'll even clean up after myself, really. It won't take you a bit of extra effort to have me here."

"The apron is what makes the image," I assured him.

"Are you going to go to the police about your car getting bombed?" Scott asked.

"I already did. And I reported that first threatening phone call, back when that happened, too. For one thing, if the cops have a record of incidents, and if there's anything that looks like an escalation, they would take that very seriously. Besides, I haven't done anything criminal and keeping the cops informed keeps them from getting suspicious. And to judge by what I got from them over the phone last night, they seem to be doing a good job. The airport cops are working very much by the book for an arson case, and I know from two past cases that the Arlington arson investigator knows his stuff. But if the people who did it are professionals, there won't be anything they can trace. The airport detective guessed it would turn out to be a plastic bottle of flammable liquid put under the car, inside a metal bowl to make it flash upwards, set off with a long strip of oil-soaked rags. Nothing traceable to any source, and chances are they didn't leave prints."

"So what are you going to do about it?"

I was getting irritated with Scott for discussing it in front of Amos, who was studiously keeping his face down in his plate and shoveling in more breakfast. "I'm not expecting this case to go much longer," I said. "So I'll spend some of Nick's money and hire a body-guard service; I've had to do that a few times for the Coalition's lawyers."

"Is that going to be enough?"

"It always has been for the Coalition," I said, with a tone that I hoped would close the argument.

After we dropped Amos off at school, Scott gave me a ride to the office, and on the way he fretted some more. We started to get into a fight about his having brought the matter up in front of Amos, and that seemed like a bad thing if he was going to be sleeping on my couch for a while, so I did my best to ignore my annoyance and put things in perspective for him.

In dealing with a take-charge guy like Scott, you're generally better off telling them the truth, so I explained it to him as well as I could. "Look," I said, "yes, having my car burned is weird and scary. I won't pretend it's not. And I don't know how much of my past experience is relevant. With the Coalition, usually anybody who is making threats is a relative of the victim or the prisoner, someone who's really emotionally worked up, and they do some crude, stupid things. As soon as they see the bodyguards, they usually lose their nerve.

"What bothers me is that I can't imagine who's doing this. Curtiss Aerospace isn't the kind of operation that you expect to hire goons. As far as I know, the federal government is on our side, even the secret agencies that sometimes do illegal action. And I've never heard a breath of organized crime being involved. So that leaves Jasper Haverford—and no slick lawyer would ever need to resort to violence, and trust me, he's *really* slick or just maybe the James family, but they're a bunch of straight arrows if ever there were any. Considering that they all grew up in the projects and none of them ever carried a pocket knife or stole a stick of gum, and that AnnaBeth and her daughters spend most of their spare time in church, I'm finding it hard to picture them sending a hit man after me."

"So what you're saying is that it is frightening, and you don't know who it is. I'm sorry I talked about it in front of Amos, but it is very serious, Thalia, you can't deny that." Scott drove another block in silence. The fall drizzle had settled in, and all the red brick houses looked washed out, as if I were seeing them through a shower curtain. "What about this 'mystery force' that Eddie Killeret keeps talking about? The one that he thinks is taking over Curtiss?"

"By definition, we don't know who they are or what they're doing," I pointed out. "I suppose it's possible that it's a mob family or something—but the Mafia's gotten burned lots of times, trying to take over legitimate companies, even when it was just garbage hauling, laundry, or supermarkets. Are they really going to try to make a big move on a company that's a vital national security asset, and be as blatant as this? It seems like they'd be asking for so much trouble."

We talked more but didn't come to any resolution. After, Scott walked me upstairs to the office, and made sure that there were a couple of people already there.

"Will you need a ride?" he asked.

"I'll get a cab—it's pretty unpredictable when I'll be done," I said. "Don't worry, now that I'm here, I'm fine."

"If you don't mind, I'll spend the day at your house," Scott said, oddly formal and shy about it. "You've got a lot of winterizing that needs doing, and besides, if I'm there, nobody will try breaking in, or planting anything."

"If you like," I said. I handed him the spare house key. I still thought he was overreacting, but surely it wouldn't hurt to have him there, anyway. Besides, whatever "winterizing" was, it was probably something that should be done, anyway.

I watched through the rain-streaked window as he drove away; I stood there for a few seconds, thinking of nothing in particular, before getting on with the day's work. I didn't think about much else until the bodyguards showed, up right on time, at eleven.

Two real surprises hit that day, which was busier than most lawyers' Fridays. The first was word from Haverford; he had filed dozens of petitions and motions in the New York court, demanding that the NASA report be suppressed and trying in various ways to claim that the actual cause of the accident should be completely irrelevant as to whether or not anyone could be sued about it. This did not look like a man who knew he was beaten and was giving up.

With a sigh, I phoned the New York court, and after a variety of delays and back-and-forthing, determined that hearings on all these motions would be next Tuesday. They all seemed so open-and-shut that I might be able to deal with them in a single day, but it seemed like a better idea to reserve rooms for a couple of days.

Late in the afternoon, I was typing out a rough draft of the out-

THE RETURN

line of my case to deny all of Haverford's motions. My basic strategy was to argue that since all of Haverford's arguments rested on the same premises and had the same intent, that if the judge dismissed any of them, he ought to dismiss all of them; that would keep Haverford from dribbling them out, an item at a time, delaying and delaying.

That was when the second surprise—one the whole world shared—began, for me, with the phone ringing. When I picked it up, it was Nick, calling from the air-cellular on the RW company plane—something he never used for personal business, so this was strange. Usually the tracking satellite uplink in the plane could deliver every call crystal-clear, but this time the call had the scratchy, fading-in-and-out quality that I remembered from long-distance calls when I had first gone off to college. "Thalia, if you've got a TV in your office, you'd better turn it on to CNN. I think Scott's case is off the front page for a while, and things are about to get completely crazy in the aerospace industry. Figured you'd better know about it if you didn't already I have to run . . . love to Amos and Scott. Maybe we can all have dinner tonight? I'll call back when I'm on the ground, in a couple hours."

"Come by my place about seven, we can all decide what to do," I said. "Call my cellular if you have to change plans."

"If it's working," he said. "Will do."

Why would he think that my cell phone might not be working? "Thanks, Nick, I'll take a look."

He hung up without saying goodbye.

When you're handling a highly publicized case, you always have a TV in the office. I grabbed the remote from the coffee sideboard and turned on CNN. As the picture emerged, I saw many worried faces, and maps with arrows and lines on them—I recognized Kashmir. The broadcast was surprisingly fuzzy, and every so often you got one of those jerky slow-motion movements that happen when there's not quite enough bandwidth for a signal. I turned up the volume and

was surprised to hear some occasional hisses and crackles, and fuzz-
iness in the tone.

Pakistan and India were at war again. Pakistani troops had crossed
the line. Fighting was flaring all over Kashmir and along much of the
frontier between the two nations. Pakistan had begun its attack by
firing a secret weapon which had worked far better than it was supposed to, which the news commentators had already dubbed the "proton bomb."

The idea had been talked about for decades. You don't need to
get up to orbital speed to go to space; you only need orbital speed
to *stay* in space. The old V-2's during World War II had gone most
of the way outside the atmosphere; they just hadn't reached speeds
that would allow them to stay in orbit. All the way back in 1949 an
Army two-stage rocket experiment had gone up three hundred miles,
twice as high as the altitude at which the first satellites orbited. Although it takes a big rocket to put a satellite into orbit, the same
rocket can put a much bigger payload into space, up above the atmosphere, for a short period of time, if all it has to do is be there briefly.

In this case, the payload had been a curious object. Superficially,
it looked like an old, crude hydrogen bomb. The body was an elongated steel egg, sixty feet long by some forty feet at the widest point.
Internally it was an ellipsoid—a shape that has two internal foci, such
that anything released at one focus will be reflected into the other
focus. In one focus rested a half-megaton nuclear bomb—a much
better bomb than the Pakistanis could make, but we didn't yet know
that. In the other focus was a 22-foot-diameter sphere, filled with
twelve tons of liquid hydrogen. The rest of the ellipsoidal had been
pumped down to a very thin vacuum.

They launched it straight up; it wasn't going nearly fast enough
to reach orbit, but it was going more than high enough. One hundred
and thirty miles above Kashmir, just as the steel egg reached its peak
altitude and began to fall back to earth, they detonated the bomb.

The first effect out of an atomic bomb is a burst of very intense

X-rays, and this bomb had been built to enhance that effect. X-rays reflect off steel like light off a mirror; the ellipsoidal focused all of them on the tank of liquid hydrogen. The dense X-ray flux instantly compressed the tank enough to raise its temperature to many tens of millions of kelvins—hotter than the cores of most stars.

Other kinds of light and radiation followed the same pathway, from the focus with the atom bomb into the focus at the center of that tank of hydrogen, but only for microseconds. Then the nuclear bomb's heat and pressure ate the steel egg and every other solid object around it.

The twelve-ton blob of hydrogen, at a temperature of just over 45 million degrees Fahrenheit, began to expand.

Hydrogen is the simplest and lightest atom: just a proton with an electron going around it. At a mere few thousand degrees, the electron and proton will separate, forming plasma. (A gas in which many electrons are separated from their nuclei is a plasma—flames, the Northern Lights, and the glowing gas inside fluorescent lights, are ordinary plasmas.)

This was no ordinary plasma. In the vacuum of space, the soup of protons and electrons expanded at hundreds of miles per second.

If the electrons and protons had been electrically neutral, they would have continued right on out of the Earth's magnetic field, and out of the solar system, with no further ado. But a proton, by itself, carries a charge of $+1$, and an electron a charge of -1, and the Earth's magnetic field acts on charged particles. The protons and electrons spreading out above Kashmir were grabbed by the magnetic field of the Earth itself, and whipped to higher and higher speeds. When they came out of the proton bomb, they had only a few hundred electron-volts of energy each—not enough to penetrate a sheet of tissue paper. But the magnetic field grabbed the protons and electrons, and pulled them along, accelerating them every instant; they accelerated at the equivalent of 5,000 g. Five minutes after the bomb had exploded, the unimaginably thin cloud of hydrogen plasma—a swirl of protons and electrons so thin that there were only about 1.5 million of them in a cubic foot—had been flung around by the Earth's magnetic field with such force that most of the particles were at relativistic velocities, and instead of a few thousand electron-volts, each particle now packed millions or tens of millions of electron-volts.

The invisible cloud swirled out to embrace the Earth; less than ten minutes after the initial explosion, so great was the velocity of the protons and electrons it had scattered, the charged particles were slamming into every object between the top of the atmosphere and 40,000 kilometers up. At such high speeds and low density, the hydrogen was no longer recognizable as hydrogen. It had become pure hard radiation, what the physicists call "ionizing radiation": charged particles moving so fast that when they crash into solid matter, they knock or pull electrons off atoms, as well as producing a nasty, dangerous spray of X-rays or gamma rays.

Traveling through hundreds or thousands of miles in the vacuum of space, whipping around the planet several times per second, accelerated all the way by the Earth's magnetic field, by the time the protons and electrons struck satellites, they had enough energy to produce a burst of hard radiation that could cut the microscopic conductors, pierce the dielectric films, burn through the transistors, chemically alter the semiconductors, send huge charges racing through ciruits never designed to carry them, and, in a hundred other ways, fry the microelectronics, on which every satellite depends, into uselessness.

The Pakistani government was loudly proclaiming that they had intended only to destroy satellites in the immediate vicinity of the detonation and to create a cloud that would wipe out satellites passing through low Earth orbit above that part of the world for a few hours. They wanted to disable India's intelligence and communication satellites, and they were willing to smash up the satellites of some other nations to do it.

If that had been their intention, somewhere they had gotten their numbers wrong. They hadn't realized how rapidly the high-energy protons and electrons would accelerate in the Earth's magnetic field, or how long they would remain trapped in the field. As the plasma cloud flew apart, picking up energy as it followed the magnetic field lines out away from the Earth, a very small fraction of it plunged down to the magnetic poles, blasting into the ionosphere high above Canada's Melville Island and Antarctica's Wilkes Land, but most of the particles were swept outward by the Earth's magnetic field, forming a denser, stronger, more powerful—and far more extensive—set of Van Allen radiation belts than the Earth had had within recorded time. That radiation would remain there for weeks, extending from 80 to 30,000 miles from the Earth's surface. While it lasted, all of the near Earth orbits would be bathed in enough radiation to destroy the electronics on satellites within an hour or two.

The hot zone reached out far enough to include geosynchronous orbit, where the communication satellites were—usually the furthest orbits in commercial use—destroying nearly all the electronic circuitry in space, making almost all of the world's satellites useless.

It had been a long time since college physics, and I had to watch the news stories several times before I understood even the basics. Meanwhile, the nations of the world were trying to get some idea of the scope of the catastrophe. The Canadians had sent up sounding rockets, and measurements taken by those showed that the protons were mostly still up there, gaining speed and energy until they either smashed into the Earth's atmosphere above the magnetic poles, or collided with some satellite and added to the radiation damage. So far the electrons were barely coming down at all, and based on the Starfish experiments, done decades ago, it was feared that they might linger in the radiation belts for decades.

It had taken the world about half a century to construct a vast network of communication, navigation, intelligence, weather, environmental, and scientific satellites overhead—and now, in less than four hours, all of them were damaged, dying, or dead. Billions of dollars of high-tech property on which the planet depended was swiftly turning to junk.

That was why telephone and television service was degrading rapidly; the satellites were dying, their microcircuitry burning out and becoming unreliable under the impact of the radiation, their radio receivers jammed by the tremendous electronic noise that drowned out the ground signals that were necessary for keeping their antennas pointed correctly and for telling them when to do correcting maneuvers, the electronic controls on their station-keeping rocket motors failing to work and leaving them to tumble helplessly under the influence of the micro-tides from the Earth and moon, as they lost the ability to correct their positions.

Fiber-optic landlines and microwave towers couldn't carry the load, especially not for trans-ocean transmission; the world's communications were snarling in one vast traffic jam.

NASA was issuing no word on what had happened to the crew of ISS; there was a "storm cellar" on the station for solar flares and other high-radiation events, but no word on whether it was adequate for the very high levels of radiation now bathing the station. There was a lifeboat Soyuz capsule docked at the station as well, but no announcement that the crew had bailed out, either. Commentators— who knew nothing yet, but had to say something—kept saying that we had to hope for the best for that crew.

The Pakistani and Indian armies had been ordered by the UN Security Council to get back out of the border areas, sit down, and not move; it appeared that the major powers were all backing the Security Council's decision. Probably the war would stop here. For all their effort at what the generals thought would be a brilliant coup, Pakistan had only managed to make an international pariah of itself, and to forfeit any support among other nations. Stories were leaking out of the Pakistani government, blaming Chinese technical advisors for having steered them wrong, but no one knew yet whether this was the truth or just a desperate attempt to shift the blame.

I sat back and stared at the screen, almost not thinking, as the information poured in through the flickering images and crackling, staticky audio. I watched a dozen experts of all kinds argue with each other. Abstractedly, I thought, this is one of those days that I'll always remember, always be able to recall where I was when I heard about it, like when Nixon resigned, *Challenger* exploded, or the Berlin Wall came down. The total achievements of the whole world's space industry had been swept away in an hour.

Well, Nick was right. At least this was going to get Scott off the front page for a while. And now I knew why Nick had thought that my cell phone might not work.

I picked up the phone, called my house, listened through my message, and said, several times, loudly, "Scott, pick up the phone."

Finally he did. "Hi, Thalia, what's up? I was just getting storm windows up; did you even do that last fall?" It was a local call, so his voice was perfectly clear.

"No," I admitted, "it was easier to just pay for more heat. That's not what I called about. Turn on CNN. I don't think it's connected with our case, but something very big just happened. You're off the front page. I also think that sometime fairly soon, they're going to need every qualified shuttle pilot, no matter what they have to pay them, so I think you're also assured of work."

After a while I knew that I wasn't going to do any more work before Monday morning, that I was just sitting there in my darkening office as a grim gray wet November afternoon wound down outside the window, matching my mood. I was just looking out the window, not really paying attention to the television anymore, half-hypnotized by the endless repetitions of the few things anyone knew about the disaster, reported by people who were all either in shock (those who understood what was happening) or confusion (those who interviewed the people who understood). I told Clara, the temp secretary, to call me a cab, and then to go home, herself.

*   *   *

TWO HOURS LATER, sitting at home, watching the news as the very last surviving satellites were fading out, the only reason we could get CNN reliably in Washington was because there was a fiber-optic landline to Atlanta. The CNN main desk in Atlanta was reporting whatever could reach them by surface methods, mainly voice telephone and email. AM radio was a roar of white noise, as the storm of charged particles began to pour into the upper ionosphere; FM radio would remain all right. The President had declared a set of national priorities, so that newscasts and government messages would go out first, and the remaining landline bandwidth would be rotated among the many competing purposes; those with satellite dishes instead of cable, of course, were out of luck.

When Nick dropped by at seven, he was in an oddly cheerful mood, insisting that we had to do "something fun, right away. This is going to be my last weekend off for at least a year," Nick said. "There is absolutely nothing anyone can do about this for a few weeks, until the Earth's magnetic field has its way and the protons have either come down, moved out, or gotten trapped in the Van Allen belts. Background radiation near the Earth will be measurably higher for twenty years, but should be down to tolerable levels for spaceflight in a month or two. Once the radiation is at levels we can cope with, we'll be building and launching as fast as we can for the next two or three years, and they may very well blow the dust off some of our Scorpion Shack proposals and let us start building some new rockets."

We all stopped talking for a minute to hear a statement from the Pakistani ambassador to the UN. Pakistan claimed that what they had intended had been a bomb set off at no more than sixty miles height, with the liquid hydrogen only providing a radiation burst directly overhead to kill satellites, and most of the effect concentrated into an EMP on the ground. They said the Chinese technical crew that was helping them had launched a bigger bomb, higher, with much more hydrogen, in contradiction to all the orders given. Some commentators believed them, some believed the Chinese denials, and in any case it hardly mattered, now, what the intention had been.

After the announcement, Nick shrugged. "If I thought this really was a case of somebody tricking the Pakistanis, I'd think it had to be us or Curtiss—between losing a shuttle for more than a year, and now losing all the orbital assets, there must be five hundred billion dollars' worth of new satellite construction and launching to do, right away. It's better than being a general contractor the day after a hurricane. Which brings me back to why I need to get away for this weekend, while there's still nothing to be done. If I should be stupid enough to go into the office, or to be anywhere where they can find me easily, I will be forced to spend all weekend reassuring people about all sorts of things that they either already know anyway, or don't understand well enough to grasp the reassurances."

"I have an idea," Scott said. He looked over to where Amos was quietly finishing his homework. "Hey, Amos, how was the trip to the cabin three weeks ago?"

"You know it was great, Dad," Amos said. "It's cold down by the ocean, but there's all sorts of things to do out on the beach, and the cabin stays warm with the woodstove."

"And your father stays warm cutting wood," Scott added.

"I wanted to try."

"I've still got to get used to seeing you swing an ax, kid, but we could give you some more practice tomorrow morning. Why don't all four of us go to the cabin? If Nick takes his cell phone, he'll be *almost* being responsible about it—even though they won't be able to reach him—and he gets two days of goofing off—"

"And cooking," Nick said, grinning. "True."

I thought about it. Nothing would be happening with the case until Monday, I could get my notes together as well down there as up here, and even if a world war were about to break out, we'd be better off at the cabin than in DC. We could be packed by seven, stop and get groceries on the way . . . "I just need to call Mrs. Banks to make sure the power and water will be on when we get there," I said. Since I was beginning to smile, just thinking about it, it might even be a good idea. "Let's do it."

THREE HOURS LATER, having done everything faster than I'd have thought possible, Amos, Scott, Nick, and I were each carrying a bag of groceries into the surprisingly clean kitchen of the cabin. For once, Scott had tidied up after himself, or maybe Amos had nagged him into it; he was becoming almost domesticated. The place was freezing cold, but Scott had left some pre-cut wood, and he got busy lighting a fire in the woodstove.

There was a note from Mrs. Banks on the kitchen table to let us know that a couple of light bulbs were burned out but the power and water were on; the refrigerator was humming, on its way to being cold, and didn't smell particularly musty.

"I haven't been back here in at least ten years," Nick said. "Is the Saturn V model still hanging in the attic? It was the last time . . ."

Amos looked embarrassed. "I have it hanging in my room at home, Uncle Nick," he said. "No one was using it here and I was afraid some summer tenant would throw it away."

Nick clapped him on the shoulder. "Perfect place for it. I'm honored."

"Friday night," I said, "is sloppy joes. Can you do those on a woodstove, Nick?"

"Can Amos stay up till midnight to eat one? It'll take Scott a while to get the fire really going, and then it takes a woodstove a while to heat up. But, yeah, sure, can do."

"Or you can use my cheater kit," Scott said, from where he was just touching off the newspaper under the kindling.

"Cheater kit?" I asked.

Scott shrugged. "Nick can cook on a woodstove, but I'm not the cook he is. I like a burner. So you'll find three electric hot plates, and a toaster oven, in the lower right cupboard next to the fridge."

"Perfect," Nick said, and reached down to pull out the hot plates. "Why don't you guys see if the television is working, and then see if there's any word yet on what's going on with the space station?"

"Amos, you're official television set operator," I said, "and I'm electing myself as cook's assistant and trainee. I still don't make them like Mom did, but your Uncle Nick does, and I'm going to learn how."

From the living room I heard Scott and Amos discovering that the cable TV was working but there were only four stations available. "Just like pioneer days," Scott was teasing Amos. "You know, when Lewis and Clark crossed the country, television was steam-powered, and only Mike Wallace was there to cover it when they reached the Pacific."

"Aw, Dad."

I had just gotten the celery and onions chopped, proudly noting I still hadn't cut myself, when Amos stuck his head in the kitchen and said, "Mom, Uncle Nick, you gotta see this," so we went out to join Scott and Amos. There were plenty of places to sit down, but once we heard the news coming from the TV screen, we stood to listen to all of it, unable to think of anything else.

SCOTT:

Much later, I was on the inquiry commission to look into exactly what happened on ISS that day. Just hearing about it was terrifying enough for me; I wouldn't ever want to be in a spot like that. But still, it was a relief to have heard the whole story. Machines failed, in extraordinary and unanticipated circumstances, but people didn't.

Alarms on ISS sound if radiation levels become unacceptable. Radiation is imperceptible to human senses; an area that is deadly looks, sounds, smells, and feels exactly like one that is perfectly safe. Injury from radiation is cumulative—the longer the exposure, the more damage. Thus it is always vital to know whether you're being irradiated, because sources of radiation are ubiquitous in space, and situations can change in a heartbeat. Solar flares, the huge gas eruptions from the sun that dump swarms of protons into the Earth's magnetic field, arrive within hours of the solar observer satellites and ground-based astronomers seeing the vast explosions tear through the solar atmosphere.

The proton bomb released far more protons than Earth receives from any solar flare. The first warning the crew got was when it set off the Geiger counters, which detect ionizing radiation. Sprays of secondary electromagnetic radiation from every piece of exposed metal set off the X-ray and gamma detectors. As successive protons had been accelerated for longer and longer before striking ISS, the energy and amount of radiation rose swiftly.

Sheer luck allowed the crew to survive. If anyone had been doing an EVA, that person might well have taken a fatal dose of radiation before being able to get back inside. But as it happened, the three "construction crew" astronauts on board were in about the best places they could be in the situation. Doris McIntyre, the medical/biological mission specialist, was asleep in her bunk, and when the alarms went off, she simply rolled out of bed and swam into the "storm cellar"— the command/control area, about the size of a motel bathroom, that was specially hardened against radiation. A moment later, as she was rubbing the sleep from her eyes with the heels of her hands, she was joined by Stephen Tebworthy, a tall thin Briton who was there as a specialist in microgravity welding. The storm cellar monitors had already come up automatically; he leaned forward, read the counts and intensities, and said, "Jesus, those numbers are unbelievable, way out of range—they can't possibly be right. It looks like the sun blew up."

Carl Tanaka, the commander and the third member of the team, swam in and closed the hatch. "What are radiation levels like here?" he asked. "Every monitor lit up like a Christmas tree."

Doris checked the internal monitors. "Shit. We're all taking a dose that could kill us in an hour or two."

"Then let's get out of here. We can figure out what it was once we're on the ground," Tanaka said. He turned to head for the hatch.

"Wait a minute, chief—right now we're in a safe spot, but it's *really* hot between us and the Soyuz," Tebworthy pointed out. "We'd better power the Soyuz up by remote, so that all we have to do is dive into it, close the door, strap down, and go."

Doris pulled herself to the storm shelter's workstation, pounded at the keyboard, and said, "Okay, it's better to go no matter where we come down, but I think it'll be the North Atlantic or maybe Europe, and there's no storms—power-up sequence is under way and—shit! shit! shit! Can you believe a system crash right now?" She pounded the keys again, hard, in frustration, making mistakes, scrambling to correct them. "Reboot and I'll have it in a minute—"

"*Maybe* you'll have it, Doris." Carl Tanaka did his best to sound calm, but the other two crew members could hear him making the effort. "There are incredible amounts of static on every radio channel. We're in the worst radiation anyone's ever seen up here. Electronics aren't going to last long, especially not if they're outside the storm cellar."

Doris had kept working with the computer while she listened to the commander. "Damn. Well, it did come up . . . okay. It should be powered up by the time we get to it."

"Good." Carl Tanaka headed through the hatch. "Let's go."

The lifeboat for the station was a Curtiss Soyuz, built from the basic Russian capsule design but with American materials and more precise engineering tolerances. Normally it sat in the dock, hatch closed and powered down, but it could be readied in less than two minutes, either by crew inside it or remotely.

The three astronauts squirmed down the long passageway that

led to where the Soyuz was docked. When they were halfway there, with a sound like thunder, the station shook. The walls lurched sickeningly around them, and everything drifted toward the walls as though they had suddenly become magnetized.

Without a word, Carl Tanaka lunged down the corridor to the Soyuz hatch. Doris and Tebworthy followed, not knowing what was going on. Carl threw the Soyuz hatch open, and plunged headfirst into the capsule. The other two followed him, squeezing into their seats beside his pilot's chair.

The board was a wild profusion of green and red lights, and the LCD displays flickered and wavered in a way they had never done in training.

Tanaka had already grabbed at the controls and was fighting with them, pounding the board in front of him in frustration. The thunder was now very loud, and the interior of the little capsule whirled like a carnival ride. He fought the controls again and again, pushed at buttons with no apparent effect, and then shouted over the roar. "Get back to the storm cellar. I'll come in and tell you what's going on in just a minute." As Tebworthy and Doris climbed back up the corridor that had suddenly become a vertical shaft, he hollered after them, "And get out the dosimeters, the film badges, and the Geiger counter."

They were halfway back to the storm cellar when the thunder stopped, as abruptly as it had begun; in the sudden silence, they could hear Tanaka swearing with fury.

As they reached the storm cellar, Tanaka came up behind them and crawled in after them. Once they were all there, he sat down, and said, "I'd say we have almost a tenth of a g in here. Nuisance, having to climb instead of swim, isn't it?"

They stared at him. He shrugged and spread his hands. "People, we're in trouble. When the Soyuz powered up, some of the attitude thrusters failed on, instead of failing safe. That's what the noise was, and that's what has started us into a slow spin. I couldn't get them to turn off. They've drained the tank. Even if we could get the Soyuz clear of the station, now, we couldn't maneuver—and that means we can't make a try at re-entry. Even if we had a spare tank of fuel for the attitude thruster—which we fucking don't, and isn't *that* stupid!" For a moment the commander looked down at his hands, clenching and unclenching them in a near rage. "Yeah, it's stupid. Well, even if we had the fuel to gas it back up, and we knew that the attitude jets wouldn't do that again, with radiation levels what they are outside the storm cellar, you couldn't get the refueling done without running some major risks. And the attitude thrusters are only what we know about. As damaged as the electronics are, the controls in the Soyuz are all dubious anyway. Who knows if we could even fly it? I'd say our lifeboat is dead; I don't think we even have a decent way to jettison it from our dock.

"The reason we have this little bit of gravity is that the thruster firing started us tumbling. I just had a look at the main thrusters for the station itself, and there's nothing working. We can't stabilize the place, so we're going to continue to tumble, and to precess, which will keep us in this fractional g for the foreseeable future and would also complicate the hell out of getting off the station, even if we still had a Soyuz."

After he let the situation sink in, he asked, "What are radiation levels like in here?"

Doris sighed. "Well, at the present level, here in the shelter, we're about five days from radiation sickness, and maybe ten from being walking dead. But the level peaked two minutes ago, and it's drifting down now. Here's what I think we ought to do. There's tons of material we can move around inside the station, and if we can pile it all up against the outside of the storm cellar—especially dense stuff like water tanks, and food, and batteries, and construction materials— then we can increase the effect of our shielding. If the radiation keeps falling off at the rate it's doing, we might be able to last for days or weeks."

"And then?" Tebworthy said, quietly.

"And then we have time to hope, and to get in touch with Houston and let them know we're alive and how bad our situation is," Doris said. "I don't know whether they'll have any way to come and get us, but they might—maybe there's an Ariane almost ready to go that could bring us a new Soyuz. Maybe they'll be able to diagnose our broken Soyuz remotely and use a Progress to bring us up a basket of spare parts to fix it, and fuel for the thrusters. Maybe radiation is going to fall to zero three hours from now, or maybe the little green men in the saucers will overhear and come rescue us. I don't care. All we have to hope for is good luck. But we can't have any good luck if we just sit here and let the radiation kill us, now can we?"

After a quick dry ration and a drink of water, they clipped on their dosimeters—which already showed alarmingly high cumulative readings—and their film badges, and set to gutting the station from the inside and strapping the pieces around their storm cellar, with "artificial gravity" from the spinning station that was just enough to make the work hard and not enough to consistently keep things where they were put.

When they finished, they crept in through the bent tunnel, formed of crates, water containers, and aluminum sheets, along with not-yet-assembled crew bunks still in the boxes, that formed the entrance to their little habitat in the center of the junk pile. By that time, most of the lighting circuits were out, and they were working by flashlight. Air recirculation could be done manually, but someone would have to crawl out and do it now and then, changing tank connections and turning hand pumps. There was food and water, and a "honey bucket," in the shelter.

Grimly, having established that none of the radios they had brought to the shelter from storage worked anymore, they sat down and began assembling components cannibalized from all of them, hoping to get a set of parts at random that were all functional. It was slow, difficult work in the dark by flashlight, and not really anyone's area of expertise, but they kept at it until they had a set they thought might work. Stephen Tebworthy drew the short straw, and climbed out into the rest of the station, briefly, to determine a rough position and trajectory from ground landmarks that swung terrifyingly by the viewports now and then. They made a best guess of when they would be line of sight to Houston, and then, attaching the antenna wire to the wall, hoping that the station would act as a giant antenna, they broadcast their appeal for help. They repeated their simple two-minute message, verbatim, for thirty minutes, hoping that someone on the ground could put it together through all the radio noise.

When, three minutes after they stopped, they received a garbled, crackling, only half-understandable message—just enough to tell them that their message had come through—and it began to repeat, they celebrated silently, afraid to miss a single word, listening over and over as they sipped their water and sat in the dark chamber that tumbled end over end, falling forever.

THALIA:

The news from the International Space Station was that the crew was alive but the station was dying. Microelectronics were slowly being blasted out of existence by the invisible proton-electron bombardment that poured against every metal surface, scattering X-rays and gamma rays. They could live some time yet—the guess was several weeks—in the dark and the slowly intensifying cold, hoarding power from batteries and fuel cells, fixing a thing here and a subsystem there (at the expense of taking more radiation in their damaged bodies). But, although no one wanted to say it outright, they probably couldn't live long enough for anyone to be able to rescue them.

"A couple of years from now, there would have been a possibility of a quick response," Nick said, gloomily. "Right now, we'd have to have a shuttle or the Russians would have to have a Soyuz ready to go, and we'd have to work like mad all the same, and it still might not make it. Anyway, with it tumbling like that, you can't dock. Even if they're alive, they aren't going to be for much longer." He stood up. "Well, the situation won't improve if dinner is burned or late. Thally, I can take it from here—it's just mixing it together and heating it up and serving it. Dinner in ten minutes." Nick headed out for the kitchen; I thought he probably wanted to do something to relax.

I knew, from having grown up around my father and my aunt, both aerospace engineers, that there's no stress quite as miserable as the stress on a ground-based engineer who is waiting for word about whether the hardware has failed and lives have been lost or are in peril. I figured a few minutes of doing something soothing was the best thing for Nick; this wasn't being much of a "day off." From the kitchen, I heard the pots and pans thumping and clanging gently, and the soft scrape of a wooden spoon in a pan, as he got the last of it ready.

"Dad, is Uncle Nick right? If they live through the radiation, after it settles down, couldn't they go get them on one of the shuttles?" Amos asked.

Scott made a balancing gesture with his hand. "They're saying a month till you can fly a crewed mission up there—and with the station tumbling and everyone weak and sick, you've got to send a person or two across to the station to go and get the crew, by the time you can go at all. I don't think any of them will be in any shape for an EVA on their own.

"Even to be ready in a month, they are going to have to rush the daylights out of getting *Atlantis* ready, and who knows how much time the survivors on ISS might have. Normally it takes several months to get one ready—and even if they accelerate it, then there's the problem of having to spacewalk between the shuttle and the tumbling station, take off anybody who's injured . . . it would be what we technically call a real bastard."

"Mom doesn't let me call things that."

"Mom is right," Scott said, glancing apologetically at me. "But there are some situations that call for adult language, and this is one of them. Anyway, it would be so difficult, and so risky, that odds are really against anything working. On the other hand, we've never left someone up there to die, and I hope we never will. It's an unwritten part of the deal they make with you when you sign up—if you'll risk your neck for any mission they ask you to, they'll risk more necks to get you back. So I'm sure if anyone can rescue them, or might just possibly try to rescue them, they'll make the attempt. But that's as much hope as there is, and I don't know of anyone who could do such a rescue."

It was just past eleven before we finally ate, but neither my ex nor my son complained about the delay. Something about the sea air or the tension had us all eating like wolves; even I had two sloppy joes. ISS was undoubtedly still on Nick's mind, but he didn't seem sad as much as quiet. Probably he was thinking about the possibilities for rescue.

After everyone had finished eating, and we were just sitting, not speaking, enjoying the sense of being warm and well fed, Nick said, "Hmm. I think I do need to get down here more often. We have the beach to ourselves, and as you all know, after September thirtieth, this little town doesn't even leave its streetlights on. So my guess is that right now we're going to have the best aurora borealis of our lifetimes. Would anyone like to go for a short night walk on the beach?"

"Absolutely," Scott said. "Just let me get the dishes into the tub to soak." He grabbed the plates, pots, and pans and scraped them into the garbage, then set them in a big iron tub on the woodstove and used a hose from the kitchen sink to fill it, adding a bit of soap. "Those should be ready to wash by the time we get back," he said.

In a few minutes, all bundled in coats and sweaters, we stepped out onto the back porch. The beach was lit in flickering red, green, and blue, bright as a barn burning half a mile away. In the northern sky, halfway to the zenith, great dancing curtains, sheets, and curving lines of color constantly changed. Vast cold films of green and blue light, laced with red streaks, appeared, curled, twisted, and disappeared like ghosts. The aurora covered the northern sky, swirling to a bright vortex just to the right of the handle of the Little Dipper, which showed faintly through the wild sprays of light.

Scott explained to Amos. "The normal aurora is caused by charged particles from the solar wind getting swept down into the upper atmosphere by the Earth's magnetic field; when the charged particles hit the upper atmosphere they hit the molecules so hard that the molecules give off light. The proton bomb created many times more charged particles than the solar wind normally ever supplies, and that's what happens when so many charged particles get into the magnetosphere. It's a big problem for the world, but it certainly is beautiful."

We stood and watched it much later than we meant to; it was just too glorious to look away from, despite all the loss and destruction it signified. When we finally went in, we were all hushed, as if we'd been to a very special church service in the world's grandest cathedral.

Scott had the dishes still to wash, and I had some things I wanted to set up for breakfast the next morning, so we spent a while in the kitchen, just quietly working next to each other, the way we used to when we came up to the Blackstone family cabin in the years before Amos was born and life got frantic.

"It feels good to be here," I ventured, after a while.

Scott set a plate in the rack to dry and said, "Yes, it does. I hadn't thought we'd ever do it again. Especially not in the fall."

"Well," I admitted, "so far this is more pleasant than the last time. Not being sick and not having rain makes a difference."

He scrubbed a pot while I pre-sliced some tomatoes and onions for tomorrow's lunch. After a while, he said, "I always thought you were a pretty good sport about that."

"I tried to be. It was important to the relationship and all that."

"Yeah."

The long silence stretched on until finally we banked the fire to get ready for bed. By then it was about 12:30. Neither of us had paid any attention to what Nick and Amos were doing. When we checked, we discovered they were asleep in the twin bunks in the attic bedroom. Amos was in the top one, sound asleep with a beautiful smile. Nick was really too tall a man for the lower bunk, but he was folded up into it anyway, snoring loudly.

"Do you think they're really asleep, or is this a routine to convince us they're asleep?" Scott asked.

"It's a convincing routine, if it's a routine," I said. "Amos hardly ever sleeps that well at home."

"Not when he's over at my place, either," Scott said. "Trouble is, this leaves us the queen-sized bed, or the couch. I suspect some manipulation here."

"Duh. You think? And Nick is worse than Amos about it. Well, the choices are that one of us gets on the couch, or I count on your being the gentleman you always have been. I've got pajamas," I said.

"Me too. I vote for sharing a bed and behaving ourselves," my ex replied. "It'll be warmer."

The next morning, when we awoke, it was a beautiful sunny morning, with light pouring in through the white curtains, and we had snuggled up during the night so that we were holding each other. Fortunately neither Nick nor Amos saw us, so we weren't raising any false hopes, and by the time they stumbled down, drawn by the smell of bacon, eggs, and coffee, we had made up the bed, dressed, and in short destroyed the evidence. Both Scott and I were kind of embarrassed by the whole situation, but it was also sort of funny, and we ended up laughing about it, as a private joke, for the rest of the day.

Just after lunch on Saturday, we all took a break to turn the television on and see what was happening with ISS. There were some brief recordings of the crew's voices, as they made a few banal comments and dished out some bland assurances. An expert told us that as radiation decreased in LEO, transmissions from the space station became clearer. Other experts assured us that the whole situation was being dealt with by ground engineers telling the astronauts how to fix everything, "Just like Apollo 13."

Scott snorted at that. "Astronauts are good at following directions. They have to be or they don't survive. But you can't fix a microchip; you can only build a new one. And right now there's no way for a capsule to dock to bring them up any spare parts, and if there were, they don't have the electronics to guide it in, and it's still way, way too hot to go EVA. I'm sure they're getting some stuff fixed, but I'm just as sure it's not much, yet, and they're still screwed."

I sighed. "Some NASA PR officer, or the Issues Management consultant if they were smart enough to hire him, is earning his keep today. They're making so much out of the parallel to Apollo 13 because they want this story off the front page for a while. So they make it sound as if it's routine—you know, Gene Kranz got them back by just telling them what to do with a roll of duct tape, and that's all we have to do whenever something goes wrong. Bullshit, but very salable bullshit."

"My parents are giving me a heck of a vocabulary," Amos said.

"I follow the same rule as your father. It's okay when the situation calls for it. And adults are the judge of when a situation calls for it."

"Amos, perhaps, as your uncle and positive role model, I should get you away from these crude, uncivilized people," Nick said. "Would you like to go throw a football around on the beach? I'll pretend I can throw if you'll pretend you can catch."

"Sweet."

The two of them took off in a burst of noise, laughing and teasing each other.

"Nick should have been a dad," I said, making conversation.

Scott shrugged. "He's better as an uncle. Busy guys just can't do what kids need them to do, which is mostly be around."

"Voice of experience?" I asked.

"Could be. Busy women probably have the same problem, hunh?"

"Yeah." We had skirted around the edge of a fight, and I, for one, didn't want to get any closer to it than we already had. For another indefinite silence, we watched the man and the boy run and throw the ball around, and the big waves roll onto the bright cold beach, and the white fluffy clouds march slowly out to sea, headed over the horizon.

"You know," Scott said, "most really dedicated engineering managers either get married right after college or right after they retire. So Nick's missed one chance and it will be a long time before the next time. Maybe *we* should start conspiring to get *Nick* married off. It would serve him right, eh?"

"It would." I leaned back against the railing of the deck, and watched Nick throw a wild pass that Amos very nearly caught. "So you think the ISS crew is going to die?"

"We all do sometime. Astronauts often die early." He sighed. "I just don't want them to die without someone having tried, down here. Like I said, it's part of the deal. And I don't have any great amount of faith in an Apollo 13 solution. I was at a reception for Jim Lovell once, and I heard him point out how much luck was involved, and how easily it could have gone some other way. I want to see us get them back down here, safely, from some combination of brains and skill and courage and pure willpower." He stared off toward the sea; I noticed how cold it was for so fine a day. "Of course I'd be damn happy to get them back, alive, by any old stroke of luck at all, right now. Want to grab some nice big mugs of coffee and walk up the beach? It's getting cold just standing here."

"Sure."

We didn't say much on the walk but the company was nice.

The rest of the weekend passed in a pleasant blur of "camp life," long walks, another spectacular aurora, and a long talk looking into the red glow of the stove. It was very much like what Scott had told me our first fall weekend here, so many years ago, would be like.

Nick spent the rest of the afternoon with Amos, doing what they called boy stuff—throwing rocks into the water, racing each other up and down the beach, and Nick explaining rockets and orbits in simplified terms. By dinner time, Amos was pestering me about letting him build model rockets, and I figured that either Scott or I would have to get him an Estes starter kit for Christmas. "Looks like genetics is winning out," I said to Scott, as we ended up curled up together in the bed for the second night.

Scott shrugged, and carefully put his arm around me in a way that was affectionate without being too familiar. The man always had been a gentleman. "It's in the Blackstone blood, I guess. Wonder if he's going to be a pilot or a robber baron?"

I had some clever reply in mind, but Scott fell asleep, and a moment later I did too, with the November ocean rumbling in the distance, and the walls still lighted by the flashes of that weird aurora.

CHAPTER NINE

NICK:

On that first Monday after the proton bomb, it seemed that the crew on ISS was far from the biggest problem the space program was facing. Estimates were that the crew up there might last four weeks without lasting health consequences. *Atlantis* could be ready to go, ASU thought, in nineteen days, with some kind of improvised radiation shielding in the crew compartment. The situation was tight, but not at all hopeless.

Email from Ned Robertson, my chief of engineering on the Starcraft project, said that some of his engineers had "an idea that might be relevant to the ISS problem." That probably meant an interesting hour sometime soon—I had enjoyed every conversation I had ever had with Robertson, and every presentation he had made. Perhaps, since I was planning to be at Scorpion Shack all day tomorrow, I could squeeze that one in, early; it would at least assure me that there would be one pleasant hour in a day otherwise filled with meetings. I sent Angie, my secretary at Scorpion Shack, an email to see if she could put together a breakfast meeting with Robertson's team for tomorrow.

I had arrived at the office in DC at 7 A. M., and there was a pile of paper the size of a small city phone book waiting for me, accompanied by a couple of meg of email. Republic Wright had some interest in about eighty communication satellites—we had built them, or built a major subsystem, or operated their station-keeping. We also had weather satellites, military intelligence, and some of GPS. In addition to the satellites themselves, all now dead and in need of replacement, we were flooded with emergency orders for replacement launches.

For every satellite, launch request, subsystem, or other Republic Wright involvement, there was a memo, about three pages long, which could be summarized as "Republic Wright must fix it for us right away." I printed them all out, sorted them into the really urgent and the merely urgent, dealt them out in piles to my assistants' inboxes, left scrawled instructions on top of each pile, and phoned for the cab.

I swallowed a big, strong coffee while I waited, and was getting into the cab to Washington Reagan by 8:30, starting on a trip that would take me about 5,500 miles before the day was out.

On the plane I pulled up the email copies on my laptop computer and read through the memos I had flagged. I would need a clear mental picture of the total situation later this afternoon, when the upper management of RW would meet in San Diego to formulate a rough strategy.

The only silver lining in that whole dark cloud of complaints and demands was the possibility that this might get me the funds, people, and resources to accelerate the Starcraft project, since the world was going to need anything at all that could deliver a satellite to orbit. Potentially a fleet of six StarBoosters, mated with StarCores, could carry satellites up faster than the manufacturers could build them. That was a potential that everyone needed to be aware of.

I had arranged to stop off at Scorpion Shack in Texas, not to hear where matters stood on the different projects—I always kept current and I already knew—but to hold a kind of halftime talk to get my engineers and scientists thinking hard about spelling out the full range of what we might be able to do, how well and how soon.

As the jet's wheels touched the Scorpion Shack runway and we rumbled toward the limo, I had just one hour to get ready for my meeting with my technical people. Angie, my secretary, was waiting in the limo with a prioritized stack of paper and a schedule. Peering at me over her harlequin glasses and pushing her unconvincing blonde wig to the side, with the kind of accent you get from living your entire life in Armstrong, Texas, she looked like she had escaped from a Gary Larson cartoon, but she'd been with me five years and there was no more efficient human being anywhere. "Twenty-one routine signatures," she said, "for stuff you already approved. You can sign while you listen."

I did.

"Breakfast meeting with Robertson tomorrow, big conference room off the cafeteria, seven-fifteen. About thirty people. And he's ordered a PowerPoint projector. Whatever it is, you're getting quite a show. Phil Tenn wants to talk to you about space junk and that thing he calls the Starbaggie, and he's penciled in for ten. A whole new flock of email arrived in the last three hours, which you'll want to see for your meeting in San Diego. Here's a copy." She handed me a floppy that I tucked into my coat pocket as I finished the last signing.

"At the rate it's coming in," she added, "I'll be giving you another floppy when you go, so make sure you get it from me. I'll run some interference to make sure that you get off the ground here in time. Now, this last thing here is a chart that I pulled off the current delivery and report schedules, the list of responsibilities, and some stuff from the organizational handbook, sort of cross-collated. I thought you might want to know what you're being held accountable for, officially, and when, while you talk to those people."

"Perfect," I said. I hadn't thought of it myself but it was exactly what I needed.

"I also took the liberty of setting up a cold buffet in your office. I checked your closet there and you have a spare suit and clothes. What you have on can go to the cleaners while you're in San Diego, and it'll be back in your apartment tonight. So we'll keep you presentable, too. Just make sure you eat in what you have on, then change.

"Oh, and there's some personal stuff too. I called your brother's lawyer to make sure, if it got too busy, there wouldn't be any delays if you don't have time to sign checks. She said everything was fine, financially, at the moment, and sounded pretty confident.

"And your nephew emailed you a thank-you note that sounds like your brother wrote it."

I laughed. Angie allowed herself half a smile before she added, "Hope you enjoyed your time off. Until time for your meeting, I'm planning to hold all calls and give you some decompression and thinking time. I've also warned all staff that if they try to catch you between the limo and the office, they may consider themselves dead."

Just as Angie had planned, I was comfortably fed, showered, changed, alert, and ready for the meeting. The table was ringed by some of the most energized technical people I'd ever seen. It warmed my heart, but there wasn't much time to enjoy it—I had seventy-five minutes until Angie would hurl me into the back of another limo and I'd be off to San Diego like a high-priority mailbag.

"Well," I said, "I wanted to talk about how this whole facility, and everyone in it, ought to respond to this extraordinary opportunity. You all know the old factoid that the Chinese ideogram for 'crisis' is a combination of the ideograms for 'danger' and 'opportunity.' What we've got to do, completely, is focus on the opportunity side.

"Here's how I see it. The world is just finding out how much they've come to depend on satellites and space travel. They will be willing to pay whatever it takes to get the space systems back up, as soon as possible. If we do it *right* this time, we can do it as a planned systematic development, instead of piecemeal across forty years. That way, when we're done rebuilding, we'll be in a much better position to expand. So no matter how busy we all get, I want you always thinking about one issue: how can we re-expand into space in a better, more systematic, more open-ended way?"

Ned Robertson, senior engineer on my staff, and also the driving force behind Starcraft, asked, "Any word on how we're getting the crew down from ISS?"

"As of the memos I had this morning, NASA is still assessing, but it looks like if they go to round-the-clock shifts, they can get *Atlantis* up there the minute the radiation people say they can go—probably with extra shielding, so they can go sooner. I think they can make it, based on the tentative stuff I saw."

Ned leaned back, surveyed the room, and said, "I don't know if you want to hear this question, just now, Nick, but is there a backup plan? The shuttle gets routine delays all the time. It wouldn't be improbable that they'd be delayed a month, even on a super-hurry-up schedule. And that could be a month more than the ISS crew have."

I thought for a moment; I had business to cover, and time was short, but I had learned that when Ned looked at me that particular way—head cocked to the side, fixing me with his right eye, lips pressed tight and curling into a little sardonic smile—there was something he thought was important, that I might not want to hear, and he was signaling me that he wanted to be asked about it.

Every time I had seen that expression, it had eventually turned out to be something I absolutely did need to know about. That's one of the effects of hiring talented people, I suppose.

"You have an idea in mind for that backup," I said. "Tell me."

"Well, suppose we skip a few steps in the current development plan. The StarBooster has been tested with Athena, and we have a StarCore I sitting there almost built, and two more coming along, right? So we just combine all the tests into one shot . . . put dual

StarBoosters on the StarCore and let 'er rip. If it all flies, then we tear down the StarBoosters, get them ready to go as quick as we can . . . and put StarRescue on top of the next StarCore, and go get the ISS crew."

"So your suggestion is that—" I tried to keep my voice neutral "—we ought to . . . fly *one* test of a major component, then fly it with a completely untested component, *plus* people?"

"Well, I didn't say it was the best way," Ned said, primly. "And StarRescue has had some drop tests. It's at least a partially tested component."

"Ned, the 'partially tested component' is a whole spacecraft. I'll be happy to hear all the ideas—even that one—tomorrow," I said. "You might convince me, but it will take a great deal of convincing."

Robertson nodded, obviously happy for the moment. He didn't need to hear "yes" all the time, or even most of the time, but my listening seemed to be important to him.

"All right," I said. "Now, even if we don't use it for anything as dramatic as the ISS rescue, the whole Starcraft series is vital. I think we'll be building more StarBooster 200's than anyone ever envisioned, and flying every configuration of Athenas and StarCores we've ever thought of with them. The question is, what *else* can we do? I know we have other rocket motors and packages in development— lots of them—and what I want us to do is *quickly* identify all the ones that could be made compatible with Starcraft systems, to add even more capability."

Phil Tenn cleared his throat. "Except for some very low altitude stuff, all the dead satellites are now long-duration space junk. We'd been messing around with an air-launched version of Starbaggie for wartime, but we could probably send ten or twelve of them up at a time on a StarBooster/Athena—or slip them in, space-a, on every payload going up. There's tons of trash now taking up valuable space in the commercially important orbits."

"Starbaggie" was a nickname; it had originally been a DARPA

project intended to be used, in time of war, to knock down surveillance or communication satellites. It was supposed to be carried aloft on a rocket launched from an airplane, much like the commercial Pegasus system, for a near-rendezvous with the target satellite, at which point it would deploy a Kevlar net about a mile across, swallow the satellite by reeling in the net, and then deploy either a small rocket motor or a long, dragging tether to de-orbit it.

Angie signaled me from the door, and I looked around the room. Probably there were six other teams with ideas, but just at the moment I didn't have time to hear all of them. I held up a hand and said, "All right, people, I know I can depend on all of you for ideas, creativity, and problem-solving. Phil, if I get a chance, I'll raise the space junk issue at the big meeting this afternoon—that could be very lucrative for us, if we can get somebody to pay a bonus on clearing junk out of orbits.

"Ned, I'm looking forward to your presentation tomorrow, but keep it as conservative as you can. For the moment, I won't say anything about that idea in San Diego.

"Everybody, I need all of your enthusiasm and support. Give your people a heads-up: we might be changing everything we're doing tomorrow, so stay creative and flexible. We're adjourned."

Nearly everyone had to shake my hand and say a few words. Angie truly had to scramble to get me off the ground in time to make the big meeting in San Diego.

On the plane, I read through the disks of email she had given me. Every other member of upper management at Republic Wright was jockeying for position, too. A quick scan revealed three groups—the ones who saw the situation as an opportunity (whom I dubbed "aggressives"), the ones who saw it as a menace (whom I dubbed "fearfuls"), and many who didn't see it at all—people who said the company should just keep doing what it was doing. (I dubbed those "oblivious.")

It was discouraging. The oblivious were the largest single group.

Somehow or other the fearful and the aggressive would have to find their way into an alliance.

When we landed at the company field outside San Diego, I was sure I'd be late. I was already mentally writing a memo to the pilot's supervisor, saying that I'd given the pilot a late start and he'd gotten some pretty bad headwinds. As it was, I wrote a note congratulating the limo driver, though I don't ever want to go through that much southern California freeway quite that quickly again. I arrived at the meeting with plenty of extra adrenaline, which might be to my advantage.

A minute after I had settled in, unfolded my laptop, and taken the first welcome sip of hot coffee, Jagavitz walked in, sat down, and said, "All right, gentlemen and ladies, I've read all your memos and notes. I can boil it down to a choice. We can do one of three things. We jump in and fight like a tiger for all the market we can get. We hunker down like a turtle and try not to lose anything we already have. Or we freeze like a goddam deer in the headlights and wait for Curtiss to take us over." As usual, when he got emotional, his slight Central European accent got stronger. "That is what I will say to the Board. Surely you all know that I will recommend the tiger, not the turtle or the deer. The Board will either agree with me, or they will fire me. If I am not fired, then all of you must either see things my way, or take a walk." He looked around the room, and from his expression, I concluded that most of my anxiety and worry about this meeting had been, blessedly, wasted. I had won before I had arrived.

Jagavitz went on. "Our policy with regard to Curtiss is that we must surpass them and win a long-run advantage. Whatever the situation was a week ago, today it is—what's the expression? in football?—today fate has punted. Loose ball, anyone's to grab. We will grab that ball, and if we have to break some noses to do it, that adds to the fun." He now had that famous expression that *Business Week* always described as "sharklike" and *Forbes* called "fearsome." "So," he continued. "So. Now we make money. Now we pioneer. Now we show everyone how it is done. Don't tell me what they told you at

Harvard MBA school, unless it tells me how to do what I want. These next few years, *we* write the book, and all the experts can study *us*."

His bald, liver-spotted head shone like a skull, but the crinkles around his eyes were warm and filled with pleasure. "I want every space launch product that can fly to be flying, as soon as it safely can. I want our sales force to be drowning in orders for all of them.

"That's what the program is, if the Board keeps me. If you think I'm going to still be the CEO after tomorrow morning—and I plan to be—then you had better get ready to work harder, faster, and better than you ever have before."

My first thought was that I hoped that I'd be allowed to hand out a tape or a transcript of that speech at Scorpion Shack.

"Comments?" Jagavitz said.

A hand went up down at the end of the table—Andrew Riscaveau. He wasn't senior management, but because so much of our work was classified, he attended our meetings as a consultant. He didn't have a vote, and normally he only spoke if security issues were involved.

"I just wanted to point out that that strategy could have very serious security repercussions. First of all, moving so much high tech out of the lab and into production, so quickly, is going to enormously increase the opportunities for espionage and sabotage, domestic or foreign. Second, and more important, the government security authorities have to be concerned about having a stable and productive aerospace industry, and that kind of market-grabbing is going to be disruptive at a time when the country really needs a smooth-functioning system. I don't think they'll let us get away with it, if they're doing their job."

Jagavitz stared as if he'd just seen a dead rat in Riscaveau's mouth. "We will be increasing launch capacity, and that is what the country needs; 'stability' is a polite expression for 'the comfort of people who are already on top.' Since, at the moment, we are not the ones on top, we have no interest in their comfort. As for Curtiss's markets, let them keep them and serve them—if they can. If not, we will.

"As for the first part, it is your responsibility, is it not, to prevent espionage and sabotage on the company grounds? And didn't you just hear me say that everyone will have to work harder? Well, work harder. Make sure it doesn't happen."

Riscaveau was nearly pouting. Instead of sensibly shutting up, he rambled for a full minute, stressing how he was just trying to help, no one understood the need for a real security perspective, and in a high-tech company that was involved in national security, every issue was a security issue.

While Riscaveau rambled, I watched him. My managers and engineers at Scorpion Shack detested him. At any meeting to which he had to be invited—no one ever invited him if it was optional—he always took great pains to assure us that he was a good security man, who could have had his choice of jobs in security. He took *pleasure* in asserting that guarding anything is always the same job, and he was the best judge of how to guard anything. He loved to remind engineers and managers that no matter what astonishing work they might do, no matter how far into the new frontier they might push humanity, Riscaveau would always be there to check their front door pass.

Riscaveau finally ran down, unable to wriggle out of Jagavitz's glare. Not hiding his impatience, Jagavitz asked for more comments and questions.

He got a few minor issues, mostly from people too junior to realize that Jagavitz wasn't a detail person, and the CFO gave him some notes about how long the company could afford to run at a loss until the new revenue streams came in. Then, at Jagavitz's request, I got up and talked in a general way about the enormous potential increase in launch capability from Starcraft. Finally, Jagavitz adjourned the meeting, and I caught a flight back to Scorpion Shack, where I arrived at about eleven P. M. local time. When the limo picked me up at the airport, for the first time that day, I could tell a driver to take his time. It had been a nineteen-hour day, and I more or less fell into bed.

CHAPTER TEN

NICK:

Breakfast with engineers is not relaxing; very few people are as nervous as an engineer compelled to socialize with management, and it is always an atmosphere of forced laughter and awkward silences. Everyone gulps the food as if someone might take it all back.

The nine people from the StarBooster, StarCore I and II, and StarBird projects suddenly developed a consuming interest in the muffins and scrambled eggs. Ned Robertson and I, who knew each other well, exchanged platitudes and pleasantries over our breakfasts, while everyone else ate in tense silence. When, after about twenty minutes, the trays had been cleared, table wiped, and notebooks brought out, and everyone was sipping coffee or tea, I said, "So, tell me your ideas."

Robertson nodded. "I should warn you, Mr. Blackstone, we stayed up till one o'clock last night getting this all together, and most of us are a little wired on caffeine. So if you ask for hard evidence for any point, plenty of it will come at you very fast and with great passion, before I can get it under control." A low chuckle ran through his engineers. He had probably been urging them to stay out of technical thickets.

"I understand. If I ask you to prove anything, what happens will serve me right."

They all smiled at me, brightly enough for people who must have been exhausted.

Robertson began. "Well, Mr. Blackstone, here's the gist: if you authorize unlimited overtime, and allow us to go straight to a full dual-StarBooster/StarCore I launch, then we would have a pretty good heavy-lift launcher. And if we put StarRescue on top of it, we could go get the crew off ISS. We might even be ready before *Atlantis*." He popped a critical path chart onto the screen and started indicating points with his laser pointer. "The two piloted drop tests of StarRescue alone, with Andre Johnston flying it down, worked perfectly. And StarCore I's working parts are almost entirely well-established, off-the-shelf technology. So, even though dual-StarBooster/StarCore I/StarRescue would be a new system, in the sense of not having flown together before, it would in fact be much more proven-out than most things we fly. Give us the word for the dual-StarBooster/StarCore I test, and we can fly it just four days from now.

"If that first test works, then in a pinch we can do the ISS rescue on about a week's notice. Even if we *don't* end up doing the ISS rescue, a successful flight will mean we've got a ready-to-go, cheap, fast satellite launcher, with heavy lift capability, right in the middle of the biggest demand for launch services there's ever been.

"If that first test fails—well, we go back to the regular test sequence, and little harm done.

"So the deal is: run this StarBooster/StarCore test. If it succeeds, we're a full year ahead, *and* in position to do the ISS rescue if anything goes wrong with *Atlantis*. If it fails, we're only a month behind."

I was impressed despite myself. "All right, you've made a case for an early StarCore test. But how do you get from that to the idea that we should then go on and fly StarRescue, *manned?*"

"Well, all right, that one is a stretch," Robertson said cheerfully.

"But the only part of the flight that would be completely unprecedented would be the return from orbit, and even that's using a well-proven method, because it comes down exactly the same way the shuttle does—we even modeled the controls off the shuttle, so that an experienced shuttle pilot needs almost no time to get up on StarRescue or StarBird.

"Now, I'm not saying that we *should* do this. I *am* saying that if the shuttle craps out, and the ISS crew is dying up there, we could be ready to go with the dual-StarBooster/StarCore I/StarRescue configuration. And if we've got people dying up there, we *have* to try to get them home, even at very great risks."

Robertson sat back down and clicked off the PowerPoint projector; when the hum of its fan went out, the room was amazingly quiet. "That's what we all think, Mr. Blackstone. There's going to be a couple hundred pages of justification on your desk for it, soon, but you know we wouldn't try to fool you about a thing like this. We think we can do it. If we have to, we can make the trip to ISS the test flight. A StarRescue mounted on a StarCore I with two Star-Booster 200's could do it."

I looked around the room. "All right," I said. "Who among you has the biggest doubts?" Finally, Caroline Ralston spoke up and said, "Red Cheney has some."

Cheney shrugged. "I think it's ninety-nine percent likely that the flight would make it and everything would be fine," he said.

"That likely?" I asked. "I don't place bets on the shuttle and it's been flying for twenty years."

"Yeah, I know. I've been over the test data on StarBooster, StarCore I, and StarRescue, though, with a fine-tooth comb, and there is just not one component, apart from the StarRescue airframe, that hasn't already been tested under stresses that are bigger than the ones for this mission.

"So apart from bad luck and human error, the only thing to worry about is a negative synergy—two things that work fine in isolation interacting in an unanticipated, undesirable way. I have somewhat more doubt than the others that our computer simulations would spot them. But the potential gain is huge, and for unproven hardware, the risks can't get much lower."

I went around the room twice, but Red Cheney really was the biggest doubter; the rest were convinced that they could have Robertson's proposed configuration fully flyable in three weeks.

Finally Robertson summed up. "You know, something people forget is that though of course they did test those early space capsules, the early astronauts all went up in unique, hand-built machines, and got back."

"They also had nearly unlimited quantities of money and public good will," I pointed out, "which makes running risks a lot easier." Still, you back your team if at all possible. I would have an extremely unhappy team if I told them to give up on the idea. "Well, there's nothing wrong with getting ahead on our test program. I'll give you the go for StarBooster/StarCore. As for StarRescue, I pray that won't be necessary, but I suppose I'd hate to have thrown the possibility away, if everything else goes to pieces. So get me your proposal and schedules, in detail, and if you manage to convince me, then I'll take it to Jagavitz. But no rosy projections, no excess optimism, no stacking the deck. Just tell the truth about how far we would have to go, and how fast, to make the plan work."

They stared at me until Ned started to clap. Then they all joined in. I'd never received a round of applause from my engineers before, and wasn't sure I liked it.

Robertson walked along with me, back to my office, to fill me in on some other points. When we got there, Angie had just received word that Jagavitz had won his battle with the Board, hands down. Robertson, Angie, and I celebrated with soft drinks from the machine, for about five minutes, then got back to work.

*　　*　　*

IN THE NEXT few days, Scorpion Shack was transformed. The break rooms and hallways were full of the kind of excited babble that only our oldest employees, who had worked, decades ago, on Apollo, Skylab, Stealth, or the SSME, could remember. I spent as much time around my excited, creative engineers and scientists as possible, but I was needed more urgently to keep well-meaning management elsewhere in the company from taking up the talent's time with paperwork, reports, evaluations, and assessments.

For half of Wednesday morning I was on the phone to Barbara Quentin, the corporate VP for Issues Management. Usually she was a sensible person, but now she insisted that we promise the public that new satellites would be invulnerable against proton bursts. Eventually I successfully explained (I think) that every pound of shielding that you sent to orbit was a pound of payload that didn't go, and that to do what she was asking, you would need several pounds of shielding for every pound of payload.

Anyway, nothing could protect the Earth's satellites against anyone who really wanted to harm them. Orbital velocities are around thirty times that of a rifle bullet, the damage done by an impact depends on the square of the velocity, and thus a satellite running into a projectile gets about nine hundred times the devastating blow it would if it were hit by that same object fired out of a gun. A ton of concrete, lofted into the pathway of a satellite, would destroy it even if you had armored it like a battleship. "In the long run, the only real way to protect space-based assets is to not have wars," I explained to Barbara.

That call had been aggravating, but it was nothing compared to the next one, from Andrew Riscaveau. "We have an interesting situation."

"Oh?" I asked.

Riscaveau said, "I have a call coming in to your private line that I need to talk to you about, before you take the call."

"You should not be intercepting my calls."

"You're the head of Scorpion Shack. We intercept everything in or out. It's just we don't usually talk with you about it."

It was an old argument that I didn't want to have again. "Is the person still on the line?"

"I told him he'd have to wait for me to talk to you. He knows it might take a while. Here's the thing. It's Killeret, from Curtiss."

"Do you know what it's about?"

"I didn't ask him."

"Is there a reason why I shouldn't talk to him?"

"Not really."

"Then why are you delaying both of us? Why don't you just record the conversation like you do all the others, and stay out of the way?"

"Look, we have good reason to believe that Mr. Killeret is about to propose something that he thinks is going to be good for Curtiss," Riscaveau said, "and it's our belief that it may be in the interests of Republic Wright as well."

I *had* been working on controlling my temper. "*Our* belief? Was there a meeting? Who was there and what's their mission?"

"Well, there's a company policy that—"

"Now, wait a minute. I *make* policy, along with other upper management. We hold meetings to do it. If this is really policy, then I should have been at the meeting where you set it."

"Well, it's not policy in the sense of a set policy or anything like that, Mr. Blackstone, but it's in the general interests of the company—"

"And there is some reason why you know the general interests of the company better than I do?"

"Well, when there's a conflict of interest—"

"Are you aware that that's a serious accusation, not just a buzz-word to sling around in the way you're accustomed to?" I hadn't blown up that way in a long time, but leave it to Riscaveau to bring it out in me.

He said stiffly, "Go ahead with your call."

When Killeret came on the line, I began with, "First of all, I've got to apologize on behalf of all of Republic Wright for the extremely embarrassing and unprofessional behavior of our security chief, who is meddling in all sorts of things he has no business meddling in." I enjoyed the thought that Riscaveau would be recording that.

Killeret laughed. "Ever the diplomat, Nick. Here's the story, and my security guy is going to wet himself about my telling you, too, but I need you to know this for the sake of both our companies. Over at Ghost Town we've been developing a new, big expendable rocket, and we've also been working, mostly on our own, on an advanced CRV, a follow-on to Soyuz. Crew of four, smaller than your Star-Rescue, but still a perfectly fine vehicle for all kinds of other functions. For example, an unmanned version would be a perfect cargo ship for sending supplies to ISS."

"So what's the good news for us?"

"The good news is that if our CRV does end up flying as a space-craft, Curtiss will be a market for StarBooster, and we'll be ordering some of them whenever you'll sell them to us. The bad news is that we might not get to do it. Yesterday there was a big meeting, corporate level, and I didn't recognize half the faces there. We've had a real turnover of upper management and various key departments, and the new people seem to be coming in from everywhere except aerospace, science, or engineering. I'd had no idea it had gone so far. And the new crew here seem to be determined to drag their feet. The company policy is that with space in such grave doubt in the public mind, we can't afford to have anything go wrong at all under any circumstances, and therefore we need to slow down, plan months of extra tests, and evaluate the 'risks' of adding a new technology to the mix. They want a yearlong slowdown on the advanced CRV."

"*New* technology?" I said. "Individual pieces might be new, but a capsule on top of an expendable rocket is the same basic technology that got Yuri Gagarin into orbit."

"Well, yeah." Killeret sighed. "So here's the favor I'm asking. The good guys don't seem to be winning the argument over here. I think that the go-slow policy is going to be made official. What I'm thinking is, maybe if you could go public with StarBooster a little sooner— or even reveal that you're planning to get competitive in expendables again—"

"We've got a test coming up very soon for something that'll knock all of your expendables out of the race for a good long while," I said. "And you're going to end up wanting to buy StarBoosters by the dozen once that happens, to get back into the race. In two weeks we'll be talking about something completely different. But thanks for the heads-up; it's good to know in advance about the potential market."

"Well, Nick, you know, Mars Four forever."

I laughed. "We were just down at the cabin this past weekend. We should have called and invited you."

"Do it, next time. How are you doing at throwing Scott and Thally back together?" He knew about that because I had told him about it during one of the long calls last week; once we started talking to each other, after years of barely communicating, we had suddenly had all sorts of things to say.

"Some progress," I said, "but I'm dealing with two stubborn people who know most of my negotiating and management tricks. I'll have to proceed carefully."

"I have faith in you," he said. "And thanks for talking to me. I read a report about Jagavitz's speech at your meeting. It must be fun to be at an aerospace company that's interested in flying."

"You can send me a résumé any time," I said. "Take care. Mars Four forever."

"You bet. Talk to you soon."

We rang off and I sat back and scribbled out the points I wanted to make to Jagavitz at our meeting the next day. The CEO's style of conversation, one-on-one with a subordinate, was often more like interrogation, and it helped to have all your ideas clear in mind before talking to him. I had just finished numbering the points when the phone rang.

Without preamble, Riscaveau said, "Now, you're really just doing things to make a mess, and I don't see any way I can do anything except report this."

I was startled. "You said you thought I should *take* the deal that Killeret was going to offer. As it turned out, he made no offer, per se, but he did discuss an area where cooperation would do us tremendous good, and so I'm cooperating. I'd have to be crazy not to. If his faction wins out at Curtiss, it could *double* the market for StarBooster. You were absolutely right. What's the matter now?"

"That wasn't what I thought the call was going to be about, and it shouldn't have been what you thought the call was going to be about, either." There was a weird tension to his voice, as if a simple misunderstanding were a matter of life and death. "I thought he would be calling to urge you to take Curtiss's new offer for your brother's case; they wanted to offer a firm contract to pay any judgment against him, so that he'd be able to just take the deal, settle the case, and get on with his life."

"Why would Killeret be the one to bring that offer to me, and why me, instead of just talking directly to Scott or his attorney? And why should Scott settle now when all the new evidence is that it's not anything the James family can sue about?"

"You and Killeret are old friends, and your first loyalty is not to your companies. You are financing your brother's court expenses totally against the interests of Republic Wright, regardless of what Jagavitz says. And yes, if you have to, you can tell him I said that. I've said it to his face. I can't believe that he's persisting in this whole crazy—"

"The Board upheld him yesterday. By a big majority," I pointed out. "And you didn't answer my question. You're also far outside your territory. How is security involved in this, at all?"

Riscaveau's voice had the kind of infuriating self-satisfaction that your kindergarten teacher had when she was insisting it was time for a nap whether you were sleepy or not. "Because you're having an irregular contact with a secure facility at our major competitor. Because accelerating the StarBooster runs a greater risk of an accident and the accident could cost the company time and money, and because if StarBooster is delivered early it's going to completely disrupt the space-launch market at a time when things are already in chaos, so it is in the interests of stability and ordered development to keep it right on schedule, not speed it up. And most of all because when you come right down to it, Republic Wright is a company that makes the basic hardware for national security, and that means everything the company does is a security affair."

I forgot all about keeping my temper. "Everything the company does is *not* a security affair. Only *some* of our interests involve security. And *when* they don't, which is *most* of the time—*particularly* at Scorpion Shack—*keep your ratty little nose out.* You are meddling outside your charter. StarBooster is not a security matter. There is no theft, treason, arson, or whatever going on. So get out of it and stay out." I hung up.

One of the advantages of being at a high level in the company is the opportunity it gives you to calm down when you need to. If I'd still been a project leader of an engineering team, right then, I'd have been so angry that I might have done something foolish in front of other people. As it was, I just had Angie hold my calls, then paced angrily around the office thinking of all the nasty things I should have said to Riscaveau. After a few minutes, I went into my private washroom and rinsed my face, went to the office refrigerator for an orange, a pear, and a big bottle of spring water, and had a calming snack while I played Pachelbel's Canon on the stereo, over and over.

Half an hour later I was a perfectly reasonable person again. With a sigh—it was nice and peaceful in here and I was about to invite trouble back in—I picked up the phone and told the secretary that I officially existed again.

Angie said, "I had two calls from Andrew Riscaveau, asking you not to return a call from Clifford Welch. Mr. Riscaveau sounded very upset. Mr. Welch did call, and left his number."

"Who is Clifford Welch?"

"Deep Blue. He said he needed to talk to you before the StarBird presentation this afternoon. And he also said he'd be at the presentation and if it's not convenient to return the call, he can come early and meet you beforehand."

"I'll return his call," I said. "Call him back. If he can't come to the phone right now, I can wait."

Much of our work at Scorpion Shack in recent years had probably been for Deep Blue, but even I didn't know exactly what or exactly how much. Everything connected with Deep Blue was "SCI"— Sensitive Compartmented Information—which is a whole set of classifications, all of which are considerably more restricted than the old "top secret" category that is still in use for more routine information. Most of the people at Scorpion Shack had a clearance for Secret, and a large minority were cleared for Top Secret, but I only had about thirty people with SCI clearances—and every SCI clearance is different, a permit to see only what is needed for the job at hand and nothing more.

Even the table of organization itself was secret; probably Deep Blue was part of the National Reconnaissance Office. The NRO itself was a completely SCI agency, the government office for spy satellites, and although it was established by President Kennedy, it was only in the last weeks of the Bush Administration that it was publicly admitted that it existed.

Deep Blue was quieter than *that*. Like many of the most secret projects since World War II, its name gave nothing away at all. My occasional interactions with them usually involved a covert space launch from Scorpion Shack's pad or by one of our experimental air-launched missiles. Deep Blue missions often were connected to some of our experimental work with spaceborne, stealth-piercing radar to track various objects that didn't "officially" exist in space; several times we had launched a small package, delivered just hours before launch, into an orbit that intercepted one of those ghosts.

I thought Deep Blue was probably the counterintelligence branch of the NRO. Perhaps what we were doing was shooting down some other nation's unacknowledged spy satellites, since those radar objects tended to disappear shortly after the covert launches. But for all I knew, Deep Blue could just as easily have been a branch of the NSA or CIA, or a freestanding body reporting to the President. And the packages might not have been interceptors; they might have been couriers, going up to stealthed American satellites to pick up material too secret to send by any other method, or tugboats repositioning the satellites, or even tiny robots to repair them. The stuff that the super-secret agencies use has always been twenty to fifty years ahead of its time; they're the only organizations on Earth that make Scorpion Shack and Ghost Town look backward.

Given what must have happened to Deep Blue's orbital assets, along with everyone else's, I figured that they probably needed one or more emergency launches, ASAP, or perhaps they had an armored probe ready to go up and take some measurements on just how intense the radiation was in orbit, something it would be good for them to know before anyone else did. As I waited for Angie to put me through to Welch, I thought of everything we had that could reach orbit. Maybe we could use the StarBooster/StarCore test to fly it . . . that way there'd be no budget line for a payload (although, as usually happened with a Deep Blue launch, there would probably be a mysterious increase in one of my budget accounts within a couple of weeks).

The only thing I was really supposed to know was that standing orders were "Deep Blue gets whatever they want and none of it ever appears in the budget; be nice to Deep Blue no matter what the cost, and more than the cost will always turn up for Republic Wright somehow," as Jagavitz had told me when I first took over Scorpion Shack.

The phone rang and Angie said, "I have Mr. Welch on the line. Go ahead."

"Mr. Welch?"

"Mr. Blackstone. We know a few people in common but we've never met. I'm part of Deep Blue, but I'm not a part you've ever had to deal with before. As for my official status in the secret agencies, I can at least say that the head of Deep Blue is a deputy director and I answer directly to him."

"Good enough," I said. That put Welch three down from the President of the United States. I was suitably impressed.

"Here's what I need from you. I'll be one of the insignificant suits in the big delegation of congresspeople and bureaucrats that's coming by to look at StarBird this afternoon. If you were planning to deputize the job of showing them around, I strongly suggest that you de-deputize it and meet the delegation."

Inwardly I sighed; I *had* planned to delegate it to a subordinate, and thus create an uninterrupted hour to catch up on business and administrivia.

"Now," he went on, "I also have one other agent in the delegation, and one in the StarBird hangar. I'm doing all this because we think that you've been penetrated by what's very possibly a violent organization with foreign sponsorship. We have reason to think they are opposed to the development of the Starcraft series in general. We'll be keeping an eye on things. There's some information I need from you, and some things it would be helpful to have you do, that might be very important, so that's why I called today."

"So you just want me to act normally?"

"At least for the moment. But we thought it might be a good idea to let you in on the overall situation. If something strange starts to happen, at least you'll be prepared for it, and maybe that will help. And at the least I want you to think about any additional security measures you can take."

A thought occurred to me. "That's very strange. We have a very gung-ho security chief, but he specifically urged me not to return your call. If what you're asking for is more security, our guy should have been delighted."

"Really? That's *extremely* interesting. Well, if he should ask if you *did* talk to me—he will—tell him no, and that you have no idea who I am."

"Got it."

"Don't call Andrew Riscaveau's attention to anything connected with Deep Blue, at all. I know that you normally wouldn't refer to SCI material anyway, and this whole conversation, and the fact that it happened, is all SCI.

"Anyway, if things go all right at the StarBird presentation, I'll be coming around to your office about forty minutes afterward, for a much more detailed conversation that will probably clear up a large number of things that must have been very confusing for you. Thank you for your cooperation." He hung up, not waiting for me to say I'd cooperate; it didn't seem to me that I had very many choices, anyway.

I checked with Angie to make sure I hadn't already delegated the job of doing the presentation. I hadn't, so all I need do was proceed according to schedule. Then I forgot about Welch, Riscaveau, and everything complicated or annoying, and got on with the paper-shuffle that has to be done, day in and day out, whether or not the whole world is going to pieces. I thought I might begin to like the monthly overtime report; it had the soothing qualities of requiring attention, not mattering much, and containing no real surprises.

To make sure the tour would go smoothly, I called Robertson. "We need to show them a good time," I said. "And if they like what they see and hear, everything will be easier. So we need a good show, and I want your staff to spend the next couple hours getting ready for one. No exceptions, no matter how high a priority. Is that clear?"

"It is. You know engineers, but I'll make 'em see reason."

"Thanks, Ned—I really appreciate that. Work areas need to look busy but don't let any of them be sloppy. If somebody just must have some huge project spread all over a table, move the table somewhere out of sight—you can move it back once the delegation's gone. Don't let the ship be seen with its guts hanging out—close up everything, hatches, access doors, the works. Now, most important of all, make sure we have a completely safe pathway for them to walk along. Nothing spoils a tour like killing a Deputy Undersecretary, and the average bureaucrat has no idea how dangerous a place like the Shack is."

"I'll be right on top of it, then, Mr. Blackstone. Clean, neat, safe, and our bird gets the best plumage we can manage. Everybody helps whether they want to or not. Anything else?"

"If you can do all that in a couple of hours, that will be plenty."

"No kidding. But we'll have it done. When do you arrive?"

"About fifteen minutes till showtime, but I might be late."

"We'll be ready at twenty till."

After I hung up, and got back to working my way through various small documents that, if not filled out, would cost precious time later, I kept thinking that the stereotype of the engineer is one of the more misleading ones. Supposedly they lack people skills, and some do, of course, but you'd be surprised how many managers and counselors are even worse than the average engineer. I was pleasantly sure that not only would everything be set up for my arrival, but Robertson would find a way to have his team in a good mood about it, though nobody hates interruptions more than an engineer on a tight schedule.

The phone rang.

Riscaveau didn't bother to say hello, and he didn't ask; he made a flat statement sound like an accusation of murder. "Your secure line was busy but our computer log doesn't show any record of a call, and we couldn't access the voice line to hear what was going on."

So Deep Blue could get an untraceable phone call into one of the most secure facilities on the planet, and scramble it so that our own security people couldn't eavesdrop. I was even more impressed than I had been before.

"Something is wrong with either your computer log or with the phone system itself," I said. "Which call are you talking about?"

"Which call? You were on the phone for half an hour."

"I'm sure I wasn't talking to Ned Robertson for that long," I said.

"Not the one to Robertson! The one before!"

"Well, there were a bunch of calls before," I said, stalling. I was not sure how good an actor I might be, and he was probably looking at voice stress meters to see if I was lying, so I decided to be blatant. "I had three or four business calls in the last two hours, but none of them was more than two minutes. Which ones are you talking about?"

"I told you, there's no record in the computer log and your line was busy—"

"Or the phone system was reporting it busy. Maybe after the call from my brother I set it down wrong in the cradle, and then I bumped it later and it came back on."

"You didn't get a call from your brother!"

"You mean, the computer log doesn't show it."

"Oh, fuck you." He hung up. At least he hadn't asked me whether I had talked to Clifford Welch.

I would have to remember to report that conversation to Welch after the presentation, when I'd meet with him.

I signed off on the overtime report and opened up the weekly budget report.

The phone rang again. I picked it up, and my secretary said, "It's your brother."

"Put him through."

"Nick?"

"Yes, Scott?"

He sounded as if he were enraged. "I just got a call from an obnoxious little troll who said he was your security person, and he seemed to think I shouldn't call you, or else he wanted me to say I'm not going to call you, or that I never call you, or something. I told the son of a bitch I'd call you when I damned well pleased, this afternoon or any afternoon, and if you didn't want the call you could just hang up on me." I was stifling laughter; when Scott and I were teenagers, he used to play "irate man," in which he'd call up some hapless business with an irrational complaint and keep building it up until they acquired the courage to hang up. What I was hearing now was the "irate man" voice, and I had no doubt it was adding to Riscaveau's confusion as he listened in. "I hope I didn't cause you any problems."

"Only problems that I enjoy having," I said. "Thanks for letting me know about that. I'll make sure there's a note about this erratic behavior in that man's personnel file. Mars Four forever."

"Mars Four forever to you too. Hope you get some time off so we can see you soon, Nick."

"I hope so too, but it isn't going to happen."

After we hung up, I leaned back in the chair and laughed myself half sick. My kid brother had never, never in his life been a snitch. When some authority demanded that he contradict something I'd said, he would look them straight in the eye and absolutely confirm it, *especially* if he had any reason to think it wasn't true. Well, he'd done it again.

Angie's alert guarding secured me an hour and a half during which I rerouted tons of trivia away from the productive people, and knocked down a pile of administrative barriers; there's an almost sadistic glee in destroying all the little traps and barriers that some managerial voles put up against progress, and letting the stream of ideas and creativity pour through, sweeping all before it. When I looked up from my monitor, I had used up most of my time, but I was roaring with energy, concentrated like a laser, and feeling like I could work forever.

I made myself take a few minutes to maintain myself. I stretched, got a cold orange juice, and splashed water on my face from the sideboard sink. Life was definitely all right with me, I thought, as I looked at the empty inbox and the bulging outbox.

It was getting to be time for the presentation, and November is a nice month in the southern Panhandle. I decided to walk over to the StarBird hangar. I let Angie know where I was going and that I wouldn't be available for at least two hours after getting back—I figured I should leave a generous allowance for the meeting with Clifford Welch.

I didn't know why I was feeling so cheerful. It might have been that I'd spared a few moments, mentally, for the ISS situation, and had realized that, bad as the global catastrophe was, it could hardly be better PR for space. The rescue would wipe the whole MJ affair out of the news and create a brand new positive spin.

Or it might have been that I was glad I had decided to do the presentation myself. There's a bit of ham in every development project manager, and one of our guilty pleasures is to pull a great new project out in front of an appreciative audience. This presentation was one of the first steps in preparing to go fully public. The bureaucrats, congressmen, and staffers in the group would leak all sorts of things—favorable things, we hoped—and with luck we might generate some favorable rumors to smooth the way. In short order, we'd be welcoming reporters in, and getting the campaign going seriously. I love that stage of a project.

Or I might only have been happy because I was getting to take a walk in perfect weather. It was about seventy degrees, there wasn't a cloud in the deep blue sky, and everything seemed to leap out of the background in extra color. The fifteen-minute walk from my office to StarBird was the most private time I'd had all day, spoiled only by the occasional golf cart full of engineers that would swoop in to ask if I needed a ride. I waved them all off, enjoyed the walk, and arrived five minutes early, fully refreshed.

And then again, perhaps the good feeling was mostly anticipation of the pleasure I always felt when I stepped into the hangar.

I stepped through the door. My breath caught. I suppose there's an overgrown child in me somewhere. Whenever I look at one of Scorpion Shack's planes or spacecraft, there's always a touch of magic about it. It might be just knowing that there isn't anything else like it in the world yet, that it's the first one, some of the future sitting in our hangars, like a newborn eagle. Maybe it's just that the most aerodynamic shapes for extreme environments—which is what we build—often look like something out of a comic book. Whatever the reason, when I walked into the hangar where StarBird I sat, in the center of a sprawl of data and power cables, I felt a touch of awe.

"The display lights?" Ned Robertson stood at my elbow.

"Definitely the display lights," I said.

Robertson gestured at someone over his shoulder. Hangars are big, and even when there are lots of bright lights, they have plenty of dark corners; a moment later, the big floods were off and the dimmer ceiling lights left the room shadowy, almost dark.

All around the StarBird, dozens of small floodlights came on, shaping a cool, white light around its smooth curves. It was a beautiful craft, no question about it—a long, slim lifting body with short wings at the back; from the front, small canard stabilizers sprouted, the wings of StarRescue if that should need to separate. It seemed like the offspring of the shuttle and the Concorde, but more graceful than either. We had painted it bright white with a black stripe down the side. The single-piece "keel" of heat-resistant composite was steel blue, its natural color, since we'd found no paint that we could trust to stick to it.

On the side the words REPUBLIC WRIGHT STARBIRD 001 implied that we hoped to build more than a hundred of them; I remembered that Robertson had told me he wished we had made that "0001," to leave room for thousands. Above that there was the logo we had settled on—a stylized eagle forming out of a spiral emerging from a star.

At the moment it was still mostly a fake, or a promise of things to come, but parts of it were almost finished. The passenger compartment that formed StarBird's nose was real enough, and had had three flights already. It was the StarRescue that we had used to flight test the StarBooster. In that test we had replaced the nose on a StarBooster prototype with the StarRescue and dropped the whole thing from a 747; Andre Johnston had flown it down to our runway, thus proving out the airframe for both StarBooster and StarBird and cutting years off our development time. Johnston had also flown two drop tests from a B-52 with the StarRescue alone. So the front one-fifth of StarBird—the StarRescue—was as real as it gets; theoretically if it were fueled up and put into orbit, it would be ready to fly down to Earth today.

The composite plate on the bottom, the advanced descendant of space shuttle tiles, was real too. And two days before, we'd slipped an old SSME and its oxygen tank into her tail, and bolted that into place. (In a sense, that superannuated SSME was the most-proven part of the whole device, for it had been to space many times, after many flights on the shuttle. We would replace it with a new one, of course, when and if StarBird 001 went to space—but for the present tests, it was the right shape and weight, and cheap.)

A few more days would see enough control electronics go into StarBird 001 to allow for a taxi test—just taking it out to rumble slowly up and down the runway to see what might fall off, and checking the throttling and landing gear, simple things that could wreck an experimental craft during takeoff and landing.

It had been beautiful to me, just sitting in the hangar, but with the display lights—I hoped—*everyone* should be able to see, right away, how beautiful it really was.

That was probably a forlorn hope. Delegations from Washington always give you a mixed response—a few like kids at a *Star Wars* movie, some determined to show you how blasé they can be, and a small percentage are actually trying to learn something.

"If it flies as well as it looks," Robertson said beside me, "then this might be the biggest publicity hit that RW—or the space program—has had in a real long time."

A staffer jogged up to ask if we were ready. We said yes, and she turned and ran for the door. Less than a minute later, the delegation filed in.

There were about forty of them, mostly men in conservative suits and women in dark dresses with matching jackets. As they came in, I could hear some of them exclaiming—little cries of "oh!," whistles, and soft "oh, wow" 's. It looked like the preliminary report was good, anyway. When they'd all come in, and had a chance to let the first impression settle, I said to Robertson, "Okay, we need regular lights for the presentation." He spoke into his phone, and a moment later the bright hangar lights came on, pushing back the darkness into the further corners, and leaving the crowd blinking.

I stepped forward and launched into the standard spiel—our line of progression from StarBooster to StarCore to StarBird, the incremental approach, how we'd developed the first total system architecture for spaceflight, and so forth. When I finished, ten minutes later, I cued a tech standing by to lower the big projection screen and bring the first slide up. Robertson came forward, and, as drawings, charts, and photos went clicking by at the three-per-minute pace that works best for keeping people interested, he gave a surprisingly un-technical account of why StarBird would be a much better ship than the shuttle, while relying almost entirely on proven technology.

A hand rose in the crowd, and Robertson said "Yes?"

My stomach turned over when I saw that it was Bingo Rasmussen stepping out of the group. He must have been a last-minute addition—I couldn't have missed his name on the roster.

In that sarcastic Midwest drawl, that, thanks to C-SPAN, made everyone in the space industry automatically wince, Rasmussen demanded, "So this thing outperforms the shuttle but uses no new technology?"

"*Minimal* new technology," Robertson said. "Sometimes the cheapest thing you can do is find a better material or concept than anything you have. For example, instead of using the heat-shielding tiles that you may recall were a problem back when the shuttle started flying, we are able to go to a new single-sheet composite, which is much stronger, much more effective, and doesn't require anything like the same amount of time or the number of skilled workers to maintain. It would have been silly to stay with the old way with such an effective new way right at hand. But for the most part, we stuck with things we understand well."

"Well, then, my question to you, sir, is why you didn't just build the shuttle right in the first place." He didn't say it like a question—it was a quotable remark that would float around Capitol Hill for the next few months, helping to poison the well for every space project. I drew in a breath, not sure what I would say but knowing that I had to say something.

Robertson got there first. "Because the reason we understand the materials, and high-Mach aerodynamics, and all the other mechanics of reusable spacecraft, as well as we do, is that we've had about twenty years of experience operating STS—which was designed in the Nixon Administration. Back then most every element of the design was a best guess. Now we have decades of real-world experience with flying the shuttle, and we know what worked, what didn't, and what could work better. So we're designing from a vastly better base of knowledge. And of course in the last thirty years we've also had a tremendous increase in the ability to do computer-aided design, supercomputer simulations, and all sorts of other tricks that depend on having lots and lots of cheap, fast computing time. And materials science has advanced very far and fast, too, so that there are better materials to make it out of. So we take much more knowledge, process it with much better tools, and build the ship out of better stuff—and you *bet* we can beat the daylights out of what a slide-rule-and-drafting-board engineer could do back when you were in grade school."

I relaxed at once. Robertson had made Rasmussen look ignorant, rather than like he was the voice of common sense. I made a strong mental note to get Robertson in front of key audiences more often. A fine engineer who can think on his feet and speak well is a resource that should be exploited.

Rasmussen, recognizing that the tide had turned, nodded and stepped back into the crowd.

I gave a quick overview, pointing out that if Republic Wright were allowed to build and operate these in a for-profit environment, depending on the government as an anchor tenant rather than as the source of funding and control, a fleet of six StarBoosters, going up two at a time with StarCore I's, could launch replacements for every important orbital asset faster than they could be built, and that the whole human infrastrure in space could be back up in less than three years. Moreover, if we went to ten StarBoosters, and added two StarBirds, we would roughly double the number of people we could send to and from ISS in any given time. "That's because of the short turnaround," I explained. "Much of the time StarBird would probably fly with fewer people than the shuttle, but unlike the shuttle it doesn't have to spend weeks or months being reconditioned on the ground—we just land it, pull the engine, shove another one in, check it out, and go again."

"Does that at least mean we could ground the shuttle fleet and stop paying for that?" Rasmussen asked.

"I doubt it. The shuttle can take up a big crew and twenty tons of cargo. StarBird carries no more cargo than hand luggage; if you want to put cargo up there with the crew, you have to rendezvous with something sent up on an unmanned StarCore. Anytime you need both a big cargo and a big crew, in the same place at the same time, there's just nothing else like the shuttle, and we've grown to depend on that ability. But for things like routine crew rotations from ISS, StarBird is highly competitive, and there can be more StarBird flights in a year, so it would tend to make station operations more convenient and practical," I said. "And StarBooster/StarCore can handle any cargo that doesn't have to have people with it. That's more than enough for any one system to accomplish."

"Why don't you just take this StarBird up there and get the ISS crew down?" a young woman asked. The older man beside her—probably her boss—looked painfully embarrassed.

"Well, because several major systems aren't in it yet," I said. "Right at the moment, it's pretty much a hollow shell. The Star-Rescue—the crew compartment, which can fly back by itself in the event of trouble—is nearly done but needs a lot of testing. The body, as you can see, is done. We just put the heat shielding on, and the engine went in two days ago. There's too many things we can't do with it yet—such as steer."

"I can see where that might be important," she said, smiling. Her boss, whoever he was, looked relieved.

Robertson handed me a hard hat and put one on himself. He picked up a small cableless video camera, switched it on, and pointed it at me.

On a big overhead screen, my image was projected twenty feet high; it's an unsettling way to see yourself, and even after a few rehearsals, I hadn't really gotten used to it. "Testing," I said, to make sure the mike in the hard hat was picking up. It came through fine, followed by a slight ping of feedback. Robertson and I walked back toward the StarBird, and after we were behind the screen's speakers, I said, as naturally as I could manage, "The interior of StarBird I is still under construction, and it's a hard-hat area, so it wouldn't be practical to take you back here physically, even if there were room for all of you. So if you'll watch the big screen, we'll give you a quick virtual tour."

Robertson and I would trade off on camera and narration duties as we went through; the script called for taking a quick tour around the airframe, starting from the newly installed engine and oxygen tank, and then spending most of our time in the crew compartment, where there would be more things that might be relevant to the audience. "Millions of pounds of thrust" sounds impressive, but "here's where the crew will heat their meals" means more to the layman.

We stood behind StarBird, looking into the immense nozzle of the SSME. StarBird as a whole was the size of a middling airliner, a fact that was not immediately apparent until we got close enough to it for people to get a sense of scale. I turned to face the camera that Ned was holding and said, "We're going to look at the SSME propulsion module—SSME stands for 'space shuttle main engine,' which is the proven technology at the heart of StarBird, and, after all these years, still one of the most impressive rocket engines you'll ever see. Then we'll take a walk around the outside before going into Star-Rescue.

"But first of all, let's take a look at what's probably the most innovative single feature on the StarBird, the single-piece composite keel that serves as the heat shield."

With Ned backing away in front of me, keeping the camera on me, I walked forward until Ned passed under the tail. From there he walked carefully and slowly backwards, keeping the camera level. I followed him in, feeling the same awe as always, as the tail of the big craft blocked my view of the hangar roof far above; it seemed amazing that anything so big could leap right off the earth. "Now, here's what we've done," I said, as Ned turned on the camera light and pointed it up at the shiny blue surface over our heads.

Something cracked like a deer rifle fired inside a garbage can. Metal groaned and shrieked somewhere nearby. I had an instant to look up and try to make sense of what I was seeing—the undersurface of StarBird tilting down in front of me. Then it hit me, and I found myself smashed against the pavement, struggling to get out from under the huge weight, unable even to free my arm to push with. In a few seconds, which seemed like hours, it got dark and quiet.

CHAPTER ELEVEN

THALIA:

We three were just back from an early movie when the phone rang. It was Angie, Nick's secretary, with the news that Nick had been hurt. Naturally I was worried about him—I could hear the tears and tension in Angie's voice—but she quickly explained that Nick was okay. He'd been knocked out and bruised all over, but there was no concussion, no internal bleeding, probably not even a broken bone.

Once I knew that, and relayed it to Scott and Amos, I stopped worrying about Nick and started worrying about Scott. He was pacing around my living room like a watchdog that heard something weird two hours ago and doesn't want to miss it if it happens again.

An hour after the first call, when the Scorpion Shack hospital called officially, they said Nick was resting comfortably, had regained consciousness quickly, and was already complaining about their plans to confine him to bed for a few days of observation. They let Scott talk to him on the phone for just a minute, and that helped.

Scott had landed a space shuttle three times and had flown 747's off remote Third World runways, but he seemed barely able to hold together at the prospect of his big brother being injured. He had leaped to the conclusion that it had something to do with the threatening phone calls and the arson of my car, and it was all his fault.

When they realized that Scott had a security clearance adequate for the Scorpion Shack hospital, they immediately invited him to come down to Texas and keep Nick company. That made Scott feel much better, and reading between the lines when I talked to them, I thought that probably what they really wanted was something to distract Nick, who was already feeling much too well to tolerate a hospital bed placidly. Mrs. Blackstone had always said she was glad she'd had two boys, because, like kittens, only they could be active enough to amuse each other.

The doctor seemed to be pretty sure that Nick had just been pinned in a way that didn't let him breathe for about a minute, until someone got a jack under whatever landed on his chest.

After we hung up, I pointed out to Scott that Nick would be cranky and trying to escape from the hospital by the time Scott got there. He laughed and agreed.

An hour later we were pulling into the private RW area at Reagan; Scott would be riding in one of the corporate jets that Nick was forever catching. "Nick cranky might be harder to deal with than Nick hurt," Scott said, "and if I'm not any help to him, at least I can be a help to his nurses and doctors. Tell Amos I'll be back soon and not to worry about Nick," he said. "I'll call when I know the day and time I'm coming back."

He kissed me goodbye, grabbed his bag, and was gone. Dropping him off at airports had been such a routine experience for me that it seemed comfortingly familiar, as if it had filled in a missing spot in my life, and I was driving out of the airport before I realized that we didn't do that anymore.

I turned and headed for the train station; my own bags were in the trunk, and I would be catching a train right away and heading up to New York City for the hearings tomorrow. Amos was at Mrs.

Talbert's, staying in her guest room, as he did whenever Scott and I had to be out of town at the same time.

A light turned yellow in front of me and I reminded myself to not try to beat it; the bodyguard car, behind me, needed to be able to stay with me safely. Anyway, it was drizzling yet again, and I was probably better off not trying to run lights. The wipers slapped out a dull rhythm, and my mind drifted off to my slightly irregular family again. I could think of nothing I hadn't thought a hundred times before.

THE TUESDAY ARGUMENTS went all right in New York, though they had to be extended into Wednesday; after hours of back-and-forth, the BB&C attorneys and I managed to get the judge to agree that the cause of the *Columbia* disaster could not be excluded from a case about who was responsible. I began to hope, again, that we might have Scott entirely out of the woods by the Christmas recess

In the court of public opinion, we were holding our own, as well. The news coverage on Wednesday night was extremely sympathetic, and the only clip they showed of AnnaBeth James was one where she had lost her cool on a talk show and shouted at a caller. The next day, the *Times* carried an editorial saying that the case should be dropped, basing it on the act-of-war principle. Radio call-in was running seven to four in our favor, and we had clearly pulled ahead in the polls.

As I was packing in the hotel room that evening for an early-morning train back to DC, I was tired, mildly annoyed by the institutionalized stupidity of civil law, but still feeling pretty good, since we'd gotten in there and won. Scott had called and said that Nick was being discharged and allowed to return to his full-time duties, so that problem was under control. It was nice, too, to be going home tomorrow morning—I'd thought about catching a train that night but I'd have gotten home so late that Amos might as well just spend the night at Mrs. Talbert's anyway.

The phone rang again, and it was Nick. I'd spoken to him briefly three or four times since the accident, but there hadn't been much to talk about. We went over the usual pleasantries—Nick could be reached at his apartment at Scorpion Shack now, instead of at the hospital, and was feeling fine, "or no worse than mildly beat up." I filled him in about our victories of the day, and said, "I'm beginning to think that Jasper Haverford is impossible to get off a case by any means except beating him in court. He gave no sign this afternoon that he was even thinking of dropping the suit, even though he must know it's doomed. Of course, the James family may still be pushing him hard to keep it going, but he should be advising them not to, and looking for some kind of face-saving deal."

"Maybe he still has a card up his sleeve?"

"I don't see how there can be. The bomb in the camera makes it an act of war, and you can't sue any of the current defendants about that. If they find out who planted the bomb, they can sue them, but that's all they can do."

"Well, you've always thought he had a hidden backer somewhere, besides the Jameses, that wants the case to go on. I suppose if you find the hidden backer, you'll find the motivation." He paused and then said, "I was supposed to call you up and tell you to expect a call from Clifford Welch."

"Who's he?"

"He's legit, he's heavily connected with national security, and he'd better be the one to tell you whatever it is that you ought to know. There's a national security aspect of the case that you should know about, and he's going to be arriving at LaGuardia within an hour; he has a tendency to just phone people or turn up, so I wanted to make sure you didn't go to bed early."

"Good idea. I was thinking about it. Can you tell me anything?"

"Just that you can believe what he tells you. And he'll probably suggest that you want to stay in New York one more day—he'll be talking to the judge in Scott's case, so he'll want all the lawyers there.

You might want to arrange to keep the room. For what it's worth, it's good news for us, I can tell you that much."

"Okay, I'm sure I can get the room. Damn, though, Amos is going to be disappointed."

"Let me give you to Scott to talk about that."

A moment later, my ex came on the line and said, "Hi, Thalia, just wanted to let you know, I'll be getting back home tomorrow afternoon, early, so I can pick up Amos and take him over to my place. Is there anything that he needs from your place?"

"Clean clothes if he doesn't have any at yours."

"Got him covered there. And I've already talked to him and Mrs. Talbert about picking him up, so it's all set."

"Great," I said, meaning it. One less thing to worry about and Amos would be glad to see him.

"Uh, listen, I'm sorry about the kiss. Flashback or something. You know, we used to say goodbye at the airport pretty often."

"Yeah, I figured. It's okay," I babbled. "It wasn't a traumatic experience or anything. I mean, not that I would expect it to be. But if you were worried."

"Uh, I was. I didn't mean anything. Uh, not that I kiss everybody, or anything, but it was . . . you know, old habit." He sounded like he was desperately trying to get away from the phone, which wasn't far from what I was feeling.

"Exactly."

"Right. Well, I'm glad you understand that."

"Oh, yeah. I'm glad you brought it up."

We talked about Amos and his homework for another long, awkward minute, and then finally we hung up. I've never been so happy in my life to get out of a phone conversation.

I always travel with two days' spare business clothes—you never know when you may get stuck with an out-of-town court proceeding going extra time—so that wouldn't be a problem, and if I stayed the extra day I could send a couple things out to be dry-cleaned and have them come back tomorrow afternoon. I phoned the front desk, got the room for another day, had a bellhop come up to take two suits and some other stuff down for cleaning, and re-unpacked into the hotel closet and drawers. I turned on the television and caught part of a silly sci-fi movie, something about a businessman trying to get control of an alien library that had been left on Mars, and had just flipped over to watch the Weather Channel instead when the phone rang.

"Ms. Thalia Blackstone? My name is Clifford Welch. Did Nick tell you I would call?"

"He did."

"I'm at my club, which is a few blocks from your hotel. I'll send a cab around for you, if that's all right, and you can come over here and we can have a talk. If you haven't had dinner, you can be my guest for that, as well."

I was about to say that I wasn't hungry when I realized my stomach was rumbling. "Sure, I'd be happy to."

"The cab should be at your hotel door in about fifteen minutes, if that's convenient. Dress for the club is absolutely whatever you care to wear—this place is intended as a retreat, not as a place to show off. The food is excellent, confidentiality is guaranteed, and I believe you'll find what I have to tell you interesting. So come as you are, enjoy dinner, and perhaps I can clear up a whole array of mysteries for you."

"It's a deal. I'll be down at the entrance in fifteen. Thank you."

"Thank you, Ms. Blackstone."

I checked myself in the mirror; I was in decent pants and blouse, so I threw on a dark jacket that matched and a pair of loafers, fussed for a moment with my hair, and decided that I was at least a notch above "absolutely whatever." I called the bodyguard in the next room, told him what was up, and had him come down and watch me until the cab came. He wasn't entirely pleased; when you get paid to keep someone safe, you don't like to let them out of your sight, and I had to promise that I'd call before I got in the cab to come back, so that he could be waiting in the lobby for me.

The cab pulled up at the front door, seemingly correct to the second, and the driver got out and called, "Ms. Blackstone?"

"That's me," I said.

I sprinted through the cold misty rain and got in the cab; he closed the door after me and then dashed around to get inside the cab himself; it wasn't raining hard, but New York's version of November rain is cold and miserable. I was glad the heater was roaring in the cab.

"Skitta-lee Club, right?" he asked.

"As far as I know. Mr. Welch didn't tell me the name of the place."

"Yeah, if it's for Mr. Welch, that's right."

Three blocks later, as we cruised down Fifth, he made a hard right into what seemed barely an alley, somewhere just south of Thirtieth Street. He drove a block into a cul-de-sac that faced the locked iron gate of a little park, then right into a long semicircular drive, around a couple of small office buildings, and finally up under an orange awning that read, in white letters, SKYTALE CLUB. Below the name there was an odd pictograph—an open eye with a dagger behind it, enclosed by a square-root sign. "This is the place," he said. "I dunno why, but Mr. Welch always asks to have me drive his guests."

"Maybe he thinks you always do a good job."

"He tips good," the driver agreed, pulling to a stop. He got out, trotted around, and had the door open before the doorman could quite get there. As I got out, the doorman was handing the driver an envelope, and the driver got back into the cab, gave me a friendly wave, and took off within a few seconds.

"You're Mr. Welch's guest, Ms. Blackstone, I presume?" the doorman said. He was a muscular type who looked like a bodybuilder and carried himself in a way that said "career military" to me.

"Yes."

"This way." He guided me in, and turned me over to "Miss Marx," a small black woman, quite young, who walked and moved like an athlete and had the kind of poise you see in good boxers and fencers; I followed her down a long hallway, through a large common room filled with armchairs, through another long hallway, and up a flight of stairs. On the way I noted that unlike many of the more secretive New York clubs, this one seemed to be racially integrated and open to women—the people in the armchairs were of all colors and both genders, dressed in everything from evening clothes to jeans.

Something about the way the employees all moved told me that they were either from some combat branch of the military, or maybe ex-cops.

It clicked for me then. The driver had pronounced it "skitta-lee." This wasn't an aviator's club, as I might have guessed, where people told tales of the sky; this was a club named after the skytale, an ancient Greek device used for sending secret messages—probably the first "code machine" ever invented—and most of the people here must have some connection to intelligence.

Well, at least my bodyguard had been worrying in vain. I probably couldn't be in a safer, or more private, place.

Welch was waiting in a small, comfortable room with a table set for two in the center, a map table along one wall, and bookcases full of old encyclopedias. The wood paneling was so dark that it was almost black, and the flocked deep red wallpaper above it was scarcely brighter. There was a small fire in the gas fireplace. It was cozy, snug, dark, and absolutely a place for discussing secrets.

A voice behind me said, "Ms. Blackstone. I recognize you from television. It doesn't do you justice."

I smiled at him and said, "Television interferes with justice; sometimes I think that's what it's for."

"A good point." He was handsome enough, and yet a curiously

nondescript man; if you met him at a big party you'd never be able to recall his appearance the next day. His hair was iron-gray, his horn-rimmed glasses made him look like Clark Kent's undistinguished brother, and he was of average height and medium build. The most notable thing about him was his voice; he spoke with great precision. "I've ordered a light red wine, a platter of mixed hot meats, the pumpkin soup—make sure you try that, it's excellent—breads, cheeses, and the vegetable platter. We can enjoy some conversation and get to know each other first; you will want to form an impression of me before you decide how much you want to believe the things I have to tell you, I'm sure."

Everything about Welch was quiet and dignified, and spoke of intense intelligence. He insisted on no business until we had finished dinner, and so we made small talk and discussed a wide range of public issues. He was unfailingly gracious and polite, and seemed to me to be very shrewd in his judgments. His interest extended to a wide range of things, and he surprised me by revealing quite a bit of knowledge about prison reform. When I complimented him on that, he smiled warmly and said, "I did some research on you during my flight here. Your positions are extremely well thought out; if prisons and victims were part of my territory, I'd be very likely to rely on you for advice."

Dinner wound down into coffee, and finally he said, "Well, time for business, then. I think you've done a remarkable job with this case, Ms. Blackstone. In all seriousness, you are good at this game, and I wish we had more talents like yours working in space policy."

"Thank you."

"I will begin with just one thought for you. If the camera bomb was the action of a foreign power—and you may trust me that it was—cui bono?"

That phrase is lawyer's Latin for "good to whom?," and it's the basic question in establishing motive—*who is better off because of this?* "I really don't know," I admitted. "I guess we all thought it must be some international terror organization, probably backed by a rogue state, like the North Koreans or Iran."

He nodded. "I think it was *intended* that nearly everyone would think that. Or that it was the work of some disgruntled NASA employee, or something similar. But terrorism *very* rarely aims at these kinds of targets. You don't need to kill Michael James in space to get publicity, when it's fifty times easier to kill a whole airliner full of passengers. Especially you don't do it and then keep quiet; the first thing a terrorist outfit does after an action is phone the networks to claim the credit, if that's the word for it. Besides, the terrorists' audience has usually been people in the Third World, who have no reason to like America. That's why they target anonymous, insignificant civilians; they're easier targets, and since no one in the Third World has heard of them, it allows the Third World types to say 'Aha, they got those Americans thoroughly this time. Good for them.'

"But Michael James was a hero all over the world, not to mention a particular hero in most of black Africa because of the good-will tours he did there and some of his charity work. So M J was absolutely the public figure they'd never kill; it would win no new friends and make many new enemies. So the whole incident just doesn't make sense as a terrorist act.

"And the chances of it being a disgruntled RW employee—I'd say none. If anything it's less probable than an international terrorist. Any engineer/machinist good enough to make that weapon was too good to be disgruntled—he'd be making a quarter million a year someplace, and have a house and mortgage, steady job and family, and all the things that make a man love peace. The people who decide to suddenly slaughter a crowd of other people are always losers— crazy people like the Unabomber, morons like Tim McVeigh, crazy morons usually. They build simple gadgets and the simple gadgets don't work very well. But that bomb-in-the-camera was a brilliant design for an armor-piercing mine, hidden inside a real camera body, which is not an easy thing to do.

"Now, that would take a lot of good engineering to make it work, including firing off some test shots somewhere. I won't say a hobbyist *couldn't* build one in his basement, but I will say it would have to be an awfully skilled hobbyist and a really well-equipped basement—how many home workshops can machine tungsten to fine tolerances? And even if he had the equipment, unless he had a proving area to test it out, he'd still need the very best of luck for it to work at all, the first few times. Yet it worked perfectly—seemingly the first time.

"So nothing is consistent with the common hypotheses. The unknown enemy's choice of target leads me to conclude that it wasn't the usual suspects out of the rogues' gallery of international terrorism. And the unknown enemy's method leads me to conclude that it probably wasn't a disgruntled RW or NASA employee. So, then, somebody must have gained something out of it; the question is, who gained what?"

I thought about it for a moment. "Well, the shuttle fleet is reduced by one quarter."

"Right," he said, pouring another cup of coffee. "And this happens just before there's a supposed accident that wipes out everything in space, so that we have to spend a year rebuilding one shuttle—and if things had gone even slightly differently, we would have lost it completely—reducing our launch capacity just weeks before the world suddenly needs more launchers than it has ever needed at any time before.

"Who benefits? Any country that has good ready-to-go space launch. *Especially* if it's new, improved stuff, because you can charge way above nominal cost on the first few launches, get your development money back right away, and make the customer bear the whole burden of developing your new systems. We have good space launch, but I can't imagine an American company blowing up the shuttle to expand their market. Arianespace has some good engineers, but they have to work tight and small. The Japanese NSDA is even tighter and smaller. And though the Russians have some of the best hardware around, they got it by being master incrementalists, making stuff a few steps better each generation. It's worked, so far, but you can still see Korolev's dead hand in everything they fly, and you can see that they don't *have* another Korolev to take them into the new century.

"Everybody is flying stuff that's decades behind what's possible, at costs that are far more than they need to be, to accomplish much less than they could, but the existing space powers have had such a long head start that they were able to just sit on that huge potential market, collecting plenty of money without doing much innovation."

"Why didn't we?" I asked. "I mean, do some innovation? Space is a big, big business. Wouldn't a better launcher have paid for itself pretty fast?"

"In a world where there was plenty of competition, that might have happened, but Curtiss and Republic Wright are essentially the whole American aerospace industry, and their only real competitors are state monopolies. They don't face much incentive. The 1950s, 60s, and 70s vintage expendable rockets are still getting stuff up to where it's supposed to go. People will pay the price for using them, plus a hefty premium that becomes your profit. If you can mark up about thirty percent over the cost of operations, why drop your cost by three-quarters, even if you can? There might not *be* that many more markets for satellites. You might trigger a price war where the other side will bring in something even cheaper. You're sitting on top of a very comfortable division of the global market—why risk it all by reaching further?

"So back to the question that started this. There's a spacefaring nation I haven't mentioned that the old comfortable launch market really *didn't* suit. A minor player that got into the game late, but has plenty of a pretty good launcher, and, if our intelligence studies can be believed, maybe even a superior one ready to go."

"You have to mean China."

"I do. Consider what's emerging about their role in the Pakistani proton burst—it looks like a team of Chinese advisors cooked the numbers and ran the launch, and the Pakistanis had no idea at all of what was about to happen. Even without the *Columbia* crash, the proton burst would have put anyone with a really good, cheap, reliable space launch system in a terrific position. If you have a good horse, but every other horse got a head start, the best thing that can happen would be for something to restart the race from the starting line.

"Add the Pakistani proton burst to the *Columbia* crash, and a variety of other things in the last six months, and the Chinese space program is in great shape. Not only that. The thing that really makes us most suspicious is they seem to have known they were about to be in great shape. I've got reports that show that they started rolling out Long March launchers a few months ago as fast as they could, but they haven't announced what they're planning to do with them. Now if we consider a few tests down at Hainan that look like a Long March II is mostly ready to go, and their sudden interest in getting a rocket section going at the Curtiss China plant in Sanxian, and I think they're making a move that they planned a while ago.

"There might even be a revenge element. The Long March launches used to be a very lucrative source of foreign exchange—and Communist countries are always short of that, because they have to buy so much of their higher tech and they produce so little that's exportable. They were launching for all kinds of Western companies and organizations, before some people in my office finally managed to convince the Clinton people that this wasn't a good thing. When we stopped buying Long March launches, the Chinese were *extremely* unhappy."

He stared into space; I had a sense that he was remembering whole volumes of clues, hints, puzzle pieces, and little, half-known things. "Now, finally, here is what I wanted to ask for your thoughts and observations on. The M J lawsuit is a whole different kind of a kick in the kneecaps to the American space effort. It could result in any amount of loss of political support, of stupid regulations drawn up in haste, maybe even things like grounding the shuttles for political reasons. It's bound to tie up vast amounts of time and energy that could go to something better, with engineers and scientists that we critically need to do creative work being squandered as expert witnesses and so forth. So if the Chinese are really operating against our commercial space programs, that's a pie where I'd expect to see their fingerprints, which are usually big clumsy ones.

"And yet, from the look of the actual operation—if there even *is* an operation—it feels all wrong for them to be doing this. They're good at espionage, and they can pull off a pretty good special-ops kind of raid. Just ask any soldier in Taiwan or Vietnam about those. But they've got no subtlety in their special ops—everything is the sledgehammer approach. They've always been lousy at any kind of systematic covert operations—heavy-handed, impatient, and usually with a poor sense of what's going to lead to what. I still don't see how they can be doing as much as they appear to be, to impede investigations and hamstring the space industry in court; that looks more like something a sharp, unscrupulous American firm that was really playing hardball could do, not like something within the capacity of a nation with a couple of hundred mostly identified agents of influence."

I said, "Well, what if someone with Chinese contacts were muscling into Curtiss? Maybe somebody way up in management, or maybe whoever chairs the search committee?" I told him everything I could remember of what Killeret had told me, and as I told him, he leaned forward and nodded vigorously.

"Now, hmmm. *That* is interesting. You wouldn't even need to put in overt Chinese agents, just timid managers, go-slow types, stuffed shirts, and keep feeding their fears. The aerospace companies already have a case of hardening of the arteries, all the Chinese would have to do would be to clog things up more. It's still more subtle than I'd expect from their regular operations . . . but then I have reason to think that this isn't the people I'm used to working against, either."

He grasped his chin with his thumb and middle finger, slowly stroking his cheek with his index finger, eyes far away. It reminded me very much of the way that Professor Dunbar had looked just before springing nightmare questions in Constitutional Law. Finally he said, "Well, we've always known that having so much of our high-tech development in private hands is a vulnerability as much as a strength. It means that no bureaucrat can just squash or bottle up a good idea permanently, but it also means control of the enterprise can change hands without anyone asking about its implications for policy.

"Curtiss has plenty of contacts in China, starting with that huge plant they built at Sanxian. To sell all those airliners to the Chinese, they had to agree to transfer all kinds of technology and build all kinds of factories over there. That isn't supposed to include high-tech or military-application stuff—but the Clinton people were pretty desperate for trade agreements, and we're still finding out what they traded away. So, for example, if Curtiss had a joint advanced launcher project going with China, or even maybe if the Long March II is partly a Curtiss development—with all the advantages of being able to use Chinese facilities outside the US, without our health and safety regulations . . . and had some major part of their planned future over there . . . well. That would explain three things at least—one, how the Chinese were able to move so fast, and two, why there seems to be such a desperate need to cover up, and three, most of all, why Curtiss is acting like they're trying to freeze the head of their advanced projects facility out of the loop."

He poured coffee for both of us, but didn't touch his; instead, he got up and walked slowly around the room, as if the answer were in one of the nineteenth-century German and French encyclopedias that lined the walls. At last he stopped by the fire; the flickering orange glow underlit his face and made his grim expression darker, grimmer, almost a gargoyle. There was nothing nondescript about him now.

Finally he said, "If this is really the last piece of the puzzle—the new people coming into Curtiss from places unknown—and it turns out to fit, well, my god, my god, my god. We might be talking about the biggest security breach since Jonathan Pollard or Aldrich Ames—maybe the biggest since Klaus Fuchs. I'm certainly glad I talked to you."

"That wasn't what you asked me here for, though, was it?"

"No," Welch said, smiling. "It wasn't. But I've found that I get some of the best mix of information about everything under the sun just by sharing all the information I'm allowed to. We had reason to think Curtiss was the deep pockets behind the MJ suit, but couldn't see any reason why a company would be covertly paying to sue itself. The answer to that is probably that the people doing it are working very directly at the behest of the Chinese. That makes all kinds of sense. And your observations helped me focus on that idea.

"Of course maybe I'm just frightening myself; for thirty years I've been in a business where paranoia is a gift. I don't know that any of what I've just outlined is going on. It's merely a line of speculation that happens to fit all the facts. But I think that I shall just breathe it in the ear of the Attorney General, and the NASA Administrator, and the CIA, NSA, and FBI, and see if I can stir up some trouble for the Chinese, with maybe a heavy reference to what might be happening to Curtiss Aerospace.

"Even if they *haven't* messed around there and the actual explanation for Curtiss's behavior is just stupidity, the Chinese have certainly done plenty of other things that I don't much like, lately, and they need a strong reminder that playing rough has a cost. Besides, at least in aerospace and other high-tech stuff, trouble for them tends to be good for us."

He sat back down. "All right, now we must get down to what I called you about. I hope you'll pardon the long digression. After forming an impression of you, I decided we could talk about more high-level matters as well, and I do trust that, if I should ever need your discreet help on some matter of national security—I am free to ask?"

I nodded.

"Good. At times I feel like the Godfather, but the accumulated mass of people willing to help *is* my most potent weapon.

"Now, here's the script for your case. Tomorrow morning, at about ten A.M., you'll get a call from the judge, and you and everyone else will gather at one P.M. At that time I'll present selected documents that will make it clear that the entire case of the *Columbia* crash is impacted by various material that, for national security reasons, must remain secret. After letting Mr. Haverford pose and shout, to keep his clients happy—this is already arranged—the judge will dismiss the case. You may then expect a storm of public criticism and uproar, but the excellent PR you've done in the last few weeks should eventually stand you in good stead, after the initial outcry. In a few months, you should have space tourism back in the public's good graces."

"Why are you intervening in this case at all?" I asked. "We were pretty sure of winning it, and any attorney other than Haverford would have thrown in the towel weeks ago. Why not just let us win in the next few weeks? There'll be less outcry if it doesn't look like a coverup."

He smiled. "Normally you'd be right, but we happen to know that there is much more evidence than has been revealed publicly to tie the bomb in the CO camera to China, and some of that evidence is out where anyone can find it, so that in the course of winning your case, you might create an international situation that ties the President's hands. We can cope with this problem rather better behind the scenes, and quietly, than the Justice Department could do overtly through the courts, and if things come out in court, Justice will have to be involved. And since trials by definition, in this country, are public—thank God—this case must never come to trial."

"Anyone that wants to make most of my problems go away in an evening is welcome to do it," I said, "and you're right, we'll be able to handle the outcry."

He got up, and I stood; clearly the interview was over. He looked at me with critical scrutiny, as if wondering if he should say anything, and then seemed to make up his mind to say it. "If what we've hit on as the possible situation should actually be the case, it needs to be looked into, and the people responsible need to be caught and stopped, but the first effect of this will be to turn up the heat on them, pressure them, corner them. And if I'm guessing right—well, people who are in over their heads are apt to do stupid things. I could be putting you and your friends into considerable danger."

I hadn't thought of that, but I wasn't going to back down now. "We'll look after ourselves," I said. "You just get to the bottom of all this. Something really has to be done."

Welch called in Miss Marx to see me out. As she guided me through the big common room, I saw an odd decoration hanging over the door that led to the front hallway—odd because everything else in the place was quiet, understated, and well kept up. This was a steel sign, painted bold yellow, scarred by rust and bent by having been broken off a wall or fence; a rusty bolt, its nut still on, dangled from a twisted hole at the lower right corner. In black gothic letters, the sign read

WHAT YOU SEE HERE
WHAT YOU HEAR HERE
WHEN YOU LEAVE HERE
LET IT STAY HERE

"That's the original," Miss Marx explained to me, as if it were a Picasso.

"The original from—"

"From the Manhattan Project. It used to hang over the gates at

Los Alamos. It's sort of the unofficial motto of the Skytale Club. It's part of why our members can feel relaxed here."

"I imagine so," I said, because I couldn't think of much else to say. She led me out, shook my hand, and said, "Pleasure to have you here, Ms. Blackstone." As she turned to go inside, the same cab I had come in was already pulling up.

"Most boring people in the world," the cabdriver said, as he pulled away. "The money's really good but hardly anybody interesting ever goes in or comes out. Since the fares hardly ever talk, I can get caught up on the news on the radio. But other than that, they could put you to sleep. Dullest club in New York."

"The food's good," I said.

"Yeah, I bet. No point in being rich if you don't eat good, eh?" He took the turn to head uptown and said, "So, if you been in there, you ain't heard about the thing that blew up at the Cape?"

My stomach dropped like a ball of lead. "No, I didn't hear about it. Is anyone hurt?"

"They don't think so. It was some rocket that they had, like, in storage or being worked on, and they had some kind of explosion with it, or maybe they thought it was going to explode. The radio in this cab, you don't always hear too clearly."

When he dropped me off, I gave him a decent tip and ran to the elevator inside the building, barreling through a tour group on my way. Somewhere in my trajectory, the bodyguard got in behind me and ran also, pacing me step for step. As the elevator doors closed, he said, "Where are they?" He was reaching into his jacket.

The elevator door closed, and he seemed to relax slightly. It took me an instant to realize. "Oh," I said. "I'm sorry. Nobody was chasing me or anything. I just got a very garbled story of something from Cape Canaveral—"

"The solid rocket booster story," he said. "Yeah, that's pretty awful."

"*What is it?*"

"Oh. Well, they had a small batch of solid propellant blow up, out in Utah, where they make those rockets. And somebody anonymous called in and said he'd doped it to make it blow up, and that he'd been doping some batches of solid fuel off and on for weeks or months. That means they don't know whether the solid rocket boosters they've got now can go or not. They're still testing out in Utah. A guy on TV was saying there's nothing you could put in the solid fuel that wouldn't be detected, and somebody else said yeah, but you have to look for it, and they've got a whole bunch of suits arguing with each other."

Well, it was clearer than what the cabdriver had said, and at least there hadn't been an explosion at KSC. The elevator door opened and I thanked the bodyguard for his alertness.

I went into my room and turned the TV on to CNN. It was pretty much as I'd heard it; chemical analysis was under way to confirm that the batch that had blown up had been doped, but they had found the contaminant in two other batches, and the fuels chemists thought that whatever the contaminant was, putting it into solid rocket booster fuel would make it very explosion-prone. And, as the engineers were explaining, there was no way to know whether it was inside any of the already-loaded solid rocket boosters; if it were deep inside, it couldn't be detected until it blew up and caused a *Challenger*-type accident.

"He may or may not have managed to get the stuff into a batch that was then loaded into a rocket," one of them was explaining. "But a solid rocket isn't like liquid. We can't just drain out the fuel, replace the tank, put in clean fuel, and be good to go. You're looking at what's basically a several-stories-high stack of solid plastic, which is supposed to burn very fast. The trouble is, if it burns *faster*—and while I can't tell you what was added, I can say it's a known catalyst that *would* accelerate the burning—well, then you get an explosion.

"Every rocket engine, to do what it does, has to operate somewhere near the edge of being a bomb. It doesn't take much to tip it over into suddenly becoming a bomb. So, yes, the threat is credible, and since we don't have any way to tear the engine down to check, without destroying it, it means basically that we have no SRB's for the shuttle."

"And without SRB's—"

"It can't make orbit. I don't know how we will get the ISS crew down, or how we'll try to, but I can tell you it won't be using *Atlantis*."

THE NEXT DAY'S charade went pretty much as Welch had said it would; the relevant papers, photos, and documents were shown, and affidavits were brought out, demonstrating that in the opinion of national security officials, both the accident itself and the James family's case were probably "sponsored and promoted by forces inimical to American national security." Everything else followed the script as well. The judge said he was going to throw out the case, Jasper Haverford raised a bunch of objections, AnnaBeth James had a good cry—I don't think that was in the script—and finally the judge threw it out. Everyone else pretended they'd never seen or heard of Clifford Welch before, so I did too.

In the hall, afterward, Haverford quietly said, "Just so you know, I was telling Mrs. James we were going to lose, ever since the NASA report. Sometimes you get a stubborn client, you know."

"I've certainly seen those," I said.

"Also, and you can believe this or not, after what was just presented, I wasn't about to take any more of that money, once I knew where it was coming from. I like to believe I'm a good lawyer, but I guess most people would say I'm a crooked lawyer. Well, one thing I'm *not* is a treasonous lawyer. See you in some other court; you're pretty good at this stuff."

He shook my hand and turned away, going back down the hall to his clients. I felt two things: flattered, and an urge to wash my hand.

CHAPTER TWELVE

SCOTT:

I was glad to hear that the case was dismissed, and it was good to see Thalia flushed with victory. Amos volunteered to go to Mrs. Talbert's for the evening, so that Thalia and I could celebrate. "Pretty transparent move, kid," I said, as I dropped him off.

"It was Uncle Nick's idea," he said, cheerfully, grabbing his bag and running inside.

It's hard not to be irritated with your big brother when he decides to run your life, especially when you've got a life and kids of your own. I turned into the driveway of her house—which had been our house. She came out in a dark dress that I'd always liked, wearing a necklace I'd given her.

As I drove to the restaurant, a favorite place of ours that was worth driving to Baltimore for, Thalia leaned forward and turned on the radio, scanning around to find an all-news station. "Basically, to give the James family enough time to get somewhere where they can have some privacy," she said, "and because of something or other, I don't know what, that Clifford Welch whispered in his ear, the judge was delaying the official announcement till 7:30."

"We still have fifteen minutes," I said. "I always set the clock in the car ten minutes fast."

"If you do that," she said, "doesn't that mean that you already know that, and just subtract ten minutes all the time?"

"Logically it would, but this works for me."

We listened till 7:40 or so, but the solid rocket booster sabotage, and the terrible likelihood that the ISS crew would remain stranded until they died of radiation sickness, seemed to be all the news there was. It was good from our PR standpoint but I could have been happier.

After a while I turned the radio off and said, "Welch is really a strange character. I met him twice out at Scorpion Shack, and I gather he had some business with Nick. He seems to have a really strange web of connections."

"He does," Thalia agreed, and told me about her visit to the Skytale Club. "I think at the end of my evening there," she said, "I half expected to be given a false passport, a wig, and a cyanide pill. Part of what makes that place so scary is that it's all so low key."

We talked for another few minutes, and finally I said, "You know, there's something I've been thinking about—not all the time or anything. I've really enjoyed seeing so much of you these past few weeks. It's the only good thing to come out of this whole terrible mess. So . . . uh, maybe . . . well, what I'm trying to say is that I'm sort of sad to have the case coming to an end, because I'm going to miss seeing so much of you."

She chuckled and said, "Scott, that's so sweet. Also so naive. The case is dismissed but it's not over. We've got weeks or months of work to do, if you're ever going to be able to get a decent job in aerospace again. You and I both know what's going on, but so far the media don't and this dismissal is going to *reek* of coverup, and I have no doubt at all that talk radio, and the Internet, and everything else will light up with accusations. What we have to do is to find out how much of the truth we're allowed to reveal, and let it leak out in some highly credible way, until eventually you look like just what you are—an innocent man that people have ganged up on for their own reasons." She sighed. "And sometimes, buddy, you're a *very* innocent man. Not that I mind. Your faith in justice is really touching, even to an experienced lawyer."

"And you're going to stick with me through that part of things?"

"Well, I don't usually leave a fight halfway through. Or leave the father of my kid in the lurch." She hesitated, and then finally added, "Uh, on the other hand . . . well, I like seeing you, too, and it's nice that we're getting along better, but I've been noticing that my life does go better without a man in it right now. There's nobody else, but I don't think I want to think about anything romantic for quite some time yet. I guess I like my independence."

I felt a sad twinge, but I had to admit that life with me had probably not been as rewarding or interesting as life without me. "Well, friends forever, then," I said. "It's good not to be angry all the time, anyway."

"Yeah," she said. "And it's good for Amos. I'm sorry that I just don't feel like getting into anything deeper."

"Hey, there's nothing deeper than the spirit of the Mars Four," I said.

"It's a little scary that you might be right."

We both laughed at that, and the silence afterwards was comfortable again. The radio still had no news at eight o'clock. Thalia thought maybe the judge had delayed announcing the verdict even longer.

We turned in at the restaurant, and the talk turned much less serious; mostly it was about Amos, and old times, and what it had been like to try to keep my big brother in a hospital bed until the doctors said it was okay for him to get out of it. "His engineers didn't help," I said. "They were in there all the time. There was a test flight that they wanted to delay until he could see it—till he told them to 'just get me a monitor in here, so I can watch the test, and that'll be good enough, dammit! Everybody involved in a test is watching it on monitor anyway!' "

"Couldn't they have used the test flight to deliver a package to ISS?" she asked.

"Uh . . ." I dropped my voice and told her. "They're pretty sick up there. They aren't going to run out of air, food, or water, because, if we don't get them help, they won't be alive long enough to run out. And nobody there is in any shape to spacewalk even in normal conditions. With the station tumbling like it is, they wouldn't be able to retrieve a package, and even if they could, we couldn't send them anything that would help. Even if we'd had a Soyuz to put on it, the rocket they were testing is too fragile in the upper stage to mount it on. And they'd have been in no shape to spacewalk over to it and fly it down. Somehow, somebody's got to send a crew up to them."

"You don't sound like you think anyone will."

"I don't. But I don't know everything. Maybe somebody's got a secret project somewhere and the President is talking to them. Maybe they're building something backstage at Scorpion Shack or Ghost Town. Maybe there really is something that they can do with a robot, that I haven't thought of."

"What about . . . uh, the thing that fell on Nick."

"StarBird I. Nowhere near ready to go, unfortunately. It's got an engine pod, and an airframe, and a lot of electronics. No hydrogen drop tanks yet, and some of the control systems aren't there, and . . . well—it looks great, but right now we don't even know how it would do just rolling to the end of a runway. Not to mention that it was damaged pretty badly." I shrugged; I'd seen the crushed metal. "Whoever did it—yeah, it was sabotage—set off the explosive bolts to separate StarRescue from the rest of StarBird. StarRescue just slumped forward on its nose, and all that they have to do is replace a couple of panels—it's a tough little ship, really well-designed, and if it flies like its simulator, about as much fun as anything coming down from orbit can be. But Starbird I is pretty much a loss. When that dropped onto Nick, the SSME broke loose and smashed up everything around it, and the bottom heat shield got a meter-long crack. Even if it had been ready—and it wasn't—it would be useless now. Hey, you should have heard what he said to the doctor who wanted to CT scan his head again, just in case—" I did my best to turn the conversation to lighter topics, because despite what she'd said before about the case not being really over, I wasn't completely sure that we'd be seeing as much of each other, and I felt like I needed to make this evening as pleasant for her as I possibly could.

It helped that she cooperated. We smiled and laughed often, completely forgot to check the radio on the way home, and we were an hour late to pick up Amos. It was a good thing that Mrs. Talbert was tolerant.

I had been crashing out on Thalia's couch often in the last few weeks, due to the threats and the burned car, generally with a ball bat that I borrowed from Amos lying under the coffee table beside me, in case of trouble. Amos went cheerfully off to bed, since he knew that I would be staying that night, and Thalia and I stayed up to catch the news. I was still hoping that the dismissal would be a minor story with no reactions, but it was the lead story on CNN Headline.

A few minutes into it, she was shaking her head and saying, "Well, you've certainly made an impression."

The announcement that the case was being dropped had been greeted by exactly the kind of uproar that the media love to report—or to make, depending on what you think it is they actually do. M J had been a world-class nice guy, and a world-class celebrity not a very common combination, in my experience—and the result was that a very large number of famous people were sad and angry that he had died. Thus it took almost nothing for a reporter to get an actor, politician, athlete, singer, activist, or whatever to declare loudly that something must be wrong.

"This stinks of coverup and I don't know if we'll ever get justice for Michael," one rapper said.

"I was starting to think this was just an accident, just one of those terrible things that sometimes happen, but now that this case is just dismissed out of nowhere, it looks like a coverup to me," an "actress/novelist" (that's what it said on the screen under her image) said on *Politically Incorrect.*

The judge had said only that there were elements of national security involved but that the files would be unsealed at the earliest possible date. That gave Jay Leno some great material, as he explained that next year the number of games the Rams lost was going to be top secret, as were "all batting averages in the Eastern Division of the National League. God knows what could happen if that fell into the wrong hands." The news that the James family had accepted the situation, and the reference to national security, gave Howard Stern room for some tasteless jokes about what M J's secret mission had been as well; I was grateful, because he drew some of the fire off of me, ShareSpace, and all the other defendants.

The next morning, when I phoned in to check by remote, there were seventy-four new messages: sixty-one from news media, ten angry threats, and three from financial services salespeople who wondered if I'd like to refinance my house. I put a stock message on my answering machine again, and Nick came up with some more cash so I could have two bodyguards in my house all the time, because every so often the picket line out there got frisky. I stayed at Thalia's house; landing a spacecraft is one thing, but when it comes to angry mobs, I'm no braver than the next guy.

Watching the picket line on the MSNBC broadcast, late that afternoon, it looked to me like a strange mixture. Such leadership as they had was coming from a few political activists who thought a black family was being denied justice. But most of the followers weren't exactly following the "leaders." Much of the crowd consisted of sports fans who thought they were doing something for their hero, plus an equal or maybe greater number of people who just liked the excitement of the crowd.

"You'd be better off with just the activists," Thalia said. "Most of them are pros at what they do. They know enough to stay off your property, they don't usually violate the noise ordinances, and they don't want to look like louts on television. Plus there's only maybe two dozen of them at any one time. You'd be able to go out, give them some hot coffee for the cold weather, have a talk with them if you wanted to. Even though they'd keep picketing, you could feel pretty safe. It's the same old principle as anything else: if you want something done right, go to people with experience. Unfortunately, most of the crowd has never done anything like this before, and they have no idea how to behave. Which is why they're acting like a damned bunch of amateurs and the police are having to work a lot harder." She slid two sandwiches onto my plate. "I hope you're staying the night again. The bodyguards get paid to deal with the hassle, and you don't. And for some reason they're targeting the evil businessman instead of his evil lawyer, so it's been quiet over here."

I looked up at the television screen, which was doing a quick recap of the days' events at my house. There was a brief statement, reasonably coherent though (I thought) unfair, from an older woman holding a sign that read "Justice IS National Security." She thought that "they" were getting away with something, and "we have to stop them." Thalia had a point—she did look like somebody I could at least try to talk to.

Then the camera cut to twenty fraternity guys in a row, each with one letter painted in red on his bare chest. They were standing out in the cold November evening, waving their arms over their heads and shrieking as if they were at a basketball game. The letters spelled out JUSTICE FOR M J WE LOVE M J. They must have seen their image appear on television, because they began to jump up and down and whoop a few seconds after the network cut to them, making it harder to read the message. When the microphone got close to one, he jumped forward and yelled, "We are totally here to support M J!" and they all started whooping again, loud enough so that the reporter never did get to ask the question, whatever it might have been. As the on-the-scene reporter was signing off, the crowd went into a long, rolling chant of "M J! M J! M J!"

"I'm glad he can't see *this*," I said. "He'd be so embarrassed."

"Oh, yeah," Thalia said, and was just reaching to turn off the television when something made her stop. The commentator was adding, "No comment yet from the White House or the State Department about the now rapidly developing rumor that the FBI and American intelligence sources have definitely traced the cause of the *Columbia* accident to deliberate sabotage by the Chinese, or about the comment by General Hofstadter of the Air Force Space Command, speaking at a retired officers' dinner earlier this evening, that the disaster that killed Michael James and wrecked a space shuttle formed 'a key move in a coherent strategy,' linking it to the proton bomb that destroyed all orbiting satellites last month." He looked straight out of the screen, and said in the sort of firm voice that they usually reserve for advertising, "We understand that this is a matter of great concern to all Americans, based on the mail we're receiving at our Web site and the volume of phone calls we're getting, but unfortunately we just don't have any more facts than what we have just told you. The only person in authority who has said anything is General Hofstadter, and he has not been available for comment since making that statement. We will keep you informed as developments happen." He turned to his left and forced a big smile. "And on a happier note, Betty, I understand that the big Christmas toy for this season is going to be pink and fuzzy!"

"That's right, Jack, and we'll have all the—"

Thalia clicked it off. "Hmm. Your public relations luck might be holding. Though I'm not sure if it's really luck, if the story that displaces you on the news turns out to be World War III. I sense the hand of Welch. If that story floats any longer, the mobs will be gone from your house, and over at the Chinese Embassy. And M J will be the biggest hero of the new century."

"Hero?" I asked. "He was a real nice guy and a great athlete, but other than that he was just standing in the way when a bomb went off."

"Trust me," she said. "If the media confirm that the story is true, then in their version of things, it will be the same thing as M J having personally died to save America. There'll be pressure on DoD to give him a posthumous Medal of Honor. There'll probably be pressure on the Pope to make him a saint. Betcha three weeks' groceries at the cabin next summer, if we have time to go."

"As long as we go together," I said.

There was an extremely awkward pause at that, and then we both found that the house needed vast amounts of cleaning up. But she didn't seem angry at me for having said it—she just suggested that in that case, we needed to put twin beds in there. "You still snore," she said, "and I'd rather have it across the room than in my ear."

WHEN AMOS GOT home, the bodyguard company decided to have me do a "back door switch," which is a pretty silly routine that Bobbi, a big strong woman who was captain of the detail, described as "an old trick that usually works as long as there's not too much light."

Dave, a bodyguard who looked something like me, would put on a sweatshirt and hat of mine, plus a big pair of black shades that covered most of his face. Then the company driver would drive us up to my house, we'd dash in with my "double" getting between me and the crowd like the bodyguard he was. Inside, I'd put on the sweatshirt, cap, and shades, and run back out as if I were the bodyguard. Amos thought it was pretty funny watching me and Dave, my double, practice the clothing exchange until we could do it in less than thirty seconds.

It went smoothly enough. As the car turned onto the street, people were running at it and yelling, and some of the more exuberant types were beating on the roof and yelling "M J! M J!" Dave looked pretty tense, and Bobbi, riding in the passenger seat, kept touching her shoulder holster.

We pulled up the driveway, and suddenly we were out of the crowd as two of the guards from the house blocked the crowd from following us. As close as possible to the door, we stopped, and Dave said, "Ready, go."

I dashed out the door, heading for my porch steps. The noise from the crowd was unbelievably loud; they sounded more excited than angry, as if this were some kind of carnival. A bottle smashed against the garage door beside me. Dave was standing tall and keeping himself between me and the mob as I sprinted up the steps and into the house.

The moment we were inside, we did the clothing exchange, and then I raced back out the door, down the steps, and into the car. As I closed the door, the driver backed up, just slowly enough so he could stop quickly and just fast enough so that people would get out of the way. We got down the driveway with no more than some hands and feet thumping the car. As I watched, the guards inside turned on a couple of lights upstairs in my house, and a brick bounced off just below the roof, inches from a window.

"Looks like we convinced them," I said.

Bobby grunted. "The old tricks are sometimes the best ones," she said. "We do this all the time for musicians. We'll be going to the company garage, if you don't mind, to do a switch of cars, too, before someone gets too clever about Thalia Blackstone's house. Anyway, we think we've guaranteed you a reasonably peaceful night."

"Thanks."

"That's what we're paid to do." She hesitated, and then said, "Can I ask you something? Don't answer if it's classified."

"All right."

"Is it really true that this is all some kind of Chinese attack on our space program, and M J was just kind of caught in the crossfire? That you, personally, didn't have anything to do with it, really?"

"Um. I don't know if that's classified or not. And I've been kept pretty far out of the loop. But that's what many people who are in a position to know seem to think."

"I'm glad," she said. "I'm sorry for Mrs. James losing her lawsuit and all, but I'm glad that it wasn't you or any American company that caused it."

There was something about her tone that made me ask, "Do you know AnnaBeth James?"

"I was guarding her last week. She's a nice lady, and she's hurting bad."

We drove on in silence until we pulled in through the doors of the company garage. There, the driver and I moved over to a nondescript little minivan, the kind of thing that suburbs everywhere are crawling with, and he drove me back to my ex's house. He didn't say much on the way, but as we neared the house, he said, "I wanted to wish you good luck and a quiet night, sir."

"Thank you. I can use both."

"MJ really was something, wasn't he? You knew him pretty well, I guess."

"I did know him. He was one of the best men I ever met. It was a terrible loss."

"Well, then, if it was the Chinese, I sure hope someone finds a way to pay those bastards back. Even if the public never gets to hear about it."

"Me too."

By the time he dropped me off at the house, Amos had finished his homework, it was fully dark, and Thalia had ordered a pizza and a couple of movies. "I thought about getting *Moonraker* and ordering Chinese," she said, "but I wasn't sure we could take the irony. So it's a great big veggie pizza, the first *Star Wars* flick to get us to bedtime, and then *When Harry Met Sally* afterwards, till grownup bedtime."

I might have been able to see irony in those choices, myself, but I thought it wiser not to point it out. We were all tired, and stressed out, so mostly we just ate and watched the movies. Amos asked to stay up after *Star Wars*, and we said he could, but half an hour of a romantic movie was about as much as he could take before drifting off to bed. After that, we sat and watched the movie; it wasn't as much fun as the first time we'd seen it, when we'd been dating.

THE GUNSHOT, JUST outside the front window, woke me up. I was off the couch and groping for the bat in an instant. A moment later I saw the flickering light of a fire through the front window. One of the bodyguards rushed past me, hissing, "Stay down."

I did. I could hear the bodyguards waking up Thalia and Amos, telling them to come downstairs, not to turn on any lights, and to keep quiet. There were voices out on the lawn, and after a while the wail of a police siren, and then the honk-wheez of an ambulance. I ventured to whisper, "What's going on?" to the bodyguard watching the three of us, but he only shrugged; he didn't know, and his job was to watch us, not to give us the news.

After a couple of minutes, I heard water running, and realized that they'd hooked up the garden hose for something; the flames flickered out. More noise outside as an ambulance arrived, and then what sounded like cops arguing with several other people, went on for about half an hour by the wall clock. Just about three A.M., almost everyone seemed to leave all at once, in a great cloud of car noises: engines skittering and thumping awake, tires crunching on the drive, headlight beams sweeping across the windows for brief instants.

At last the chief, or captain, or whatever you call the bodyguard in charge, came in and said, "None of ours down, one of theirs. And it turns out it's a national security affair. There's someone here to talk to you all—he'll be inside in a couple of minutes."

We all sat up on the couch, and on an impulse, I went into the kitchen and turned on the coffeemaker, since it was already set up for the morning. The familiar smell and noise seemed to stir me out of this bizarre dream. Something big had happened out on the front lawn that I had mowed, right where I'd taught Amos how to throw a football. I didn't know exactly what, yet, but they'd said there was "one of theirs down," and the presence of fire and ambulance crews sounded like violence.

While I was in the kitchen, I heard the front door open and close a couple of times, and soft conversation.

I came out of the kitchen with a tray of eight cups of coffee, figuring everyone could use some, and discovered that Clifford Welch was sitting in the armchair across from the couch, looking a little weary himself. I set the tray of coffee down on the table and took a cup myself; Thalia grabbed another, and Welch and the lead body-guard also picked up cups. "You might want to take a cup to each of the other guards, and to my man out by the garage," Welch said, dropping an obvious hint.

The lead bodyguard nodded and went out with the tray; I figured he wouldn't be back until somebody told him to.

"It sounds like Amos should maybe go back to his room for a bit," Thalia said.

Welch nodded. "If you're still upset, and would rather be out here with your folks, Amos, maybe you could just put on headphones and listen to some music, or watch something on TV?"

Without saying anything, Amos sat down and hooked himself up to the television with headphones; I was about to tell him not to tune in anything violent, or where they talked dirty, but he was way ahead of me—he found some fifty-year-old cartoon with singing flowers and bees, and seemed to zone right into it. When I saw that he was settled for the moment, I asked, "What's going on?"

Welch grunted. "Well. Things very nearly got out of hand, and it was lucky that they didn't go any worse. I came out here with one man, to keep an eye on your house, and found your security detail was pretty alert, so it took some time to work our way through them and sit down to keep our watch in the shadows in front of the garage. Then a man ran across your yard with something on fire—which turned out to be a Molotov cocktail. I didn't have any other way to stop him quickly, so I shot him. He fell over and landed on the Molotov cocktail, which went off before we could get to him, and it set his clothes and hair on fire."

"He's dead?" Thalia asked.

"Not yet, but if he's conscious, he must wish he were dead. God, what a way to go. He was burned all over, and it looks like my shot smashed one thighbone. If they can save his life, he won't thank them for it." He sighed. "But the paramedics still had a heartbeat when they left, and I've known of cases that looked just as bad and survived."

"Why did you come here tonight?" I asked.

Welch made a tight little smile. "I was here as a backup, in case Andrew Riscaveau came here; we thought he'd be either running for the Chinese Embassy or more likely just trying to leave the country. It was just a gut instinct or something, a feeling I had that he might try something before running out on us. And I *think* it was Riscaveau. I didn't get a good look at him before, so it could conceivably be someone else, but it was about the right height and weight, and I don't know anyone else who would have had any reason to do this kind of thing."

It was finally beginning to sink into me; I said, "But—uh, Andrew Riscaveau is, or he was, the security guy at Republic Wright—"

"Yep. And also a defector—or at least he was planning to defect. For cash, we think. Heavy alimony, gambling habit, daughter at Smith, a bunch of cash withdrawals from most of his investments, over the last three years, that don't coordinate with his gambling binges, but I'd bet will turn out to trace to a drug habit or maybe a relationship with a high-priced prostitute. Andrew Riscaveau was yet another one of those strung-out cases, a guy in over his head who never really had any loyalty to anything except his career." Welch sighed. "No matter how many times the intelligence agencies get caught by these clowns, we always get surprised when another one comes along. And it's always the same guy with hardly any difference except details: it's your basic jerk under pressure, who realizes that he could solve his financial problems by selling a few pieces of information. And he says to himself, heck, the other side probably has all that information, already, anyway, so where's the harm? Besides, nobody appreciates how hard he works. And besides all that, as a political realist, he knows that the two sides are really the same anyway. They all tell that same story to themselves.

"Anyway, we'd tied Riscaveau to the fire that destroyed your car, Thalia—nothing a regular cop would go to a grand jury with, but he was in town, he was unaccounted for at the right times, and it turned out he'd had a petty arson conviction as a teenager. Then he turned up again as probably the guy who dropped StarBird onto Nick; at least, between the lists of suspects, he was the only overlap. So we started checking, and sure enough, when you looked at his debts and expenses, he looked like a guy who, about three years ago, really needed a spare quarter of a million tax free—and found it. Shortly after a vacation in Thailand, which no accountant would have thought he could afford, there were some interesting deposits into his bank accounts, mostly transfers from offshore sources.

"So we went to have a nice chat with Mr. Riscaveau, at the DC office for Republic Wright Security, and . . . he took off. Saw us drive into the parking lot and just went straight out the back, jumped on the Metro, got a car on a fake ID and credit card, and was moving fast. We thought he'd just run to his Chinese bosses, but we couldn't be sure."

"Why did he come here to bomb this house?" Thalia asked.

"There might be several reasons. You can take your pick, and chances are we'll never know for sure. Could be personal—your family had gotten in his way one time too many, and he was mad at you. Or he was hoping, maybe, that you would all run outside, the bodyguards would be confused, and he could take one of you as a hostage.

"But the most likely thing, to me, is that he was being twisted into one last action. The Chinese work their agents hard and always treat them as expendable. I think probably they told him that he'd have to do one more thing before they'd take him out of the country. Even if he'd survived, I doubt he had any information that would have been any use to us—so from their standpoint, it was better, because it was cheaper, to try to get one more bit of action out of him, especially if we killed or captured him and spared them the nuisance of maintaining him. They didn't stand to lose anything except an unreliable employee who no longer had anything to offer."

I shuddered. "How can anyone work for people like that?"

Welch spread his hands and smiled slightly. "They're very nice while you still have anything they want. And if it's disgrace next week, or maybe getting caught two years from now, well, some people will pick the latter. Anyway, we don't know for sure, yet, that it's Riscaveau, but it fits the pattern. And we've already started to move on some interesting characters at Curtiss, as well—though that's a much tougher job. Unfortunately, dragging your feet because you take orders from Beijing happens to look very much like dragging your feet because you're stupid, or because your company is fat, dumb, and happy and doesn't like change.

"But we'll have the whole nasty lot of them, I think; the Chinese couldn't have made this work without confederates in our government, Curtiss, and RW, and they moved so fast and hard, and overplayed their hand so much, that most of their agents in place will have had to scramble around to keep up with it. We just look for who's been scrambling lately, and why.

"All this is just a reminder that you're never secure against anything that the other side wants to do badly enough. Any agency out there can do almost anything, if they don't mind getting caught big time; during the whole Cold War, the KGB could always have shot the President, if they'd been willing to take the outrage, and luckily for us, there was never a situation where it was worth it. Our clever friends in Beijing—or more likely, just at Hainan—thought they might be able to gain so much that it would be worth the price. At this point, they're not going to get much . . . and the bill is coming due." He stood up. "I strongly suggest that you all go back to bed and sleep in. Scott, you'll be needed at a meeting tomorrow at three P. M., and you might want to dress up for it."

I was almost past the point of worrying about how much I got pushed from place to place, but when it looked like Welch was leaving, I asked, "Uh, where is this meeting?"

He smiled. "At the White House. I'll be there, and your brother Nick, and some other people you know. We have a job for you."

CHAPTER THIRTEEN

NICK:

The phone rang at six o'clock in the morning, just as I was getting out of the shower. It was Jagavitz. "Nick, I need to meet with you and Robertson in your office, seven o'clock. I've ordered breakfast. You'll need to be in a decent suit because we're off to talk to some bigwigs this afternoon. The good news is, this is my last day in your office."

It had been typical of Jagavitz that after I was injured, he temporarily took over Scorpion Shack himself, and saw them through that first, flawless StarCore I launch, and the by-the-book re-entry and safe landings of both StarBoosters. He claimed, anyway, that he hadn't had so much fun in years—not since his days with a small start-up company. Whatever the truth was, the day before, when I had at last gotten into my office to see how things were going, he'd had the whole place up to date and ready; there was no backlog of work for me to worry about.

"I'll be there," I said. "When and where's the meeting?"

"2:30, in DC. After we meet and discuss, we'll get right on the plane. So bring your bag. Can you get all that in an hour?"

"I live packed," I said. "See you at seven."

A few minutes later I was rolling down the white-painted asphalt path in the back of one of the company "golf carts," bag and briefcase beside me. The driver wasn't talkative—hardly surprising at the hour—and the sun was just up, barely clearing the horizon, a warm presence that would turn the humid air hot by eleven.

I figured this was going to be about a twenty-thousand-mile month; I have those. Maybe I could squeeze in time for a dinner with Thalia and Scott, before flying back here.

Jagavitz and Robertson were already there; it was too early in the morning for many pleasantries, so we just grabbed the bagels, cereal, and coffee and got our blood sugar up to where we could all be coherent. By 7:15 we were sitting down with a large stack of paper, each.

"After your accident," Jagavitz began, "when I came in here to take over, I found Ned's short report on the dual-StarBooster/ StarCore I/StarRescue system. I discovered I agreed with both of you—that Ned was right, that there would be a better than fifty-fifty chance of success, and that you were right, that it was still far too much of a gamble as long as we had any other way to do it. But after the situation developed with the solid rocket boosters on *Atlantis*, I asked Ned to prepare a somewhat lengthier document."

Ned plunked a big pile of paper in front of me and grinned in a way that made me even more nervous than I was already from seeing him in a non-rumpled suit without any pens in his pocket. "You don't have to read any of this," he said, "at the moment. You can spend the whole plane flight going over it with me. Just turn to the first page."

I did. It was a picture of a StarCore I, with a StarRescue and service module sitting on top of it. A cage that looked like a heavy-duty playpen wrapped the Centaur stage.

"Oh, man," I said. "You have to be kidding."

"No joke," Robertson said, and leaned back, putting his hands over his head. "The StarRescue was undamaged in the sabotage, and it's already built, and has had a number of flight tests of one kind or another. The dual StarBooster/StarCore I has just had a successful test shot all the way to orbit. The airframe checkout on the Star-Boosters, after the test shot, two days ago, showed that there wasn't a thing about them that needed fixing. And that service module is just an aluminum wrapper around a couple of the same big thrusters we've been making for decades. So the only really untested technology is the I-bar cage around the Centaur, and that's already built, Nick. We have enough old-fashioned shop floor engineers around, and enough good machinists, so that they all worked through the night. The whole thing is being assembled out on our Pad Two, right here at Scorpion Shack."

"It's the only hope we've got for getting them off ISS in time," Jagavitz said. "Would you rather we didn't try?"

I stared at it. In my mind's eye, almost against my will, I could see it working, and in addition, a good engineer and my boss agreed that it would. "I think I can accept it, mentally," I said, "but it may take a few hours. Emotionally, maybe a few days. We're going over all the specs, I assume, on the plane."

"Yep." Robertson reached out and flipped two pages.

The page now in front of me was a crude drawing of six astronauts, inside the crew compartment of the StarRescue, all being eaten by a giant amoeba. I stared at it for a long moment until I finally saw that the label below said ENCLOSING WATER RADIATION SHIELDING.

"You're going to put . . ."

"Water beds, basically," Ned said. "Big flat heavy vinyl bags of water. Also mostly built, now. They cover every inside surface. You're taking a ton of water along as radiation shielding. The pilot flies it from a keyboard/simulator with a cable that runs into the regular control panel, since that has to be covered up. The bag over the window is transparent, and we have a little pump for moving water in and out of it so that the pilot can go visual when he needs to. And since that's a lot of extra mass, we've got a neat little gadget that lets you dump it just before you start the aerobrake part of re-entry—a centrifugal pump from an old liquid-fueled rocket project that got canceled. Pressure tests are going on right now on the sections they've finished."

I sighed. "I guess it's better than not trying."

"There is that," Robertson said.

"Also," Jagavitz added, "it pains me to say it, because I'd like this to be totally an RW operation, but our counterparts over at Ghost Town, as the prime contractor on ISS, know the station much better than we do. They were able to work up a gadget that will let you stabilize the station when you get there, since none of the crew aboard are in any shape to cross over via EVA. So the job is for you to get up there with the pilot and the guy from Curtiss, make the jump to ISS, install the stabilizer, stabilize the station, push the Soyuz out of the dock, dock the StarRescue, load in the ISS crew, and come back home. About fifteen dental X-rays' worth of exposure, which will make your blood chemistry funny for a while but shouldn't have too many other consequences. Simple list of tasks, eh?" There was a strange twinkle in his eye.

"You are talking," I said, "very much as if you expected me to go, personally. And now that I think of it, Ned's been talking that way, too."

Jagavitz shrugged. "We've been working out who to send. The list is pretty short, to tell you the truth. Curtiss has just one guy that they think understands their miracle-stabilizer gadget as a whole— the supervising engineer from that one—so he goes. We were able to find just one qualified pilot who is already aware of the political situation. That was important because they don't want to brief another one. This mission will be flown, very much against my better judgment, as a covert mission after the old Soviet style. That is, if it works, they will announce it, and if it doesn't work, they never heard of us. I think it's a stupid way to do things, but that's why I'm a businessman and not a politician.

"Now, just for the sake of safety, we think we should send along someone who does know the total system architecture and could take action in an emergency—an engineer who's really familiar with the whole system, StarBoosters, StarCore, StarRescue, and all. You probably see the problem that we ran up against?"

I did. "Hardly anyone has an overview. Practically all our engineers specialize in just one aspect or another. The total system view is in the hands of, oh, I don't know, maybe seven or eight people. The four engineers in the master design review team, Ned, and my two deputy managers. Seven, I guess."

"Eight," Jagavitz said. "There's you. *And* you're the only one that's also a pilot with any significant time in jets. *And* three of your senior engineers and one manager are past sixty with heart problems—that's what a desk job with generous quantities of stress will do for you, it can cost you the chance to be blown up later in life, eh?" His chuckle was not reassuring. "Nick, you know we can't order you to do it, but of all the engineers who could go on this flight, you're the only one with no dependents, a broad knowledge of the total system—and no body of specialized knowledge that would be hard to replace. That doesn't mean you're not valuable—"

"But it does mean I'm the best candidate," I said. "No offense taken. So what it boils down to is, I go along as general repairman and Mr. Fixit?"

"The official title will probably be flight engineer."

I thought for all of one second. "When do I start?" I asked.

"Today. You spend three days studying and we let you play on the flight simulator. Then you go. The crew up there doesn't have much time."

Robertson added, "Just so you know, I volunteered to go and they pointed out that I have high blood pressure and I'm forty pounds overweight and I have two kids in junior high. But I'll be rooting for you anyway, you lucky bastard. Especially because if we ever get the big tourist ships flying, I'm buying a ticket on the first one."

"Hell, I'll buy you one," I said.

"I regret to say you'll also need to spend an hour or two being briefed by Caitlin Delamartin and Barbara Quentin about how to present yourself at the press conference afterwards."

I shrugged. "Oh, well, it's all showbiz nowadays." Then a thought struck me. "I don't know who the pilot is."

Robertson grinned. "Well, remember, this whole thing is being run as SCI, everything on a need-to-know basis, only people who already know being included in things. Now, the controls of the StarRescue were deliberately copied from the shuttle, so that a pilot who can handle one can handle the other, though the StarRescue will probably handle even more like a concrete block than the shuttle. As it happens, there is one shuttle-qualified pilot who has been in on most of this affair right from the beginning, and who knows about all the national security issues connected with it. Admittedly, he's on the reserve list, because he's gone civilian . . ."

I suddenly realized. "Oh my god. You mean Scott."

"Unh-hunh," Robertson said. "While he wasn't visiting you in the hospital, we even had him play on the StarRescue simulator. Great hands, quick thinker, super intuition, all that stuff you want a test pilot to be. When you all get back, we're going to offer him a job, and I hope he takes it."

I shook my head a few times, to clear it. "Oh, he's qualified enough. I'll feel perfectly safe, with Scott flying us, I'm sure. But . . . uh, did the poor idiot child ever mention being stuck in a swamp in the backwoods of Bangladesh for most of a day?"

CHAPTER FOURTEEN

SCOTT:

Nick enjoyed the heck out of watching my jaw drop when the President of the United States explained to me that I would be flying the StarRescue, but Nick's own jaw dropped pretty far when Eddie Killeret came in and was introduced as the third crew member. It made as much sense as anything else, though; the President wanted a small operation, kept as close as possible, because he was determined that if it failed, no one was to know anything. I thought about mentioning to him that for thirty years Presidents had been getting into more trouble for the coverup than for the offense, but that seemed like borrowing trouble.

He did have a point; he didn't want his hands tied in space, the way that Reagan's had been after *Challenger* blew up. "Mr. Reagan just had a couple years of trouble doing maintenance, and had to cancel some missions. If Congress went nuts on me and shut down or slowed down launches, we might never be able to regain our position in space at all," he said. "The crew dying on ISS would be bad—but having the public see the rescue attempt crashing would be worse."

Less than seventy-two hours later, I had landed StarRescue correctly eighteen times—on a simulator—and made sixteen correct rendezvous. Both of those were out of twenty tries, so I was giving my last day over to getting the rendezvous up to snuff. In this practice session, I was four for four, and was going for number five, when the simulation run was interrupted, as they often were, for another briefing.

Killeret's "tarantula" had finally arrived from Ghost Town, and he and Nick were practicing with it. Supposedly after making it over to the truss of the ISS, they would attach the first thruster next to the solar cells; then climb "up" the truss (since centrifugal force would be against them, it would feel like up) to a pre-selected strut where they would attach the first digital camera; from there to the center modules, where they would tie on another camera and another thruster, and add the CPU; then "down" the other side truss to put one more camera in the middle and one more thruster on the end. After some discussion, it had been decided that rather than try to re-rendezvous with StarRescue, they'd just climb into ISS and ride things out. In computer simulations, anyway, the tarantula had only taken about fifteen minutes to end the tumble.

It was called the tarantula because the cameras and thrusters all came off from the CPU on long coaxial cables, like the arms of a tarantula. Using a celestial navigation program, the CPU was supposed to be able to figure out the spin of the station, and then use the thrusters to damp it out in the most efficient possible way. I was nervous about letting a computer program do that job, but its record in simulations was much better than mine. Besides, if they had to, Nick and Eddie could hand-fire the thrusters, and probably get a good enough solution for me to be able to bring StarRescue in to dock.

Nick's engineers had built a full scale model of the ninety-foot-long truss in the hangar, and put it on a motorized turntable. What Nick and Eddie were doing was practicing going up and down it, counting struts, memorizing where the tarantula's units had to be connected. The major thing I was realizing was that, with two guys who had never gone EVA before, this would be the hard part. They seemed to be having fun, but I couldn't help thinking how much I'd rather have two experienced astronauts on the job, and let these guys phone in the fixes from the ground.

Finally they let me go back to flying simulations. I did three more correct rendezvous in a row, and told the engineer team that I felt about as ready as I was ever going to feel. They said that Nick and Eddie were going to do one more run in the buoyancy tank, practicing the attaching maneuvers, and then declare themselves ready. The next window to intercept ISS would be early the next morning, so their strong suggestion was that I have a good dinner and get to bed early.

I was just about to turn in when on an impulse I grabbed the phone and called Thalia. She and Amos knew what was up, and Welch had assured me that that line had been secured, so we could talk freely. I talked with Thalia for a while, and she said that, from a PR standpoint, if the mission came off, she thought my name would be about as clear as it was going to get. I talked with Amos for a minute or so—it was very awkward—and then he blurted out, "Dad, if you don't come back, I'm going to miss you a lot."

"I know," I said. "But, you know, for what it's worth, everyone has to worry about that. Sooner or later you don't see somebody again, because they die. And you miss them. But if you didn't love them in the first place, you'd have missed out on *everything*. I'll do my best to come back, but aren't you glad we got to have our time together, anyway?"

He sniffled. "I guess I'm greedy. I want more."

"Then I'm greedy too." It seemed like a good note to say "See you later" on, so I did. I stretched out on the bed in the Scorpion Shack visitor dorm, and noticed I had tears running down my face. Well, it was natural enough. A few minutes later I was sound asleep.

*   *   *

WE WERE IN StarRescue's cabin, which at the moment was like being inside a rolled-up water bed. "You know, they could have put a few goldfish in there to keep us entertained," Eddie said.

"Bad human engineering," Nick said. "We'd get attached to them and wouldn't want to pull the plug when the time came."

"Well, damn this working-with-humans thing, anyway," Killeret said. "Next lifetime, I'm working with well-trained monkeys."

I was busy with my checkouts, supposedly checking everything for the second time, actually for about the fifth—the level of paranoia I was reaching was pretty amazing. The first generation of astronauts had been nearly all test pilots, and they had been *used* to the idea of climbing into a tremendously complex machine that no one had flown before, and taking it up to see what it did. This was my first real experience of the kind.

Well, if I only did this once in my life, that would be plenty for me. And at least I'd have talking rights in the world's most exclusive locker room.

Nick and Eddie were doing their checkouts too, when the voice crackled and said, "T minus forty minutes and counting. All systems are nominal."

"Strange that they only need to tell us every ten minutes," I said, "this late in the count."

"Simple system," Nick said. "That's what we built it to be. The countdown time is just for us to do multiple checks; everything was nominal by seven this morning. If we didn't have to wait for the 8:43 launch window, we'd have been able to go an hour ago." Something caught his attention on the screen in front of him, but whatever it was didn't merit more than a moment's frown and a couple of touches of his keypad. After a minute he said, "You suppose that we'll ever get to where we don't do a countdown? Where all Mission Control says is 'Now departing from gate two, concourse six?' "

"Never," Killeret said. "Airliners never have to hit a moving target; spacecraft always do. If it moves, it's got a window, and you have to make your time for the window."

"Besides, there's the romance and tradition," I said.

"Pilots," Nick muttered, under his breath.

The countdown worked its way down and everything stayed absolutely fine as far as any instrument could tell. Occasionally we'd get a "best wishes" or "good luck" from one department or another, which I always acknowledged with a short "Thank you." A long time after, when I was reviewing the tape, I discovered that I had thanked the President of the United States and my brother's secretary in exactly the same way. I don't think either of them was offended.

If everything went well, the checkout was the last time before orbit that I would be really doing a pilot's job. For the ascent, I was just a passenger; my piloting would come later. On a hurry-up mission like this, without much time for training, and over American territory where we had plenty of radar and transmitter stations available (our path would take us almost parallel to the Gulf Coast, almost directly over Memphis Columbus, and Montreal), it made sense to launch and fly completely under ground control. They'd get us all the way to orbit before it would be time to throw off the Centaur, power up the service module, and do any real flying.

The StarBooster engines thundered alive under us—two Atlas first stages pushing us upward, the effect rising to a roar. The takeoff was smoother than on the shuttle; for the first two and a half minutes, we were in pretty high acceleration, held down to our couches as if we were under a heap of sandbags. The sky swiftly darkened toward violet. The voice in my earpiece read off a litany of things that were going fine.

Booster separation felt as if someone had thrown a switch and turned off the gravity. The twin StarBoosters shut down and released the StarCore simultaneously, and though I couldn't see them, I knew that they were flipping over away from us, turning over to get their bellies back toward the Earth, and beginning their glide back to Scorpion Shack. We were about twenty-five miles above the ground, moving upward at Mach 5.

For five seconds, to give the boosters time to get away, we moved upward on pure inertia, in free fall and therefore weightless. It seemed much longer.

Then the Castor 120 engine in the first stage of StarCore cut in. Weight returned and we were again roaring upward, gaining velocity rapidly. A minute and a half later, with a brief shudder, the first Castor 120 dropped off and the next one in line ignited; we had another ninety seconds of boost, and by now the sky was black as night. We were just under sixty miles up in the sky and at almost Mach 20; nearly the whole of the Earth's atmosphere was behind us.

The gravity "switched off" again, as the second Castor motor fell away and took the interstage adaptor with it. We hung weightless for most of half a minute, coasting upward, while the Centaur engine under us went through chilldown. Mission control read off a long list of things that were working right and told us we were "go for insertion"—that is, we would fire the Centaur stage and climb to orbit, rather than jettisoning it and trying to fly back down. They had barely finished confirming the go when the Centaur fired, and for the last time we were shoved back into the seats. The Centaur is a high-performance rocket, originally developed to be an Atlas upper stage, and it packs a mighty kick. Four minutes of the Centaur, and it cut out. We were weightless and in orbit.

"Scorpion Peripheral," a voice said in my ear, "this is Scorpion Central. You are on course for your rendezvous. Jettison extra equipment in three minutes. Are you prepared to take over manually?"

"Yes, Central, I am."

Clifford Welch and his boys had worried about somebody with a scanner picking us up, so we were using misleading code names. As far as I was concerned, Scorpion Central would still be "Mission Control"; I was just hoping I wouldn't forget and call them "Houston."

And I hated having my craft called "Peripheral"—it made it sound like I was flying a floppy drive.

Everything looked green on my board, and the time counted down slowly. "How are you guys doing?" I asked.

"Just fine," Eddie Killeret said, "except that I don't quite believe I'm here."

"We're doing fine," Nick said, "and radiation counts are lower than we were afraid they might be."

I waited out the time, and then the voice in my ear said, "All right, over to you, Peripheral."

I checked out the service module. Everything was fine. I reached forward, threw the first switch to arm the jettison system, saw the green light, and said, "Jettisoning the Centaur." I flipped the second switch.

There was a thud that you could feel all through the StarRescue, and the Centaur in its I-beam cage separated and tumbled backward away from us. In our low orbit, its perigee would be low enough to deorbit it within a few days. I got busy with Scorpion Central, getting the figures for our first burn, to take us into the higher orbit that would eventually bring us up to ISS. "Stay belted in," I told the other two, unnecessarily. "You'll get to play in weightlessness once I put us on our way."

A BIT OVER two complete orbits, three hours later, we were closing in on ISS. Less than 500 meters away, huge in the window, it was weirdly distorted by the bag of water I was looking through. The central core was a giant set of cylinders, each the size of a double-wide trailer, forming a rough T-shape. The truss extended from it on both sides, triangular in cross section, three feet on a side, ninety feet long; at each end of the truss, the solar panels, dwarfing the station itself, spread out like rigid rectangular wings.

I had been watching the crippled station while depressurizing StarRescue. Rotation was slow, thank heavens, but still, swooping in between the panels to match velocity with part of the truss for a split second—and then getting back out without hitting anything—was going to be an interesting little problem. "Open the door now," I said, shutting off cabin pressure. "I don't want to get kicked sideways when I'm trying to do something precise."

Killeret did, and the three of us, in our pressure suits, were committed to the vacuum of space.

"Let's go for it," Nick said.

"I'm up for it too," Killeret agreed. "We can be ready in a couple minutes."

"Take your time," I said, "I just want to study this thing."

Behind me, they were setting up the bag with the tarantula in it, clipped to Nick's belt; Nick roped himself to Killeret with a three-meter cable; and Killeret, as the guy who had been better with the grapple in practice, was by the door. "How close can we get, Scott?"

"Close," I said. "No long throw. Wait for me to tell you when we're coming up on closest."

ISS was tumbling and precessing; what I was looking for was any place where I could be reasonably sure of getting in close enough to the solar panels that swung past like immense tennis rackets, with us as the potential ball. I approached, using little squirts of thrust to get closer, then killing the resulting relative velocity. Finally I was co-orbiting just about five meters from the edge of an imaginary sphere that roughly marked the outer path of the great whirling wings. I continued to watch, began to catch the rhythm, and finally said, "I can probably go right through, once, to let you guys try for an overhead grab. Riskier till you get there but easier once you do. All right, here we go . . . starting . . . NOW."

I canted the small craft, waited for a solar panel to move to the place I judged right, and gave us a quick forward thrust. We shot in, crossing the space in less than half a minute.

I had us positioned so that Killeret would have the truss passing just over the top of the door opening. Killeret was back to back with Nick, and Nick held the tarantula on his chest; they didn't want to get caught or tangled going out the door.

"Okay, Eddie," I said, "coming up on your throw, five, four, and—three, two, and . . . one, and—go!" My cadence was irregular because I was still adjusting to the tumbling station and the way we were passing through its terrifying whirling arms.

At my "go," Eddie tossed his grapple in an underhand throw; it snagged in the truss, and the moment Killeret saw it catch, he said "Good."

Nick kicked gently backwards with both legs, throwing himself and Killeret out the door. StarRescue lurched in reaction. The wing slid by beneath them silently, and they were clear of the ship. I let momentum take me back out of reach of the whirling ISS, then nulled relative velocity with a couple shots of the thrusters, and slowly yawed the co-orbiting StarRescue 180 degrees, so that I could keep ISS in the window continuously. I had coasted about twenty meters beyond the farthest reach of the solar panels. I was plenty close enough to see what was happening to Eddie and Nick; they were still swinging on the cable attached to the truss, most of the way out toward the solar panel on the "short side" of the hub. Eddie was climbing steadily hand over hand, and as I watched, he caught the truss in his outstretched hand, pulled himself to it, clipped on, and hauled Nick and the tarantula in to him.

"Scorpion Central, the team is on the truss and looks fine," I said, into the radio. "Guys, can you hear me?"

"Right here, Peripheral," Nick's voice said. "Everything is looking pretty good. Got to work now. More when we know more."

Though it was nothing like the rapid death it would have been to be EVA up here a few weeks ago, the radiation was still much more than anyone wanted to take for long. For the moment, I had the safest seat up here, and all I could do was wait and watch.

NICK:

Every one of the hundreds of pilots and engineers I'd ever worked with, sooner or later, had always told me that drill is different from real, theory from practice, drawing from product, and I'd have sworn I knew it as well as any of them, but I don't think I grasped it until the moment when Killeret and I started to install the tarantula. I knew, in principle, that we needed to climb the truss more or less like a ladder, but nothing had mentally prepared me for the problem we were in with the slight centrifugal-force gravity where he had connected. That meant there was relatively little force between boot and truss, and we slipped and skidded constantly as we struggled downwards. You'd plant your feet a step below, and suddenly they'd fly outwards, waving around, as your mass tried to tug your grip loose from the truss, and the sky and Earth whirled slowly, inexorably around you, until your feet drifted back to the truss again and you began the whole process again. For safety, we worked on a short tether line the whole time, and it was astonishing how much harder it was to move the clip than it had been back in the Scorpion Shack hangar.

Nonetheless, we made our way all the way down there, and I gingerly opened the bag. Killeret reached in, grasped the thruster and camera units on the top—everything had been packed carefully so that things would come out in the right order, and not tangled, we hoped. The cable came smoothly. So far, so good.

I closed the bag, belayed it to the truss, carefully counted struts twice until I was sure I had the right one, and then wrapped my feet around one side of the truss and got to work clamping the thruster to the strut. Despite the Clancy clamps, which are designed to spin closed and thus not require any direct twisting force, I still managed to put considerable torque against my body, and nearly lost my foot-grip. It took twice as long as it ever had on the ground, and I was sweating and sore in unfamiliar places before I was done.

I felt a little twinge of competitive pleasure when I saw that Eddie didn't quite have the camera unit on yet; as I watched, grunting and swearing, he finally got it dogged down. "Okay, let's climb," he said, and we made our way up the truss to install the next camera and thruster.

There was only one twist in the whole bag, right after the tarantula's controlling computer, and it only took us about seven or eight minutes to straighten that out. The hub was a weird place to do it; gravity was almost zero, but changed very rapidly as you reached away, so that it was noticeably different between your feet and your head. That was disorienting, and of course there was the sensation of endless tumbling as the sun, Earth, and moon, all cavorted about us. After that, perhaps because we were going from a new task to a less-new one, climbing down the other side of the truss went much more smoothly, and the remaining cameras and thrusters went on without trouble.

"Okay, Scott," I said in the headphones. "Let us get up and inside, and then you can turn on the tarantula—and hopefully tame this rotating beast."

"Roger."

We scrambled up the truss to get to the airlock hatch; it was designed to be operated manually from either side. Stephen Tebworthy had gone out into the exposed part of the station, briefly, a few hours before and made sure the inner door was closed. We pushed into the airlock—in pressure suits, nearly weightless, it was like packing a phone booth while scuba diving—closed the outer door, and cycled the lock; pressure rose quickly to standard, and we opened the inner door and climbed the dizzying tunnel in front of us.

It was slightly worse in here, where you couldn't see the spinning, and the only light came from the improvised headlamps on our pressure suits, but we had practiced this many times, and to my great relief, we proceeded directly to where the Soyuz was docked, without getting lost or disoriented. We had thought it best to be here, for the next step, before trying to stabilize the station, because if anything went wrong we might get disoriented or thrown around, and we didn't want to lose any more time than we had to.

"Got a handhold, Eddie?"

"Yep."

I made sure my own grip on a railing was secure, and then said, "All right, Peripheral, we're go for the tarantula."

Scott's voice crackled in my earpiece. "Tarantula is powering up . . . checking out . . . ready to go in five, four, three, two, one . . . go."

There were a series of weird lurches and yanks as the thrusters gradually brought ISS under control and eventually into its prescribed alignment with the sun. The jolting, yanking, and swerving lasted about five minutes, as the controlling computer fired first one thruster and then another, trying to line up the cameras first with the horizon and then with the sun. We could feel it succeeding—each time the world shifted, it shifted less violently, and the pseudogravity caused by centrifugal force was less. At the end of it, we were weightless, though still in the dark.

"Got it, Scott," I said. "We're good in here."

"Good out here too," he said. "Let's proceed to our next step; we have just about one orbit till we have a descent window, and I'm sure we'd all like to get out of here."

The next part of the plan was simple; first we had to get that dead Soyuz out of the dock. We hoped that we would be able to work the manual eject system, which was basically a device for turning the couplings loose from each other. Since we had no way to reliably power the dead capsule up, after that, Scott would come up close, open the door of StarRescue, "lasso" the Soyuz solar panel with a big loop in a stiffened cable, and, using the thrusters, gently tug the Soyuz away from the station, putting it into motion so that it would drift out of our way.

The couplings separated at once, and we radioed the good news to Scott. About a minute later, we heard a whispering scrape as the dead capsule slid away from the station.

"I got the Soyuz moving," Scott said, over the radio, "and boy do I feel like a cowboy. I'm about fifty meters beyond the station and I'm going to jettison the tow cable, now; the Soyuz is definitely leaving for good. Then it's going to be some minutes more to repressurize and get ready to come in for a docking. Also, guys, I did start a very slight tumble in the station again, so hang on . . . tarantula fires again in five, four, three, two, one . . . there."

There was a faint rumble, and then we were stable and weightless again.

Less than five minutes later, with a thud, the hatch of StarRescue mated with ISS. "Okay, open up," Scott's voice said in my ears.

We did, and he swam in, dragging the medical kit and the three special pressure suits, folded into their bags, with him. He checked the air sampler and said, "All right, the air's okay in here," and we lifted visors for the first time.

The stench was terrible. Radiation poisoning slowly destroys the skin, sets the bowels going, leads to fluid loss through every available route; and the crew had been getting weaker and weaker, less able to care for and clean each other, eventually barely able to haul buckets of waste out into the other parts of the ISS. We all gagged, and Killeret retched.

To minimize exposure, the ISS crew had been told to stay in the storm cellar until we came for them. They had little or no cumulative dosage left to mess around with.

We zigzagged through the maze of improvised walls they had made from anything easy to shift; since radiation travels in straight lines, they had laid their improvised barriers out so that there were no straight paths to the storm cellar.

In preparing the rescue mission for what we might find up here, they had shown us photos of the *Lucky Dragon* crew, of some workers from the Chernobyl plant, and of the messy death of Louis Slotkin—

all the cases of genuinely massive radiation poisoning that might be comparable with what we would find here. The ISS crew looked worse than some of the pictures, and better than others, but still, nothing can prepare you to encounter the real thing: the feel of the raised lumps of flesh through the thin working gloves of our suits; the stench of blood and shit and sickness; the scattering of teeth by each bed; the little floating blobs of fluid horror, and the smears on the walls; the clumps of hair sticking to our gloved hands with static and bodily fluids; worst of all, the twitches and winces of misery on the human faces.

Carl Tanaka was by far the sickest of the three. He had insisted on his right as commander to make more excursions into the outer, dangerous area than the other two did. He was puffy and red, as if he'd been stung by a swarm of bees; hundreds of little open sores on him leaked blood, and his hair drifted away in clumps when we went to move him. As gently as we could, we cleaned him with antibacterial wipes, trying to remove some of the feces, blood, and mucus without breaking or crumbling his ravaged skin, and gently powdered him so that we could slip him into his suit without doing more damage. He passed out as Killeret and I worked on him, which was probably for the best.

Doris McIntyre and Stephen Tebworthy were mostly able to clean and powder themselves, though they too were losing hair, leaking blood, and had patches of raw skin that looked like the worst case of poison ivy you could imagine. Scott helped them through that process, and had them in the pressure suits by the time we got the unconscious Carl Tanaka into his. "Vital signs *not* good," Killeret said, looking at the monitor. "Can we still make that first descent window to Edwards, Scott?"

"Yeah, if we hurry," he said. "If he's zipped in, let's go. You guys move him along. I'll help Doris and Stephen."

I don't exactly know how much trouble Scott had getting his two charges down the corridor to the dock; comparatively not much, I think, since he got them belted in and came back to help Killeret and me with the unconscious commander. Carl Tanaka's body had gone limp, except when it was racked by spasms that threatened to slam his head or his overworked kidneys against the metal walls around him. "Probably nervous-system damage," Eddie muttered, as we guided him around yet another bend, Eddie leading, Scott and I keeping arms and legs from jamming or catching.

Taking things as carefully as we had to, it took five minutes to move him twenty meters, but Scott said we still had time "—if we move fast—" as we strapped the unconscious Tanaka to the seat. We pulled down our visors and strapped in ourselves. "Ready," I said, just as Eddie Killeret said it.

"Scorpion Central, this is Scorpion Peripheral. Can we still hit the window?"

"Transferring data. Answer is yes. Details are being loaded to ship's computer . . . all right, Scott, our screen says you've got all the data."

"Transfer was successful," he agreed. "All right, we're coming home."

SCOTT:

Heading into a window that's closing isn't intrinsically harder than any other re-entry, except that you have narrower error bars on everything; but any good pilot plans to hit right on the money. So what does it matter where all the wrong places are? You aren't going there anyway.

I used the service module thrusters to push us back from the dock. The attitude jets swung us around until we were orbiting tail first, the service module preceding us. Then I turned control over to the computer; I wanted this burn to be timed more precisely than my own hands and brain could do unaided.

Scorpion Central counted down for me, but the computer was doing all the work; at precisely zero, the big thrusters thundered, shaking the StarRescue for a ten full minutes, pushing against the direction of our orbit, and nearly exhausting their tanks. It was only about a one-percent drop in velocity, but that was enough to start us dropping toward the Earth.

ISS orbits, very roughly, a million feet above the ground; our loss of momentum from firing the thrusters caused us to begin a long fall into a much more eccentric lower orbit, one that would swing so low as to pass inside the atmosphere, where we could use the air's drag to slow us down and bring us in. Gingerly, I rotated us 90 degrees in two different axes, until we were pointed straight down at the Earth, looking at the wide blue South Pacific. Samoa flashed by the window like white dots on the interstate.

Half an hour later, the jagged curve of Baja sprawled out across the horizon to my right, and I was watching for the California coast dead ahead. StarRescue was more than halfway down—we were at about seventy-five miles above the Earth, still in space but coming down fast; the horizon of the Earth was still curved below us and the sky was jet black in broad daylight. Firing the service-module thrusters for the last time, I tilted StarRescue's nose up forty degrees to get it into re-entry attitude, with the heat shield pointed directly forward.

When I was sure that was satisfactory, I said, "Jettison coming up . . ." and hit the button. With a brief, mild lurch, the service module slid back and away behind us; unshielded from the heat of re-entry, and with less wind resistance than we had, it would tumble on ahead and burn up.

Twenty minutes later, we were down to 250,000 feet—about the altitude where you start feeling the air. There was thunder under the wings and fuselage. Weight returned and built up as the acceleration crept up toward three g's. StarRescue was re-entering.

"Time to see how good your plumbers are," I remarked to Nick.

In space, it hadn't mattered that we had tons of water aboard as radiation shielding, but in the atmosphere, the increase in Star-Rescue's density would make it impossible to maintain an appropriate rate of descent—a fancy way of saying we were too heavy and we'd go in too steep. So Nick's team had come up with a set of pumps and tubes to empty the "water beds." I tripped the switch, and the shaking and rattling of StarRescue became more violent, but the bags all around us shrank steadily into the walls as we sprayed the water into the atmosphere. It was gone in three minutes—spread across hundreds of miles of sky, much higher than any cloud ever forms. At the time, I was too busy to realize that we were smearing the biggest contrail anyone ever saw across the clear blue Pacific sky, pointing northeast up to Los Angeles—a thousand-mile-long streak that drifted eastward for days before dissipating.

At 180,000 feet, with the sky still black and the curve of the Earth much farther away, streams of white-hot air flowed past the front window; we were entering the high-heat regime, and as we descended ten more miles toward the Earth, we were cut off from contact by that white plasma that blocked all radio.

As if a switch had been thrown, at 130,000 feet, the window cleared, and I looked at a dark blue sky. We were still screaming along at four times the speed of the fastest jet fighters, higher than the Blackbird reconnaissance planes flew, but we were flying, not orbiting, and that was a long step closer to home. "Hello, Scorpion Central," I said. "Looks like we're coming back fine."

"Glad to hear it, Peripheral. You're go for Edwards. Very little wind today, so if you want to aim for the shuttle runway per original plan, go for it."

"Roger."

StarRescue was never intended to be flown like the shuttle; it was a lifeboat, and its job was to get passengers to where they could be rescued. We had no landing gear and our rate of descent would have made a landing dangerous.

Instead, the idea was to get close enough to the ground, and then deploy a parawing, essentially a big, steerable rectangular parachute, to get us the rest of the way down. With no wind, and nothing in the way, it made sense to steer for the shuttle runway—it was a huge target, easy to hit, flat ground on which a landing would be safer, and most of all, equipped to get emergency vehicles out to an arriving aircraft.

The rest of the flight on wings was not much different from landing an extremely-high-performance jet or a super-fast glider; I pointed us in the right direction, kept us on the beam, and waited until it was time to do something else. The curving Earth became flat, the sky lightened, and after a while Catalina and San Clemente rushed by below us, and then the great brown smear of Los Angeles itself.

When the shuttle runway was looming huge in the windshield, and we were just a few thousand feet up, I pulled the lever, and the parawing popped out. With a hard shake, as if a giant dog had just caught us like a Frisbee, we dropped speed quickly down to only around 150 miles per hour. Working the less-familiar rudder and line control system, I brought us down to a final, grinding, bumpy touchdown on the tarmac. I released the parawing, which fell over in front of us like a giant jellyfish. By the time we got the door open, the ambulance crews were already there, waiting to rush in and grab the ISS crew the moment we got out of their way. Nick, Eddie, and I piled out of StarRescue, removing our helmets, into the hot California desert sunlight, blinking at the harsh light, noticing, for just a moment until it became normal again, how much gravity they have down here.

CHAPTER FIFTEEN

THALIA:

Scott and Nick hadn't really been able to tell Amos and me anything at all about where they were going or what they were doing. All we got was that it was an emergency, and it was important, and that they'd both be back in a few days. Then over the weekend, I got a call from Clifford Welch, who said he'd had a thought that Amos and I might like to see something at Edwards Air Force Base. That put four good clues together for me: that was where the shuttle often lands, Nick was involved with a project to build a new spacecraft, the shuttle couldn't do the ISS rescue in time, and Scott was a qualified pilot who had just spent time at Scorpion Shack. I agreed that we would like to see that, and we flew out with Welch.

When we got there, the combination of secrecy and VIP treatment was more than enough to give the rest of the story away. They set up raw feed in our guest quarters, so we were able to look over Scott's shoulder for much of the flight.

When Scott fired the rocket motors and started the return to Earth, there was a knock at our door, and when I opened it, Welch was standing there, saying, "We thought you'd like to go out to the runway, where he'll be bringing it in."

The van made a number of stops at other guest rooms. We picked up Eddie Killeret's father, and then a larger group that was the families of the ISS crew.

As we rode in the big van out to the runway, we listened to the communications between the ground and StarRescue. The blackout during the high-temperature part of the descent was maddening, of course, but it wasn't much different from what I'd been through during three shuttle landings. By the time that we were parked, and had stepped outside the van to watch, the StarRescue crew were back on the air and coming in, with everything fine.

For a while all there was to look at was the great white streak, high up in the southern sky, that was the weird contrail you make by dumping a ton of water in a straight line through the thermosphere. "I'd bet it's visible from Baja to Vancouver," Welch guessed.

Amos spotted the little dot of gleaming metal first, and stood up and yelled. I stood next to him, and then everybody saw it. It was coming in pretty fast and was quite high up; as we watched, it descended until we could just make out that it had wings and a fuselage. Lower and closer, we could see the shape of the stubby wings, the rounded nose, and the windshield. Then something that looked—just for a second—like orange smoke billowed out behind it. The parawing deployed fully, and StarRescue slowed and began its gentle descent to the tarmac.

"As long as we don't get in the way of the ambulances, I would imagine we can drive on over there," Welch said to the driver.

We parked in a row of a dozen other vans. Welch, sitting next to the driver, turned around and said, "Now, folks, we're eager to see them, but it's going to be a few minutes. Just in case something goes really wrong at the last minute, we want you all to stay here in the van—there's enough window space, you should all be able to see them come in. Once they're down, they'll dump the parawing, and a crew will run out to get that under control so it doesn't blow around and cause accidents. At the same time, the ambulances will go get the ISS crew—I'm afraid they all have to go direct to the hospital, but this van will take their families to the hospital to meet with the doctors who will be treating them. You'll be able to talk to your loved ones just as soon as the doctors say it's okay.

"For those of you with friends and family in the StarRescue crew, after the ambulances go, there's going to be one van that goes up and greets the crew before we do. That should only take about five minutes. Then this van will go up there so you can greet the crew. It will drop you off, and take the ISS crew's relatives to the hospital. You'll have about five minutes to say hello, and then your friends and relatives in the crew will have to do about half an hour of shaking hands and talking to press people, and then finally you'll all ride in the bus with them back to the main base. Everyone clear on how it's going to go?"

Any agreement was drowned out by our rush to the windows, to watch StarRescue make its final descent to the runway. It came down at a steep, almost vertical angle, seemingly slowly as an elevator, hanging beneath the huge canopy. It touched down without a bounce, and the canopy released and fell over to one side. Out of the corner of my eye, I could see ground crew running toward the collapsing parawing, but I was watching the hatch on the side of the nose. It swung inward, leaving a round hole about the size of a small kitchen table, about three feet above the pavement, and ground crew people ran out to put a set of steps underneath it.

Scott, still in his pressure suit but with the helmet off, climbed out, followed by two other crew people—whom I suddenly recognized as Eddie Killeret and Nick. "Wow," Amos breathed, beside me, and I had to agree: "You're right, kid, wow."

The ambulance crews went in with a stretcher, and came back out carrying Major Tanaka. They went in again, and a few minutes later, Doris McIntyre emerged, supported on either arm by the paramedics. Stephen Tebworthy followed, also supported between medics, and managed a feeble wave. Each time, as soon as the patient was loaded in, the ambulance shot off, hurrying to get them to the hospital.

About the time that the ambulance with Tebworthy in it was just a dot down at the end of the road, a van swung out of the line and pulled up by where the crew was still standing.

"Mom, why do the people in that van get to see Dad before we do?" Amos asked. "I know they had to get the sick people to the ambulance, but why does—"

Then we saw who was getting out of the van to shake hands with the crew, and Amos fell silent. "Well," I said, "he *is* the President, and it is a pretty big day."

The radio crackled on, and we got to hear the last of what the President was saying: "—who have not only accomplished so much for a grateful nation, but whom we also honor because of the further trails we expect them to blaze in our advance into this new frontier. Thank you all, God bless you all, and welcome home." The entourage applauded, the President stepped back, and they pulled out.

It was our turn next, and it was only as the door was opening that I realized I had no idea of what I was going to say to Scott. Amos shot out ahead of me, anyway, and by the time I got there he was hanging on to his father very, very tightly. So I thought about it for an instant, and decided that if Scott didn't like this, I could always claim it was old habit. I walked up and gave him a good long kiss. After a moment's surprise, he kissed back. When we stopped kissing, I was reasonably sure that he had liked it. "Now what?" he said.

"That was it," I said. "I don't intend it to lead anywhere. I just thought on a day like this you deserved more than a handshake."

THE DAY AFTER Thanksgiving—which was at our house, cooked by Nick, and attended by Eddie Killeret, and thus was the first real "Mars Four Reunion"—AnnaBeth James finally took Jasper Haverford's advice, and made the case go away.

By then, the cry of "Justice for MJ!" was fading, slowly worn away by bad weather, the coming of the holidays, and most of all the tendency of the press to lose a story when a bigger one turns up. The ISS rescue dwarfed the old news, and M J was beginning to fade into the sort of permanent, less-active story that Princess Di had become—still brought up, instantly recognizable, but only occasionally covered.

That was just what I had been aiming for.

The day after Thanksgiving is normally a slow news day; the typical story is about how big the crowds are at the malls and the downtown department stores, and what the hottest-selling toys are. But late that afternoon, at the Algonquin Hotel in New York, Jasper Haverford brought AnnaBeth James out in front of a hastily assembled pack of press and media, and she sat down to talk to them.

She was in a plain, almost severe, black silk dress, with her hair pulled back, and though her face was dry today, she looked as if she had been crying for a century. She nodded at the press, clear-eyed and calm, and said, "When I first launched this lawsuit, there was so much we didn't know. We didn't know if Michael had been killed by negligence, or if someone had lied to him. We didn't know that it had been a terrorist attack, or that it had been intended to destroy the whole shuttle and leave no trace. Sometimes somebody starts a lawsuit just because they want to know why, why, why such a terrible thing could happen. And now, it seems to me, I know.

"And then there was anger; anger that no one had said that this would happen, anger at ourselves that we hadn't tried to keep him on the ground, anger at our loss . . . and that can keep something going for a while, too, you know.

"After that it can get to be so that you just feel like you'd be betraying him, like it would finish him off and make him completely dead, if you didn't carry through with this, even if maybe there wasn't much to the case anymore. Oh, God, he was a hard one to let go.

"These past few weeks, the family has been searching our hearts, looking for the right thing to do, because Michael James was always a one to do that, to know he was right before he made a move. And we've prayed, and talked, and watched so many of our old tapes of him . . . I want to thank you folks at the networks, for letting us have copies of so much, it's been such a comfort to us . . . and finally we had to say, what would he like? What would Michael have felt good about?

"And I think I know now. I do. I think his eyes were always upward, he was always wanting people to reach and to do and to try, himself most of all, but everyone. And if I were to press this suit . . . well, there's people out there that murdered Michael, and we all know that there are. But they aren't the people that built the shuttle, or flew it, or even the ones that sold him a ticket.

"And there are people out there that would be pretty happy if the whole human race just stayed home forever, and people that will do anything to hurt America, and probably people that thought a black man, or a civilian, or any number of other things that Michael was, has no business going to the stars. But they aren't the ones who are reaching for the stars. And it's the ones who *are* reaching that M J wanted to be around, wanted to work with and spend time with.

"And if I press this suit, I'm very afraid that I would be hurting his friends, and helping the people he would have wanted us to fight." She looked around the room. "And I would say *that*, I like to think, even if I hadn't been allowed to look at some secret information from our government. And I trust and believe the men who told me what they had found out, though I can't discuss it here. It was a matter for national security, and it was a good thing to drop the case. But most of all, as I've learned more of what really happened and how it happened, I've come to conclude that there's no justice in this suit. I'm not ashamed or sorry to have started it, back when we knew nothing—but I'd be ashamed and sorry to continue it now.

"Like I said, it wouldn't be any kind of memorial for Michael.

"And that's why I didn't put up a fight when the case was dismissed. And that's why I'm asking all the people who have been so

generous with their support, and their desire to see justice done . . .
my friends, your hearts are good, and I am oh, so grateful for your
willingness to stand up for MJ, but we honor him more, now, by
letting this drop. It's over. Please, no more protests, no more
marches, just accept what's happened; a terrible thing, but sometimes,
when you reach for the stars, you don't live to get there. That's part
of the cost, and MJ knew he might pay it, and as it happened, he
did. Honor him by carrying on his dreams. Thank you."

There were a few, generally polite questions from the reporters,
about her future plans (she had very few; he had provided generously
for his family in his will, and probably none of his relatives would
ever need to work again). She made a couple more brief statements,
thanking Haverford, expressing her relief that the ISS crew had been
rescued, and reminding people to pray for Carl Tanaka, who was to
have a marrow transplant the next day.

When Nick finally clicked the set off, we all sat silently for a
while. "You know," he said, "no matter how well someone handles a
tragedy, I always think how much better it would have been to see
them at an occasion of joy."

Scott nodded. "I think maybe we just got a look at how MJ got
to be MJ. Oh, we'll go on and we'll manage to make a better world
out of this, but I think we'll always wonder how much better it might
have been to have all our new successes and challenges in space—*and*
Michael James."

EPILOG

THALIA:

"Did he say who he was bringing?" Scott asked.

"No," I said, and glanced over to where Nick was turning over an array of steaks and chicken legs on the grill we had set up on the deck. "Should you have started those before they get here?"

Nick smiled. "If Killeret is late, it will be the first time, ever. And this stuff takes a while to cook." He checked his watch. "He'll be here within eight minutes. Guaranteed. Bet me if you like."

"No bet," Scott said. "I saw enough of him when we flew. You can set your watch by the man. I wonder who he's bringing, though."

"It's going to be fun to have a Mars Four reunion here," I said, "in the summer, and at the cabin." We'd all gotten together about once a month since Christmas, but generally just at a restaurant in whatever place happened to be mutually convenient, for a shared meal and some conversation. "Eddie said after he drives his guest back, he'll be able to come down and stay a couple of cabins over, for the whole week."

Late June on the Virginia coast is great if you like temperature contrast; the sunny beach is hot, but the Atlantic is still chilly enough so that only tourists and kids are really anxious to go in. I watched

Amos splash around in the shallow water, playing some complicated game with a group of kids he'd taken up with. It was good to see him having a social life again, and not clinging to Scott or me. As I watched, the kids, all shivering from the cold sea, rushed up and threw themselves onto the towels in the sun; I could hear them yelling and calling things to each other, but couldn't make out what.

"So if we were the Mars Four, what will those five be?" Scott asked, casually.

Nick flipped over two huge steaks and smeared sauce on the exposed tops. "Probably the Mars Five. Even with all the breakthroughs we're getting, it's still going to take twenty more years before people can go there. Once we've learned to handle interplanetary distances and expeditions of several years, then, maybe, the rest of the solar system will gradually open up . . . but Mars will be the frontier for another generation, I should guess, and maybe even longer. That's okay. A frontier nourishes a civilization; we don't have to have a new one until the old one closes."

There was a crunch of tires on the gravel out front, and Nick, looking at his watch, said, "Two minutes early." Scott and I sprang up and went through the house to meet Eddie Killeret and his guest. Eddie was already coming up the steps to the screen door, and directly behind him was Clifford Welch, in a suit and tie that looked particularly peculiar considering that all of us, including Eddie, were in gym shorts and T-shirt. "Unfortunately, I have a meeting in Washington late this afternoon," he said. "But Mr. Killeret has kindly offered me a spare bed in his cabin for the next few days, and I've just about decided to take him up on it."

I played hostess for a minute, making sure everyone had a cold drink, and then we went out to sit and watch Nick cook. He'd begun to throw heaps of sliced vegetables onto the grill, and was sprinkling some special sauce or other over that. "Dinner in twenty, or so," he said.

Welch nodded, sipped his iced tea, and said, "Actually I came here because yesterday, when I bumped into Ed, he told me that you'd all be here, and it seemed like a great opportunity to fill you all in, at once, on some things that I'm now at liberty to talk about. And if it's twenty minutes, that's plenty of time to cover it, before Amos gets back up here."

Nick nodded. "I can cook while I listen. What's up?"

"First, a small and perfectly public piece of news. The Federal order for StarBoosters will be stepped up to twelve. The four they have flying right now, with StarCore I's, are doing a great job, and NASA and the Air Force are realizing that this is saving their bacon— so they've decided to make sure it *stays* saved. Four more StarBoosters for NASA, four more for the Air Force—and maybe some up-front money toward getting StarBooster 350 into development, too. Also approval is going to come down—at least if everyone in Congress stays on the side they say they're on—for getting StarCore II and StarBird moving, as well, on a hurry-up schedule. So I think that at least two of you here have secure jobs.

"Second piece of news, also interesting, probably won't be reported in the media. Two nights ago, on Hainan, where they're developing the Long March II, the Chinese suffered a tragic accident. For some inexplicable reason they're blaming it on sabotage or a commando raid by Taiwan, Vietnam, the Philippines, and sometimes us. They seem to have a hard time sorting out their villains, and exactly what happened.

"That may be because there's not much left on the ground. The Long March II booster, which was supposed to be the first test flight later this week, blew up while a group of dignitaries and specialists was taking a tour. Among those killed were three men who I have very good reason to believe created and ordered the plan that killed MJ, and two physicists just back from a tour of duty as advisors to Pakistan. The Chinese government has made a number of ugly accusations without proof, which I doubt that our press will even bother to report. At least, they won't, if they want any more news leaks in the next twenty years.

"That brings me to some highly confidential stuff. We've finally closed the investigation into the late and unlamented Mr. Riscaveau and his friends at the Chinese Embassy. It would appear that Mr. Riscaveau was probably a talented petty liar all his life; he forged some of the credentials that got him each job, until eventually he made it to chief of security for RW. A couple of RW managers seem to have failed to notice several good reasons for not allowing him to be promoted, and we're looking to see whether that was a matter of incompetence, successful deception by Mr. Riscaveau, blackmail of some kind . . . or perhaps something more sinister.

"But before his incompetence was detected, he found a golden friendship, during his little trip to Thailand. The Chinese, you see, weren't just a source of income. Intelligence services tend to know a lot about other kinds of spies—and always have a few spies and snitches of their own that they are eager to get rid of. Riscaveau was getting a list every few weeks, from the Chinese, of people he could 'catch,' to make his reputation grow."

"And it did," Nick said. "Everyone in the company always said that he seemed not very smart, and he was very annoying, but you couldn't argue with his results—he caught spies like nobody else."

"Same gimmick that Aldrich Ames used," Welch said, nodding. "Along with a dozen other double agents throughout history. It works as long as your bosses have enough small fry to sacrifice. Perhaps they were running out of petty traitors and rival spies to turn in, and decided to end the charade. More likely Riscaveau was at the end of his usefulness, and they decided to expend him in one big operation.

"At any rate, it would appear that when *Columbia* made it back down to the ground with much of the evidence intact and some of the crew still alive, the plot began to unravel, and all sorts of things, including the Pakistani proton bomb, were moved up in the schedule.

That also meant that enormous pressure was put on Mr. Riscaveau to keep the lid on and prevent anyone's taking effective action for a few weeks. A cleverer man might have found ways, but Andrew Riscaveau prided himself on his mastery of standard procedure and his ability to treat things as routine, no matter how extraordinary they were. I think it was Isaac Asimov who said that 'Violence is the last resort of the incompetent,' but he was wrong; real incompetence gets violent before it needs to, or when it doesn't need to. There were hundreds of subtler and trickier ways he could have helped the James lawsuit along, and stymied the Starcraft project, but when a man spends his life thinking like a thug, the thoughts that come naturally to mind are threats, arson, and sabotage. I suspect that if Riscaveau had made it to China, after a couple of years, they'd have shot him themselves, just as a matter of convenience.

"As far as we can tell he acted with Chinese help, but not on their orders, and he acted alone. There's no larger conspiracy or ring out there waiting to get either Thalia or Scott. You can safely pull the bodyguards whenever you like."

"Actually," Nick said, "since there had been no incidents since Riscaveau's death, we pulled them a month ago."

Welch shrugged amiably. "You're all a bunch of amateurs. And it's probably a good thing that we live in a world where you can safely *be* amateurs. But no hurt, no foul, as MJ might have said, and I wish he'd had the chance to say it.

"All right, now here's one more piece of news, and I've saved the best for last. After that, I have a trivial question for you all. The news is this: the President will be giving a space policy speech in July or early August, and he's going to be announcing a whole series of commitments to space. He'll talk about streamlining and simplifying the laws so that launch services are easy to buy, and about a federal anchor tenancy so that there's a guaranteed market for space—and about committing to buying the whole Starcraft series, right up through StarBird II's and StarCore III's, from Republic Wright.

"American companies will be launching hotels in space, and hundred-passenger ships will be carrying people up to them, and by the end of the decade we'll probably have increased the number of Americans who have flown into space tenfold. And by 2015, we'll have a vast experience with long-term habitats and all the other expertise needed to get the process going, and mount a serious Mars expedition of fifty or a hundred people, most of them scientists, that will be able to stay over for a couple of years on the Martian surface and do real exploration.

"If all goes well, they might even arrive there in 2019, for the fiftieth anniversary of the first lunar landing. The frontier is open again."

Nick sighed. "Well," he said, "there go a few more vacations, I bet."

"On the other hand, there's only one member of the Mars Four that hasn't been to space now," I pointed out, "and all this talk of commercial passengers and space hotels sounds like there might very well be a chance."

"Funny you should mention that," Welch said, leaning back and looking about as relaxed as he was ever going to. "Because one thing we discovered, when we broke into Riscaveau's encrypted files and obtained some decrypts of various messages to and from the Chinese, was that for the last few months that he was working for them, right up to his death, he was absolutely certain that there was a secret project going on, some big leap in American technology or some secret military operation, called Mars Four. He and his Chinese bosses expended hours and hours trying to find out what it was and who was involved and so forth. They thought that either Nick or Ed must be the leader or head of it, and that all of you were in on it, and they had a long, long list of things it might be and how it might be carried out, and I would guess that one out of every ten Chinese agents in the USA was working on the problem.

"Now, I happen to know that there is no project anywhere in our government called Mars Four, but then I have some advantages over the Chinese in finding that out. It's worked out pretty well for us, these past few months, because anyone who seems to be trying to find out what Mars Four is, and where it's located, turns out to be a Chinese agent. So we're poised to roll up some of their intelligence network, and to feed the rest all kinds of disinformation for decades. Call it just another little payback for their recent bad behavior."

I was trying very hard not to laugh, and I noticed that Scott was choking and turning a deep red. Ed Killeret and Nick Blackstone weren't doing any better job of controlling it. Welch looked around, smiled broadly, and went on, "It would appear that the Chinese are convinced that Mars Four is going to be some kind of super-secret ultrahigh technology which is going to catapult us ahead of everyone in space for generations to come, something more like magic than technology, if you see what I mean. Probably they arrived at this opinion because Mr. Riscaveau had a knack for exaggerating his importance and stretching the truth, in the first place, and secondly because of the tendency of intelligence agencies to think that anything you haven't penetrated yet must be very big.

"Rather in a spirit of fun, we've begun to include the words 'Mars Four' in some of the gibberish that we send out routinely as filler in our coded transmissions, and we've done a few little things to make it look like some very unimportant weather stations in remote locations, and some basic research at the national laboratories, has something to do with Mars Four.

"But we'd really like to know what it really is, and the four of you turned up frequently in Andrew Riscaveau's original notes on the subject. Now, from the way you're all laughing, I think you probably can tell me what it is."

So we did tell him, in bits and pieces, then, and over lunch, as we would remember one incident or another. Amos and a couple of his friends were there, whispering to each other; I wondered if maybe Scott had been right, and we were seeing the start of another secret society.

Lunch ended with everyone having over-eaten—a hard thing to avoid when Nick was cooking. The adults went out to sit on the deck and watch the afternoon waves roll in from the blue-green Atlantic, and sit and talk for an hour or so until Eddie would have to drive Welch back up to DC. Welch went so far as to take off his coat and vest and put his necktie in his pocket. "You'll see," he said, grinning. "When I come down here to stay with Ed, I'll bring along boat shoes and maybe even a pair of shorts and a ball cap."

For a while we just watched the kids running back and forth and yelling to each other, and let our eyes drift off to the far horizon. I wasn't sure there would be any more conversation.

"Funny," Welch said, after a while. "The Chinese thought we must be planning to leap to the stars—that somewhere there had to be the superproject that would do everything. And yet the whole point is, we're not leaping. We're taking one careful step at a time, better booster, better upper stage, better orbiter, each one just enough better to make it worth the cost and risk of developing, each one working a small improvement. We've learned not to be Superman—we don't leap a tall building at a single bound—we climb it, one foot and handhold at a time, staying on belay the whole way. We always knew that was the right way, and now we're doing it."

"The reason they looked so hard for Mars Four was because they thought there had to be one," Nick mused. He leaned forward and pointed to the gathered circle of kids, who had surrounded something or other that had washed in from the tide, and appeared to be deep in argument over it. "And yet that's all it was." He gestured at the intent ring, the boys and girls packed in close as they examined whatever they had found.

Welch sat forward and said, "Maybe they weren't so very wrong, in that regard. Take a human child, give it lots of time and attention, a secure place to come home to but plenty of things to explore. Let it find all kinds of challenges and let it stumble and make mistakes and learn to get back on its feet. Eventually you get something that can go to the stars. Sure, you also get armies of kids who use their time and freedom to watch television, and their security and support to get complacent and smug. But if you just leave the door open to the big world . . . some of them go through it. Like your Mars Four. They find out about small steps and big failures and how to *use* their confidence and *use* their doubt. . . . and finally there's nothing that they can't do or find out about. Maybe my opposite numbers, over on the other side of the world, *did* find out the name—or one of the names, anyway—of our secret. They just didn't know what *kind* of a secret it was."

Amos came running up the beach then, followed by his four friends. "Hey, Dad, can you look at something with us, and tell us what it is?"

"I can look," Scott said, easing out of his chair, slipping into his sandals, and walking down the wooden steps onto the beach, where the gaggle of children surrounded him. "That's always the first step. After that, who knows?"